The Hailwic Chronicles: The Forgotten Prince

By: Kendra Slone

Cover design by: Christian Bentulan
Edited by: C.M. Santoro's Editorial Service

ISBN: 9798328162821

This book is dedicated to my parents, Lynn, Ken and Vicky. Without their constant love and support, I would never have been able to follow my dreams. Thank you for everything, I love you!

In Memory of Michael Hagan

Chapter 1
The Lost Prince

Bem

The silence of the crisp night air threatened to drive Bem mad. The only relief granted to him from the deafening stillness was the rhythmic wingbeat of the crimson dragon he rode upon and the pounding of his own heart in his ears. Bem clung to his bow with white knuckles, an arrow already positioned in its notch.

He wasn't sure why he relied on such a feeble weapon. An arrow wouldn't protect him from the shadow creatures he was so desperate to find. Fire would be much more useful in this predicament, yet the familiarity of his bow comforted him. Bem wasn't confident that he could summon fire, not yet. Even though he was a sorcerer, his magic was still new to him.

The pain in Bem's head from his battle wound was intense. He had wrapped a scrap of cloth torn from his shirt around his head to stop the bleeding. Falcon hadn't taught him how to heal himself yet. It was something he would have to ask the sorcerer about sooner than later.

His nerves frayed. Bem grabbed onto one of the smooth spikes on Theo's back, the crimson dragon, and stared into the darkness below. Where had the shadow creatures taken the prince? His mind swirled with endless possibilities.

He prayed Theo was searching for the prince, just as he asked. Even though Theo could understand him, Bem couldn't comprehend what he might say. Dragons could only speak a language of their own, which only sounded like grunts and growls to him. He wished there was a way to communicate with him when Nyel, the dragon Shifter, and Bem's brother, wasn't around to translate.

Bem swallowed past the dry lump in his throat. He ran his hand through his shaggy blonde hair in thought. What were they doing? It was extremely foolish of them to go looking for the shadow creatures on their own, especially in the dark. It was impossible to know how many of them could be lurking—waiting for the right moment to attack.

But he couldn't stomach the thought of Carver out there with them alone. He also feared what they were going to do with him. They wouldn't kill him, that much Bem was certain of. The shadow creatures only had one goal when they crossed paths with any human or dragon, and that was to possess their body. He just hoped they weren't too late.

Bem shuddered. No, he mustn't think that way. He couldn't stomach the thought. Carver was a strong sorcerer. They couldn't overtake him. But he couldn't help the nagging voice in the back of his mind that tried to argue otherwise. With gritted teeth, he pushed the anxious thoughts aside. He had to stay focused on saving Carver or he was going to lose his mind.

At that moment, Theo raised his massive head and sniffed the air. His nostrils sucked in air deeply while he slowed to a near halt. He remained suspended in the air as he focused. Bem felt the dragon's sides expand beneath him as he took deeper breaths and studied the area. A growl rumbled in his chest. Bem shifted the bow nervously in his clammy hands. His eyes scanned left and right along the ground, searching for whatever had caught Theo's attention, but failed to find it.

"Have you found them?" He whispered when he couldn't take the suspense any longer.

The crimson dragon turned his head slightly and nodded once with an affirmative grunt. One piercing golden eye stared back at Bem. He knew that the time to find answers had come.

Theo glided in silence to the ground below. He landed with careful precision, still sniffing the air. Bem slid off of his back and held his bow at the ready. The temptation to summon his magic to his hands was strong, but Bem feared it might bring unwanted attention to them. So, he waited. They descended on the edge of a monstrous, shady forest. Bem held his breath and listened. If he strained his ears enough, he could make out faint whispers further within. He glanced at Theo, his nerves twisting his stomach into tight knots.

"He has to be in there," Bem murmured in a small voice. He was afraid to speak too loud. Theo nodded again; concern evident in his eyes. Bem considered their options as his pulse continued to drum in his ears. There weren't a lot of choices, but he knew which one he had to make. He turned and craned his neck back to face Theo. The dragon's head towered a good three feet over him.

"I should go alone. You'll draw too much attention trying to squeeze through those trees," Bem added, studying Theo's face for his response.

A soft, yet firm, growl erupted from Theo's mouth. His upper lip curled, and he shook his head. It was clear he didn't like Bem's plan at all. Bem placed a hand on the dragon's scaly leg. The red scales were smooth and solid. His shoulder was slightly taller than the top of Bem's head.

"I hear your protest; I wouldn't want you to go alone either. But it's the quickest way. If it looks too dangerous, I'll turn around and come straight back. Then we'll come up with a different plan. Ok?" Bem offered to soothe the dragon's concern.

Theo lowered his head to Bem's level and stared at him with large, golden eyes. At one time, Bem would have feared for his life at the sight of those slit pupils. His gaze drifted to the scar along

Theo's eye, the one he got the very first night they had encountered one another. The sight of it set Bem's resolve in stone. He'd never let his friend suffer that cruelty ever again.

A puff of hot air blew from Theo's nostrils and ruffled his hair, interrupting his thoughts. Bem chuckled. "I'll be quick," he promised and turned back towards the woods.

Theo shuffled with unease, but he didn't stop him. Bem studied the forest for a moment. He couldn't see far past the thickness of the trees that turned into pitch black darkness. He clenched his jaw and ventured into the tree line as quietly as he could.

His breath rattled as he crept further into the quiet forest. Bem cursed himself for being so nervous. He wished he could control the tremor in his hands, but it was no use. The silent woods grew darker with every cautious step he took. Whispers of the unseen shadows hissed in his ears as he tiptoed through the brush. Bem's grip tightened on his bow. The trees loomed over him. Their scraggly branches resembled arms reaching out to grab him. He paused and tried to shake the fear that built in his mind before he pressed onwards. They didn't know he was there, not yet at least.

He crept along his chosen path for what felt like ages, his footsteps silent with the skill only a huntsman could achieve. The outline of something massive came into his sight. Bem stopped and squinted, trying to make out what it could be. It looked like a small hill at first. Until he noticed the form rose and fell with every sigh that escaped from it. A gasp caught in Bem's throat as realization struck him. The massive hill, only a few feet away from him, was that of a sleeping dragon.

Bem waited for his eyes to adjust as he watched the dragon for any signs that it might wake up. He held his breath for what felt like an eternity. When the dragon continued to sleep, he let out a sigh of relief. He scanned the area around it carefully. To his relief, the dragon seemed to be alone.

In the cover of darkness, Bem watched as the dragon's side rose and fell with every deep breath it took. His scales were the color of bronze coins. Bem nearly gasped again. It was the dragon that the Shadow Master, Kollano, had been riding on when Carver disappeared! It was one of the unfortunate few that a shadow creature had possessed. Which meant, or at least he hoped it would, that the prince must be close. Bem backed off and made a wide circle around the sleeping giant, praying his footsteps wouldn't disturb him, and carried on. Facing the possessed dragon was not something he was prepared to do on his own.

The whispers intensified as he made his detour and crept further into the woods. He was getting closer. A scream erupted from the woods ahead of him that made his stomach lurch. Bem recognized the voice in an instant; Carver.

Bem abandoned his attempts at stealth without a second thought. He crashed through the trees, his adrenaline forcing him to run as fast as he could towards the source of his fears. Low-hanging branches whipped his face and shoulders as he raced through the dark forest. Many times, he barely escaped coming face first with some trees.

A sudden burst of light illuminated the night. Bem shielded his eyes from the blinding light. He squinted through his fingers to reveal the bloodied form of Carver with a ball of fire hovering over his palm. With a grunt, the prince hurled the ball of fire at a group of shadow creatures that crept towards him. Their dark, ghost-like bodies slithered off the ground while their glowing orange eyes gazed at the prince with hunger. Wisps of smoke-like tendrils rolled off of their bodies. Each bore a malicious grin that matched the predatory glint in their eyes.

The fireball smashed into them, and they shrieked with rage before they vanished into thin air. Yet more took their place. Carver conjured another ball of fire and sent it soaring towards them. Bem felt an overwhelming mixture of relief and concern at the sight of the prince. He almost called to him when a movement caught his eye.

While Carver was distracted with the cluster of others, a lone shadow floated behind him. Fear gripped Bem's chest. An arrow alone wouldn't be enough to save him. Bem squeezed his eyes shut and focused on the swirling store of magical energy within himself. When he could grab hold of it, he uttered a silent plea for it to turn into fire. His right palm tingled until it became hot. Bem opened his eyes and sighed in relief when flames sprung from his fingertips. He grabbed the tip of his arrow and willed the flames to remain there, not trusting himself enough to throw magical fire in Carver's direction.

In one fluid motion, Bem aimed and launched the fire-arrow at the shadow creature. The creature shrieked with fury as the fire made it vanish into nothingness. Carver whirled around in astonishment. When his wild eyes landed on Bem, a huge grin spread across his face.

"Bem, you're missing the fun!" he called as he hurled another ball of fire at the creatures.

"Where's Kollano?" Bem asked, rushing to Carver's side. He drew another arrow and set the tip on fire once more.

Carver shrugged. "He tried to take over my body when he couldn't get Nyel's. I was stronger and used magic to cast him away. I think I used too much at once, because it knocked me out cold. One moment I'm in the air, stabbing Kollano in the back, and the next thing I know I wake up here surrounded by shadows."

"Thank goodness you're alright," Bem sighed. He grabbed hold of Carver's biceps. "Let's get out of here before more show up."

"Good idea," Carver agreed. Bem led the prince in the direction he had entered the woods. The remaining shadow creatures screeched with fury and followed them.

"You have no idea where he is?" Bem asked again. He shot another flaming arrow through a shadow creature, who tried to block their path. Bem plucked the arrow from the ground as they hurried past.

"Like I said, everything is a blur," Carver replied. Fire erupted from his hands and sent it soaring into a group of the nightmarish creatures. "I remember an explosion of orange light when I stabbed him and that was it. I think I killed him."

"That's not enough to convince me he's dead. Besides, the shadow creatures are still here," Bem said in between breaths as they ran through the forest. They used the light of Carver's fire to navigate through the darkness. They were getting close to the edge of the trees, Bem realized in relief. Until a monstrous roar thundered ahead of them.

Bem and Carver skidded to a halt as a massive, scaly body rose to all fours from the ground in front of them. It was the dragon Bem had snuck past earlier. In his rush to get them out of the forest, Bem had forgotten about the sleeping dragon.

The bronze scales of the possessed dragon's rugged face reflected in the prince's firelight. Bem cursed under his breath when the dragon's piercing, ember eyes landed on them. He grabbed Carver's hand and shouted, "This way!"

Carver followed him without protest and they bolted to the right to avoid the stream of fire that shot from the dragon's mouth. The shadow creatures screeched behind them as they were extinguished by the light. Bem kept a firm grip on Carver's hand and pulled him through the trees, making their way to the outer edge of the woods.

An angry roar followed close behind them. They spun around to see the bronze dragon barreling towards them, his ugly glowing eyes the only light in the darkness. Bem raised his bow and shot an arrow at him, hoping to gouge one of his eyes. But the arrow only bounced off of the dragon's protective scales. Carver stopped and faced the charging dragon. He placed his feet shoulder width apart and held out his hands at his side. Both of his hands burst into a blaze of fire, preparing to cast it at the dragon.

Suddenly, the ground beneath their feet trembled. Bem looked around in confusion, unsure of the source. Until he spotted a blur of red scales run past them towards their attacker.

Theo charged towards the bronze dragon with his sharp teeth bared. Theo swung his head underneath the dragon's chin and shoved the shadow dragon's chest with his paws. The bronze dragon fell to the ground in a massive heap. Theo stumbled; his breathing heavy, while the dragon dragged himself to his feet. It was at that moment when Bem remembered Theo was still injured from their fight with Kollano only hours before. Bem's heart sank with fear and guilt. Theo wouldn't be able to defend himself for long in his condition.

Thinking fast, Bem used Theo's body to shield himself from the dragon's view. He reached over his shoulder until he felt the soft feather of an arrow on his back. Bem plucked the arrow from its quiver and notched it into place with careful precision, as he had done thousands of times before. While Theo distracted the possessed dragon, Bem shuffled around his side and aimed the arrow at the dragon's glowing, ember eye. The bronze dragon roared, ready to attack Theo with full force. He had to make this arrow count.

Bem sucked in a sharp breath and let the feathered arrow slip through his fingers.

The dragon screeched in pain as the arrow sunk deep into his eye socket. He swung his head violently from side to side, trying to shake the arrow out. Thick, red globs of blood landed on the ground around him. Bem grabbed Carver's hand once more and drug him back to Theo. He helped the prince climb onto Theo's back and hurried to sit behind him. Without any prompting, Theo leapt into the air. As he climbed higher into the air, they could see the shadow creatures emerge from the trees and floated into the air to pursue them.

"Quick Bem, summon your fire," Carver commanded, while he did the same. Bem focused once again on the ball of energy buried deep within his chest until he lit two fingers on his right hand.

Carver nodded his approval. "Good. Now use your breath. Breathe in, allow the flame to grow. I want you to throw it when I tell you to." When he caught a glimpse of Bem's nervous face, he added, "I know you can do it, Bem. Believe in yourself, like I believe in you."

Bem did as he was told, focusing on his lit fingers with each deep breath. To his surprise, the fire built in his hand. Carver grinned at him and yelled, "NOW!"

Together, they hurled a fan of flames out at the shadows before they could leave the ground, blocking their path to them with a shield of fire. Theo pumped his wings faster to put more distance between them.

Carver swayed to one side. The energy he had used to block the creatures took its toll on him. Bem gasped and hurried to wrap his arms around the prince's waist to steady him. Carver peeked over his shoulder at him and smirked.

"Thank you, Bem," Carver sighed. His arms slumped to his sides and went limp against Bem's chest. Bem buried his face in the crook of Carver's neck and hugged him close. A heavy weight lifted off of his shoulders, knowing that Carver was safe in his arms. He then lifted his head to rest it against Carver's.

"I was afraid that I might have been too late," Bem whispered into his raven hair. He could feel Carver chuckle. Carver reached a hand back and traced the tips of his fingers down Bem's cheek.

With a mumble, Carver closed his eyes and uttered, "You won't get rid of me that easily, love." He let Carver rest, holding him close so he wouldn't fall. Bem glanced back to make certain they weren't being followed. To his relief, they were alone.

"Good job, Theo," Bem grinned. Theo looked back at him and huffed. His eyes flickered behind them with a guarded expression. Bem followed his gaze.

"Do you think the creatures might be following us?" Bem asked nervously. Theo glanced at him in concern and then returned his attention ahead of them.

Bem remained silent for a long time after that, anxious as Theo sped away from the forest and the creatures within it. Carver had fallen asleep in his arms. He didn't realize how exhausted the prince must have been, especially to be able to fall asleep hundreds of feet in the air. Bem was eager to check Carver for injuries, but decided to let him rest for now. They all needed a rest, Bem realized as the exhaustion settled over his own body.

Theo soared through the air for a long time until, finally, he relaxed and slowed his frantic pace. Bem sighed. The nightmare was over. Now maybe they could return to the others. They remained in silence as Theo went a different way than they had previously. Bem could only assume it was to be certain they weren't being followed. Without being able to understand his response, it would have been too complicated to ask him that question. But it didn't matter, he trusted Theo with his life.

At long last, Theo hummed happily deep in his chest. Bem let out a sigh of relief. They made it back to Theo's clan. Even in the dark, Bem couldn't believe how beautiful the area was. The sound of a waterfall crashed in the distance. A welcoming sign that they were close. Theo angled upwards to ascend the tallest mountain; his pace grew quicker with anticipation to land. Bem tightened his grip on Carver with one arm to keep him from slipping off of the dragon's back. With the other arm, he tried to hold on to one of Theo's spikes. He cursed under his breath as his muscles strained, wishing he had a saddle or even some rope to help keep them from falling.

Something solid suddenly descended upon them from above. Two dragons emerged out of nowhere and met Theo mid-flight, forcing him to stop his ascent. Bem recognized them as Guardians of the clan. They growled at them with deep, menacing snarls and glared at Bem and Carver. Bem gulped. Why weren't they letting Theo pass? Where were the others? He grew worried, wishing he knew what was being said.

"Theo!" exclaimed a familiar voice. Bem spun around to follow the voice up the mountain and in an instant, all his worries faded away.

It was his brother, Nyel! Without another word, Nyel dove head first towards them off the steep cliff. This would have scared Bem, if not for the two enormous emerald wings that sprouted from Nyel's back. His new wings caught Nyel in the air and carried him towards the dragons. Once he was close enough, Bem noticed his brother's face twisted with pain. Was he hurt?

They caught each other's eye. Nyel's face relaxed, relieved to see the three of them in one piece. Then, a moment later, his expression turned into anger. Bem winced under Nyel's glare. He knew he was in trouble.

Nyel pulled himself up to fly beside Theo and turned his attention to the two Guardians. He argued with the Guardians, who looked at him in disgust. He snarled something incomprehensible to Bem, pointing first to Theo's face and then to Bem and Carver's.

The two Guardian's grumbled and snorted with displeasure. They then spun around and left as quickly as they had arrived, soaring away from the mountain. Nyel cursed and pushed his shaggy brown hair back from his face. Whenever he was overwhelmed or frustrated, he always did that, but this time Bem feared he caused it. Nyel's green eyes flickered, and he motioned for Theo to follow him. Instead of continuing upward, they drifted down the mountainside.

"Where are we going?" Bem called, surprised by their sudden change in direction. Theo had seemed eager to fly up the mountain only moments before.

Glancing over his shoulder, Nyel replied in a saddened tone, "To a funeral."

Bem's face paled and his heart sank. He wanted to ask who's, but his words caught in his throat. The faces of their friends flashed through his mind in an instant. Bem was afraid to ask, even though he would soon get his answer.

Bem hated funerals. He clutched at the small blue crystal that rested against his chest. It was once his father's crystal, before he passed away. His father was also a sorcerer, though Bem didn't know it at the time. He wished he had more time with him. Maybe his father could have taught him everything he knew about magic. Bem sighed and let go of the crystal. It was no use to dwell on the past. His father was gone.

They landed at the base of the mountain in a quiet, grassy meadow. The grand, white-scaled dragon known as the Ascendant and the leader of the Ryngar clan sat patiently. His name was Ivory, and he was the oldest dragon Bem had laid his eyes on thus far. Though his scales were snow white and clean, they were also rough and weathered. They didn't catch the light like Theo's did in the sun. By his side were two young dragons the size of large dogs. The boy was a brilliant blue, while the girl was a vibrant red, even brighter in color than Theo's scales.

To Bem's relief, Falcon and Iris stood a few feet away from the dragons, their eyes downcast, with silent tears rolling down their cheeks. Falcon's left arm was in a makeshift splint, with a sling made of old cloth wrapped around his neck to hold it up. Lying on the ground beside them with his arms folded carefully onto his chest was Sargon.

He knew Kollano, the leader of the shadow creatures, when he last saw him had possessed Sargon. Yet in death, his face looked the most peaceful. The most human. Remembering Falcon's stories of this man from their time in the fortress on the lake, Bem wished he had the chance to have known him too. He silently cursed Kollano and his swarm of shadows for the pain and havoc they had already caused.

Bem gave Carver's shoulder a gentle shake to wake him and helped him to the ground. They both wobbled for a second, tired and unused to using their own legs after the long flight.

"What's going on?" Carver asked as he looked around in confusion. Carver leaned against Bem for support, still exhausted from his use of magic. Bem swallowed past the lump in his throat.

"I'm sorry, Carver. Your uncle…he's gone," Bem whispered. The prince's eyes opened wide and darted over to his tear-stricken sister and the silent Falcon. His eyes then slowly traveled down to Sargon's body, and he breathed, "Oh."

Bem grabbed his hand and gave it a squeeze.

Nyel's body transformed as his scales and wings retracted inward. He grimaced the entire time. Bem hadn't noticed the makeshift bandages before. They were placed on his neck and shoulder, stained with dried blood. In Nyel's hands, he carried a worn shirt he had kept tucked away in his bag. He winced as he put one sleeve on and then the other, before he joined the others.

"Should we say something before we bury him?" Nyel offered in a gentle tone, glancing from Falcon to Iris. Iris quietly nodded. Silent tears ran down her face.

Falcon cleared his throat and shuffled on his feet. He stared up at the sky, as if searching for the right words. Finally, he lowered his gaze and spoke in a gruff voice. "There are not enough kind words I could say about this heroic man. Sargon saved my life when I was just a boy. He saved me a second time when he took me under his wing as his apprentice…and as his son. He taught me everything I know, even though I didn't make it easy for him in my youth. Despite facing criticism, Sargon always chose to go his own way.

His own brother banned him from the castle and yet he still waltzed in to comfort his niece and nephew when their mother died, like nothing ever happened. I thought he was dead for sure that day," Falcon chuckled. "Sargon, I'll miss you for the rest of my life. I don't know what you got yourself into while I was gone, but mark my words, I intend to find out. And I intend to avenge you. We won't let this darkness win."

Iris slipped her hand into his and squeezed it. It was silent for a moment as the princess took a few deep breaths to steady her sobs. Then she spoke, "Uncle, you were foolish for getting into this mess. I'm going to be angry with you for a long time. And yet, you're still the smartest, kindest, and funniest man I'll ever know. No one can replace you, no one. You should have been the King of Hailwic, not my father. I will never understand why you didn't take his place. Instead, you accepted the life of a banished prince. But know this, uncle. I, too, vow to put an end to whatever evil is lurking in this world. And I promise to fight for your dream of man and dragon's uniting. And to bring our people out of hiding. I love you and I'll miss you."

Bem peeked up at Carver, waiting for him to say something. Carver only stared blankly at the man on the ground, his gaze distant. Iris moved first. She knelt on the ground beside Sargon and placed a single wildflower on his chest. She then stepped back, wrapping her arms around herself as she cried. Falcon studied her for a moment. Deciding against his thought, he turned and asked, "Bem, will you help me?"

Surprised by the question, Bem nodded and released Carver's hand to take his place on the other side of Sargon. He paused and bowed his head to Sargon out of respect. Then he turned to Falcon, unsure if he could do what he was about to be asked.

"Just take a deep breath," Falcon said in a quiet voice. His voice was barely a whisper. His eyes remained focused on Sargon's still face. "The ground around him will become like quicksand."

Bem nodded and drew his magic from within, feeling the energy build up inside of him. His hands warmed and glowed. Bem watched Falcon closely and mirrored his actions. They raised their hands above Sargon's body and willed the ground to morph around him.

Slowly, the earth shifted underneath Sargon. The once hard ground resembled muddy sand. Bem watched as Sargon's body sank into the ground beneath him like thickened water. Nyel put an arm around Iris and held her close as she sobbed into his chest. The dragons bowed their heads respectfully as his legs and torso disappeared.

And as Sargon's face quietly slipped beneath the earth, a single tear escaped its prison and ran down Falcon's face. And he whispered, "I love you…father."

Chapter 2
Divided Roads

Nyel

After Sargon's burial, the small wounded group returned to Ivory's cliff to heal. There was a sense of despair and exhaustion amongst his friends. Nyel couldn't help but feel the same. When he shifted his wings away, a terrible pain pulsed throughout his entire body. It took everything he had not to scream through gritted teeth. Whatever magic Kollano had used on him was still affecting him. Nyel stayed in his human form for the time being until he absolutely needed to use his dragon form. The very thought of shifting into a dragon made his stomach queasy.

Iris dried her eyes and worked on Falcon's broken arm. Her hands began to glow a warm, golden color as she got to work. She gently glided the palms of her hands over his arm, tracing his injury. Her long, raven hair hung in her brilliant blue eyes, but she didn't seem bothered by it. Falcon sat on a smooth boulder outside Ivory's cave in silence. The sorcerer's blank gaze drifted towards the ground, his face emotionless.

Nyel hadn't known Falcon long, but he knew him well enough to know that Falcon was already bottling up his feelings for Sargon's passing. His mane of silver hair hung loose and tangled in its leather hair tie. His amethyst eyes remained still, unwavering and empty, as he allowed Iris to heal him.

Nyel sighed and let them be. He wanted to give them space to grieve together. They were each other's greatest support in this unfortunate death. Theo emerged from below the cliffside and flew overhead to land beside Ivory's cave. On his back were Carver and

Bem. Nyel approached them and offered his hand up to Carver. The prince accepted it without protest and allowed Nyel to help him off the dragon's back. Bem followed closely behind him on his own.

Carver wobbled on his feet and fell forward. Nyel lurched with him to support his weight, startled by the prince's response.

"Sorry, I'm exhausted," Carver grumbled. He looked terrible, sickly even. Dark circles had formed under his eyes and his face was as pale as a ghost. A pit formed in Nyel's stomach as he took in Carver's appearance. He snuck a quick peek at Carver's eyes and was relieved to find the same striking blue color that he shared with his twin sister.

Bem hurried to Carver's other side and wrapped an arm around his waist.

"I've got him, Nyel," Bem assured him. He held Carver close to his side.

Nyel released the prince while saying, "You guys look awful. Why don't you go into Ivory's cave and rest? You'll be safe in there; the other dragons wouldn't dare enter without the Ascendant's permission. I'll join you guys in a little while."

Bem gave Nyel a nod while a tired grin formed on his face. "Thanks, brother."

The couple made their way into the cave's entrance, leaning against each other. After a moment's thought, Nyel turned to Bem once again and said, "Oh, and Bem?"

His brother halted and glanced over his shoulder at him in response. "If you ever chase after a swarm of shadow creatures again without me, I'll end you."

Bem chuckled and shook his head. "No, you wouldn't. I'll try to consider that next time."

Nyel shuddered. He hoped there would never be a next time.

Theo cleared his throat from high above. He seemed much larger to Nyel when he wasn't in his dragon form. Nyel eyed the crimson dragon and said, "That goes for you as well."

Theo rolled his yellow eyes at him and snorted. "I'd like to see you try…"

"What made you think it was a good idea to go out there on your own?" Nyel growled, his previous anger returning. "You both were in serious danger, or worse, at risk of being possessed!"

Theo lowered his head, and a deep growl rumbled in his chest. His large yellow eyes glared at Nyel in response. "I don't know if you've realized it, but I consider Bem my brother as much as I consider you my brother. His mate risked his life to save all of us, and Bem was distressed. It would have been shameful of me if I had ignored his plea."

Nyel stared at Theo in shock. He didn't realize the strength of Theo's loyalty to them had grown so strong. It warmed his heart. Nyel took a deep breath and let out a long sigh. He reached up and placed a hand on the dragon's snout, feeling the warm, smooth scales under his palm.

"I can't argue with that, I suppose," Nyel admitted, meeting Theo's tired gaze. "Thank you for watching over him." Theo puffed a cloud of hot smoke from his nostrils, ruffling Nyel's hair and causing his eyes to water.

Without another word, the two retired into the cave to join the others for a much-needed rest.

It had been a few days since Sargon's quiet funeral. Nyel circled above the quiet river that ran around the base of Ivory's mountain. The water was clear. Perfect conditions to spot a fish from overhead. He had spent the early morning sharpening a stick into a spike with Bem's dagger while the others slept. Nyel thought that they all deserved a warm meal after everything they had been through. And they could eat as they discussed their next move.

A fat, greenish-blue fish popped up close to the water's surface. The water rippled as the fish's tail fin broke the surface. Nyel gripped his makeshift spear with one hand and took aim. In one fluid motion, he hurled the spear into the water with a loud splash. He quickly dove and yanked his weapon out of the water, and grinned victoriously. Thrashing at the end of it was the large fish. That made his fifth catch of the morning. He landed on the shore as he pulled the fish off the spike and shoved it into his empty bag. He wished he had a basket to carry them in, but the bag would have to do.

"I would have never thought to use a twig to catch a fish," an unfamiliar voice observed from his left.

Startled, Nyel looked up and searched for the voice. His eyes scanned the area until they rested on a female dragon. She was tall and more slender than Ivory or Theo. Her scales sparkled in the morning sun in marvelous shades of purple while her throat and underbelly shone silver. Two sharp horns rested on top of her head, but she didn't have as many spikes along her jaw and neck as her male counterparts. Suddenly, the realization hit him. She was the one who had plucked him from the sky after his battle with Kollano.

"That's something you'll quickly learn if you spend time with us humans. Most of us need tools to survive," Nyel replied, waving the stick as he spoke. "We normally don't have sharp fangs and claws for hunting, I'm afraid."

"You're not most humans," she countered, staring at him with pale gray eyes. They were fierce, yet also provided kindness towards him. He was not used to seeing this from the rest of the clan. "You should try hunting in your strongest form. You'll easily catch more with your jaws."

"How do you know if that's my stronger form?" Nyel chuckled. He slung his bag of fish over his shoulder. "Besides, I don't know if my friends would appreciate their food coming from my mouth. I'll have to try it sometime."

He paused for a moment, both of them stood in silence. Then, he added, "I meant to thank you for saving me the other day. I know you don't know me. You may not even like me, but I appreciate you doing it. What is your name?"

She cocked her head at him for a moment in contemplation. He was curious about the thoughts racing through her mind at that very moment. Finally, she replied, "I am Lorna and I do not dislike you."

"Thank you again for saving my life, Lorna," Nyel grinned after a moment of surprise. She was the first of the clan to approach him without Ivory's prompting. "And for your advice."

Lorna studied him for a long time. She seemed intrigued by him, yet skeptical. She lowered her head closer to his eye level and said, "You are not as I thought you were."

Nyel gulped and let out a nervous laugh. "I hope I haven't disappointed you."

Lorna tilted her head once more and chuckled in amusement. "On the contrary. I find you rather fascinating. You're nothing like the stories I have heard of your kind. I haven't encountered many humans myself, to be honest."

"I know what you mean. I felt the same way about dragons. I think we're all just trying to survive. If we just stop and take the time to listen to one another, maybe we'll have a better chance of understanding. Then again, there are a lot of evil men out there, too. But I aim to not be one of them if I can help it," Nyel smiled.

He then swung his bag around to his front, retrieved a fish from within, and offered it to her. She stared at him a moment longer, contemplating his words. Then her eyes lit up and hummed her approval.

"Well said, Shifter," said Lorna. She leaned forward and gently took the fish from his hand with her sharp teeth. She tossed her head back and, with one gulp, she swallowed the fish whole.

Lorna then bowed her head to him and said, "It would be an honor to fly with you, if ever you need me."

"As would I," Nyel grinned. Lorna nodded and continued on her way.

Nyel's footsteps felt lighter as he leapt into the air and continued spearing fish from the water. His mood had lifted at the thought of possibly making a new friend in the clan. Once he caught enough fish for their group, he gathered the fish in his bag and returned to the Ascendant's cliff. By then, the others had emerged from the cave and started a small fire to warm themselves from the morning cold.

Nyel hadn't considered making a fire when he woke. It had slipped his mind that the others might be cold. Ever since he had been given the Ascendant's power, his blood ran warm like a fire burned inside of him. He grabbed a smooth, flat stone and placed it in the middle of the fire to allow it to heat.

Seeing the bag of fish in Nyel's arms, Bem hurried towards him and took it from him with eager eyes. Nyel wasn't the only one ready for a warm meal. "I'll get to work on these. Thanks!"

Bem grabbed his hunting knife where Nyel had left it and removed the scales. Nyel grabbed another knife from his own pack and helped him. He tried not to imagine his own scales as his knife slid against the fish's skin. Iris sat beside Falcon across the fire, already at work on his arm once again. Nyel only knew as much about magic as Mari, his stepmother and a healer in their small village, had taught them. However, she only relied on crystals to heal the most extreme injuries. She wasn't a true sorcerer like her son. She made use of the crystals she obtained, which contained small amounts of magical energy.

Iris, on the other hand, used her own energy to heal Falcon's injury. She had to take frequent breaks so she wouldn't exhaust herself. Falcon grumbled from time to time to let it heal on its own, but she waved his refusals away with a flourish of her hand.

As Nyel moved on to the next fish, he noticed Carver hadn't joined them yet. The prince was probably still resting in the cave.

Nyel worried about him. He knew how it felt to come close to a shadow creature's possession. Its very presence could paralyze a man with cold and helpless fear. The effects of just one were enough to render Nyel unconscious. He could only imagine withstanding a swarm of them. The prince had to have been strong to fight his way out without passing out. He made a note in the back of his mind to speak with the prince, and to thank him for putting himself in that situation to save him.

"So, what's the plan from here?" Bem asked, not taking his eyes off his work. But Nyel knew Bem directed his question at him.

Nyel stole a glance at Iris, who remained focused on Falcon's arm. "I'm not sure. I haven't spoken with Ivory yet."

That seemed to arouse Falcon from his silence. A spark of annoyance flashed in his bright eyes and growled, "We can't keep sitting around here doing nothing."

"You're not 'doing nothing'," Nyel countered, sending a flurry of scales flying towards the fire. "You're recovering. And together, we're also showing the dragons that we can live together in peace."

"That would be true if they didn't avoid us," Falcon grumbled.

Nyel couldn't argue with that. Even though they allowed them to stay, most of the clan wasn't welcoming to any of them. Not yet, anyway. They only followed the orders of their Ascendant. After the battle with Kollano and his shadow creatures, the clan had stayed clear of Ivory's cave. Nyel knew he had to figure out a way to get through to them. And to do that, he had to stay in Ivory's good graces as well.

"We'll make this work. It will just take some time. I think we will have to work together to be rid of these shadow creatures once and for all. It's going to take all of us to do it," Nyel said.

"That's very noble of you," Falcon grumbled with a roll of his eyes. "Working together won't matter if we can't figure out how to defeat those hellish creatures. Sargon's dying breath gave us a clue on how to stop them. He said something about his journals back in his cabin that could help us find out what that is. We need to go there and find what he spoke of."

Nyel hesitated as he considered Falcon's words. He had spent so long dwelling over becoming the Shifter and trying to convince the dragons to accept them. He never really thought of how they were actually going to destroy the shadows. Fire and light seemed to weaken them, but it didn't stop the creatures from regenerating. Nyel couldn't leave the duties he had tied himself to, not yet. But that didn't mean their efforts had to be put on hold.

"You're right, Falcon," Nyel finally said. "You should go and find out what he wrote in his journals."

Falcon gaped at Nyel, surprised that he agreed with him. Bem's eyes flickered up from the fish in his hands and stared at Nyel in confusion. "Wait, why are you singling him out?"

"Because Nyel can't leave the clan," Iris answered, her brow furrowed in concentration. Although her focus wasn't on Falcon's arm anymore. Nyel could almost see the gears turning in her head as she studied him. "We'll have to split up again if we want to get ahead of Kollano's plans."

Falcon arched an eyebrow at her in speculation. "We? You mean we'll have to leave Nyel behind, right?"

"No, not exactly. I'm going to stay with Nyel and assert my allegiance with the dragons," she said firmly.

In one swift movement, Falcon leapt to his feet with a flash of anger in his eyes.

"No, you won't! They could kill you!" Falcon argued. She shook her head with a gleam of determination in her eyes.

"I'll be with Nyel. I trust him with my life," she said. Her statement surprised Nyel. His heart skipped a beat in his chest without fully understanding the reason. "And he's right. You need to retrieve those journals. Find out what Sargon has discovered about Kollano and the beasts that serve him."

"I'll go with you," Bem suddenly volunteered. This also shocked Nyel. He had expected his brother to argue with him. "We need to find out more about those nightmares. Maybe the dragons can take us there? It would save a lot of time and we can return to Iris and Nyel in no time!"

Falcon winced. "I'm not so sure about that."

Bem arched an eyebrow. "What are you not sure about, me or the dragons?"

Nyel crossed his arms. "That's not a bad idea, Bem. If we want to unite with the dragons, then we need to show them we can work together. Theo can go with you; I know he won't lead you astray. I think Steno would be a good choice too. He's more understanding of us when he's not around Syth."

Still fuming, Falcon growled, "How do you expect us to communicate with them if you're not going to be there?"

"They can understand what you're saying," Nyel explained as he placed a couple of the gutted fish on the now hot stone. "Just listen to each other. Study their expressions, be patient. You'll do just fine."

The crunch of rock under foot made Nyel stop and glance over his shoulder. Ivory stood not far behind him, quietly listening to their discussion. He hoped the elder dragon wouldn't be mad at their idea. "What say you, Ascendant? Would you be willing to allow a few Guardians to fly them into the kingdom? Sargon's journals could have an answer to all our problems."

Ivory's blue eyes sparkled with intrigue. "Hmm. I'll allow it. But they must swear to protect each other. Treat my Guardians like their own flesh and blood, and they will do the same. If any human captures my Guardians, there will be consequences."

"Trust me, they do," Nyel smiled. He turned back to the others. "It's settled. Ivory has allowed a few Guardians to take you to Sargon's cabin. What about Carver?"

Bem hesitated. His hands hovered over the fire as he cast his eyes to the ground, his expression troubled. "I'm worried about him. He's slept a lot since we've returned, and he doesn't seem to want to come out of the cave. Carver either used too much magic or he was around those shadow creatures too long. He's drained."

"To be honest with you, it surprised me he wasn't possessed." Falcon shared the same fears Nyel had tried to ignore. "Are you sure that he wasn't?"

"I'm absolutely sure!" Bem countered at once, meeting Falcon's interrogating gaze with confidence. "He was able to fight them off. I saw it with my own eyes. I think that's why he's so exhausted. Go examine him for yourself if you don't believe me! His veins never turned black and his eyes are still his beautiful shade of blue."

Falcon frowned, unconvinced. His back stiffened suddenly, looking past Nyel and Bem.

They turned to find Carver had just stumbled from the cave. A goofy, relieved grin spread across Bem's face when his eyes landed on the prince. He bolted from his seat and hurried to offer Carver his support, but the prince waved him away.

"What are you all blabbering about?" he asked in a raspy voice as he joined the group. He sat in Bem's place beside Nyel. It took everything in Nyel not to gasp aloud. He had seen little of Carver for the past few days, but he looked worse than the night he had returned. His skin was pale and there were dark circles under his eyes. His breaths were shallow, as if he had caught an illness. Nyel had never seen the prince look so fragile and aged.

Iris hurried over to him at once. She knelt and grabbed her brother's shoulder. "Carver, what did those demons do to you?"

"What are you talking about?" Carver asked defensively. He eyed the rest of the group in annoyance while they gawked at him.

"You look like you ought to be on your deathbed," Iris replied as she hurried to pull out a smooth, palm sized crystal from her bag. Nyel hadn't seen her use crystals before. Perhaps she had some saved in her bag for emergencies.

Carver scoffed and rolled his eyes. "I'm fine, Iris. You worry too much."

"Just swallow your pride and allow me to mend you. Do you think you can do that?" Iris sighed, kneeling in front of him once more with her amethyst crystal.

Carver rolled his eyes again, but didn't argue with her. That would be a losing battle. Iris got to work at once. The crystal glowed in her hand as she held it against his chest. She closed her eyes in concentration.

The prince turned to Bem and said, "I'll ask again, what were you guys talking about?"

Bem hesitated. Nyel stirred, and quickly answered, "We were discussing what our next move should be. Iris and I are going to stay with the dragons while the three of you will go to Sargon's cabin."

Carver arched an eyebrow in confusion. "Why would we need to go there?"

"You're not going," Bem said firmly. Carver laughed.

"Bossy, aren't we, love?" Carver asked. Bem didn't reply, so he continued. "I'm fine. It's just taking a while for my body to recover from being surrounded by so many of those creatures at once. You can attest to me, yes?"

He turned his attention to Nyel, who nodded once in agreement. Being touched by one of those things was bad enough. He could only imagine a swarm of them. Nyel shuddered at the thought.

"Hold still so I can do a proper healing session on you," Iris commanded, her patience wearing thin. Carver was about to protest, but thought better of it after catching the look in her and Bem's eyes.

"Fine, I surrender," he sighed. After a moment of silence, he said to Bem, "I am going with you, love. You can't be rid of me that easily."

Nyel flipped the fish around with a long stick, then stood to stretch his legs. Bem and Iris were fixated on the prince, so Nyel decided to give them some space. He moved to the edge of the cliff and looked down at the beautiful scene below. The slow-moving river he had captured the fish from ran down the valley between the mountains. Groups of dragons, young and old, soared through the skies below. Their scales were gorgeous in the morning sunlight. It was a calm and peaceful sight. It almost convinced him there wasn't any trouble in their world.

A pair of footsteps followed him to his perch, interrupting his thoughts. He didn't have to look to know who had joined him.

"So, everything's settled," Nyel began, but Falcon stopped him.

"I know I can't change Iris's mind. You better protect her with your life," Falcon threatened. His glare could have burned holes into Nyel's head.

Nyel let out a deep, not-so-human growl. "Do you think I wouldn't? Have a little more faith in me, Falcon. I thought you could trust me by now."

They stared each other down, neither one wanting to be the first to back down. Falcon was the first to break the silence. When he spoke, his voice was nearly too low to hear. "She's all I have left."

His words struck a chord in Nyel that reverberated deep in his soul. His anger towards the sorcerer evaporated in an instant. As his shoulders fell, he turned his gaze away from Falcon's pained expression. He wasn't expecting the princess's protector to be vulnerable with him. Nyel took a moment to choose his words carefully, before turning back to Falcon.

"I promise you; I will guard Iris with my life," Nyel began in a soft tone. He paused before he placed a careful hand on Falcon's tense shoulder. He met the sorcerer's intense gaze with his own. "But you should know…she's not all that you have. Not anymore. We may not always see eye to eye, but I hope you realize that we're family now. Bem and I will always have your back."

Falcon blinked in surprise. The sorcerer looked away from him to the valley below. Slowly, he patted Nyel's hand once before removing it from his shoulder. Nyel smirked and turned to watch the valley, too. He expected nothing less from the stoic sorcerer.

Behind them, Bem and Iris spoke to each other as she worked her magic. Bem seemed relaxed, grateful to have Iris to look after her brother and teach him more about what their magic could do. Carver remained still as a statue with his eyes closed, as if he were meditating as they talked.

Falcon leaned towards Nyel, surprising him.

He whispered, "You don't think Carver's possessed, do you?"

Nyel hesitated, then shook his head. "No, he couldn't be. I mean, I can't say that the thought hasn't crossed my mind as well. But he would show signs of possession, right? I believe he's just recovering from the effects of being around the shadow creatures. It's a traumatizing experience, to say the least. I feel sick to my stomach even thinking about it."

Falcon still seemed skeptical as he watched Carver closely. "How do you think he avoided being possessed? Why did they carry him off without one of them getting him?"

"Bem said Kollano's dragon was there as well, right?" Nyel said, also watching the prince meditate. "I think when they fought, that dragon captured Carver and took him away. He must have escaped and tried to run. Bem said he was putting up a good fight when he found him."

Falcon scratched his chin absentmindedly and muttered, "Perhaps you're right. What do you think ever became of Kollano?"

Nyel stared at him for a moment, then said, "Carver stabbed him and saved me from possession. Whether or not it killed him, I'm not sure. But I think it definitely would have weakened him, if nothing else."

Falcon turned and watched Carver. "You don't think that Carver could have been…"

Nyel shook his head. "No way! Kollano's too self-absorbed to be quiet this long. I think whatever Carver did to stop him worked. His shadow creatures must have helped hide him somewhere safe to regenerate. So we have to use this time wisely to find a way to be rid of him once and for all."

Falcon nodded in response, still watching the prince in thought.

Nyel patted his back and said, "Do me a favor and help Bem keep an eye on him, will you?"

Falcon studied Nyel for a moment. "Of course, I will. And just so you know, I do trust you."

Satisfied, Nyel turned and made his way to Ivory, who was laying outside the cave entrance watching them. Nyel stopped a few feet away from him and asked, "What do you need of me?"

Ivory raised his head from the ground and looked down at Nyel. "I'm relieved you're taking my words to heart."

Nyel crossed his arms and raised an eyebrow. "Did you think I wouldn't?"

Ivory chuckled. "You're very loyal and caring. I'm only glad you can make room for all your commitments."

"We've sorted out their plans," Nyel replied after a moment. "So, what are ours?"

"Tomorrow morning, we are going to fly to the neighboring clan," Ivory said. "We know their Ascendant was possessed, but we don't know how the rest of the clan is fairing without him. I would get some rest if I were you. It will be a long flight and I'll need you in your best condition. Which brings me to ask, why have you stayed in your human form? It would be better for you to remain in your dragon form while staying with us."

Nyel sighed in frustration and kicked a stone across the ground between them. "Kollano's magic continues to pain me. Any shifting I try to achieve has been excruciating. I promise I'll change as soon as the others leave."

Ivory's gaze softened. A puff of smoke flew from his nostrils and rustled Nyel's hair. "Get some rest, I implore you."

Nyel nodded and gave him a half-hearted smile. He felt more unsure of himself than he did when he first arrived at the clan. Nyel tried to push those feelings aside and instead thought about the day ahead of them. They each had a mission of their own to follow through to the end. But it didn't stop him from wishing they could stick together. Nyel looked around at his friends, each of them preparing for the journey ahead of them. They had only just got back together again, only to be separated once more in a short time. Even though he knew it was necessary, it filled his heart with dread.

He watched Iris inch her hands from Carver's head to his chest. He did look rather ill. Nyel cursed under his breath at the thought of those creatures trying to possess the prince's body. He must have put up a good fight to be that exhausted and weak. Nyel's eyes shifted to Bem's face. A sense of admiration for his brother came over him. He could see the concern and love in Bem's eyes every time he looked at Carver. Nyel had never seen that look on him before. Carver should go with Falcon and Bem for his own good, but he also felt that it was for Bem's best interest, too.

Nyel stretched. He looked back out over the peaceful valley below once more. There was someone else he needed to talk to before they went their separate ways. He had to find Theo and explain their plans to him. Theo had left them to help the other Guardians watch over the valley. The clan had increased the number of dragons assigned to protect them at all times of the day. The more eyes, the better.

He took a deep, shaky breath. Nyel felt the change swirling throughout his body, but he only focused it to one area. His wings sprouted from his shirtless back. A sharp wave of pain shot through his entire nervous system like a bolt of lightning coursing through him. It took everything he had not to scream in agony as his emerald wings towered over him. Nyel doubled over with his hands on his knees and gasped for air. If he didn't know any better, the pain was getting worse. But why?

"Nyel?" Bem paused in concern. He could hear Bem get to his feet to approach him, but Nyel was quicker.

Without a backward glance, Nyel sprinted towards the open valley and leapt off the cliff's edge. His wings spread open and caught him midair. The pain subsided into slow, uncomfortable spasms as the cool air rushed against his face and chest. Nyel closed his eyes and sighed in relief. He preferred this transformation the best, without the pain, of course. Half dragon, half human. His true self.

He found Theo at the west end of the valley and landed beside him. A puff of smoke burst from his nostrils in greeting. The crimson dragon looked much better since the battle with Kollano. Nyel had feared the worst when he found him and Bem on the side of a mountain at Kollano's feet. Nyel sat on the ground and wrapped his arms around his knees.

"I assume you bring news?" Theo guessed, as he continued to watch the surrounding mountains for any signs of danger.

"I do," Nyel confirmed. He then explained their plans for both Ivory and Falcon and who would accompany each group. Theo nodded as he absorbed the new information in silence. The Guardian dragon seemed to be surprised, though he tried to hide it from him. Nyel realized Theo had been expecting to accompany Ivory, his grandfather, to the next clan. Even though Nyel knew it was selfish, he hoped Theo wouldn't complain about his position.

Theo was quiet for a moment, so Nyel asked, "Will you convince the others to join you? I don't know if they will listen to me."

"I'll do my best," Theo sighed, turning to look Nyel in the eye. "It's one thing to get them to go to the lake. It's an entirely different matter to try to get them to cross it."

"I know. That's why I need your help," Nyel said, tossing a rock across the ground. He hoped that Sargon really had something of value in his cabin. He'd hate for them to be separated and send them into dangerous territory for nothing. Nyel pushed that thought from his head. If Falcon and Iris trusted Sargon's word, then so would he.

"Thank you for being so…accepting of everything we throw at you," Nyel said, glancing up at Theo.

Theo chuckled. "You've thrown nothing at me. We protect and provide for our own; always."

Nyel grinned and patted the dragon's scaly leg, feeling a sense of relief that Theo would oversee the other dragons.

Together they stood in silence, comforted by each other's company as time slipped away much too fast.

Chapter 3
Farewell

Nyel stood in the center of a dark cavern. He looked around in confusion. The trickle of a small stream was the only sound he could hear. How did he get here? Where was he? But no one was around him. Out of nowhere, a breath echoed in his ear and he quickly turned, anticipating a presence. But he was still alone.

"*Return to me,*" a sudden voice whispered from somewhere in the darkness. It was so quiet, hardly a whisper that echoed around him.

Nyel strained his eyes, but still could see nothing in the dark cavern. He called, "Who's there?"

"*Come back to me,*" replied the voice. Nyel took a step forward and a flash of bright emerald light blinded him.

With a gasp, Nyel bolted upright and looked around with wild eyes. He was back in Ivory's cave. Nyel sighed in relief. It was only a dream. How strange, he thought. But it was just a dream.

He rubbed the sleep from his eyes and blinked, looking around in a daze. Everyone else was still asleep. Nyel and his friends had taken over a corner of Ivory's massive cave. His friends laid in bundles of blankets that they had found in the boat they used to cross Lake Peril. Nyel didn't need his blanket, so he gave it to Carver the night Bem brought him back. He wondered if it could have been the dragon fire that burned within him that kept his body at a constant high temperature. Nyel meant to ask one of the dragons about it, but it sounded silly even to him.

Nyel stood and stretched. He peered down at his friends as they slept. Ivory, Theo, and the younglings lay curled up in their own nests. Bem fell asleep slumped against the cavern wall with Carver's head in his lap. A line of drool trickled out of the corner of Bem's mouth and threatened to run down his jaw. Off to the side, Falcon and Iris snuggled close together for warmth. They faced each other, with Falcon's arm draped protectively over Iris. Nyel couldn't help but feel alone looking at them.

With a sigh, he averted his gaze and snuck out of the cave. Heavy steps crunched pebbles behind him. Nyel turned to find Theo had awoken and followed him, trying not to make a sound. Nyel groaned as soon as he exited the tunnel to the outside. The sun hadn't even risen yet. The urge to turn around and go back to bed was strong, but not enough for him to act on it. He wished he could have slept more. His anxiety of the day ahead, however, made it impossible.

Theo chuckled. "For one so small, you make a big fuss out of mornings."

"It still looks like night to me," Nyel grumbled, unhappy. Theo nudged his side with his snout and chuckled. Nyel grinned at him, but it soon vanished as he remembered their journey ahead.

"Today marks the start of our flight to the Malachite clan," Nyel proclaimed.

Theo nodded. "We fly to the human's territory."

Nyel hesitated as doubts about their plans swarmed in his head. "Do you think we should all go together instead? I feel terrible that we're separating again. What if you're spotted?"

Theo looked toward the south in the direction of the kingdom thoughtfully. "Don't worry, we can fend for ourselves. According to Falcon, we won't be going into heavily populated areas. Remember, it's not my first time flying into your homeland."

"Just be careful," Nyel pleaded.

Theo chuckled again. "Don't worry about us, Shifter. You'll have enough to worry about convincing the other dragons not to eat you. We are the nicest clan, after all."

Nyel gulped. "You're not serious, are you? We don't stand a chance then."

Theo gave him a toothy, dragon-like grin. "Well...we're all savages when it comes to our territory."

Nyel rolled his eyes and smacked his leg for good measure.

Ivory was the next to emerge from the cave. He let out a boisterous yawn that vibrated the air around them and stretched his massive body. His joints creaked and cracked in protest. The old dragon's age showed. His scales didn't shine as bright as Theo's. He had lost one of the two horns on his head in a fight long ago. Even his wings had small holes and tears that never quite healed all the way through.

"I advise you to wake your friends, Nyel. I'd rather them leave before we do. It wouldn't do well to leave them on their own with the rest of the clan," Ivory suggested.

"They're not on their own, grandfather. They'll have me to protect them," Theo reminded him.

Ivory grunted, "Even so."

Nyel nodded and returned to the cave. Once he reached the cavern where his friends slept, he studied them once more. They seemed so peaceful, like they didn't have a care in the world. Nyel smirked as a thought crossed his mind that was too good to ignore. He planted his feet firmly on the ground, sucked in a huge breath, dug deep, and let out a monstrous roar from his chest. It was the mightiest roar he had ever mustered in human form. It bounced off the walls, surrounding them with its mighty call.

The cave erupted into chaos. Everyone jumped to their feet in fright, screaming and shouting all the way as they grabbed their weapons or summoned their magic. Nyel burst out into a fit of laughter at the shocked expressions on their faces. Bem was the first to whip around and notice Nyel in hysterics in the tunnel's mouth.

"Nyel, what the hell," Bem groaned. Carver and Falcon scowled in disgust and annoyance at being tricked, while Iris ran over to him and swatted him with her boot.

"How could you?!" she roared as she slapped him over and over with the sole of her shoe. Nyel tucked his head away from her while he laughed.

"What? The Ascendant wanted me to wake you guys up and what better way than a friendly dragon's voice?" Nyel snickered.

"You're a child," Falcon grumbled, rubbing his temples. His long silver hair lay in messy waves around his face.

Nyel smirked at him. "At least I know how to have a bit of fun."

Bem's mouth twisted into a grin, and he began to laugh as well. "He's right. We should all lighten up a little, try to enjoy life."

Iris rolled her eyes as she pulled on her boots, finished with her attack on Nyel. "Just don't make a habit of roaring at us in our sleep. Or else I'll use something other than my boot on you!"

"I'll try to resist," Nyel grinned impishly.

Nyel decided to make it up to them and left the cave to scrounge up some breakfast. He found a loaf of stale bread in one of their bags and a jar of apple jam. He cut the bread into slices and spread the jam on each piece. As he did this, his mind wandered to his father and Mari. Mari made the best breakfast. His mouth watered at the thought of the spread of meats, eggs, and fruits she laid out on the table for them. His stomach lurched. They were a long way from home now. Nyel did his best to push them from his mind. He hoped they were safe and doing well.

Once everyone emerged from the cave, they all sat around the remnants of their last fire in silence. The group was content with each other's company, knowing that it wouldn't last long. Iris was the first to stir as Nyel brought the bread and jam and passed the first piece to Carver to eat.

"Falcon, will you gather some of my uncle's crystals and bring them back? It would help to have as much reserved magic as we can, just in case," Iris asked.

Falcon nodded right away.

"I was already planning on that. I'll check every corner of his cabin for anything of use," Falcon promised. Iris thanked him as Nyel handed Falcon his bread-slice, who immediately passed it to Iris.

"Are you sure you'll be alright on your own? Theo won't be there to help you if you get into trouble," Bem asked Nyel. His brow furrowed in concern. "I mean, we're talking about a whole new group of dragons who aren't expecting to encounter humans!"

Nyel sighed. "I think we'll be fine, as long as Ivory is there to reason with them."

"Just be careful," Bem implored again. Nyel passed around the remaining slices, and they returned to silence while they ate. He wished he would have gone hunting once more to give them more than the stale bread and jam, but it would have to do.

A steady, rhythmic sound reverberated up the mountain towards them. It was the sounds of multiple dragon's wings filling the air. Nyel stood and peeked over the cliff's edge to find Theo, Syth, and Steno climbing towards them from the valley below. Seconds later, they soared above them, circled through the air, and landed all around the group, one by one. Swirls of wind from their wings stirred around them in a cloud of dust and pebbles.

"Why do they all look miserable? Did they eat spoiled meat? I'm the only one who has the right to feel such misery," Syth grumbled. He examined the group with a look of disgust.

"We've only just reunited as a group," Nyel explained after finishing his bread in a few bites. "We're not so keen to part ways again."

"Well, we're not either, but it's not like we won't see our clan again," Syth grumbled.

Nyel had to stop himself from rolling his eyes at the stubborn dragon. At least Falcon, Bem and Carver couldn't understand his complaints the entire journey to the cabin.

"Are they ready to go? We want to leave as soon as possible," Theo questioned, his eyes scanning over his riders. He seemed anxious and in a hurry. Nyel quickly relayed the message to the others. They wiped off their hands and collected their things, preparing to leave. As they did, Nyel turned and addressed the three dragons once more.

"Please promise to be patient and careful with them? They won't be able to understand you, so you'll have to figure out a way to listen and communicate to one another," Nyel instructed, his eyes resting on Syth.

"We promise," Theo replied. Steno nodded at Nyel while Syth grunted as he watched the others make their preparations.

Nyel patted Theo's scaly leg and said, "Thank you," then lowered his voice and added, "Keep your eye on Syth, will you?"

Theo snorted in amusement, but nodded in agreement. Nyel sighed. He was nervous, but he knew he had to take their word for it.

He returned to the others just as they finished packing. Iris embraced her brother first, followed by Bem and then Falcon. Bem made his way to Nyel and wrapped his arms around him in a tight hug. Nyel squeezed him in return, suddenly not ready to let him go. They patted each other heavily on the back.

"Be careful, brother. We'll be back as soon as we can. Don't get eaten," Bem grunted in Nyel's ear.

"You too, Bem. Remember to stay hidden and keep away from any villages," Nyel cautioned. They let each other go, and Nyel turned to find Carver standing beside them. Carver reached out a hand and Nyel took it.

"Watch over my sister," Carver warned. He tightened his grip and stared into Nyel's eyes with a fierce glare. It took Nyel aback for a split second, but quickly regained his composure.

"I will. Look out for each other,' Nyel replied.

Bem and Carver joined their dragons; Bem to Theo and Carver to Syth. Falcon followed behind them, but paused in front of Nyel. They nodded to each other, and then Falcon climbed onto Steno's back.

Ivory joined Nyel's side to see them off. "May the winds carry you safely on your journey. We look forward to your speedy return."

The dragons bowed their heads to their Ascendant and then, one by one, they soared into the air. The three dragons circled overhead once, each of their riders waving to Nyel and Iris below. With three departing roars, the dragons took off southwards towards Lake Peril and, beyond that, the kingdom of Hailwic. Iris joined Nyel as they watched their friends fly away through the mountains. Nyel hoped they could work together as a team.

As the last dragon disappeared from sight, Nyel let out a weary sigh. A sudden heavy loneliness crept into his heart, a feeling he didn't expect to feel so strongly. It made him want to fly after them. A gentle hand grabbed his shoulder and gave it a comforting squeeze. Of course, he wasn't alone, Nyel remembered. He had Iris by his side. He pushed away his troubled thoughts and turned to her. Nyel forced a smile, trying not to show her the unease he felt.

"Well, shall we prepare for our own departure?" he asked, attempting to sound more confident than he really was.

Iris grinned in response. "Yes, we shall."

She turned and led the way back into the cave, where they gathered their things. Nyel decided not to bring his bag with him on this trip. All he needed was his sword and the belt Iris had enchanted for him. He could never understand magic, especially when it came to enchantments. Somehow, she found a way to make his belt keep whatever was attached to it in his human form, even after he transformed into his dragon form. It allowed him to be ready for a fight whenever possible.

Nyel fastened his belt tight around his pants and fixed his sword onto his left hip. He also forwent his shirt and boots. He only had one set of each and didn't want to risk shredding them to pieces. There was no plan on him staying human around the group of dragons, anyway. Nyel glanced over his shoulder and watched Iris finish packing up her blanket. He spotted a few different sized and colored crystals in her bag before they vanished out of sight.

Iris's long, raven hair hung in her blue eyes. Her brow furrowed, as if she were deep in thought. Watching her, Nyel realized how nervous she must be. She put on a good show, but even he was still somewhat scared to be around a clan of dragons who mostly hated humans. His urge to protect her grew stronger at the thought. Iris could fight for herself, but even a talented sorceress like her couldn't stand up against an entire clan. No matter what Ivory expected out of him, Iris's safety had to come first. No matter what.

Iris stood and slung her bag over her shoulder. "Are you ready?" she asked, catching his eye. Nyel nodded and gestured for her to follow him up the tunnel.

"Are *you* ready? To be amongst a pack of ravenous dragons, I mean?" Nyel asked her as they walked side by side.

Iris adjusted her grip on her bag, considering her answer. Finally, she said, "I'm nervous, yet strangely excited. More than ever, I'm ready to see my uncle's dream come true. I'm ready to fight alongside the dragons and create a better life for us all. Also, having you by my side helps."

"What, as your translator?" Nyel chuckled as he gave her a playful nudge.

Iris laughed. "There's that. You also give me the confidence and strength that we can do anything."

"Oh…thank you," Nyel blushed, unsure of what else to say.

They emerged from Ivory's cave to find the sky had awoken while they were away. The sun still hid behind the mountains, but Nyel could make out its faint pink glow, promising a clear and sunny day. He breathed in the crisp spring air to calm his nerves. The others would arrive soon to join their Ascendant.

Ivory stood by the cliffside, his eyes locked on the valley beneath him, waiting for their arrival. Nyel joined him and crossed his arms over his chest, following his gaze as the clan came to life.

"We're ready whenever you are," Nyel offered.

Ivory grunted. "I suggest you shift into your dragon form soon."

Nyel's brow furrowed. "I will, but not until it's time to leave."

Irritated, Ivory snorted and shook his head. "You're rather stubborn. Why do you not just do as I say?"

"They need to know both of my forms," Nyel said, a little annoyed that the Ascendant didn't understand his intentions. However, what he didn't voice was his concern about the pain he felt when shifting the last few attempts. Nyel pushed those thoughts from his mind when he spotted movement in the distance. A group of three dragons flew towards them from the valley below, followed by another group of four.

Nyel gulped and inched closer to Iris, readying himself for anything.

Chapter 4
Flight of the Guardians

The first to arrive on Ivory's cliff was someone Nyel recognized at once. Lorna landed beside them; her bright purple scales gleamed in the rising sun. Two other female dragons followed her, one with a mixture of gold and copper scales that sparkled in the dazzling display of light and a smaller one with turquoise scales that were more subtle. They were a lot like Lorna, with slim frames, bright white horns and small spikes running along the back of their neck. Lorna's companions kept their distance from Nyel and Iris, gazing at them with curiosity and caution.

Before he greeted them, four more Guardians landed beside the remnants of their campfire. The lead dragon took one look at the remains and angrily swept them off the cliff with his massive tail. The air vibrated as a rumble of growls erupted from their throats, four pairs of angry eyes glaring at them. Nyel stepped in front of Iris with his hand on the hilt of his sword, but Iris grabbed his arm and pulled him back.

"Let's use our words before our weapons, yes?" she suggested. She met Nyel's glare with a stern, authoritative gaze. Even though they wanted the same thing, he also swore to protect her. Reluctantly, he let his hand fall to his side, but kept an eye on the newest cluster of dragons.

There were three males and one female, each more vicious than the last. Some of them had dulled and scratched scales, or were missing scales altogether. Nyel realized these were some Guardians who were not to be messed with. They seemed wilder and more intense than any other dragon Nyel had worked with before. He made a mental note to keep an eye on them.

Lorna snorted. Her upper lip curled up to reveal her sharp fangs and lowered her horned head at the newcomers in defense, unfazed by their gruesome display.

"You dare disrespect your Ascendant's wishes before we can even begin the day?" she growled at them. She was also one to not mess with, Nyel realized with a shudder.

The dragon who had swept away their campfire stepped forward and snarled at her in anger. Nyel's stomach lurched at the sight of his mangled face. Deep old gashes carved around his right eye socket. A wrinkle of amber scales and scar tissue bunched up where his eye should have been. His existing eye, however, shone with a fury that would make the mightiest dragon slayer turn and flee.

"He disrespects us by forcing these feeble pests upon us!" the dragon hissed in a raspy voice that sent chills down Nyel's spine. He had to be as old as Ivory himself, if not older.

"Calm yourself, Orden, or else you might strike yourself ill," Lorna retorted. She wasn't about to let him intimidate her. "You have no right to speak of the feebleness of another when you're present."

Orden roared. Iris, still holding onto Nyel's arm, yanked him back a few feet in response. Nyel glanced over his shoulder at her for a moment and caught a glint of fear in her eyes before she forced it away. At least she realized these dragons were dangerous.

"ENOUGH!" Ivory boomed from behind them. Nyel winced as his voice echoed in his ears.

The group of dragons stilled and turned to face him. "I won't tolerate any fighting amongst ourselves! You will control yourselves, and you WILL respect my wishes. Anyone who disagrees, we will leave behind. Understood?" he threatened.

The group grunted their affirmations. Orden glared at Ivory with contempt, but gave one harsh nod in understanding.

"Good," Ivory huffed. "Now be silent until the rest of the group arrives. You're hurting my head with your drivel."

Nyel sighed in relief when Orden turned away to join the others he had arrived with. He grabbed Iris's hand and hurried her over to Lorna, who watched them with pale gray eyes.

"Iris, I'd like you to meet Lorna. We shared some fish at the river the other day. She was just defending us against that dragon. Orden, I believe?" Nyel explained in an attempt to make peaceful conversation. "Lorna, this is Princess Iris of Hailwic."

Iris bowed her head to the dragon. "It's nice to meet you, Lorna. I want to thank you for defending us."

Lorna's eyes gleamed with amusement as she studied Iris. "Why does she bow to me?"

Nyel shrugged. "Out of respect, I suppose."

"Well, tell her to stop it," Lorna huffed. "It makes me uneasy. I won't bow to her, nor should she bow to me." Nyel quickly relayed her message and Iris flushed with embarrassment.

"Apologies, I meant no offense," Iris replied, standing straight up and meeting Lorna's gaze.

Lorna chuckled. "I hope her backbone is as strong as her kindness. Otherwise, she won't make it long out here amongst the beasts. She must be fierce to survive out here."

A growl formed in his throat, surprising both Iris and Lorna. "You've no idea how capable of greatness this woman is, so I suggest you hold your tongue," he warned, his growl lowering his voice beyond normal.

Lorna lowered her head and met his intense gaze with her own. "Here's some advice. Control your emotions when you're in our world. Otherwise, your anger will get you killed, my young two-legged friend. I admire your spirit all the same. Come, meet my sisters while we wait for the others."

With that, Lorna turned and strode towards the two dragons that accompanied her earlier. Nyel's skin prickled as he seethed in anger. He glanced down and noticed small emerald scales forming on his arms and chest. He took in a deep breath to steady his nerves until they began to fade away.

"What was that about?" Iris asked in shock. "Did I do something wrong?"

Nyel shook his head in frustration. "You did nothing wrong. Follow me. She wants to introduce us to her sisters."

Iris didn't respond, only followed Nyel in silence. The gold and turquoise dragons stiffened when they spotted Iris and Nyel approaching them.

"These are my little sisters," Lorna said. She nodded towards the golden dragon. "This is Casca. And this," she continued as she motioned to the turquoise dragon, "Is Aura."

Each of her sisters gave them a stiff nod. At least their greeting was kinder than the others, for which Nyel was grateful. He placed a hand on Iris's shoulder and then said, "It's nice to meet you. I'm Nyel and this is Princess Iris."

"How strange must it feel for a mouse to turn into a bear?" Casca noted aloud. Her cool gray eyes sparkled with mischievous delight.

"Casca!" Aura gasped, horrified.

Casca scoffed. "What? Aren't you intrigued by how our ancestors' power has abandoned us for a weak little human? Even you're more deserving of the Ascendant power than he is."

"Of course I am! I wasn't going to say anything about it," Aura hissed in a much too loud voice.

Nyel winced, but tried not to show it. He was prepared for the anger that would arise from the clan when they discovered he had inherited Ivory's powers. As an Ascendant, Ivory held the power to heal himself and others in his blood. One dragon after another, the Ascendants passed on their power for generations, each dragon wielding their own unique abilities. Ivory used his gift to heal Nyel when they first met. They discovered in shock that the Ascendant's power had transferred to Nyel, granting him the ability to shift into a dragon.

Lorna gave them a soft growl. "Don't cast this one aside so quickly, sisters. I've watched him hold his own against the shadows. He has the potential to be one of us."

Casca grunted. "We shall see."

More dragons arrived on Ivory's cliff. Many of them glared at Nyel and Iris, fuming that they were in the same proximity. They remained cold and silent as Ivory watched on.

"I suppose you should change soon," Iris suggested, shuffling from one foot to the other with growing impatience. Nyel sighed and braced himself for what he knew was to come.

Nyel focused on the foreign bubble of energy that hid deep within his core, coaxing it out. Immediately, scales formed across his skin. With another shaky breath, Nyel forced himself to shift all the way through. He held back a scream as his body exploded in pain. His arms and legs bulked up and his head and neck grew long and heavy. Claws sprouted from his fingertips while spikes erupted from the base of his skull, down his spine and to the tip of his newly formed tail. The last thing to emerge were his enormous wings that shot out of his back and spread themselves open.

He gasped for air as his transformation finished. Nyel's legs shook as he struggled to contain himself. He hadn't experienced such pain since the first time he shifted. Whatever magic Kollano had used on him hadn't gone away. It had only become worse.

"Nyel?" Iris voiced in concern. She grabbed hold of his lower jaw, supporting his head as he panted.

"I'm ok," he said in a rush, pulling his head away from her reach. The last thing he wanted was for her to worry about him. He could handle it, no matter how badly it hurt. Iris stared at him with a flash of hurt in her eyes before nodding.

Nyel turned away and noticed the others staring at him in shock. They hadn't seen him shift into a dragon before, and it had stunned them into silence. Many looked away from him when he met their gazes, but a few seemed intrigued by him. One of them being Casca, who pranced over to him with the same mischievous look in her eyes.

"Well now, that was a sight to see!" she exclaimed in delight. Casca sniffed at his neck, his chest and wandered towards his backside.

"Hey, watch it!" Nyel growled, whipping around and snapping his teeth at her.

Casca chuckled. "He's rather feisty, isn't he? Careful darling, boy. You're outnumbered here. I was only amazed that you no longer reeked of humans. It's not a trick of sorcery. You're truly a dragon!"

"Indeed," Nyel huffed, feeling a bit violated.

"Casca, leave the poor thing alone," Aura scolded. "You pester too much."

"And you are too reserved, fledgling. You're no fun," Casca returned with a roll of her eyes.

Aura growled at her. "Rotten lizard."

Casca burst into laughter. "I never expected *you* to defend the human. Sometimes you surprise me, little sister."

Before she could reply, Ivory grunted as he stood on all fours. The group went silent. All eyes fell on their leader. Ivory scanned the dragons that surrounded him, meeting each of their gazes.

"I count twenty of you," he announced. "I want ten of you to accompany us to the next clan. The rest of you will remain here and guard our home. Know this, if you choose to go with us you must show our guests respect. Do you understand?" Some of the group grumbled unhappily.

Lorna stepped up immediately. "My sisters and I will graciously accompany you, Ascendant. If you allow it."

"I do," Ivory nodded in approval.

A young dragon and two others about his age also came forward and said, "We will go. To prove ourselves of our new Guardianship roles."

Ivory nodded.

One after another, more Guardians slowly stepped in and offered their allegiance to Ivory for the journey ahead. The last to step up was the older dragon from before, Orden, who glared at Nyel for a fraction of a second. "I will go, Ascendant."

Ivory wavered as he studied him. "You addressed the concern earlier. Can I trust you to treat Nyel and Iris as one of your own?"

Orden's good eye turned on them once more. In a scathing voice, he said, "Of course. I will do nothing to harm them, so long as they don't harm one of us. It goes both ways, after all."

Nyel felt a pit in his stomach as he watched the old dragon carefully. He didn't have a good feeling about him.

"Very well," Ivory sighed. "The rest of you, return to your posts and keep our home safe. We will return as soon as possible. You're dismissed."

The remaining ten dragons bowed their heads and leapt into the air one at a time. Nyel watched as they soared away, a little too eagerly. If he didn't know any better, he could bet they were happy not to have to be near him and Iris.

"I want each of you to pick a companion to fly with, in case we must separate. Choose well, for you will guard each other with your lives until we return."

The group whispered amongst themselves. Nyel translated what was being said while nervously glancing around. Now there were twelve dragons in their group, including Ivory and himself. Who would choose to fly with them?

A snout nudged his neck, causing him to jump in surprise. "Care to be my companion in the sky?"

He turned and found Lorna awaiting his reply, amazing him. Nyel nodded at once, relieved. He was certain he could have flown with Ivory. But here was an opportunity to get to know another dragon from his new clan. He smiled to himself with a new sense of gratitude towards Lorna for giving both he and Iris a chance to prove themselves worthy. Once he explained this to Iris, she smiled up at the purple dragon.

"Thank you, Lorna!" Iris said, placing a hand on her heart. "It will be an honor to fly with you."

Lorna lowered her head and stared at Iris with one large eye. "Likewise, my dear. I'd like to hear about the trials of being a princess."

Iris grinned after Nyel's translation. He sighed in relief once more.

Ivory cleared his throat, and the talking amongst the Guardians ceased. "I expect all of you to work together and protect your clan. Your family. These creatures of darkness are not to be taken lightly. They are extremely dangerous, and the possessed are even more so. Be vigilant. Now, to the skies before we lose daylight!"

With that, Ivory leapt into the air. A variety of beautifully colored scales launched into the sky after him. Casca and Aura followed while Lorna moved to the cliff's edge. She glanced back at them expectantly. Nyel lowered himself onto the ground to allow Iris to climb onto his back with her things.

"Are you ready?" he asked, looking over his shoulder at her.

Iris adjusted herself for a moment, ensuring her bag was secured to her back. She then grabbed hold of the spike in front of her and nodded. "Ready."

Lorna dove off the cliff, with Nyel following close behind. She led him downwards along the mountain's face instead of up like the others. Iris shrieked in surprise and delight as they dove towards the ground. The air rushed past them, sending Iris's long black hair into a fit behind her. Nyel couldn't stop the grin that formed on his reptilian face as the familiar feeling of weightlessness overtook him.

They pulled up into the air about halfway down, ending their descent, and climbed into the air to rejoin the others.

"I must say, I'm impressed by how well you've taken to the skies. I would have thought your nature would have made you frightened by the very thought of it," Lorna called to him from ahead. She was much stronger and faster than he was. Then again, she had flown her entire life and didn't have to worry about someone on her back.

Nyel chuckled. "Of course, I was terrified! Sometimes those fears must be pushed aside. I also had wonderful teachers who helped me."

"Ah yes, the younglings," Lorna laughed. "They were a good crash course. You'll have much to learn out in the wild with fully grown dragons." Nyel fell silent as his concerns raced back into his mind. He had barely made friends with the dragons of this clan.

"What are you two talking about?" Iris asked after a moment, bringing Nyel out of his troubled thoughts.

"Lorna was commenting on my flying skills," Nyel explained. "Or at least, she's suggesting that I still have much to learn."

"I'm sure she's right. You can only learn so much in a short amount of time," Iris agreed.

They joined Lorna's sisters at the back of the pack. Ahead of them, Orden and his companion turned and glared at them with hatred in their eyes, but said nothing.

Out of pure instinct, Nyel growled at the sight of them. "We're going to have trouble with that one."

Iris didn't have to ask who he meant. She stared at the massive dragon and gulped. "Yes, well…we'll just have to watch each other's back."

As their group of twelve left the clan's territory, they fell silent. Although their group was larger than he expected, Nyel knew they couldn't depend on their numbers being enough to defend them from being ambushed along the way. Nyel already spotted the

Guardians scanning the area above and below them as they went. Anticipating any type of danger.

They continued to fly like this throughout the day over the treacherous mountains that passed around them. It made Nyel thankful for being able to fly. It would have taken them days to pass through the Dragon Mountains on foot, if not weeks. To his knowledge, the Dragon Mountains were the largest mountain range in all of Hailwic.

Back at home, Nyel was used to the Emzer Mountains. They appeared to be filled with more trees than rocky terrain, as these seemed to be. On the tallest mountains they flew past, Nyel could even see snow clinging to the tops of them. Below them were various valleys of woods, rolling hills, and even large boulders that had fallen from the mountains long ago and lay in a pile of rubble. The scenery was breathtaking beyond words, but at the same time, the most dangerous terrain he had ever laid eyes on.

Time seemed to pass by as they made their way east. Hours had passed before Iris stirred and broke their silence.

"Have you heard any other news?" Iris called to him over the wind. She seemed a little more relaxed since they first started flying. He was glad to see her enjoying the view as much as he was.

"No. I assume we'll probably stop somewhere for the night," Nyel answered while he studied the surroundings far below.

"We could be there by early morning if we fly straight through the night," Aura commented from ahead. It was the first time she had spoken since they left Ivory's mountain.

Lorna turned her head to look at them and replied, "Yes, but we must consider the shadow creatures. Watch out, sister, they could be hiding anywhere."

"We'll be sitting ducks if we stop for the night!" Casca interjected. "We'll be much safer if we stick to the skies until we get to the clan. They will have more numbers readily available if those creatures decide to show their ugly faces!"

"She has a point, you know," Aura said in a small voice. She was much quieter than her outspoken sisters. Nyel wondered how they could be related.

Casca smirked. "You see? Even little Aura thinks so."

"It's not my decision. You'll have to take it up with the Ascendant," Lorna sighed, obviously not wanting to argue with her hard-headed sister.

"What's going on?" Iris asked in confusion. Nyel glanced back at her to find her brow furrowed in frustration.

"They're arguing whether we should fly straight through the night," Nyel hurried to explain.

Iris adjusted her weight as she gave it some thought. "It would make more sense to keep going. Will you at least have them stop at some point to allow me to stretch my legs? Riding on these scales is brutal on my legs."

Guilt flooded Nyel in an instant. He hadn't considered how uncomfortable it would be to ride a dragon for an extended amount of time. It was something he hadn't had to think about for himself. He agreed with her and quickly called out to Ivory, "What do you think, Ascendant? Should we continue flying through the night?"

There were grumbles from a couple of dragons who were more interested in resting their wings, while the rest of the group shouted out their agreements.

"Very well. We will travel throughout the night," Ivory decided. "However, we must be ever vigilant for any signs of danger in the darkness. These shadow creatures are becoming stronger with each passing day. There is a small lake not too far up ahead. We will stop for a drink and rest our wings there."

Nyel relayed the message back to Iris, and she sighed with relief. The rest of the flight was quiet until they reached the lake moments later. It was a perfect display of peace to Nyel. They rounded a corner through a long valley to reveal a small lake that sat nestled in the mountains. The water was still and crystal clear.

The Guardians followed Ivory as he descended onto a sandy beach that surrounded the lake. Nyel would have never guessed it was there if he hadn't seen it for himself. He spotted about four or five elk standing knee deep in water on the opposite side of the lake. As soon as they noticed the swarm of dragons heading towards them, the elk bugled loudly and took off into the safety of the forest behind them.

Nyel was careful to land away from the other, more aggressive dragons. As soon as his claws sunk into the coarse sand, Iris slipped off of his back and stumbled onto the ground. Nyel shifted back into his human form and stifled back a groan as pain shot through his body once more. He ignored his pain and hurried to help Iris to her feet.

"Are you ok?" he asked in concern.

Iris laughed, "Yes, I'm fine. My legs went numb! If dragon riding is going to be a common way of travel from now on, we are going to need proper saddles."

Hunched over the water yards away, Orden raised his massive head from the lake and stared at them with his cold, piercing eye. Water dripped from his jaw as he curled back his upper lip and snarled at them. "We are not your filthy pets!"

Nyel stepped in front of Iris without hesitation. "We understand that. She's only saying it would be more comfortable to have something other than scales to sit on for hours on end."

"You insult us by even suggesting such a thing! Don't think for a second that this will be a permanent union," Orden hissed, enraged. "Dragons aren't meant to befriend humans. You are below us, next to the grubs in the dirt."

"Why did you choose to fly with us if you are so against us?" Nyel countered. His skin prickled with the scales that threatened to return, ready to defend himself. "You had a choice to stay behind and protect the clan."

"I'm only here to ensure that you don't pull any tricks on the Ascendant," the angry dragon spat. He took a few threatening steps towards them. Nyel flung a protective arm out in front of Iris to push her backwards. "And to protect my fellow clan-mates from dirty humans!"

"Did I upset him? I'm sorry, that was not my intention," Iris spoke up, trying to connect the dots where she couldn't understand Orden.

Orden growled at her instead, deep and menacing. Iris didn't need a translator for the message he was sending her. With a surge of his own anger, Nyel crouched and let out a fierce growl in return. He didn't care if the dragons threatened him, but he wasn't going to allow them to threaten Iris.

"Orden, back off or I'll have to take you down...again," Lorna warned as she trotted over to them from her spot a few yards away and positioned herself between them.

"Stay out of this Lorna, you traitor," Orden threatened, his tone harsh. The other dragons looked up at them with curiosity. Lorna didn't flinch.

"I'm not a traitor here, Orden. If you harm these humans, you will go against your Ascendant, and we will force you to leave the clan. Is that what you want?" Lorna inquired. Her tone was calm, but her eyes shone with wicked defiance. It seemed this wasn't the first time she had stood up to the old Guardian.

Orden growled at her with growing hatred, yet he didn't say another word. Instead, he let out a quick burst of flame into the lake, causing vapors to twist up into the air as it hit the water. Orden then stalked further down the shoreline to be alone. Nyel and Iris watched him for a few moments, remaining completely still as they did.

"Let him cool off. He'll come to his senses soon enough," Lorna said, turning to face Nyel and Iris. Nyel's tense shoulders relaxed, and his scales vanished a few seconds later. He looked down and his eyes widened. He didn't even realize that he had clasped onto Iris's left hand during the commotion. Or did she grab his hand?

When he looked back at her, he noticed Iris's other hand glowed a hue of blue, ready to use her magic to defend them. As if realizing for the first time what she had done, Iris released it and quickly pulled away from him. She gathered her leather canteen in silence and went to the lake to fill it.

"Thank you, Lorna, for all your help. I owe you one," Nyel sighed, casting a sidelong glance at Iris, wondering if she was alright.

Lorna chuckled. "Perhaps you will. But for now, make sure your mate is unharmed. She looks a bit shaken."

Nyel's head snapped back, and he gawked at Lorna with wide eyes. His face burned bright red, even though he knew Iris couldn't understand what she had just said.

"Iris isn't my mate! We're just friends," he hissed in embarrassment. He prayed Iris couldn't hear him, as even his ears burned.

Lorna gave him a curious look. "Is that so? The way you defended her and looked after her just now would tell me otherwise. We dragons defend our mates with our lives, especially if they are expecting hatchlings."

Her eyes drifted over to Iris and studied her for a moment. "Are you not expecting hatchlings?"

Nyel's face burned with the intensity of the sun itself. For a moment, he couldn't breathe, as if someone had just hurled their fist into his stomach. He shook his head and waved his hands, trying to shoo the very question far away, out of sight and out of mind.

"No, no, no! You've got it all wrong!" he stammered. "We're just friends, honest! And there are certainly no hatchlings involved. We, as in humans, are more complicated than that."

Lorna snorted and rolled her eyes at him. "You mean to tell me you have the senses of a dragon, and yet you can't sense the racing hearts when you're near each other?"

Nyel stared at her, dumbfounded. He swallowed past the lump in his throat. "As I said."

Lorna shook her head and chuckled, unconvinced. "You have a lot to learn, fledgling."

Nyel was about to protest further, however Lorna turned without another word and returned to her sisters. He stared after her as his unspoken words died away. What did she mean by racing hearts? Of course, he found Iris beautiful. Anyone would. But Iris had Falcon, didn't she? She didn't look at him the way he knew he looked at her.

"Is everything alright?" Iris called from the lakeside. Nyel jumped in surprise, lost in his own thoughts. He spun around and almost lost his balance as his foot dug into the sand. She took one glance at his red face and raised a curious eyebrow.

"What's going on? What did she say to you?" Iris interrogated.

Nyel's heart could have stopped dead in his chest right then. His throat went as dry as the sand beneath his feet. He coughed a few times to clear it and turned his face away from her while another wave of embarrassment swept over him. "Oh, it was nothing. She...uh...was just making sure we were safe."

"You haven't convinced me," Iris said, crossing her arms. Her stunning blue eyes pierced daggers into his very soul.

Nyel took a deep breath and met her gaze. For a moment, he wanted to tell her the truth. What would she think about their conversation? His lips parted as he stared at her, the words ready to spill out.

"Just trust me. You don't want to know," Nyel said. He wanted to kick himself at his cowardice. "Can we drop it? Please?"

Iris studied him for a moment. Finally, she dropped her arms and let out a sigh. "Very well. It's maddening not being able to understand your conversations. I appreciate your translations, however, it's not the same. What's the plan from here?"

Grateful for a change of subject, Nyel knelt beside the water and cupped handfuls of water into his mouth. Flying had become more natural to him, but it was still exhausting. He wiped drops of water from his chin and eyed the cluster of dragons along the shoreline across from them.

"I believe we are going to travel throughout the night. So I need you to stay alert the entire time we are in the air. No sleeping," he warned, his eyes flickering back to her as he spoke. "I don't want you falling off."

"Trust me, I wouldn't be able to sleep up there even if I wanted to. I've had one too many free falls in my short time of flying and I don't plan to repeat it," Iris groaned, sitting next to him in the sand. She wrapped her arms around her knees and watched the distant dragons as they drank from the lake.

Nyel placed his arms behind him and lowered himself into the sand to rest beside her. He snuck a peek at her from the corner of his eye. Nyel couldn't help Lorna's prying questions from floating back into his mind. He would always admire Iris's beauty. She tied her long black hair into a careful braid to keep it from getting tangled in the wind. Her blue eyes sparkled like the lake in the sunlight as she gazed across the calm water.

He glanced away, not wanting to stare too long at her. If a dragon could tell that he was attracted to her, did that mean she could tell, too? He hoped she couldn't sense it, but why?

"We'll have to be prepared for anything. Make sure we have our firepower ready," Nyel offered to distract himself. Iris remained still until slowly she nodded.

"Do you think we are fighting a losing battle?" she asked in a near whisper, her usual confidence suddenly wiped away by fear.

Nyel stared at her, astonished by the sudden change. She had always seemed so certain of herself, yet now he could hear the doubt in her voice. The trials of the day must have gotten to her more than he had realized. He turned to face her and leaned forward until she met his eyes.

"Of course not! It was never going to be an easy fight, but I have faith that we'll get at least some dragons on our side," Nyel offered, trying to encourage her.

"I sometimes fear that my father may actually be right about me," she whispered. Her eyes brimmed with tears. Nyel felt surprised by the change in her demeanor. He quickly wrapped a comforting arm around her and gave her shoulders a squeeze.

"Listen, don't take this the wrong way. Your father is a narcissistic ass," Nyel said with a smirk. Iris chuckled through her tears. "You're the strongest, bravest, and most intelligent woman I know. You have so much more to give to our people than your father ever could. Please never doubt yourself!"

"It's just, it was always my uncle's idea to unite men and dragons together. The stories he told Falcon and I, the adventures he took us on, it was impossible to fall in love with his dreams. When I saw him possessed by that demon Kollano..." Iris shuddered. "Sargon wasn't evil. He was always curious about how the world worked and finding the peace within it. If whatever he was planning with those shadow creatures backfired on him, I wondered, could something like that happen to me on my quest? Is something terrible going to befall us all because of me?"

Nyel placed a finger under her chin to bring her gaze back to him. "I won't let anything happen to you, or the others. And I know you won't let that happen, either. Sargon's mistake was working alone. But that's not you. That's not us. We're your army and your family now. Wherever you lead, we will follow, because we believe in you."

Iris stared at him with wide eyes, silent tears rolling down her cheeks. Their faces weren't very far apart from each other at all. With a swarm of emotions racing through him, Nyel resisted the urge to look down at her lips. With his heart drumming in his ears, he gently pulled away from her and got to his feet. Nyel then reached a hand out to her and smiled.

"Dry your eyes, Iris. You're a warrior," Nyel whispered.

Iris grinned up at him as she wiped away her stray tears. She took his hand and allowed him to pull her to her feet. Once she stood in front of him, she hesitated. Nyel's heart skipped a beat as her face leaned towards his and placed a quick peck on his cheek. "Thank you, Nyel. You always know what to say. I'm glad to have you by my side."

Nyel's hand traced his cheek where her lips had grazed it as Iris turned to gather some food from their pack. Her face had changed from uncertainty and fear, to determination and courage by his words. He felt proud that she trusted him, but was he telling her these things because he was a loyal protector and friend?

His heart thudded in his chest and his cheek still tingled where her lips had brushed it. Did he care about her and protect her so much because she was the princess? Was he just doing his duty as a good servant to what remained of the true goodness of the royal family? He shook his head; Lorna's words were getting to him.

Iris looked up at him and gave him a warm smile as she handed him some bread and jerky, forcing him to eat the most dreadful meal time and time again. He took it from her hand and ate a few slow bites, watching Iris pause to watch the lake once more. Her eyes were suddenly fierce and ready for anything as she stared, deep in thought. When she returned her gaze to Nyel, this time, he didn't look away.

"Let's go talk to Ivory about the next clan. I want to know everything about them before we get there," she said. She turned without waiting for him, marching towards the pack of standoffish dragons without a trace of fear in her stature. Ready to brave the greatest beasts that any darkness could muster.

A grin broke away from his frown, a feeling he had not felt for a long time as he wiped his hands of breadcrumbs. A spark of excitement, hope, and desire ignited inside him as he watched her descend on the unsuspecting dragons. He couldn't hide from himself any longer. He wouldn't douse the flame that burned hot in his chest. There was one thing he had left to admit to himself, and it was finally time to acknowledge it without hesitation. He had to ignore the fear of what it might lead to if he said it out loud, but at least for now, he could whisper it in the safety of his own mind.

He had fallen in love with Iris.

Chapter 5
Flight of the Dragon Riders

Bem

Have you any idea what they're arguing about?" Carver groaned as the three dragons circled each other midair. They had been that way for longer than any of their riders would have liked. Around and around again, hundreds of feet in the air over mountains and trees, it seemed it would never end. The prince's pale complexion appeared to be green over time while he clung to Syth for dear life.

"How should I know? Does it look like I speak dragon?" Falcon growled in annoyance. He crossed his arms tightly against his chest. At least, it seemed, he had grown accustomed to the height and the sway of Steno's movements.

However, Carver wasn't the only one who grew nauseated by the constant circling. Even Bem, who had flown more than the others, had felt his stomach twist and churn. He quit counting how many times they'd looped around each other after his head became dizzy from the attempt.

Carver let out a sarcastic laugh, trying to focus solely on Falcon across from him. "Well, you seem to know everything else! I figured you'd have that one in the bag, too."

Falcon's eyes narrowed on Carver with a look of disgust.

"Says the golden-child prince who had everything handed to him on a silver platter," Falcon countered.

"You know nothing of my life," Carver shouted. For the moment, he seemed to have forgotten where he was. The prince seethed with rage, and his hands glowed red.

Bem was quick to intervene. The last thing they needed was a fight amongst themselves. "Stop it, both of you! Have you not thought about asking the dragons instead of bickering at each other like children?"

"I doubt you've inherited your brother's gift," Carver spat, but his hands dimmed until they returned to normal. Bem had to resist rolling his eyes at him. It hadn't even been a day since they left the others and the two sorcerers were already at each other's throats. If Bem wasn't there to settle their constant bickering, he was almost certain they'd still be sitting on Ivory's cliff.

Bem ignored Carver's unhelpful comment. Instead, he leaned closer to Theo's head and yelled, "Theo, what's going on? Are we just going to fly in circles like this until the shadows find us?"

Theo grunted and glanced back at his rider, as if suddenly remembering he was there. The red dragon changed course with a strong flap of his wings. Theo pulled up higher into the air and away from their endless circle. He pointed towards the south with one claw with a grunt, and once more towards the east.

Then the dragon glanced back at Bem expectantly.

Bem groaned. "I'm sorry, I don't understand."

Theo snorted in frustration. He glanced down at the ground far below and then seemed to address the other dragons. Without warning, the three dragons dove towards the ground. Their riders wrapped their arms around the dragons' necks in fear as the ground raced towards them. Theo opened his wings and caught himself, slowing his descent for the final stretch. The dragons landed on a soft patch of dirt and knelt to the ground, impatient for their riders to climb off their backs.

Falcon, Carver, and Bem hesitated to dismount. Their limbs shook from the unexpected plunge from the sky. One by one, the riders dropped to the earth with a sigh of relief and a curse under their breath.

"Don't ever do that again!" Carver moaned, resting his hands on his knees. His face went pale and scrunched in a way that suggested he was giving everything he had to hold back his breakfast.

A rough gurgle sounded in Syth's throat: a chuckle. He found a plentiful amount of amusement in tormenting the prince whenever he could. Nyel had warned Bem to watch out for Syth. Even though the moody dragon agreed to help them, it didn't mean he felt enthused about it. When Carver regained his composure, they rejoined their dragons' side, still uncertain why they were on the ground.

"We don't have time for this," Falcon sighed. He looked to Bem in annoyance, as if he were in control of the dragons. Bem shrugged and shook his head. He didn't have a clue either.

Theo growled at him to get his attention. With one sharp extended claw, Theo traced triangles into the dirt, followed by a large oval. On the other side of the oval, he traced a few squares. They stared at it for several moments.

"He's a terrible artist," Carver observed. Bem elbowed him in the side.

Theo let out an agitated rumble. The dragon pointed a claw at Bem and then pointed to the squares. He then pointed to himself and then pointed to the triangles.

"It's a map," Falcon noted. He knelt beside Theo's drawing, intrigued.

Theo hummed in his chest with approval and nodded his head. He then placed an X at the left of the triangle mountains and motioned a circle with his paw at the surrounding group.

"The X represents us?" Bem asked, uncertain.

Theo nodded enthusiastically.

He held up one claw and drew a line from the X straight down across the lake and into the kingdom of Hailwic. He then held up two claws before drawing a second line from the X across the dragon's side of the map all the way to the right and then down across the lake from there.

"They're discussing two options on how to get to the cabin," Falcon explained. He scratched his chin where the stubble had grown while he studied the map. Falcon told the dragons where Sargon's cabin was located after they left the clan earlier, but hadn't told them the best way to get there.

Carver stepped in and drew a new line as he said, "Why not just go from here diagonally across the lake to the east kingdom?"

Syth growled in obvious protest. Carver sneered at him in frustration. "It just seems like the obvious choice. It's the quickest path! Why make an extra trip along the lakeside when we could simply cross over it?"

"Don't you have soldiers out there on the lake to guard against dragon attacks?" Bem asked.

"With a missing prince and princess last seen sailing into dragon territory," Falcon added, "they would heavily guard the area." Carver sighed and gave up with a wave of his hand.

"Fine, you guys choose the course. Don't listen to me," he sighed.

Theo watched them as they stared at the drawing. Bem looked at Falcon and said, "We have a risk of running into Kollano and his shadow creatures if we stay on this side of Lake Peril. If he's even still around."

"I think shadow creatures are a risk no matter where we go at this point. However, there's an added risk if we cross too soon and get spotted by one of the King's soldiers. Every dragon hunter for miles will be drooling at a chance to slay the dragons and hunt us down for an extra profit. I'm certain the king has a bounty on all our heads,' Falcon explained. He looked up at the three dragons and continued, "I think it would be wise to stay on this side of the lake as long as possible before crossing. I don't have a map of

Hailwic on me, but if my memory serves me right, I'd guess it could take us two days' time to fly there."

Syth was the first to nod in approval. Bem wondered if it was because he didn't want to go into the kingdom at all, but they would have to cross that bridge later. The other dragons shrugged and waited for their riders to return begrudgingly to their backs.

"I guess it's settled?" Bem asked Theo. He nodded and took off into the sky once more and led the others eastward. It was midday by the time they finally had a plan they could all agree on. Bem was eager to cross the lake. He could see it in the distance as they flew along the edge of the mountains. The clear blue water sparkled in the sunlight, beckoning to them to return. The dragons seemed more comfortable staying close to their homeland for safety. And he couldn't blame them for that.

Bem looked to his left at the looming mountains and felt his stomach twist in knots. Kollano could still be out there somewhere with his shadow creatures, maybe even watching them now. Or worse, they were following Nyel and Iris deeper into uncharted lands swarmed by human-hating dragons. Bem swallowed past the lump in his throat. All he wanted was everyone's safety, yet he feared that wouldn't be the case for any of them.

"Is everything alright, love?" Carver called out to him. Bem followed his voice to find Carver resting his body and head against Syth's neck. His striking blue eyes watched Bem with curiosity. It made Bem's heart leap in his chest.

"Oh, yeah. I was just lost in thought," Bem said, giving him a weak smile.

Carver arched an eyebrow at him, unconvinced. "Don't be afraid to speak your mind."

Bem hesitated. "I was wondering if we were being followed. I'm growing weary of having to look over my shoulder all the time."

Carver straightened up, but kept a firm grip on one of Syth's spikes. Bem knew he was afraid of flying, but Carver tried not to show it. "I understand. Don't worry, I think we should have enough fire power between all of us if they do show up. What's important is getting that journal so we can really solve our problems."

"Not all of them," Bem said. When Carver gave him a questioning look, Bem continued, "We're no doubt fugitives in the kingdom. They'll kill us on the spot if they capture us."

"Well, maybe you at least," Carver pointed out. Bem rolled his eyes, and Carver laughed.

"I'm joking, Bem! Take it easy," Carver chuckled at Bem's sour face. "Don't worry so much. We'll be fine, have some faith! In the meantime, I think this is an opportune time to practice your magic."

Bem sighed and tried to let go of his concerns for the time being. "What do you have in mind?"

Carver reached into his pocket and pulled out a small, smooth stone. He held it in his palm until it began to glow. Without warning, Carver sent the glowing stone over to Bem with his magic. As it reached Bem, it stopped glowing and dropped. Bem scrambled to catch it before it fell to the ground below.

Confused, Bem studied it and said, "Do you normally make it a habit to carry rocks in your pocket?"

Again, Carver chuckled. "No, airhead. It's a gift I got especially for you!"

"Gee, thanks," Bem teased, unsure of where he was going with this.

"Try to make that hover above your hand," Carver instructed.

Bem gave him a skeptical look. "You realize the wind will knock it out of my hand, right?"

"That's part of the challenge," Carver explained. "Find your balance. Line up the stone in the middle of your palm while fighting against the wind. I want to see you hold it all the way out to your side before we stop for the night."

"I have conjured fire before…" Bem stated, unenthused about his assignment. Carver sighed.

"Are you going to argue with me about this the entire way? Yes, I know you've made fire. Felicitations, I'm overjoyed for you! But there are many aspects to using magic and you need to get a feel for each one. Do you think the enemy will pause and give you time to conjure up your magic? Of course not. Now less complaining and more magic please, or I'll show you what a true sorcerer is really capable of," Carver instructed.

Bem grumbled in protest, but did as he was told. He placed the smooth stone in his palm and stretched his hand out in front of him. For several moments, Bem stared at it as he reached within himself to call upon his magic. The usual tingle sensation traveled up his arm and into his hand, followed by a warm glow, but nothing happened.

Bem suppressed a gasp. It astonished him how long it took for his magic to focus on the stone itself. Determined to not look like a fool, Bem clenched his jaw and forced his magic to grab hold of the stone. To his relief, the stone lifted away from his palm. Just as it rose an inch above his hand, the wind whipped around Theo's neck and knocked the stone backwards into his lap. Bem panicked and flailed his arms to grab the stone before it could be lost in the clouds below.

Embarrassed, Bem peeked up at Carver to see a knowing, if not somewhat teasing, smile form on his lips.

"Try again," was all the prince said in a gentle tone.

Bem sighed and focused on the stone once more.

He tried to lift the stone over and over for the next hour as the others flew on in silence. He managed to make the stone go a little higher, but couldn't keep it steady in the wind for very long.

Frustrated, Bem balled his fist around the stone and chucked it as far as he could. As he watched it soar away, a glow formed around it and stopped it mid-flight. The stone zipped back up past Bem and into Carver's outstretched hand. Bem was too angry at himself to care about the annoyance on Carver's face. His magical abilities weren't as good as he thought they were. Carver sighed and pocketed the stone.

"You'll get it, love," Carver called to him. Bem ignored him, too disgruntled to reply.

Bem turned away from Caver and rested his head against Theo's neck. He watched the scenery change beneath them. The mountains changed into hilly terrain and the vast open field running along the lake sprouted clusters of pine trees that dwarfed any found around Folke.

Even in his frustration, he couldn't deny the beauty of nature. He loved to explore the wilderness. He suddenly found himself wishing that he and Carver could go explore the area on their own with no one or anything to worry about for a change. No angry dragons or parasitic demons to chase them away. No brainwashed soldiers or a murderous king to threaten their lives. Just the two of them, on their own adventure, discovering new plants and animals along the way.

Bem sighed. It was a nice thought.

Steno growled low in his chest, alerting the others towards the mountains. Everyone's attention snapped to their left and when Bem followed their gaze, he froze. Descending from the mountain's edge was a group of five dragons flying in a V formation. Bem felt the rumble of Theo's growl against his legs. He cursed under his breath. This could only mean trouble. The dragons snarled and grunted at each other and suddenly they jolted forward, moving faster than before. It took everything they had for the riders to hold on as tight as they could.

"Do you think it's Kollano?" Bem yelled to the others over the roar of the wind rushing past his ears.

"It's possible. Or at least the possessed dragons," Falcon replied. He eyed the newcomers with apprehension. "I don't think our friends would react like this otherwise."

A groan resounded behind them. Bem twisted around to find Carver clutching his head in his hands. His eyes squeezed shut in a grimace and he grit his teeth. Concern swelled inside Bem's chest, and he called out, "Carver, are you alright? What's wrong?"

"My head…is pounding," Carver gasped.

Bem scrambled for his bow and put an arrow into place. Whatever was wrong with Carver, he was in no shape to fight. Bem's guts twisted into knots with worry for Carver, but he had to push his concerns aside. The five intruders had almost caught up with them.

"Theo, are they possessed?" Bem shouted. He aimed his arrow at the lead dragon before he got an answer. Their leader snarled at him with malice in his eyes. Theo glanced back at them and nodded. That was all the validation Bem needed.

In one swift motion, he let his arrow loose, aiming for the soft spot just under the dragon's jaw. The enemy dragon ducked its head, allowing the arrow to bounce off its scales with ease. Bem cursed. They needed better weapons, something that could penetrate their scales. He pulled another arrow and aimed again, this time for the eye. But the dragons were smarter.

Before Bem could even release the arrow, the possessed dragons split up and began circling around their group in different directions. Bem's eyes darted left, right, and all around him trying to keep track of them. With a grunt, Bem raised his bow and sent an arrow straight above him at the belly of a passing dragon. The dragon merely tilted away from him as it passed, avoiding his arrow entirely.

Syth snarled, impatient as he watched the swirl of dragons. He caught sight of their leader and lunged for his leg. His sharp teeth sank through scales and muscle. The leader shrieked in pain and the others hurried to his aid at once.

"No!" Bem shouted, afraid for Carver's safety. He seemed unaware of his surroundings, still clutching his head in pain.

Theo responded to Bem's desperate cry without hesitation. He spun around to face one of the dragons flying towards Syth. Bem could hear the rumble deep in the dragon's chest before Theo let out a blast of hot, blinding fire straight into the possessed dragon's face.

The dragon shook its head and teetered to the side. He squinted as the fire had reached his eyes. Without missing a beat, Theo grabbed the dragon's throat in his powerful jaws and shook him ferociously. With a sickening snap, the dragon's body went limp.

As the dragon's lifeless form fell from the sky, a thin wisp of a shadow withdrew from the body like a stream of smoke. A cold shriek filled the air as it met the light of the sun and disappeared. Bem sighed in relief. At least they had the sun to their advantage.

They heard a painful squeal as another dragon fell from the sky. Falcon's fingers danced with electricity while he watched the dragon fall.

"Nice work," Bem called to him as they flew past Falcon and Steno. Falcon nodded in thanks before turning his attention to the next one.

Theo made his way towards Syth, who had released the lead dragon to fight off two others. Carver shot a ball of fire out at one of them, but then doubled over in pain once more. A large, earth-toned dragon swooped down to bite into Syth's throat, unaware of Theo's approach.

Bem aimed an arrow at the earth-toned dragon and released it. As his arrow sunk into the dragon's right eye, he was rewarded with a painful roar. The dragon turned angrily towards them and Bem sent a second arrow into his left eye. The dragon shrieked with rage and agony. Theo grabbed the blinded dragon by the throat with ease and snapped its neck, just as he had with the last one. Another shriek filled the air as the shadow creature vanished in the sunlight.

The remaining two possessed dragons glanced at each other and without another thought, they turned and fled back the way they had arrived.

Furious, Syth chased after them, but Theo let out a roar that stopped him mid-flight. They appeared to argue back and forth before Syth snorted his displeasure. Instead, he changed direction to return to their previous path.

Bem sighed with relief. "Thank you, Theo."

He was glad Theo watched after them. It made Bem hopeful that maybe the others could learn from him. He made a great leader. Theo and Steno were quick to catch up with Syth as they continued on their way.

"Carver, are you hurt?" Falcon yelled, surprising Bem.

Carver looked back at them with a nauseated look on his face and forced a smile. "I'm fine. The feeling is less intense now."

"Those things did something to you when they captured you," Falcon observed. His face was stern, but there was concern in his voice that Bem rarely heard.

Carver scoffed. "They wouldn't have captured me if I was in my element. It's not often that I freefall from the sky to attack the enemy."

"Carver-" Falcon began, but Carver was quick to cut him off.

"I said I'm fine, Falcon!" Carver snapped. "I don't need you to be my nursemaid. I'm not my sister."

"That you are not," Falcon said through gritted teeth. Carver ignored him.

Bem eyed Carver, and his insides twisted into little knots once more. What *had* those creatures done to him? He wasn't himself anymore, even though he tried to be. Bem was certain that he hadn't been possessed. He ran through the obvious signs once more in his head. His eyes never glowed orange, nor did his veins appear pitch black across his body. Of course, he was certain that he was not possessed. Bem scoffed at himself. To be in the shadow creature's presence was enough to weaken him. They left Nyel unconscious with their touch.

Carver stared ahead; his face had fallen, thinking no one was watching him. The look on his face made Bem's stomach sick with dread. Carver was worried about something; it was written all over his face. And what made it all the worse, he hadn't shared his worries with Bem.

They returned to their silence as the hours passed. The Guardians quickened their pace ever since their encounter with the possessed dragons. Were more on the way? He was worried about the possibility. And he was sure the dragons were too. Bem glanced over his shoulder every few seconds to make sure they weren't being followed.

Suddenly, Theo grunted to the others and they all veered to the right towards the lake.

"Are we finally crossing over?" Carver groaned and stretched his arms above his head in an attempt to make his stiffened muscles more comfortable.

Falcon rolled his eyes, yet held his tongue.

"It seems we are," Bem grinned in relief. "We'll be back in the kingdom before you know it!"

"Don't let your guard down. Just because we're leaving the dragon's territory doesn't mean we're out of danger," Falcon forewarned.

"Falcon... shut up," Carver sighed in annoyance.

Falcon shook his head, but again said nothing. It was a losing battle to argue with the moody prince, and Falcon would rather choose peace.

Bem leaned closer to Theo so only he could hear him and asked, "Are you sure you don't need to rest? It's been a while since we've stopped."

Theo turned his head so that one of his large, bright eyes could look at him and nodded. Bem sighed, "I wish it was easier to understand you. It's hard when Nyel's not around to translate. I enjoy our conversations."

Theo's sides vibrated as he chuckled to himself before returning his gaze forward once more. Bem smiled and shook his head in defeat. He wasn't sure why Theo was laughing, but he was glad to have him by his side even so.

As the day drew longer and the sun crept along the sky closer towards the horizon, the small group of dragons and their riders began to grow more tense. Each of them watched the skies and the water below for any signs of shadow creatures, possessed bodies, or the king's soldiers.

The sky turned orange and pink as the sun descended to their right. Bem turned to watch the last of the light when he spotted something in the water in the distance.

"Hey Falcon, look over there!" Bem noted.

Falcon followed his gaze to see a small island with something towering over the rest of it in the center.

Bem asked, "Is that another fortress?"

"Indeed, it is," Falcon replied with intrigue.

"Do you think it's abandoned?" Bem wondered out loud.

Falcon pondered for a moment. "It should be, but I can't be certain. There's one way to find out."

"Do you really think we should stop now?" Carver shouted from up ahead. Syth rumbled his disapproval beneath him.

"I think we all deserve a rest," Falcon answered. "Plus, it's nearly nightfall. We shouldn't have to worry too much about encountering shadows there. Whereas if we continue on, who knows what will be lurking in the darkness of the woods once we reach land."

Carver grunted, "Yes, but there could be soldiers there waiting to report any sign of us."

"The last fortress was abandoned," Falcon countered. "Why should this one be any different? Besides, I've been to this one before."

The prince sighed and gave up with a shrug. Perhaps he, too, was ready for a break. Or at the very least, to stretch his legs. Bem knew his legs had grown stiff and sore from sitting on Theo's scaly back all day. It made him miss the softness of a leather saddle in comparison.

"Shall we go then, Theo?" Falcon called.

In response, Theo turned towards the right, and the others followed suit without complaint. They flew straight towards the distant island in complete silence. Bem scanned the surrounding waters for any kind of ship or vessel that could be out on the lake or docked at the island. He also trained his eyes to the sky in search of any dragons that may have been trailing them.

Once they were closer to the island, Theo grunted to Syth. Syth nodded to him and they split apart in opposite directions to circle the island. Steno and Falcon followed close behind Theo, and together they studied the waters and rocky beaches for any signs of human life. As they did, Bem observed the tall fortress in the center of the island. It was identical in build as the first fortress they stayed at not long ago. However, this one seemed a little more intact. There wasn't as much fallen rubble and the walls and four smaller towers that surrounded the tallest tower remained strong.

Syth met them on the other side of the island and snorted. Theo turned his gaze to Falcon and gave him a nod.

"It seems the island is secure," Falcon announced. "Now we should check the fortress on foot."

The Guardians glided across the rocky isle and landed close to the gates of the fortress. Bem slid off Theo's back as soon as the dragon's feet hit the ground. He had to catch himself against Theo's elbow. His legs trembled as if they had turned to jelly after sitting for so long on the dragon's back. Carver and Falcon struggled to regain their ground as well. Bem was determined now. He had to talk the Guardians into wearing saddles if their companionship were to continue. He could make them easily with the right materials and measurements. But he knew now wasn't the time as the others grabbed their weapons and crept towards the open gates.

Falcon went first with his sword drawn, followed by Carver. Bem stayed a few paces back and readied his bow. He scanned the outer walls, first along the ground and then following the ivy-covered stone up to the top of the wall. All seemed quiet.

Carver and Falcon approached the entrance and went to either side of the gate. They eyed each other, as if having a silent conversation. Without a word, they charged inside the fortress, swords ready. They halted in the center of the courtyard and scanned the area. Bem followed close behind them and hurried for the tower entrance. He took his time checking each room as he climbed the spiral staircase to the top. Everything appeared deserted. Once he reached the top of the stairs, he unlatched the wooden door at the top and flung it up to open.

Bem walked out onto the top of the tower and looked down at the rest of the towers. A sigh of relief escaped his lips. They were alone.

"All seems secure," Carver said from behind.

Bem grinned at him and nodded. "Falcon would never lead us astray."

Carver scoffed. "He has his moments, I suppose."

Bem stared out in the distance towards the setting sun. Brilliant colors of orange, pink, and blue filled the sky. It reflected over the calm waters of Lake Peril. Bem was in awe of the beauty of it. He could imagine having a nice, cozy home by the lake and watching the sunset every night from his porch or window. No, he wished his parents had that life. His mother would love it, he thought with a small smile.

The prince sheathed his sword and wrapped his arms around Bem's waist from behind. He rested his chin on his shoulder and followed Bem's gaze. "My, what a pretty view the dragon slayers have provided," he mumbled in Bem's ear.

A chill went down Bem's spine as Carver's breath hit his neck. "Well, they were lucky to claim the territory for it. You seem to be feeling better," Bem chuckled, trying not to look back at him.

"Much better," Carver mumbled, his lips grazing Bem's ear. Footsteps hurried up the steps behind them.

"Let's set up camp before- " Falcon began, but went silent. He halted in the trap door entrance in an awkward balance between finishing his ascent or turning on the spot. "I'm sorry, am I interrupting?"

Bem's face went hot, and he pulled away from Carver. Carver's smile vanished in an instant. He clenched his teeth and spun around to face Falcon.

"Can we not have a moment alone without you skulking about?" Carver shouted in anger. Bem was taken aback. *Where did that come from?* Bem wondered.

Even Falcon's eyebrow raised in surprise as he studied the prince. "Apologies. It's just that we don't have much time before the sun sets. We need to have our space in order before then, to be ready for any shadow creatures."

"We're on a deserted island in the middle of a lake. I don't think we need to worry about those demons here!" Carver snarled at him.

Bem placed a hand on his shoulder. "Take it easy, Carver. Falcon's right. We should set up camp before it gets dark. This tower is more intact than the last one. I saw plenty of rooms that would be perfect for you to rest in."

Carver shrugged out of his grasp and growled, "You're always taking Falcon's side. What a shock! If he wasn't so infatuated with my sister, you'd be perfect for each other!"

With that, Carver stomped back down the stairs, shoving Falcon out of the way in the process. Bem's mouth dropped open in disbelief.

"Carver, wait!" Bem called. He chased after him, but Falcon stopped him as he grabbed his arm.

Falcon eyed him with his usual stern expression and said, "Bem, let him go for now. We need to talk."

Bem hesitated, watching Carver disappear around the curve of the staircase before turning back to Falcon. "I'm sorry about that. I don't know what's gotten into him."

"That's what I wanted to discuss," Falcon replied. He quietly closed the trapdoor and sat against the ledge of the tower. Bem joined him, placing his bow down at his side.

"What's on your mind?" Bem asked, although he already suspected what Falcon was going to say.

Falcon sighed and pinched the bridge of his nose. Bem waited patiently, tracing a rut in the stone beneath him with his finger.

Finally, Falcon turned his gaze back to Bem and this time, his face had softened. "Bem, we need to be careful with Carver. Ever since those creatures took him, he hasn't been himself. Or at least, he's worse than he was before."

"Well, do you remember when a shadow creature almost took Nyel? It messed with him for a couple of days after," Bem countered.

"I remember," Falcon sighed. "But what if Carver was possessed? They had plenty of time and opportunities to do so."

Bem shook his head immediately. "I don't believe that. You should have seen him putting up a fight against them. Besides, you remember how someone puts up a fight when they are possessed? Carver didn't look like that at all, not even for a second!"

"Then I have to wonder why he didn't get possessed?" Falcon returned, studying Bem. "Have you considered that?"

Bem stared at him in shock. "You think he's sided with them?!"

Falcon shook his head in annoyance. "No. What I'm getting at is, what if they are growing stronger? What if they can hide the signs of possession?"

Bem picked at the side of his boot for a moment in thought. "I don't think so. I haven't seen anything to support that theory. I think a hoard of those creatures exposed Carver, and it has affected his entire demeanor. I think maybe they either fought over him or they were using him as bait to get us to come after him; more bodies to possess. Things will be different when we get to the cabin. Carver will be fine after a few days of proper rest, you'll see."

Falcon sighed and placed a hand on Bem's shoulder and waited until Bem met his gaze. "Just promise me that if you see any signs of danger from him, any at all, you'll let me know. I don't want you getting hurt."

A small smile formed on Bem's lips. He knew Falcon was only coming from a good place. He was a protector, after all. Bem nodded in agreement, got to his feet, and grabbed his bow. He held out his other hand to Falcon and said, "Shall we set up camp?"

Falcon smirked and grabbed his hand, allowing Bem to hoist him up, "We shall."

And together they opened the trapdoor and descended the stairs to meet up with their dragon partners once more.

Chapter 6
Welcome Home, Falcon

The next morning, they packed up their belongings at first light. Bem had barely gotten any sleep. He had volunteered to take the first watch. He had too much on his mind to get any rest.

He spent some time watching the moon float across the sky, sometimes hiding behind the shadows of the clouds. Bem hoped it wasn't a bad omen of their journey ahead. How many of the men and women of Hailwic had the shadow creatures overtaken? He hoped his parents were safe from them. Bem tried to shake that thought from his mind as a shiver ran down his spine. By the time he realized he should wake up Falcon for the next watch, it was nearly too late.

Bem yawned and flung his bag over his shoulder. He chewed what little breakfast he could scrounge up as he made his way across the courtyard.

"Bem," called a calm, low voice behind him. He turned to find Carver standing sheepishly in the doorway of the tower. "I'm sorry for what I said last night. I don't know what came over me."

Carver looked better this morning than the day before. Bem let out a sigh of relief before he could stop himself. Perhaps his conversation with Falcon had him too worried about sleeping last night as well. He offered Carver a smile and hurried over to him.

"It's ok, love," Bem offered, using Carver's nickname against him. "You didn't scare me away."

Carver stared at him in surprise and then a mischievous smile tugged at the corner of his mouth. "That would be a shame."

Then before Bem or anyone else could say anything more, Carver grabbed the back of Bem's neck and pulled him in for a kiss. Bem wrapped his arms around the prince and held him close. He missed Carver, who had decided to stay inside one of the tower rooms by himself overnight. But more than anything, Bem was relieved that he was alright. He didn't want to let him go, afraid that he may return to his sullen self once more.

When they pulled away, they were all smiles. Carver shouldered his own bag, grabbed Bem's hand, and led the way back to the dragons.

"Did you sleep well enough last night?" Bem asked Carver as they approached Theo.

Carver shrugged. "I don't think I slept much at all, to be honest. I wasn't tired."

Bem raised an eyebrow in disbelief. "You looked exhausted yesterday. How could you not have slept?"

Again, the prince shrugged. "As I said, I tried. Sleep wouldn't come to me, though."

"Next time, you're taking the first watch," Bem yawned. Then he turned to Theo and asked, "Well, did *you* at least get some sleep last night?"

Rested and eager to be on the move once more, Theo snorted and stretched his wings upward in response. Carver gave Bem's hand a squeeze before releasing it and left him to join Syth. Bem pulled himself onto Theo's back and diligently secured his things to his body.

They waited for Carver and Falcon to climb onto their own dragons. Once everyone was ready, Theo grunted his commands to the other Guardians. With that, the dragons leapt into the air one by one. Bem would never get used to the ground hurtling away from him. It was thrilling yet terrifying every single time.

The rays of the morning light were warm and welcoming. It comforted Bem to see a long way across the lake; to him, it meant that the shadow creatures couldn't sneak up on them.

He scanned the lake below and around them for any signs of ships, but they were alone. He was surprised that they hadn't come across any soldiers on the lake. Perhaps the king didn't find it useful to send his men into the open water to be sitting ducks for any dragons that may pass by. The two abandoned watch towers in the middle of the lake were enough evidence for Bem to support that theory.

They flew southeast for a time in silence, keeping an eye out for enemies on the water or in the sky. Without saying a word, Carver lifted his palm into the air and sent his rock over to Bem with his magic. Bem caught it with a groan. With a sigh, he held out his hand and practiced lifting the rock once more.

He focused on his task, losing track of time as the rock stayed above his palm a little longer with each try. When he took a break, he looked up and, to his surprise, he could make out the shore of the approaching land. A wave of relief and excitement washed over him. Bem pointed it out to the others, who seemed just as relieved.

"You'll have to take the lead now," Bem called to Falcon. He was the only one who knew where Sargon's cabin was located.

"The cabin hides deep within the Troden Forest," Falcon explained. He leaned forward in anticipation as he spoke. "We should be able to make it there before the day's end," Falcon explained. He leaned forward in anticipation as he spoke.

"Lead the way," Bem replied, gesturing with his hand. Falcon nodded and instructed Steno where they needed to go. To Bem's surprise, Steno didn't resist and even pumped his wings faster, eager to leave the lake behind. Bem was certain the dragons were ready to get back home as fast as they could. He hoped it wouldn't be hard to find the journal Sargon had mentioned before he died.

The trio of dragons stayed well above the wisps of clouds that hung in the morning sky. They wanted to avoid any detection from any wandering eyes below. Steno led them over the changing landscape of Hailwic. Bem sighed in relief.

Even though they were still far from Folke, Bem felt like he was home again. The thought of his mother and Fridolf made him feel homesick for them. His eyes drifted toward the direction of Folke, miles and miles away from them. Carver took note and turned his head to follow his gaze.

"What are you looking at?" he called.

Bem looked at Carver and answered, "I was just thinking about my parents. I hope they are doing ok with their shop without Nyel and I to help them."

"I'm sure they're fine," Carver offered.

"I hope so," Bem sighed. "I worry that the shadow creatures could wander that far. Or Brock will give them problems."

"Who's Brock?" Carver asked. His head tilted slightly.

Bem made a face that made Carver chuckle. "He tried to kill my brother when he defended Theo and his family. He was also awful to our father. I sent him flying into a building by accident."

Theo's ribs vibrated beneath Bem's legs as he laughed.

Carver's eyes widened. "Bem, you beast!"

Bem shrugged and laughed. "He deserved it."

"You're right, he did," Carver chuckled once more.

It felt good to talk to Carver again. He seemed more like his old self. Bem grinned. For now, his friends were his family. And one day, he wanted to introduce them all to his parents.

They were fortunate that there weren't any villages in their path to the Troden Forest. Bem spotted a couple of riders coming from the lake, but they didn't seem to see the dragons high above them. Thankfully, it was cloudy enough of a day to hide them.

The rolling fields below them quickly sprouted tall spruce trees until it was all they could see beneath them. It felt odd to Bem not to see any mountains, just a vast amount of forest below. It reminded him of when he and Nyel ventured through the Silent Woods. He shuddered at the memory of the first shadow creature they encountered that tried to sneak up on him. And they realized that what they called Midnight Sickness was even more dangerous than they thought. That was so long ago, it seemed. Even though it wasn't.

They continued their flight over the forest and the trees still did not thin out as they flew. Falcon wasn't kidding when he said Sargon wanted seclusion. Bem doubted anyone else would ever want to live or even travel this far into the forest. His whole life he was told tales about the forests of Hailwic. The oldest of them all was the Troden Forest. He never thought he'd see the day that he would visit it.

According to legend, the forest was ancient and filled with mystical happenings that few could explain. Bem remembered his real father telling him once when he was a boy that magic was born in the Troden Forest. He always believed these stories were nothing but myths, but then, they had already encountered enough mysterious things to put those doubts to rest. It made him eager to explore what secrets the forest held.

"There!" Falcon shouted. He pointed at a small opening amongst the trees.

The Guardians hurried over to the spot and circled it with uncertainty. Sure enough, the Guardians discovered the outline of the roof of a small log cabin nestled within the confines of the trees. The opening itself turned out to be a small clearing of land that surrounded the cabin. Bem wondered if the clearing was natural or if Sargon had cut the clearing out and used the downed trees to build his cabin.

The clearing was just big enough for all three dragons to land in one at a time. Syth was the first to descend. As he landed, he quickly folded his wings and moved closer to the cabin to allow the others to land as well.

Theo was the last to land. As he folded his tired wings, Bem slid off of him and almost fell over. His legs had gone numb from sitting in one position for so long, his muscles stiff. He wobbled over to Carver and offered to help him down.

"So glad to be off that giant lizard," Carver grumbled.

Syth growled a warning at him.

"You might want to attempt to be nicer to them. They left their clan to help us out after all," Bem noted. Even though he had seemed to be feeling better, Carver was in a poor mood yet again after another hour or so of flying. Maybe he just needed some rest. No, Bem was sure he needed rest.

Carver waved a dismissive hand at him. "Whatever."

Frustration swelled up inside Bem's chest, but he decided not to dwell on it. They had more important things to do than get into an argument. Bem went to find Falcon instead, who stood in silence, staring at the quiet cabin. Even though the sun was high in the air, the light had not yet reached the small home.

Bem observed Falcon for a moment. It seemed as if the sorcerer was holding his breath. He stood as still as a statue. Bem could only imagine the thoughts and emotions that must be swirling around Falcon's head. He wanted to say something to him to comfort the sorcerer, but his own words failed him. As if reading his mind, Falcon cleared his throat and spoke.

"Being here...I almost expected him to come strolling out the door just now. No doubt to scold me about something that I had forgotten to bring him," Falcon whispered. His face almost seemed to age backwards instead of forwards, resembling a lost, frightened boy. A man filled with grief and confusion had replaced the usually guarded and strong Falcon; his violet eyes shone with the threat of tears.

Bem followed his gaze back to the small cabin. It was old, but in decent shape. Not as nice or as big as his home in Folke, but all the same, just as cozy. There was a small, empty stable built a few yards away from it, big enough for a couple of horses. A stone well protruded from the ground not far off from where they stood. The field where the dragons sat looked well kept, as if someone had used it for growing crops. Though there was none to occupy it. It was a peaceful place to live. Bem would enjoy a quiet life in such a secluded place. He wondered how close the nearest village was.

Bem placed a hand on Falcon's shoulder. "You must miss him. I'm so sorry we couldn't help him."

Falcon sighed and pulled gently away from Bem's touch. "I do. But we mustn't dwell on the past. We need to find his journal as soon as possible."

"Hold on," Bem stopped him before he could go into the cabin. "First, I think we all deserve a little rest. I'm sure we're safer here than the outlook last night. We'll worry about finding it afterwards. It can't be easy returning here without Sargon. Please, take your time to mourn. I know what it's like to lose a father. Don't try to bottle up your feelings, it will only make you feel worse. I think he would want that for you."

Falcon stared at him, contemplating for a moment. Finally, his shoulders dropped and he let out a tired sigh. He looked as exhausted as Bem felt.

"Perhaps you're right. Come, I'll show you around."

Bem turned to Theo, Syth, and Steno and said, "Thank you for getting us here safely. Are you alright to rest too?"

Theo nodded while Syth puffed out smoke through his nostrils. He didn't seem at ease in the crowded woodlands. The three dragons looked for a cozy spot to curl up. He could hear them grunt and growl at each other, but again had no idea what they could be discussing. Bem motioned for Carver to follow them inside. The prince followed him in silence.

The cabin was a single large room with a bed in two opposite corners. A stone fireplace and an oak table with two chairs rested between them. On the other side of the cabin were trunks, a desk, and shelves mounted to the walls. On the shelves were numerous crystals of all shapes, sizes, and colors.

"Wow, that's a lot of crystals!" Bem noted. Even from where he stood, he could sense the power stored within them. His mother would love a collection of crystals of that magnitude.

"Sargon always liked to be prepared when it came to storing magic energy," Falcon said as he grabbed one of the bedposts and observed the room. "It looks like he left here planning to return. Nothing seems to be missing or out of place."

After a moment of silence, Falcon pointed to the other bed and said, "You can put your bags down over there for now. I guess we might as well get comfortable."

Bem took Carver's bag from him and placed them beside the empty bed. Carver sat on the bed with a tired sigh and leaned his head back against the wall. "Now what?"

"Now you rest. We will look for Sargon's journal," Bem suggested. He moved to the end of the bed, flung open the trunk, and gasped. Beneath various clothing, scattered crystals, and other miscellaneous objects were stacks of leather books. He looked up at Falcon, only to find him waving handfuls of books at Bem he had found on the small desk beside his bed.

"It may take a while to find the right one," Falcon answered in an apologetic tone.

Carver groaned. "Shouldn't it be there on the table somewhere? It must have been the last ones he wrote in."

Falcon shook his head and sighed in frustration as well. "Knowing Sargon, it could be anywhere. He kept many journals at a time and organized them how he saw fit. But if we work together, we should be able to find the right one."

"We're never going to find it. You realize that, don't you?" Carver grunted.

Bem picked up a stack of journals from the trunk and tossed them on the bed beside Carver. "Not with that attitude. If you're not going to rest, then make yourself useful and start reading!"

Carver gave Bem a dirty look, but picked up the closest journal and flipped to the first page. Bem grabbed his own stack and sat at the table across from Falcon, who was already flipping through pages. They were all made the same. Smooth, brown leather covers with uneven pages bound between them. A small leather cord wrapped around them with care, as if to keep prying eyes out of them.

Bem carefully untied his journal and opened it up to the first page. The cabin fell silent as the three of them read through their stacks of journals. Although the first few journals were older, Bem became captivated by the glimpses of Sargon and young Falcon's lives. The first seemed around Falcon's teenage years. Sargon described in detail his attempts to train the young sorcerer while Iris was visiting one summer. It read:

As much as I love my niece's company and would prefer her to live here with me over her father's godforsaken reign, the boy is far too distracted when she's here. He knows I have tasks for him to complete almost daily. However, every time I turn around, they've gone running off into the woods to explore or he's showing off his magic to her. I'm going to send that boy off for supplies before too long…Iris needs proper training without him on her heels.

Bem chuckled to himself and set the book aside. There wouldn't be anything current in that one. He grabbed the next journal and skimmed through its pages. Halfway through, he stopped at a small note that was underlined.

Took Isaac to the Telling Tree today for the first time. He doesn't feel it yet, but he will in time. I believe in his strength. Even when he doesn't.

"Who's Isaac?" Bem blurted out to the silence.

Falcon's journal had hidden his face except for his eyes, which looked up in alarm. "Oh…that's my name."

Bem's jaw dropped in astonishment. "Your name is *Isaac*?"

Falcon's eyes dropped back down to his pages and muttered, "I don't know what mother would name their son Falcon, do you?"

"I never thought much of it," Bem replied with a chuckle. "It's a good name. Why do you go by Falcon?"

Falcon sighed and answered, "A story for another time, Bem. We should really focus on the task at hand."

Bem glanced at Carver, who only shrugged. "He's been a bird-brain as long as I've known him."

"Well, clearly, you don't know me then," Falcon growled.

Carver was about to make a retort, but stopped at Bem's glare of warning. Instead, Bem changed the subject to the other curiosity that befell him. "What is the Telling Tree? Sargon mentions he took you there, but you couldn't 'feel it yet'?"

Falcon placed his open book facedown on the table for a moment and said, "Now that's something remarkable on its own. Before we leave, I must take you to the Telling Tree. But for now, let's keep looking for the right journal. It has to be here somewhere."

Bem burned with curiosity of what the Telling Tree was, or why Falcon changed his name. However, he did as he was told and continued reading through his pile of books.

The three of them spent hours combing through the pages of Sargon's many journals. Occasionally, Bem would ask Falcon about a small detail about their lives as he stumbled upon something of interest. He found the things Sargon jotted down over the years amazing. He spoke highly of Falcon, as if he were his own son. He rejoiced in his triumphs of magic or his combat skills. He commented on where Falcon could improve.

And yet, as Bem crept closer to more current times, Sargon and Falcon explored the surrounding areas more than practiced their magic. He made journals that were more specific only to the things he found interesting. Bem found a record of plants for healing, eating, or for poisoning; a journal filled with the different types of crystals and how they could make certain enchantments stronger; and most intriguing of all, he found the journal in which he recorded his time spent in the land of the dragons.

From what Bem could gather from skimming over the pages, Sargon had ventured around Lake Peril for years, instead of crossing it. He was able to observe dragons from a distance and scribble a rough map of the route he took to get there. On it he circled a mountain beside a waterfall further north. He was amazed at how far he had traveled. Bem flipped a few pages, looking for a clue as to why he circled that area, but he couldn't find anything to show why it was important.

A groan broke the silence and startled Bem from his thoughts. Carver lay flat on his back on the bed as his last journal thudded against the floor. "This is pointless. We're never going to find the right journal. The old man probably lost it!"

Falcon scowled at Carver and said, "We must keep looking. Sargon wouldn't have sent us here if it wasn't important!"

Carver's arms shot up in the air and exclaimed, "The man was possessed! How do you know if his brain wasn't even more scrambled than it was already?"

"Carver!" Bem gasped as Falcon jumped to his feet.

"Don't ever speak of him as if he were nothing," Falcon seethed through gritted teeth. "You didn't even know him, thanks to the king."

Carver sat up, rested his arm on his knee, and smirked. "My apologies, bird-brain. It's just a fact that he was a bit uncanny. I knew him well enough to know that much."

Falcon's hands balled into fists. Bem spotted a faint glow through his fingers and sprung into action before things got out of hand. He jumped from his chair and put himself between them. All they needed were a couple of angry sorcerers to fight in an already unorganized mess.

"Enough," Bem commanded. "Carver, stop talking about Sargon and read the damn books. Falcon, maybe you should go outside and take a breather. Some fresh air would do you some good."

Bem could feel Carver's glare on the back of his neck. To his relief, the prince remained silent. Falcon rubbed his temples and sighed. "Perhaps you're right."

As he turned towards the door, Bem knelt to pick up Carver's discarded book and froze. There under the bed sitting against the back wall was a lone journal.

Chapter 7
The Malachite Clan

Nyel

Ivory led his Guardians onwards through the final stretch until they would reach the Malachite clan. Along the way, Ivory explained the clan was smaller than their own, but was a tight-knit group. This new information only made Nyel all the more nervous and filled his head with even more questions.

"How many clans are there?" Nyel asked after a pause. Ivory glanced at him out of the corner of his eye.

"There are four clans all together."

"That's all?" Nyel asked in disbelief.

Ivory nodded. "No clan is the exact same as the next. Most of the clans, including ours, formed throughout generations as strongholds to protect mothers and their hatchlings until they grew enough to fend for themselves. Those mothers will join a clan she deems suitable and after her hatchlings are strong enough on their own, she will either choose to stay or go on her own once more."

"So, dragons aren't always in a clan?" Nyel asked.

Ivory shook his head. "No, many are loners or travel with their mates until their younglings can survive on their own."

"Interesting. I haven't seen any lone dragons," Nyel observed. Again, Ivory shook his head.

"My daughter, Seren, was a loner," Ivory said quietly. "Until she had Theo, that is. Theo was born alone, while his siblings weren't. She came to me out of the blue one day after many years. We hadn't seen each other in nearly a decade. Seren could have easily fended for the both of them, but still she chose to come back to her home

The

clan. I was thrilled!" The old dragon's eyes sparkled as he spoke of his daughter.

Nyel felt a tug at his heartstrings as Ivory continued. "I was never much of a loner myself; you see. I always worried about her when she left the first time. Her mother died when she was still a hatchling, so it was just the two of us for a while. When Theo became of age to go off on his own, he decided to stay by her side instead. He is very much like me in that aspect. I think that's why it's so hard on him that she's gone. He felt like he needed to be her personal Guardian."

"I didn't know that," Nyel replied in a soft voice.

The white dragon cleared his throat and averted his gaze elsewhere. Nyel let him be for the moment. Through all the chaos they had seen in the past weeks, Nyel had almost forgotten about Seren. He wished he could have done more to help her, but they didn't even know what became of her. In the state he found Theo in, he wasn't sure if he wanted to know what happened to Seren.

"It shouldn't be much longer until we reach the next clan's territory," Nyel called to Iris. "Are you ready?"

Iris chuckled. "As ready as I can be, I suppose."

Lorna swooped down from her spot in the clouds to fly beside them and shouted, "I enjoy the Malachites. They're a rough, irate bunch, and protective of each other. If our clan wasn't the best in the land, I'd say theirs were."

"That makes me feel confident, thank you," Nyel growled, his voice thick with sarcasm.

Lorna chuckled. "You better be sure-footed. They can smell fear a mile away and won't hesitate to snuff it out." Nyel's heart raced as a wave of panic coursed through his body. He snorted in an attempt to hide his true feelings.

"Don't tell him such things, sister. I can hear the drumming of his heart from here!" Casca called out with a smug expression. Nyel cast a sidelong look at her and growled in annoyance and embarrassment.

"I'm only being honest," Lorna retorted. "It won't do us any good to leave him in the dark."

"It would do me some good," Nyel grumbled in misery.

The two sisters laughed at him in unison. Nyel's blood rushed to his face, thankful that his scales hid the redness that would usually be there. A mud-scaled dragon by the name of Niko drifted closer to them as the sisters laughed at Nyel's woes. Nyel had noticed him a couple times before flying with Casca, but not engaging much in their conversations. He looked younger than most of the guardians by his smaller frame, bright scales, and lack of scars.

"My brother was born to live in the Malachite clan," Niko said after a lull in their laughter. "All brawn and no brain."

Casca rolled her eyes. "Confess, you're just jealous they wouldn't let you into their little pack."

"I am not! Rane wanted me to join up with them and that's the only reason I tried to in the first place. Lucky for both of us, they thought I was too weak and lazy," Niko grumbled.

"I'm not following," Nyel stated in confusion.

Niko glanced at him with a look Nyel couldn't quite place. His golden eyes had flecks of green in them that Nyel hadn't seen before. Just when he thought Niko was going to ignore him, the young Guardian answered, "The Malachite clan will never turn away a mother and her brood. However, the Malachite clan requires males and any subsequent younglings to prove their fitness and strength in order to stay; otherwise, they will be discarded like spoiled meat."

"You don't speak highly of them. Why bother trying to join them?" Nyel asked, still confused.

Niko snorted. "Much of my bloodline lives or has lived in that clan. It's where I grew up. I learned everything I know there. How to hunt, how to fight, and most importantly, how to protect our own. I was never strong or fast enough, but I had many friends and family there. I was a fool to think they would make an exception for me."

"That's awful!" Iris said after Nyel's translation.

Niko stared at her; his gaze wary. Without another word, Niko pushed hard with his wings and soared high above them and away from the conversation. A quiet, frustrated sigh escaped from Iris's lips. It was going to take a great deal of effort to get the dragons to accept her presence. It made Nyel all the more nervous to bring her into the Malachite clan. He hadn't realized how ruthless they were until now.

Nyel's stomach twisted into knots as he realized they were getting closer to the clan. The Guardians in the lead talked eagerly amongst themselves. From the sound of it, many of them had friends, even a few rivals, within the clan that they hadn't seen in ages. At the same time, Nyel wondered if he had lost his mind when he agreed to let Iris accompany him into a new clan filled with fierce dragons, unaware of their presence.

It was at that moment Lorna drifted closer to him and caught his attention. "I want you to know you're not alone. We protect our own, no matter what. Just remember to keep a level head and a powerful spirit," she offered in a low voice.

He nodded his thanks in return, unable to trust that he could speak above his nerves. Her words offered him a little comfort, but he wouldn't let his guard down. Just because Ivory forced them to accept him into their clan, doesn't mean they would treat Iris the same.

A hiss resounded from the front of the group, startling them into silence. Ivory halted their flight in an instant, hovering up and down in place with each beat of his mighty wings as he stared ahead with an intense glare.

"What is it?" Iris asked Nyel half a second later. Nyel didn't answer her right away as he leaned heavily into his enhanced senses.

At first, he didn't notice anything. The group had gone quiet. The rush of the wind pulsating through the air from their wings was the only sound he could hear. Nyel scanned the area ahead, trying to find the source of their repulsed reactions.

Then it hit him like a punch to the face. A smell that was stomach churning and undeniable. The stench of death. Bile rose in his throat as fear filled his heart. Nyel swallowed past the lump in his throat and told Iris in a quiet voice, "Something terrible has happened…"

"Orden, take half of the group and circle around from the opposite direction," Ivory commanded at once. His tone was sharp, but his face revealed nothing but dread. "I'll lead the rest of the clan from here."

Orden grunted in affirmation, and his group raced ahead, angling in a wide circle towards the left.

"The rest of you, follow me. And keep a wary eye out for any signs of trouble," Ivory urged.

Nyel hesitated as the rest of the Guardians pressed onwards. He glanced back at Iris and said, "I don't know if I should take you into this place."

Iris immediately slammed her fist into his shoulder, which only felt like a tap against his armor-like scales. "Nyel, may this be the last time you worry about my safety? I am NOT a child that needs looking after. Falcon is already bombarding me with that nonsense, and I don't need it from you as well. I am a warrior, just like you, remember? The only thing I expect from you is to treat me as your equal. Understood?"

Nyel studied her with one eye and knew what she said was true. He pushed down his own concerns and nodded in agreement. Whatever was ahead of them, they were in this together. He hurried to catch up with their group of Guardians and kept close.

"I don't see anything. What's going on?" Iris mumbled as they scanned the skies and the ground below.

"I smell death," Nyel replied, his voice grim. "A lot of death."

"Ivory!" Aura suddenly shouted from their far left.

The Ascendent rushed to her side, and she pointed below with a claw. Lying on the side of a mountain, they could make out the motionless body of a dragon. The group rushed to the lone dragon in unison, with Ivory leading the way. They landed around the dragon and immediately the sounds of gags and coughs filled the air.

The dragon was dead and had been for a while. His body had caved in on itself, his throat slashed with what could only be the claw marks from another dragon.

"Who could have done this?" Aura asked in a meek voice.

Ivory growled as he took in the grim sight. "I have a theory. Kollano did this!"

"The Shadow creatures got to the Malachite's Ascendant. Could they have gotten to the entire clan as well?" Nyel wondered aloud.

"Impossible!" Niko snarled. "They couldn't have taken on the entire clan. I'm sure their Ascendant sacrificed himself to protect them."

Ivory snorted and opened his wings. "We must hurry."

The Ascendant soared into the sky, followed closely by his Guardians. Nyel's heart sank as he realized the stench that filled his nostrils only grew stronger as they continued forward.

When they arrived in Malachite territory, there was no one there to greet them. They circled overhead in silent horror at the grotesque sight below them. Bodies of dead dragons scattered the ground throughout the area. Even Iris gagged at the stench that rose towards them in the burning sun. Orden and his group joined them moments later, and another wave of anger erupted throughout the clan.

"No, this can't be real!" Niko groaned as he stared at the dreadful scene in dismay.

One by one, the Guardians landed in the grassy meadow below amongst the deceased. They bellowed in fury and anguish. Bile rose in Nyel's throat once more, threatening to cause him to vomit. He knew whoever wasn't lying there amongst the dead had to be possessed, just like their Ascendant. Iris slid off of Nyel's back and slowly scanned the area with tears in her eyes.

She moved in silence, careful to step around a male dragon's body as she made her way through the scene. Perhaps in search of survivors. Nyel kept a close eye on her, but decided for the moment he needed to stay with Ivory.

"This is worse than I feared," Ivory hissed as he scanned the devastation before him. Orden followed his gaze. A seething growl resounded from his throat.

"I'm going to burn every last one of them!" Orden seethed with hatred.

"Patience, Orden," Ivory said in determination. "Patience. We don't know how many we're up against."

"I'm sick of patience. I want vengeance!" Orden growled at him. "Don't you see what those things have done here? Have you forgotten Azar lost his life as well? We aren't immune to these creatures' path of destruction!"

The others growled in agreement. Their rage overtook their sorrow at the devastating scene.

Ivory remained calm. "I haven't forgotten. We don't know exactly how many creatures we are dealing with now; both in shadow and the possessed. We need to be careful. We need a plan."

"If you don't come up with one soon, I'm going after them myself," Orden spat. His anger and hatred were palpable. "Anyone who slaughters our brethren won't live to see another day!"

Ivory snarled, his snout only inches from Orden's. "Are you questioning your Ascendant?"

Orden growled in response, standing his ground. "Not as long as he does his duty as our Ascendant. It's your responsibility to defend any of us as a chosen one, and I fear you may be forgetting your place."

Ivory growled and snapped his jaws close to Orden's face. They grew louder as they continued to argue with each other. The other Guardians stood by, watching them intently.

Nyel sighed. This wasn't going to be easy. A gasp made Nyel whip his head around. *Iris!*

He rushed over to her as quickly as he could before anyone else noticed her by herself. "Iris, what is it?"

Iris was bent over in a hollow in the earth. Nye's jaw dropped in revulsion at what she had found. Pieces of what could only be broken eggshells lay scattered around them. They didn't even spare the lives of the hatchlings. Nyel ignored his pain as he shifted into his human form in an instant. He grabbed her shoulders to pull her away.

"Iris, come on," Nyel urged her, pulling her gently. "You don't need to see this."

But when she stood to face him, her eyes were wide with wonder. "Nyel, look!"

In her hands was a pale white egg the size of a watermelon. Nyel stared at it in shock. He had never seen a dragon egg before. He never had the opportunity to be close enough to a mother with a clutch of them, and he wasn't stupid enough to try. Nyel looked around and spotted a slim, jade colored dragon lying a few yards away from them. The mother died trying to protect her nest.

"What should we do? Do you think it's still alive?" Iris whispered, staring at him with concern.

Nyel wet his lips, trying to decide. His eyes darted from the egg in her arms, to the broken shells, to her arms again. How long had the egg been there all alone? Was it too late to help the poor defenseless egg? He placed his hands on the egg. It was warmer than he expected it to be. Nyel closed his eyes and pressed his ear against the eggshell. A small flutter resounded in his ear.

He spun and ran to find the only dragon he felt safe enough to ask.

"Lorna, come quickly!" Nyel hurried. She looked down at him in confusion, probably wondering why he was in his human form. But she followed him without question. The others were still busy arguing amongst themselves to pay any attention to the humans of the group.

She followed him to the nest and gasped in horror. "No! Those demons will pay for murdering those precious hatchlings!"

Nyel placed a comforting hand on her shoulder and pointed. "Look what Iris found!"

Lorna's gaze lowered and suddenly widened. "Oh, no…"

"What can I do to help the egg?" Iris asked her at once.

Lorna sighed and shook her head. "I don't know how long it's been. Our eggs can survive for many days without a mother's warmth. But, judging by the dead around us, I don't know…"

After Nyel's translation, Iris looked down at the dragon egg and held it close. "I won't leave it to chance. It will certainly die if we leave it behind. I'll take care of it."

Lorna's eyes widened. "I respect your decision, but the others will be furious even seeing you holding that egg, let alone taking care of it. And what happens if it hatches?"

Nyel squared his jaw. "Then the clan will have to accept it. We can't leave it here to perish."

Lorna studied them and sighed once again. "Very well. But try to keep it to yourselves for now. We need to focus on the matter at hand. You can put it in your leather pouch. Don't worry, it takes a lot of force to crack a dragon egg." She winced at the last part as her eyes settled back on the broken pieces of eggshell scattered on the ground.

Nyel grinned and translated to Iris.

She beamed up at Lorna and placed a hand on her snout. "Thank you."

Lorna pushed gently against Iris's hand and then left to join the others before they noticed her missing.

"Are you sure about this?" Nyel asked Iris as she pulled things out of her bag to make room for the egg.

"I'm not going to leave the poor thing here to either die or hatch alone," Iris whispered.

Nyel nodded. He agreed with her wholeheartedly. He only hoped the others wouldn't be too furious when they found out about it. They couldn't hide it forever. As she repacked her bag with the egg inside it, Nyel shifted back into his dragon form. She held something close to her chest. Her palms glowed brightly for a brief moment. She then placed the object in her bag. Satisfied with her work, Iris climbed back onto Nyel's back and tied her bag securely to her.

"I've enchanted a crystal to create some warmth around the egg for now. It doesn't have a lot of energy in it, but it should last for a few hours," Iris explained as Nyel made his way back to the group.

Nyel nodded his approval as they drew closer to the others, not wanting to bring attention to themselves. The Guardians were still arguing with each other. On one side, Orden and his followers were eager to hunt down whoever had attacked the Malachite clan and rip them to shreds. The rest of them wanted to return to their own clan, fearing they might be targeted next.

Nyel turned a wary eye to the sky. The sun had already crept lower towards the mountains beneath it. He then scanned their surroundings with a growing pit in his stomach. Although they hadn't seen any shadow creatures, it didn't mean they weren't lying in wait for the perfect moment to strike.

A glint of light high in the sky caught Nyel's full attention. The flash turned into sparkles before his eyes. As distant as they were, it only took Nyel moments to realize what he was staring at. "Dragons!"

Chapter 8
Rapid Waters and Secret Dwellers

The Guardians fell silent and turned their attention to Nyel. Orden joined him and examined the skies with a piercing gaze. A menacing growl rumbled in his chest.

"They're approaching from the east," Orden stated in a venomous tone.

"Maybe they are survivors? It could be some of their Guardians?" Niko offered hopefully.

Nyel wasn't so sure. He didn't know how dragons treated their dead, but he felt they wouldn't leave their family and friends' bodies out in the open for so long. Ivory's silence proved his own doubt as he moved forward to get a better look. Nyel quietly relayed the newest information to Iris and warned her to be ready to fight.

As they watched the dragons grow closer to them, Lorna shouted from the back of the group, "There's more approaching from the west!"

Ivory's head whipped around faster than the others. They saw another group of dragons moving towards them. Nyel squinted and glanced back and forth between them. With a sinking feeling, he realized the danger they had placed themselves in.

Nervously, he called to Ivory, "I think we're being surrounded!"

Ivory's piercing blue eyes moved back and forth between the two groups of dragons. In response, Ivory's wings opened in a flourish and he looked to his clan.

"To the skies!" Ivory roared.

The Ascendant leapt into the air with the agility of a younger dragon. The Guardians followed him in quick unison, eager to rid themselves of becoming easy prey. Ivory led them north, not daring to take the chance of leading them back to their own clan. Together, they watched all sides while the strange dragons hurried after them.

To their dismay, another cluster of dragons emerged from behind a mountain not too far ahead of them. The first two groups began to fly towards their rear in an attempt to surround them. Nyel knew with one glance there were far too many for them to fight against. Their only choice was to flee.

With a grunt, Ivory immediately dove towards the mountains below. The Guardians followed close behind and tried to use the mountains to shield them from the enemy's view. The sound of the pursuing dragons' wingbeats became louder, closer.

The group of dragons ahead of them also dove towards the mountains to try to cut them off. As they rounded the rocky face of a mountain, five possessed dragons dove from a hidden ledge and shot a stream of fire at them.

Ivory pulled up as hard as he could to avoid the fire, and the rest followed. Iris's arms flung around his neck in a tight grip to keep from sliding off his back as he angled his body to shield her from the fire.

"We have to fight them off!" Orden yelled before letting out his own fire at a few of the dragons.

"There's too many of them," Lorna argued. She too released a torrent of flames. The enemy dragon's orange eyes gleamed in the firelight. Their scales had paled in comparison to their own scales, with faint lines of black webbed within them. It reminded Nyel of the ghostly film over an elderly person's eyes. They were no doubt shadow dragons.

"They're possessed," Nyel spoke up. "If they're here, then the shadow creatures are not too far behind them. We can't fight them all on our own."

"It's the dragons from the Malachite clan," Casca spat, enraged. "Or what's left of them."

"Split up! Maybe we can lose their trail," Ivory commanded.

The group hesitated. "Is that wise, Ascendant?" Lorna asked with uncertainty.

"It is all we can do. Otherwise, they'll corner us somewhere where we can't fight back. Now go!" Ivory roared.

With that, the Guardians broke off into the groups of two they chose before they left. Lorna appeared by Nyel's side without question and together they veered to the right, away from the others. They could hear the possessed dragons shrieking as they too, split into smaller groups.

Soon, the rest of the Guardians were out of sight, leaving Nyel, Lorna, and Iris on their own. The unnatural screeches of the possessed followed them, urging them to fly as fast as they could.

Lorna took the lead and flew deeper into the mountains. These mountains were more rugged, filled with rock and sharp edges. Not as lush with trees and life. The roar of a rushing river echoed ahead of them, far down in a ravine. Nyel and Lorna exchanged nervous glances before they dove into it in an attempt to take cover. Iris clung to Nyel's neck with all her might. The ravine was wide enough for the two of them to fly side by side.

The river was dangerous and unforgiving. It twisted and turned around boulders and ledges within itself. They followed the crashing white-water with the sounds of angry dragons close behind them. Nyel looked back, and to his dismay, saw they were far outnumbered.

"What do we do?" Nyel asked in a panic. Lorna glanced at him and even she looked frightened.

"We'll have to try to lose them," she finally replied. "We can out-fly them! The shadows may have power over their bodies, but it doesn't mean they can use them properly."

"Do you recognize any of them?" Nyel asked between breaths. He was straining himself to keep up with Lorna and didn't want to think about having a newly acquired body as a disadvantage.

"A few. It looks like they are what's left of the Malachite clan," Lorna confirmed, her tone grave.

Just then, a black-scaled dragon soared towards them and nearly bit Nyel's back leg. In one quick motion, Lorna swerved and kicked the dragon in his jaw before he could reach his target and sent him hurling backwards in fury. She snarled victoriously as they picked up speed.

"Are you alright?" Iris yelled in a shaky voice.

Nyel nodded. Then to Lorna, he called, "Thank you."

They glanced back at the Shadow Dragons. There were ten in total. They were following close behind them, however they weren't using their fire or lunging at them with brute strength. It seemed they were more preoccupied to slow them down.

"They're not trying to kill us," Lorna observed.

"They want to use us as more puppets for their friends," Nyel replied in disgust. Ahead the sound of crashing water grew louder. Nyel squinted and saw the river abruptly drop at the end of the ravine in a cascading waterfall.

This time, the entire group of Shadow dragons flew at them all at once. They grabbed onto Nyel and Lorna's legs and tail with their sharp teeth or claws at the same time. Their cries echoed throughout the cavern around them as pain shot through Nyel.

Nyel halted his panicked flight and tried to shake off the two dragons holding onto him. Lorna kept going ahead of them. As Nyel fought against the creature's hold on him, he looked back at the remaining possessed, and his heart sank. To his dismay, he spotted shadow creatures that slithered down the rock walls towards them. The ravine provided enough darkness for them to come out of hiding.

Iris was the first to react. She pulled out her sword and stabbed the first dragon in the soft part of its throat. His scales protected him from a fatal wound, but it was enough to force him to let go.

She then twisted around and swiped her sword across the eye of the second dragon, who roared in pain. Blood spattered through the air. The possessed dragon roared in fury and swatted back at her with a massive paw. They didn't have time to react. His paw struck her hard in the chest.

The force of the blow sent Iris flying off of Nyel's back. Nyel watched in horror as Iris descended into the rushing waters far below.

"Iris!" Nyel screamed.

He struggled to get away from the five dragons that surrounded him, two of whom were angry and bleeding. They kept blocking him at every twist and turn he tried to make.

Time seemed to slow down and speed up all at once. He watched helplessly as Iris disappeared underneath the rushing water far below. In a moment of panic and frustration, Nyel turned towards the group of shadow creatures and sucked in a deep breath. A blast of fire spewed from his open mouth and directly into their faces.

He roared in fury as the shadows shrieked and vanished in his fire blast. The possessed dragons flinched away, blinded momentarily by the flames. It gave Nyel enough time to get away from their clutches. Without a second thought, Nyel shifted into his human form and dove headfirst into the treacherous waters below.

The cold, strong water grabbed hold of him and pulled him into the swift current. His body flipped up and around as the water carried him away. Desperate for air, his lungs struggled to keep what little he had as he tumbled through the dark, cold, choppy waters. His back crashed against a rock, causing his breath to bellow out of his mouth.

His lungs screamed for air. His body ached in pain from the attack and from shifting. He knew if he didn't regain control fast, the water would swallow him whole.

Summoning all his strength, he used his arms to right himself and kicked as hard as he could off of a boulder with his legs. Until finally, Nyel forced himself back to the surface.

Nyel gasped for breath as soon as his head broke free from the unforgiving water. Relief filled his senses, thankful to be alive. But he didn't have time to celebrate. His head whipped back and forth as he scanned the churning river for Iris. Fear gripped his chest when he spotted her head bobbing down the river ahead of him.

"Iris!" he screamed when he realized she was face down and dangerously close to the waterfall.

The dark creatures above hadn't spotted him yet, perhaps because they were looking for a dragon and not a human. He used the opportunity to swim after her. He pumped his arms and legs as fast as he could to propel himself with the current to get closer to her. All he could see were glimpses of her face and long black hair in the treacherous, icy water. But he soon realized he wasn't fast enough.

Nyel watched in horror as her body bobbed up once more in slow motion. She seemed to linger there for just a moment, long enough for him to see she was still unconscious. And then she dropped out of sight over the edge of the waterfall.

A rogue, angry cry escaped from Nyel's throat. Once more, he summoned all of his extra strength and swam with the river. He couldn't give up on her. He struggled to keep his head above water as he raced towards the edge of the cliff. When he reached the river's end, Nyel connected his feet to the slippery rock of the cliff's edge and launched himself off of it.

Wings sprouted from his back as he fell, feeling as if it had ripped through his skin. But he ignored the pain. Nyel angled himself downwards, parallel with the waterfall. He used his wings to grab the air and force himself to plummet after her. He opened and closed his wings twice with gritted teeth. "Come on," he mumbled. "Faster, faster!"

Just before they reached the rocky bottom of the waterfall, Iris came within arm's reach. In one fluid motion, he grabbed Iris around her waist and opened his wings. His wings caught the air, and it hoisted them upwards, saving them from a nasty fall.

Water pushed against his back and drummed against the membranes of his wings as he tried to regain his balance. But the force was too strong, and it pushed them back into the waterfall and out the other side. They fell behind the waterfall and into a shallow pool next to a pebble beach. Nyel slid a few feet backwards on his back in a spray of rocks and mud with Iris cradled against his chest.

Nyel groaned as he came to a rest against the cool, wet rock. His entire back stung from scraping against the rocks below. His wet hair hung in his eyes as he carefully sat up, still supporting Iris in his arms.

Slowly, he got to his feet and coughed, spitting out retained water. Somehow, he saved them from the fall. He glanced around at his surroundings. To his surprise, he saw they were sitting in the mouth of a cave, which was perfectly hidden behind the massive waterfall.

He panted as he dragged Iris out of the water and into the cool, hidden cave. It was too dark to tell how far it went, but that was far from Nyel's mind. He laid Iris carefully on the smooth cave floor and shook her shoulders. When nothing happened, he patted her cheek and said, "Come on Iris, wake up!"

In response, her head slumped to the left and pointed lifeless towards the ground. He stared at her in dread as his eyes adjusted. Two wide and nasty gashes ran from her left collar bone to the top of her right breast. He put his ear down to her chest and listened. A faint heartbeat was all that remained of the strong princess.

Nyel quickly brought his hands together over her breastbone and pumped them against her chest, forcing her heart to beat faster. He paused to put an ear to her once more, only to realize that she wasn't breathing. Nyel held her head in one hand, clamped her nose in the other, and quickly put his mouth against hers and gave her a breath of air.

"Come on, Iris!" He yelled at her as he started pumping her chest once more.

He repeated this process twice, shouting at her to wake up and cursing between breaths when she didn't. Tears burned in his eyes. Panic clawed at his soul. He cursed his fear away as well. He wouldn't allow Iris to die, not here…not like this. "Don't leave me Iris, fight!"

As he was about to bring his lips to hers for a third time, Iris's chest suddenly convulsed, and water sputtered from her mouth. Nyel helped roll Iris to her side as she emptied her lungs of the river water and gasped for breath.

"Breathe, Iris! Just breathe. There you go," Nyel cried in relief as he gently rubbed circles on her back. His own heart hammered against his chest.

Once Iris had regained her breath, she looked up at him in exhaustion. "... You saved my life."

Nyel smiled, wiping cold sweat off his brow, and replied, "Yeah, I guess I did."

Iris looked at his hands, and her eyes widened at the sight of blood on his palms. In the excitement, Nyel had forgotten about her own wounds. He looked around for something to help her and realized her bag was missing.

Calmly, Iris removed a necklace from her neck that held a rose-colored crystal hidden under her shirt. She placed it in his hand and said, "Will you heal me?"

"I'm not a sorcerer," Nyel countered in confusion.

"You don't have to be, remember? It's enchanted to heal wounds," Iris answered in a strained voice. She winced as the pain settled in after her initial shock.

Nyel remembered. On rare occasions, his stepmother Mari would heal people with crystals if she thought they were beyond her medical capabilities. He nodded to Iris and knelt closer to her. He unbuttoned the first few buttons of her shirt, and carefully peeled the cloth back just far enough to reveal the long gashes.

Nyel took a slow, shaky breath to calm his nerves. The wounds weren't too deep, but if left alone, there was a possibility that she could lose too much blood. He held the crystal firmly in his hand and willed it to heal her.

The rose-colored crystal glowed warm and bright. It's comforting light shone between his fingers. The small crystal vibrated in his hand as he placed his other hand over her torn flesh. Slowly, he followed the gash with careful precision. As he did, Nyel could feel the flow of the magic trickle up one arm, across his chest and shoulders, and down the other. He watched with fascination as the skin he left behind mended itself together, leaving a pink scar in its place. Nyel did this with both gashes, using all his concentration to follow each one to the end.

Finally, the crystal's glow died, and he sat back to admire his work. The only remnants of Iris's wound were two long pink scars. Nyel let out a sigh of relief and handed Iris the empty crystal.

"You handled the crystal's magic well. Thank you," she said as she took the crystal from him.

Nyel grinned. "Bem's mother taught me how to use them for healing. She's a good teacher."

"I must thank her one day," Iris breathed. "Remind me to replenish the crystal's energy later."

Even though she had been healed, Iris sounded exhausted. She fixed her shirt as best as she could and got up, but Nyel placed a gentle hand on her shoulder to stop her.

"Please, you need to rest. I think we're safe here for the moment," he insisted. Iris turned her head and studied the waterfall. Suddenly, Nyel felt her shoulders stiffen.

"The egg!" she gasped in horror.

Nyel's eyes grew wide, and he cursed under his breath. He had forgotten about the egg. Without a second thought, he hurried towards the cave's entrance and launched himself through the waterfall. He landed on a jagged rock that stuck out of the water, grabbing it with his hands to keep himself balanced. Nyel studied the sky first to see if there were any dragons or shadows above him. To his relief, he saw nothing.

He then turned his gaze to the river beyond him and scanned the water. It didn't take long. He spotted Iris's bag drifting far away from the waterfall, almost rounding a slight bend in the river. Nyel's wings emerged from his back and he soared after it. In just a few short seconds, Nyel lifted the bag from the water and held it to his chest. "Sorry little one."

A screech echoed from high above. Nyel craned his neck and saw a couple of dragons circling above the waterfall. Nyel grit his teeth. Perfect, he thought.

His eyes wandered over the water as an idea came to his mind. He just hoped it would actually work.

Nyel strapped the bag to his back, took a deep breath, and dove underwater. Using his wings, he swam back towards the waterfall and clung to the rocks beneath it, using them to pull himself through the fall of the rough waters. Finally, he emerged from the other side in a spray of water. He collapsed onto the pebbles, gasping for breath and clutching the bag to his chest.

"Nyel! Are you ok?" Iris gasped, hurrying to her feet.

Nyel's wings disappeared a moment later, and he forced himself to sit up. "The creatures were up there. I had to hide in the river before they could spot me. I got it."

He held the bag up to her. Iris gently grabbed it from him and opened the bag. A sigh of relief escaped her when they saw the egg intact. Nyel got up and helped her return to sit against the wall. This time, she hugged the egg tight to her. It remained intact; Nyel could even feel the warmth of the crystal through the bag when he held it.

"We almost died," she whispered, staring at the crashing waterfall. He could barely hear her over the roar of it, but he saw the look of fear that overcame her usually strong demeanor. A twinge of sympathy overtook Nyel.

"But you didn't. I won't let that happen," Nyel promised, stroking her cheek before he could stop himself. But it was true. She almost died, along with the egg. The thought of it twisted his guts into knots. He couldn't bear to think about what would have happened to her if he hadn't gotten to her in time.

Iris returned her gaze onto him, a look of wonder sparked in them for a fleeting moment. As if she had just noticed him for the first time. Then, as fast as it came, it was gone. She looked away and asked, "Where's Lorna?"

Nyel let his hand drop to his side. "I don't know. I lost sight of her after I went into the water."

"I hope she's alright," Iris shivered.

"I'll go look for her soon. Let me check this place out first and make sure it's safe for you to rest here," Nyel offered.

"I'll be alright Nyel," Iris protested, but Nyel stopped her.

"Please, just let me look," he said as he rose to his feet. "You need time before we return to the skies, if we can help it."

Iris nodded in surrender. As he turned towards the back of the cave, Iris said, "Thank you for saving me, Nyel. I owe you my life."

He glanced over his shoulder and smirked at her, "You don't owe me anything. Just rest, princess."

She wrinkled her nose at him in disgust. "What did I say about you calling me princess?"

Nyel only waved at her as he headed into the darkness of the cave, still smirking to himself. He traced his hand along the rough, rocky surface as he made his way deeper inside. His vision quickly adjusted to the darkness, allowing him to see more of his surroundings. Something on the ground caught his eye, causing him to freeze in place.

Lying on the ground a few feet in front of him was a tattered leather pouch and an old hammer by its side. He looked around the area in bewilderment, half expecting to see its owner somewhere nearby. But he saw no one. Nyel knelt on one knee and placed tentative fingertips on the bag. How was this possible?

"Hello?" he called, looking around the cave. His voice echoed off of the walls around him. Only the distant roar of the waterfall answered him. Nyel examined the wall next to the leather pouch and found gouges in it where the hammer must have struck. There were people out this far in dragon territory? What were they trying to dig up? And why?

Nyel grabbed the items and retraced his steps back to Iris, eager to show her what he found. When she came into view, he held up the pouch and approached her with wide eyes.

"Did you just find that?" she asked in bewilderment.

"Yes! Along with this," he replied, holding up the hammer for her to see. She took the hammer from him and studied it closely. Nyel dug into the pouch for more clues.

First, he pulled out a worn chisel. He studied it and realized that's how the gouges in the rock were made. Next, he pulled out a moldy piece of stale bread and stared at it in surprise. It was as hard as a rock, but it told him it hadn't been too long since the owner had been here. The last item he pulled out was a silver ring with a green crystal embedded in it. Nyel examined the ring for a moment and then handed it over to Iris.

She examined it thoroughly before placing it in the center of her palm. She stared at it in concentration, never breaking eye contact with it. Her hand glowed as she summoned her magic, focusing intently on the ring. When finished, Iris let out a sigh. She still felt drained from the ordeal before.

"This is fascinating! It's a crystal I have never encountered before," she explained, twisting it around in her fingertips.

"Did someone enchant it?" Nyel asked, intrigued. He sat across from her with crossed legs.

Iris handed it back to him to examine as she said, "No, it's a crystal that produces its own source of magic. There are only a handful of them we know of that exist. And someone has deemed it important enough to wear on a daily basis."

Nyel placed the ring on his pinky finger. "It's small. A woman's ring?"

Iris nodded. Her brow furrowed in deep thought. Nyel offered her his hand. She held out her right hand with a curious look. Nyel gently grabbed her outstretched hand and placed the ring on her second to last finger.

"You should keep it with you, then. It may be important and you're the only one who can figure out what its purpose is," he said. Iris brought her hand closer to her face to study the crystal once more.

"What else was in the bag?" she asked, distracted.

His eyes flickered to the items sitting beside him and replied, "A rock for bread and a chisel."

"Looking for more crystals, perhaps?" Iris wondered out loud. Nyel scratched the scruff on his chin, at a loss for words.

Finally, he blurted, "Who would be out here in dragon territory? More importantly, how did they make it this far without being seen by one?"

Iris gave him a pondering look as she answered. "I would like to know the answer to that question. I would have never thought that someone else might be out here amongst the dragons. Especially without the Shifter to help them communicate if they got caught."

Nyel felt uncomfortable by her words and looked back at the waterfall. "We should go, just in case something or someone finds us here. Do you think you are able to?"

Iris nodded at once. "Yes, of course."

Nyel got to his feet and offered his hand to help her up. Iris carefully placed her bag and the egg over her shoulders. Together, they began walking towards the entrance of the cave, hand in hand. Nyel took a few steps ahead of Iris and allowed his green scales to cover his body.

Iris watched him with a look of amazement. "I'll never get used to that. There are all kinds of magic we must not know about out here."

"All magic is new to me," Nyel chuckled. He motioned for her to wait and made his way closer to the waterfall. Slowly, he stuck his head out of the cave around the edge of the waterfall and looked around. The waterfall emptied into a calmer river than the one they hurtled through above. It twisted around the base of another mountain and out of sight. He didn't see any shadows or enemy dragons anywhere. But it didn't mean they weren't close by.

He stepped back inside and said, "It seems to be safe; all is quiet."

With a look of concern, Iris started, "Hopefully we can find the others-"

"You stole my bag!" shouted an angry voice from the back of the cave.

Startled, Nyel and Iris whipped around. A spark of light ignited in the darkness. A flash of a torch lit up the back of the cave to reveal a young girl standing there with a hardened expression. She held a torch in one hand and a dagger in the other. She couldn't have been older than eleven or twelve. Nyel was too stunned to say anything, but he quickly released his scales to not frighten the girl.

She marched towards them and stopped a few yards away. She pointed her torch at them with an angry snarl. "Thieves! I'll cut your hands off for stealing from me!"

Nyel was taken aback. He didn't know what to think. She was young and yet stood confidently on her own against two adult strangers. She couldn't have been expecting to see people there. Could she?

Iris was the first to speak. "I'm sorry. We were just surprised to learn that someone else has been here." Filled with concern, she asked, "What's your name? Are you all alone out here?"

The girl held up her dagger threateningly, showing no fear. "You're the thief. I don't have to answer to you! Now give me back my bag. I won't say it again!"

Nyel raised his hands up in the air with the pouch in one hand and slowly walked it to the girl.

"Put it on the ground!" she commanded, the light of her torch illuminated her caramel skin and short, wavy black hair.

Nyel did as he was told, not wanting to scare the youngster. He couldn't help but admire how bold and fearless she was in the face of possible danger. He couldn't be sure if even he would have been as brave at her age.

"We don't want to harm you, honest," he offered. She snatched the bag from the ground yet didn't lower her dagger.

"Where's my ring?" she interrogated.

Iris held up her hand and removed the ring from her finger. "I'm sorry," she apologized again. "I was just intrigued by its magic. I've never encountered such a crystal before."

The girl lowered her arms slightly, a look of confusion in her eyes. "You know it's magical?"

Iris smiled and nodded her head. "Yes, I'm a sorceress. I can make and sense magic, see?" She let her hand glow and lit up the cave even brighter than the torch in the young girl's hand.

The girl cocked her head and said, "So can I."

With that, she twirled the hand that held the dagger and the water from the waterfall streamed into the cave through the air and flew around them in a perfect circle. Nyel and Iris stared at her in disbelief.

"How did you get all the way out here?" Iris asked in amazement as the girl returned the water to the river with ease.

"I've always been here," the girl answered coolly. "The real question is, why are you here?"

Iris looked at Nyel, and he shrugged. What was the harm in telling the truth?

"We're here to make peace with the dragons," Iris finally said. "My name is Iris, princess of Hailwic. And this is my friend Nyel. We are here with a group of dragons, but a group of shadow creatures found us and separated us."

"You're a princess?" Her eyes widened, and she brought up her dagger and torch so fast, that Nyel stepped in front of Iris to protect her in fear that the girl would lunge. "You're here to find sorcerers for the king, aren't you? Well, you're out of luck. There's no one else here! And you aren't taking me. I won't let you!"

Iris raised her hands and shook her head. "No, no! We are truly here to speak with the dragons, nothing more. The king is the one who captures sorcerers and kills dragons, not us. We are completely against the king's judgment, I promise!"

"I don't believe you!" the girl shouted.

Nyel took a few steps back and shifted into his dragon form. The girl yelped and leapt back, raising her torch high to follow his head as it rose towards the ceiling.

"Do you believe the king would work with me?" Nyel asked in a booming voice that echoed into the cave.

The girl stared at him in disbelief until slowly, she put her dagger away. As Nyel shifted back into his human form, the girl began to smile. "Wow, wait until the others see this!"

"Others? What others?" Iris asked.

"Oh, you'll see," the girl answered excitedly. "Come with me, I'll show you a better way out of this cave. Unless you want to be found by those creatures again. Where do you think they hide when the sun is out?"

Nyel and Iris glanced at each other. This time, Iris shrugged and said, "Very well, show us the way."

The girl held up her torch and walked back into the cave. Iris stopped her by asking, "Wait! What's your name?"

The girl glanced over her shoulder with a cheeky grin. "You can call me Shara for now."

"Nice to meet you, Shara," Iris smiled. She held out her hand with the ring in her palm and continued, "I'm sorry if we startled you. We didn't mean to steal your things."

"No worries. In fact, keep it. You'll need it more than I will," Shara replied with a wink. With that, she skipped into the back of the cave, leaving Nyel and Iris to wonder what else this land had to reveal to them.

Chapter 9
The Telling Tree

Bem

Bem fell to his hands and knees and crawled to reach it. "Wait, Falcon, I found another journal."

Falcon met him at the end of the bed and waited eagerly for Bem to open it. "There's only a handful of written pages!" Bem gasped.

Falcon grabbed it from Bem's hands and flipped through the pages so fast, Bem wondered if he could read them. And then Falcon's jaw dropped open.

"What, what is it?" Bem implored.

"There are pages missing," Falcon muttered. He turned the book towards Bem and Carver to show a rip down the center of the book.

"But why? Why would Sargon do that?" Bem asked, staring at the journal in shock and dismay. "Do you think it's the one we've been looking for?"

Falcon nodded his head. "He speaks of dark magic in the beginning. Sargon wouldn't rip pages out of his own journal…but maybe Kollano would."

Bem let out a frustrated sigh. "Is there anything there that can help us?"

Falcon read over the pages carefully. "He speaks of an abandoned mine of some sort. He found it one afternoon while picking mushrooms. But he doesn't say where."

"Sargon mentioned that the two of you explored a lot in your time together. Have you ever come across a mine before?" Bem asked, hoping to jog Falcon's memory.

This time Falcon let out a sigh of frustration. "No, we hadn't."

"So let me get this straight," Carver interjected. "He wrote of dark magic and a mine, but didn't specify where or why he wrote it down? It could be anywhere!"

Falcon dangled the open journal in front of Carver and said, "Again, there are pages missing. He could have written the location down. Or better yet, how to put a stop to the shadow creature's existence. We just don't know."

Carver crossed his arms and said, "What do we do now without those pages?"

Falcon dropped the book on his bed and sat beside it with an exhausted sigh. "I don't know. I need to think."

Carver rolled his eyes and stood up. "Well, I'm not waiting around for you to make up your mind. I'm going hunting. I want some real food in my belly. Bem, are you coming?"

Bem hesitated. After a moment's thought, Bem grabbed his bow and arrows and offered them to Carver. "I'm going to help Falcon. You can use my bow if you'd like."

Carver snorted and raised a hand. "I'll be fine with magic. But thank you."

With that, Carver trotted out the door and out of sight. Bem turned back to Falcon to find him with his head in his hands. He waited for a moment, contemplating on what their next course of action should be.

Finally, Bem said, "Why don't we take a walk to clear our heads for a bit? You need a break."

"I'm fine," Falcon murmured, not meeting his gaze.

Bem crossed his arms and stared at the sorcerer until he lifted his head and met his eyes. "Come on."

Falcon sighed and stood without further protest. He moved to the door and opened it saying, "After you then."

Bem grinned and hurried outside. As Falcon shut the door behind them, Bem examined the sky. The once bright blue sky mixed with fluffy white clouds had given way to dark, gray clouds. Theo, Syth, and Steno rested in the field in front of the cabin.

When Falcon started for a small path leading into the woods, Theo raised his head from the ground and grunted at them.

"We're just going for a short walk," Bem called to him. "Be back soon!"

Theo snorted and laid his head back down. Bem wished once again he knew what the dragon wanted to say to him. Perhaps he disapproved of them leaving the area? Or maybe he didn't care in the slightest. Either way, Bem had to jog to catch up with Falcon, who seemed to be on a mission. Once Bem caught up with him, he matched his pace and looked around the shady forest.

This area became more densely populated with trees. The dragons wouldn't be able to move comfortably through them unless they were to knock some down along the way. The path they followed appeared to be a frequently used footpath, possibly created by Sargon and Falcon themselves. Bem was glad to be in the woods once more. It felt more like home to him than the monstrous mountains. However, he knew better than to let his guard down.

"Where are we headed?" Bem asked.

"You'll see soon enough," Falcon replied.

He was right. About a quarter mile from the cabin, they left the path into a glade around a hundred feet in diameter. And in the center of the glade was an enormous, twisted oak tree. It seemed out of place beside all the spruce trees that surrounded it.

"The Telling Tree," Bem said in realization.

Falcon nodded.

"This is where Sargon trained you," Bem stated, taking in the flat, grassy area around them. Falcon nodded once more, before moving towards the tree with Bem close behind him. He turned his gaze upwards as they stopped underneath the old tree and stared at it for a moment.

"In my youth, we used to come here almost every day to train. Sargon taught me everything I know about magic right here under the branches of this very tree," Falcon said in a hushed tone. His eyes stayed fixated on the old oak tree. He was no longer there with Bem, but in another time all together.

A distant rumble of thunder tore Bem's eyes away from Falcon and the tree to gaze at the clouds above. "I think we should probably head back before the rain comes."

Falcon nodded without a word. He placed his hand on the bark and muttered, "If only I knew what you wrote on those pages."

Suddenly, Falcon's hand glowed and a web of light shot from his fingertips and twisted around to the other side of the tree. Falcon's eyes went wide in astonishment.

"What's going on?" Bem gasped.

Falcon disappeared around the other side of the oak tree. Bem scrambled after him, eager to find out what had happened.

They stopped at the opposite side of the base of the trunk and followed the purple lines upwards. There above their heads, almost out of sight, was a hole in the tree. It was about as wide as a hand. Falcon stood on his tiptoes, reached inside, and froze. He met Bem's eager gaze with a look of shock before pulling out the contents.

In his hand were pieces of parchment rolled together and tied with a leather cord.

They stared at the rolled-up parchment in Falcon's hand as another rumble of thunder rolled overhead. Drops of chilly rain sputtered around them, bringing them out of their daze.

"We should go back before it pours," Bem suggested. "You need to keep it dry. What if those are the missing pages?"

Falcon grinned and nodded in agreement. He carefully put the parchment in his cloak pocket. They hurried out of the glade as the rain poured around them. The trees provided little protection as the leaves and branches swayed in the wind. As they ran down the path, a flash of lightning illuminated the dark sky above them. It reminded Bem of the battle in the sky against Kollano and his creatures. He shuddered at the thought of it.

When they reached the clearing, they could see the glow of a fire in the cabin. Bem sighed in relief. He was glad Carver made it back before the rain. Falcon hurried inside and Bem hovered by the door with a twinge of guilt. The dragons laid closer to the tree line with one of their wings raised above their heads to protect their faces from the rain. Bem grimaced and went inside. He couldn't do anything for them. There was no way even one of them could fit inside the cabin.

Bem and Falcon took off their soaked cloaks once they were inside and had shut the door. Carver sat beside the fireplace with a couple of rabbits roasting over the fire. He shook his head at their appearance. Panting from running through the mud with grins on their faces.

"That was fast. You already have a meal ready on the fire," Falcon noted as he eyed Carver.

Carver rolled his eyes. "Magic makes life easier sometimes, especially when you're hungry."

The prince then studied them and tilted his head curiously.

"Where have you two wandered off?" Carver asked as he rotated the rabbit meat. Bem's mouth watered. He hadn't realized how hungry he was until the smell of the meat hit his nose.

Bem tried to ignore his stomach and answered, "We went to the tree and you won't believe what we found!"

"Don't keep me in suspense, love. What did you find?" Carver asked, arching an eyebrow.

"We don't know for sure yet," Falcon replied, pulling the parchment out of his cloak. He grabbed the other chair and pulled it close to the fireplace. He pulled the leather cord loose and carefully unrolled the pieces of parchment.

Bem and Carver waited for a moment as Falcon examined it. Falcon looked up at them and said, "This is it. Sargon hid the pages in our tree for me to find."

"Why would he do that?" Carver asked, staring at the pages in disbelief.

"He must have thought it was important enough to do so," Falcon responded.

Bem sat on the bed beside Carver and urged, "Well, what does he say?"

Falcon flattened out the pages in his lap. Despite being dirty and torn in some places, the words on the pages in Falcon's lap were still clear and legible. Sargon's handwriting was neat; however, it was all over the place on the pages. As if he jotted down random thoughts immediately upon opening the journal. Falcon pointed to a section halfway down the page.

"*I found a curious place hidden deep within the forest, deeper than our cabin,*" Falcon read. "*I was hunting for a certain species of mushroom when I stumbled across an old mineshaft. There's something off about it. The place was hidden by magic. Fortunately, I was able to sense it, but it would have been difficult for anyone who isn't sensitive to magic to find it. I'm going back tomorrow when I have the proper tools with me.*"

"Does he say anything else about it?" Bem asked

Falcon continued, "*It took me longer than I anticipated returning to the mineshaft, but today I finally found it again. I sense an old magic in and around it. I'm writing this down as I go, in case something unexpected happens. It's something I've not encountered before. I'm eager to uncover whatever is hiding inside, but I encountered a blocked path halfway through. I'll be taking some extra crystals with me. Don't want to be trapped in there all alone!"*

Falcon's face fell, troubled. He took a slow, deep breath as he flipped the page and continued reading. *"I was able to blast my way through the entrance. It's an old crystal mine! Decades old, if not centuries. There are some small crystals left behind in there, but most of the big chunks are gone. It doesn't seem to go very far down. Why would someone abandon a crystal mine?"*

"I'm not sure…it's probably in my head from being alone for so long. But I swear someone called my name in that dark mine shaft a few moments ago. I've looked everywhere, but I haven't seen anyone. I'm losing my mind, I'm sure of it…"

Bem and Falcon shared a look before he continued.

"I must be going crazy! A whispered voice called out my name once more, only this time I saw someone's shadow pass over the entrance of the mine. I tried to follow it, but again, no one was there," Falcon paused for a moment, closing his eyes tight, as he read, *"I wish I had Falcon with me, even though I know he'd agree that I'm losing my marbles."*

The pain that sentence brought him was evident in his face. Bem stood and reached a gentle hand for the pages and took them from him.

Bem continued where Falcon left off, *"I'm not crazy! Today when I went for another look at the crystals, I walked in to find a being of smoke and shadow floating in the center of the room. I nearly fainted at the sight of it. Its eyes glowed as orange as the fire I was about to cast over it, but it stopped me when it spoke my name. I was…no; I am still intrigued yet frightened of this creature. It speaks in whispers, but I could only make out one word. One that I know I have heard before, but I can't place where. Kollano."*

The three looked at each other in silence, taking it all in.

"Kollano? Why was he in a mine shaft?" Carver questioned, taking the meat away from the fire and placing it on a plate. "What does he say next?"

Bem presented them the pages to show that it was the end.

"Why would he stop there?" Carver exclaimed, throwing his hands up in the air in exasperation.

"Maybe that was the last time he was able to write before...," Bem glanced at Falcon's ashen face and continued, "Before he was possessed by Kollano."

"We have to find this mine," Falcon stated, rising to his feet at once.

Bem nodded in agreement, but Carver remained seated. "Can we at least wait for the rain to subside? The mine isn't going anywhere. Besides, I just cooked some lunch!"

Falcon scowled and turned his gaze to the window. Drops of heavy rain pelted the glass and the roof above them. "Fine, we'll wait. But we go as soon as the storm clears."

"Do you even know where to look? We could spend days, if not weeks, running circles around in these woods!" Carver questioned, passing out the food as he spoke.

Bem wondered the same thing. How were they going to find the mine? Falcon had never given a hint he knew its location. Bem took a bite of the small meal he had been given and stared down at the pages spread out on the table. He saw nothing there that would tell them where to search.

"I have one idea where to look," Falcon answered quietly, watching the rain pour outside. "Exactly where we found those pages."

"The Telling Tree?" Bem asked in confusion. Then he remembered the web of purple light that led them to the pages in the first place. "What exactly happened when you found those pages?"

Falcon tore his eyes from the window and turned to face Bem. "A wonderful form of magic Sargon taught me long ago. He left those pages there for me to find in more ways than one."

To answer Bem's look of confusion, Falcon said, "I'll explain when we return. For now, I suppose we should rest and eat."

"That's the best idea I've heard yet!" Carver sighed, wiping the grease from his mouth. Leaving the bones on the plate, he stood from his chair and plopped onto the bed beside him. Falcon grabbed his own portion of the food and chewed it slowly.

Bem wiped his hands and hesitated. He examined Falcon and said, "I'll watch for a change in the weather if you'd like."

Falcon shook his head. "It's useless for me to sleep. Besides, you need rest more than I do. Thank you, though."

Bem nodded his head and stood. He glanced at the empty bed, and then to Carver.

"What are you doing?" Carver asked as he watched Bem with a blank gaze.

"I'm going to rest," Bem replied. "We all need a proper sleep. So, lie down in that soft warm bed and close your eyes, and so shall I."

Carver's eyes narrowed at him. The prince scooted until his back was against the wall. Carver patted the bed beside him and said, "Leave that bed for Falcon. I can share."

Bem grinned at him and shook his head, feeling his cheeks warm. He took his boots off and set them next to the bed beside his bow. Bem draped a wool blanket over Carver and lay beside him on top of the blanket with his arms crossed against his chest. They lie facing each other in silence. Bem could feel the warmth of the fireplace on his back as he examined Carver's face in excruciating detail. He took in the prince's mischievous smirk and kind, tired gaze. They hadn't had a quiet moment to themselves. It was nice to just be in his company.

"What are you thinking?" Carver whispered. A distant boom of thunder rumbled overhead. If Bem had to guess, the thunderstorm was going to last well into the night.

"I was just hoping that you're feeling alright. Ever since the shadows took you, you've been different. On edge," Bem whispered back. Unable to resist any further, he raised his hand to stroke Carver's cheek with his fingertips. Carver gave him another impish grin that Bem had grown to love as he reached out and swirled patterns across his collarbone with his finger.

"I'm marvelous right now," Carver teased as his hand traced his jawline. Bem's heart skipped a beat at the prince's touch. He slowly reached for Carver's hand and brought it up to his lips.

"You need your rest. Don't worry, I'll watch over you," Bem whispered as he planted a gentle kiss on Carver's knuckles.

Carver chuckled softly; his black hair fell into his eyes. "My ever-proper Bem. Fine, I'll sleep. But you should too. There are three fire breathing lizards outside and a brooding sorcerer at the door. I'm sure you can rest easy." He then propped himself up on one elbow, leaned down to Bem's face, and gave him a long, slow kiss on the lips.

Bem's face burned red as Carver pulled away, grinning as always. "I'll never tire of that blush," Carver teased as he settled into the bed. Bem playfully shoved him and turned his back on him to face the room instead. As the minutes ticked by to the sound of the rain outside, Bem felt himself relax. A yawn escaped his mouth, and he knew he wouldn't be able to fight to sleep much longer.

Carver wrapped his arm around Bem and pulled him close against his chest. Bem smiled and placed his hand on Carver's. At that moment, Bem didn't care about anything else in the world. Just having Carver by his side was enough.

Chapter 10
The Crystal Mine

Bem woke to a firm hand shaking his shoulder. He cracked his eyes open to find Falcon standing over him. The fire had gone out, and it was dark, except for the faintest glow of the sunrise. Bem's eyes widened as he sat up in bed.

"We slept that long? You could have woken me sooner," Bem gasped, rubbing his eyes.

Falcon shrugged, grabbing a bottle of what looked like wine from a shelf and taking a swig. "The rain stopped late last night. But I figured there was no sense in leaving until daybreak. We should hurry."

Bem nodded and shook Carver until he woke.

"What?" Carver groaned. He sat up and his hair was askew. He stared at Bem as if he had insulted his name. "Why did you wake me? I was sleeping so well..."

"It's time to go search for Sargon's mine," Bem replied, pulling on his boots and lacing them up tight.

Carver groaned and buried his face in the pillow. Bem smacked his back and said, "Let's go, your majesty!"

"That's your royal highness to you," Carver growled, dragging himself out of bed. The three ate a quick breakfast of bread and jam as the world slowly turned brighter outside. Bem chewed his last bites of bread as he examined the crystals on the shelves.

"You are more than welcome to take a few," Falcon offered. "I am."

Bem thanked him and grabbed a few yellow and blue crystals that held a good vibration of magic within them. As he slipped them into his bag, he made a mental note to be more prepared, like

Sargon. He would have to store his own magic in crystals for emergencies, too.

Falcon reached inside one of the chests at the end of the bed and pulled out a long blue tunic. He held it at arms length and studied Bem. "Sargon was about your size. You can have this if you want it."

Bem looked down at his own dirty, torn shirt. Then he looked up at Falcon and said, "If you're sure it's alright."

"Of course it is," Falcon sighed. "Otherwise, I wouldn't have offered it to you."

They got dressed, tied on their cloaks, and gathered their weapons before heading out of the cabin door into the morning sun. Carver groaned as he entered the warm rays of light, shielding his eyes with his hand.

"Are you alright?" Bem asked.

Carver groaned. "Yeah, I'm fine. The sun just gives me a nasty headache."

He hurried to the shade of the trees and kept his eyes down on the ground, allowing them time to adjust to the light. Theo looked up at them as they approached him. He was the only one there. Steno and Syth must have left to go hunting. Bem hoped that was the case, anyway. He quickly explained what they had discovered, and that they were going to go look for the mine.

Theo stood up as if to follow him, but Bem shook his head. "I need you to wait here for the others. And I'm not certain you can fit through the trees. Besides, you're the only one who can really control them," Bem added.

Theo snarled and glanced up at the sky, as if hoping his friends would fly back at that very moment.

"We'll be back as soon as we can," Bem promised. Theo snorted. A puff of smoke bellowed from his nostrils and he sat in the grass with a thud. Bem patted his leg and then turned to Falcon. "Where do we even start looking?"

Falcon's eyes shifted to the trees. "I know where he might have gone. This way."

He then strode into the southern forest without another word. Carver and Bem silently followed him a few yards behind. Out of the corner of his eye, Bem caught Carver rubbing his left temple and whispered, "You can stay back and rest if you want to."

"Bem, stop treating me like a helpless child. I said I'm fine!" Carver spat. Bem stared at him in surprise. Carver took one look at Bem's face and let out a frustrated sigh.

"I'm sorry. I appreciate you caring for me, but you don't have to worry. I'm tougher than I look," Carver said and offered Bem a small grin. Bem returned the smile and reached for Carver's hand and gave it a reassuring squeeze.

"I'll always worry about you," Bem mumbled.

Carver chuckled. "I know. That's why I love you."

Bem froze as Carver continued, walking a few steps ahead. Carver loved him? Nobody outside of his family ever told him they loved him. Bem's chest swelled with happiness, suddenly feeling light as a feather. But he still felt scared. Was this real? And the biggest question of all, did he love Carver in return?

Carver glanced back over his shoulder and called, "Come on, love, while the sun is still up!"

Bem hurried after him and grabbed his hand once more. Carver brought Bem's hand to his lips without looking at him and placed a soft kiss on his knuckles. For now, this was enough until he could sort his thoughts.

Falcon led them to the glade he and Bem had found the pages. And the Telling Tree, as Falcon called it. Soon, the small clearing came into view, where the large oak tree stood tall and strong in the glade's center. Falcon paused at the edge of the tree line whence they came and stared at the massive, moss-covered tree, just as he had the day before.

"We used to come here almost every day to train when I was young," Falcon said in a hushed tone. His eyes stayed fixated on the oak tree.

"It's a beautiful place. I can see why he liked it so much. What made him want to live all the way out here, anyway?" Bem inquired, joining him at his side.

"Don't you remember? My father banished my uncle from the castle. Sargon knew my father didn't care about these woods, so he hid out here," Carver explained. He glanced around the area uninterested and unbothered that Falcon glared at him.

"Although he wanted to get away from your pathetic excuse of a king and have his freedom," Falcon started. Carver gave him a dirty look, but Falcon continued, "This forest is a very special place to a true sorcerer. This forest holds powerful magic within it."

"It does?" Bem wondered.

Falcon nodded. "Oh yes. I've seen it with my own eyes. Magic is a part of nature. You just have to know where to look." He then walked over to the oak tree and placed his hand on it. "This tree, for example. It might not look like much, but it is one of many guardians of the forest. Place your hand on it and open yourself to its power. You'll see."

Bem joined Falcon and did as he was told. He focused on the rough bark under his palm and closed his eyes. At first, he sensed nothing. Bem tried to settle his mind and took a deep, calming breath. Then he felt it. A soft hum came to his ears as the bark under his hand vibrated and buzzed like a swarm of bees. Bem's eyes opened wide in astonishment. Falcon smirked at him, pleased.

"How is the tree a guardian?" Bem asked. He left his hand in place to feel the magic running through the tree. It tickled his palm.

"Just that. It is one of many that protects the other trees, the animals, the insects, and the land. Out here, we respect this forest. In turn, it will protect us," Falcon explained.

Bem dropped his hand, and the glade fell silent once more. He stared up at the giant tree above him in bewilderment. The amount of magic that filled the world around them amazed him. He would never have guessed it was so real; so alive.

"Remember when I told you about the orbs of light in the Silent Woods? Were they guardians too?" Bem asked.

"Yes, I believe they were. They sensed the magic you were trying to keep hidden. They are a protector of magic and wanted it to live as they were living," Falcon explained.

"Magic isn't alive. It's just extra built-up energy that our bodies produce," Carver argued, running his fingertips over the bark of the tree. Bem wondered if he was trying to feel the tree's magic too.

Falcon frowned. "Some magic does have a consciousness, so I'd be wary of what you say. Especially here."

Carver placed himself face to face with Falcon and said, "You forget that I'm also well versed in the art of sorcery. So, I'd watch what you say to *me*. Don't forget, I am your prince."

Falcon's eyes narrowed, but his face remained calm. "Are you feeling alright, my prince? You've been out of sorts of late."

Carver gritted his teeth. "I'm fine," he growled.

In an attempt to diffuse the tension, Bem stepped in and said, "Alright Falcon, where do we go from here? I didn't see anything in the pages that pointed in any particular direction."

Falcon kept his eyes locked on Carver's for a few more seconds, before answering, "We'll ask the tree."

Carver rolled his eyes.

Confused, Bem responded, "Ask the tree?"

Falcon moved away from Carver and pulled out Sargon's journal from his pocket. He placed the ripped-out pages back inside the journal they were torn from and securely tied it up to keep them in place. Falcon undid the leather cord and read over the pages for a moment. He then tied the journal shut once more and pressed his hand against the tree, and closed his eyes. Bem and Carver watched in silence as Falcon's hands glowed purple.

Suddenly, the tree creaked. It was a slow and steady sound. The leaves above them shook back and forth, though there was no wind to rouse them. The purple light from Falcon's palms burned brightly until it shot down the trunk of the tree all the way through to its roots. Bem and Carver yelped and jumped backwards as the light flowed past them.

From there, the purple beam zipped out along the ground in a pattern much like lightning. In quick, precise movements, the light shot off to their left and disappeared deep within the forest.

"What was that?" Carver asked in alarm.

"That's a form of magic that your king doesn't understand," Falcon said as he placed the journal back in his cloak pocket and followed the purple trail. "Respect for the origin of our magic."

Bem couldn't believe his eyes as he hurried to keep up with Falcon. As Falcon moved forward, the light disappeared behind him.

"How did you do that?" Bem asked in astonishment.

"As I said, Sargon and I respect the nature of magic. And I was certain that if he would leave me a map, it would be here. That's why we called it the Telling Tree. We would leave each other maps on where to find each other," Falcon answered with a sad smile.

"So, he enchanted the tree?" Carver asked a few paces behind them, still skeptical.

Falcon sighed. "The tree is enchanted, in a sense, yes. But not by him nor I."

"You've once again lost me. We enchant items to do something for us with magical properties. It seems like the logical answer," Carver grunted.

Falcon fell silent for a moment as they followed the trail crossing through the trees deeper into the forest. There were no paths they followed now, other than the light.

A sudden realization came to Bem. "The tree isn't an item or weapon, though. It's alive," Bem observed.

Falcon grinned at him. "You're getting it."

"So, what? Sargon asked the tree to tell you where to go if you came along and ask it?" Carver asked. The sarcasm in his voice was enough to make Falcon roll his eyes.

"Essentially," Falcon replied. Carver sighed in frustration and gave up asking anymore questions.

They followed the light trail down a steep ravine. Further down they went, the area grew darker. The canopy of the trees grew thicker. As the tree trunks grew closer together, the sunlight was even more blocked out. The vegetation began to wither and brown the farther down they went. The air grew surprisingly cold. A chill went through Bem's body as they reached the bottom of the ravine and saw the purple light twist around a moss-covered boulder and out of sight. The three companions hesitated and glanced at each other with uncertainty.

There was a shift in the group. A sudden anxiety crept over Bem as they stared at the boulder. Instinctively, Bem dropped his bag and retrieved his bow and an arrow from his back, and held them at the ready. Falcon's hands glowed once more, while Carver drew his sword. They looked at each other and, one by one, they nodded.

Together as a unit, they moved toward the boulder. Falcon led the way, carefully stepping around it to reveal where the trail would lead them. Carver and Bem followed close behind him. It didn't take long to discover where they were.

The purple light ended at the entrance of what Sargon had called a mine shaft. Bem wasn't sure that he'd call it a mineshaft at first glance. One thing he knew for certain; it was dark, manmade, and it angled downward in an immediate, dangerous slope. Bem realized the boulder must have once blocked the entrance from view to keep people out of it. Or, Bem thought with a shudder, to keep someone in.

"Didn't he say that the mine was hidden by magic?" Bem asked. Falcon nodded.

"He must have broken the illusion when he found it," Then, after sucking in a deep breath, Falcon mumbled, "Well, here goes nothing."

Bem glanced back at Carver, and the corner of his mouth twitched in a nervous smile.

"Together?" Bem whispered to him.

Carver leaned down and kissed Bem's cheek. "Of course, love."

Falcon led the way with a glowing handheld high above him to illuminate their path. He looked back at them and mumbled, "Careful, the path looks steep and slick. There's a lot of loose rock."

They ventured down into the depths of the earth with caution. Bem's feet slid a few times on the slick rocks, but kept his balance all the while. The sides of the tunnel consisted of stone and dirt. Every few yards, they passed tall wooden beams that supported the structure from caving in. Bem hoped they were strong. The thought of a cave-in terrified him. The further down they traveled, the muskier the air smelled.

They ventured down deep into the earth by the time Falcon stopped in his tracks and waved his hand from the left to the right against the wall. Bem squinted his eyes to see what appeared to be blast marks.

"This must be where Sargon removed the blockage," Falcon said, tracing a finger along the wall. Bem looked over Falcon's shoulder and gasped.

"What's that?"

Falcon aimed his hand ahead and his light reflected at him in a hundred different places around a small room. They stepped inside to reveal a small, rounded empty room with crystals embedded within the rock. Bem reached out and touched one with his fingertips. It was as large as his hand and was smoky-black, like the others surrounding them. A sudden tingle shot through Bem's arm, causing him to yelp and jump away from it.

"What was that?" he exclaimed, holding his hand with his other as the tingling sensation wore off.

"These crystals aren't natural here," Falcon observed in alarm as he examined the room. He, too, traced his hand across the wall of crystals. "There's some magic in here, but not as much as what it must have once held. And it looks like it held a vast amount of magic. Someone created this, but why?"

Bem wondered out loud, "Maybe they made it to hold Kollano in here. After all, this is where Sargon found him. What do you think, Carver?"

He turned to look at the prince and froze.

The blood drained from Carver's face. He stared wide eyed at Bem; his eyes were wild with fear.

"I can't move," Carver rasped. Falcon spun around in alarm while Bem's heart jolted with dread.

"Why can't you move?" Bem asked. He rushed towards him to help.

"Stop, Bem," Carver yelled, his voice changing into total panic. Bem halted right away, the fear in Carver's voice the only thing he could hear. Bem was scared, and when he looked over at Falcon, he could tell he wasn't the only one.

Carver licked his dry lips. "It's him. He…he's in my head…it's Kollano," Carver croaked. His body convulsed. Beads of sweat appeared on his forehead. Bem's breath caught in his throat. He knew he should have been more careful. He should have seen the signs that something was wrong. Falcon had even warned him, but he was too blind to see it.

"What do you mean, he is in your head?" Falcon demanded, raising his magic-wielding hand in defense.

"I can hear his voice. He's whispering terrible things in my head. I've been having nightmares every night since the shadows took me.

Because he's been in my head all along!" Carver groaned. Tears swelled into his eyes. "I'm sorry! I'm so sorry. I tried to tell you, but something stopped me every time. It was him! He's trying to take over me!"

"Fight it, Carver!" Bem shouted in fear. He wanted so badly to run to him, to chase away the demon inside him.

Tears ran down Carver's cheeks and he let out a shriek of terror as his eyes flickered from his beautiful blue to black as night. His veins darkened throughout his face, spreading down his neck and down to the rest of his body like little snakes searching for a way out.

"Carver!" Bem yelled, unable to stand still any longer. He raced towards him, but something tackled him from behind. Bem glared over his shoulder to find Falcon clutching him firmly to his chest.

"Let go of me. I have to help him!" Bem roared. He struggled against Falcon's arms, but he was too strong.

"Don't! If Kollano has been in there this whole time, it means that he doesn't want to be in here. We are safe from him here," Falcon urged.

"Let me just grab Carver and he'll be safe too!" Bem screamed. Hot tears rolled down his own cheeks as he never took his eyes away from Carver. He screamed in pain, clutching his head and pulling out strands of his own hair. As if he was trying to pry Kollano out. It was agony to Bem.

"We don't know what it will do to Carver if we do that! What if it kills him?" Falcon shouted in Bem's ear. At those words, Bem stopped struggling and slumped against Falcon's arms.

His tears streamed down his face as he helplessly watched Carver crumble to the floor in agony. His screams filled the cavern and echoed into Bem's skull. Carver cradled his head as if to keep it from exploding.

"I'm here Carver, look at me, I'm here! You can fight it! You must!" Bem pleaded, falling to his hands and knees to be on

Carver's level. Carver's screams died down, and he looked up at Bem with black eyes and whispered, "Bem…"

Suddenly, Carver gasped as if someone had knocked the wind out of him and doubled over once more. Bem pleaded for him to get up, to fight it, to be alright.

One hand before the other, Carver pulled himself to his hands and knees. Slowly, Carver stood with his head hanging low. Bem felt hopeful. Maybe he was able to fight him off. Maybe he was…

Carver looked up at him, his eyes as black as night, and gave him a malicious smirk. "Well, well, my love. Bem, was it? We could have some fun, you and I."

Time stopped all at once. All the air seemed to fade away from Bem. He wasn't Carver anymore; he was Kollano. Kollano studied the crystal walls from afar and then his cold, dark eyes settled back on Falcon and Bem.

"I'd love to join you, but those pesky crystals might get in the way," Kollano grinned, making Carver's handsome face look twisted and unfamiliar. "Please, don't think you have to come out here to me. I'd love for you to enjoy my old home. Cozy, isn't it? I think it's perfect for my special friends. Please enjoy. I'll see myself out. Farewell!"

With that, Kollano brought Carver's power out in full force. He curled both hands into fists and struck the rocky walls on either side of him. Falcon shouted something and tried to shoot a blast of magic to stop him, but nothing happened. The rocks crumbled in front of Kollano and collapsed into the only exit they had. As the remaining rocks fell, the last thing Bem saw was Carver's distorted face grinning wickedly at him. Then the cavern fell into darkness and all they could hear was Kollano's sinister laugh growing faint as he left them behind.

Chapter 11
The Servant and the Soldier

Nyel

Nyel and Iris followed the girl further into the deep, dark cave with caution. Iris allowed her hand to light up the otherwise dark passages as they journeyed deeper inside. The tunnels Shara led them through were wide at first. But the further they went, the narrower they became. Nyel ran his hand along the damp stone wall and discovered that tools had chipped away some of it. These tunnels were man-made, or at least, someone had carved them to accommodate their size.

"How long did you say you've been here?" Nyel inquired, still observing the walls with the help of Iris's light. The girl skipped ahead of them, unfazed by the narrow tunnels. Perhaps it was because she was still small and didn't notice the tight fit that forced Nyel and Iris to squeeze their body through.

"My whole life," Shara replied as she hurried ahead of them. "I was born in these caves, so I know them like the back of my hand."

"You have family here?" Iris asked, keeping her lit hand above her to get a better view of the surrounding cave walls. At times, they had to crouch because the ceiling was too short. And other times, they marveled at the tall ceilings where stalactites hung above them.

"Yeah. It's just my mom, dad, brother, and I," she said nonchalantly.

"Did they carve these tunnels out themselves?" Nyel asked.

Shara stopped and nodded, looking back at him. "Some of them, they did. My mother used her magic on some, but my father had to do most of it himself. Mother was really sick when they found this place."

Before they could ask any more questions, she called, "Come on, this way!"

Shara made a sharp turn and leapt down from a ledge and into a hidden passage. She sprinted down the second passage, humming to herself. Nyel and Iris hurried after her, fearing they might lose her and become lost themselves. They climbed down the ledge, their already soaked clothes catching the mud as they did.

Suddenly, Shara stopped when a distant frantic voice shouted, "Shara? Shara, where are you?"

It was a woman's voice and she sounded very worried. Shara spun around on her heel and whispered, "Dim your light!"

Iris did as she was told and grabbed the back of Nyel's left arm at the same time. "Let me talk to her before she sees you," Shara whispered. They silently nodded and watched Shara disappear around the corner, leaving them in total darkness.

"I'm not sure I like this. We don't know who these people are or what they're capable of," Nyel whispered to Iris. He could feel her hand tighten around his upper arm.

"I have to know how and why they are out here on their own," Iris replied just as quietly.

Nyel focused his eyes until they shifted into the slit-pupiled dragon eyes, revealing the outline of the tunnel before them. "I can see a little. Hold on to my shoulders and we'll get closer," he whispered. Iris did as she was told and Nyel carefully led the way in the direction Shara had left them.

As they drew closer, they could hear muffled voices just ahead of them. "How many times do I have to tell you not to wander off on your own?" the woman scolded in a stern voice. The dance of a torchlight illuminated the area just around the corner. Nyel and Iris made sure to stick to the darkness of the cave.

"I stayed in the tunnels, mother," Shara groaned. It was obvious it wasn't the first time they'd had that conversation.

"Your father just returned and told us there are demons all over the place out there! You can't be anywhere near the entrances. If they get you, that's it!" Shara's mother cautioned angrily.

"I know, mother," Shara sighed. Nyel peeked around the corner to see Shara's mother standing over her with her arms crossed against her chest. She looked furious, but also frightened. She had dark, rich skin and the same wavy black hair as her daughter.

"You were trying to visit those dragons again, weren't you?" her mother questioned, her hands now going to her hips as she waited for her answer.

"No mother, I was just looking for my bag I lost yesterday," Shara quickly said, but winced as another voice entered the conversation.

"We've told you over and over not to mess with the dragons!" a man's voice shouted as his large frame entered the small room. "You will never listen to me, will you? You leave me no choice but to block that tunnel off. That way, we can keep a better eye on you!"

Nyel heard his footsteps coming towards them. Shara shouted, "Wait!"

"Not another word, young lady. I'm tired of you not listening to us," the man growled as his voice drew nearer. A brawny man with short red hair and a long red beard turned the corner and froze when he caught sight of Nyel and Iris hiding against the wall.

"Evanna, get Shara out of here. Now!" the man commanded, pulling out a sword from the sheath on his hip.

Nyel moved to stand in front of Iris, but she was the first to react. She summoned fire to her hands and aimed them at the redheaded man. The man hesitated. His knuckles turned white as his grip tightened on his sword.

"You can't have my family, witch," the man growled, his hazel eyes focused on her hands.

"We're not here to harm you," Iris answered in a calm voice.

The man scoffed. "I find that hard to believe," he growled as he motioned at her hands.

"Father, wait!" Shara called, trying to escape her mother's grasp. "She's telling the truth. She's a princess!"

The man's eyes shifted from Iris's hands to her face. A look of recognition changed his face from stunned to pure hatred in an instant. He raised his sword again, causing Nyel to draw his own sword in response.

"Shara, they've fooled you! The royals are the reason we are out here amongst these scale-bellied beasts!" he roared, his eyes alight with rage.

The fire dwindled and faded as Iris slowly lowered her hands. Nyel was not so willing to let his guard down. He kept a wary eye on the man towering over them, ready to fight if it came down to it.

"Yes, I am the princess. Or rather, an exiled princess. Whatever my father has done to you, I would like to make it right," Iris offered. "Please, we mean you no harm."

"Tell your guard to hand over his sword," the man ordered, not budging with his own.

"How do I know you won't attack us after I hand it over?" Nyel grumbled, glaring at the man.

The man returned his glare, unblinking. "I won't let you in here with my family armed to the teeth. You understand, yes?"

Iris nodded at Nyel. He reluctantly dropped his sword to the ground and kicked it over to the man. As he quickly picked the sword up, Evanna glided past him and held up a bracelet with a large smoky black crystal embedded into it. She stopped in front of Iris to allow her to examine it.

"You will need to wear this as well, princess," Evanna instructed in a firm voice. Iris eyed the crystal and looked at Evanna in amazement.

"Where did you get that?" Iris asked in surprise.

Evanna simply held it out to her in response, so Iris reluctantly raised her arm and allowed her to snap the bracelet in place. Nyel's eyes narrowed on the bracelet. He realized it resembled a shackle more than a piece of jewelry. It even had a place for a key to unlock it.

Satisfied, Evanna stepped back and said, "Follow me. We will talk somewhere more comfortable. Don't try anything stupid, or Garian will gut you."

Nyel glanced back at the brawny red head and the look in his eye told him that she was serious about that statement.

Evanna grabbed Shara's hand a little too forcefully and began walking further into the cave yet again. This time, the walk was shorter. As they carefully walked down a steep slope, they entered a large room that was surprisingly cozy. There was a stone fireplace built in the center of the room. Nyel looked up and saw stars way above them through a crack in the ceiling, which surprised him. There were only a few candles lit in the surrounding area.

There were also four somewhat comfortable looking beds, a roughly made table and chairs, and a few other decently made furniture that scattered the underground room. It looked as if they had been living here for some time.

"Sit," Garian ordered, nudging Nyel in the back with the tip of his sword.

Nyel resisted the urge to growl at him. He knew they wouldn't get very far if he suddenly turned into a dragon right before their eyes. Instead, he obediently followed Iris to the table. He ensured to sit beside her and took long, deep breaths to calm himself. The last thing he wanted was for his nerves to trigger his power and put Iris in danger.

Iris carefully placed her bag on the floor by her side. Nyel tried not to look at it. He didn't want to bring their attention to the egg inside of it.

Evanna cautiously sat across from Iris. Her eyes lingered on the crystal shackle she had placed around her wrist, as if to make sure that it was still there. Garian stood behind her, sword still in hand as his careful eyes remained on their guests. Shara sat quiet as a mouse on a nearby bed behind her parents. It was obvious she wanted to stay within earshot and was doing everything she could to make sure her parents didn't send her away.

After studying Iris for a long moment, Evanna finally broke the awkward silence. "I recognize you, princess Iris." Her voice was just as calm as Iris had been, although her brown eyes shone with fierce resentment. "You've grown into a beautiful young woman. And well-practiced in your magic, I'm sure."

Iris placed her hands in front of her on the table, relaxing into her chair. However, the look of shock was clear on her face. "You know me?"

"Of course I do. I first laid eyes on you when you were about Shara's age," Evanna replied. She glanced over at her daughter, who pretended to be interested in the pillow on her lap. When she looked back, her voice turned scathing. "Your father was giving you and your brother a tour around the servant's quarters, boasting about his marvelous system of secrecy. But it wasn't servants, was it a princess? No, he showed you his prisoners. He was quite pleased with himself."

Iris winced as if Evanna had reached across the table and slapped her in the face.

"Ah...yes, I remember that day vividly," Iris replied in almost a whisper. She twisted her fingers together nervously as she spoke. "That was the day I lost what little respect I had left for my father. It was the first time I realized where the magic-filled crystals truly came from."

Her words were filled with horror as she spoke, her fingers fidgeting together.

Evanna arched an eyebrow in disbelief. "You didn't know?"

Iris shook her head. "I was naïve. Kept in the dark until that point. Even then, he insisted you were all of royal blood, or at least descendants; but traitors of his cause, nonetheless."

"Servant quarters?" Nyel interrupted. He hadn't heard mention of servant quarters until now.

"A more pleasant name than dungeon. My father enjoys twisting his words," Iris grimaced. "It's one of a few places my father had built to keep any sorcerers who begged not to be killed when they were discovered. He forced them to store all of their magical energy into crystals for him to sell to his people in controlled amounts. He took anyone willing to serve him, no matter how young, old, poor, wealthy, or race."

"Our living conditions were brutal there too. They barely fed us," Evanna said through gritted teeth. "They treated us like vermin, expecting us to fight for scraps amongst ourselves. Many died from exhaustion every week and were simply tossed out like garbage. But more would replace those who we lost soon after. When we weren't fueling their crystals, we were placed in cells embedded with magic repelling crystals like the one around your wrist to prevent any attempt of us using our magic to escape."

Iris paused, looking from her to Garian. Finally, she asked, "How did you escape?"

Evanna buried her face in her hands as if fighting off a painful memory. Garian placed a large hand on her shoulder. "I helped her escape with a few others," he answered. His voice softened as he watched Evanna.

"How?" Nyel asked, intrigued. Garian dragged the last chair out from under the table and sat. The wood of the chair groaned under his weight. He placed the tip of his sword to the floor and leaned it against his leg.

"I was a soldier in the king's army from a young age, and a damn good one at that. I rose to every occasion, followed every order, until I rose high enough in rank to be a guard in the castle," he replied. "They don't reveal the king's secret sorcerers until they trust you to be a guard of the castle or one of his other prisons. After they tell you, you are either assigned to hunt for more sorcerers or to keep watch over the captured ones in one of the three secret locations throughout Hailwic.

"Fortunately, they entrusted me with the task of guarding the servants throughout the day to ensure that none of them would go astray with their magic. We were told that if we let the sorcerer population get out of control, they would try to overthrow the king and put all of Hailwic in turmoil. I didn't feel comfortable with how they treated the prisoners, but I assumed the king knew what was best for our kingdom. And I had heard that the other prisons, which held captured sorcerers, were far worse than the castle."

Garian sighed and rubbed his left temple with his hand. "I was so stupid back then. Young and stupid."

Evanna placed a loving hand on his whiskered cheek and gave him a small smile. "No, you were fooled. Like many of us were."

"So, the soldier fell for the servant," Iris observed with a sad smile as she watched them care for each other's pain. Evanna nodded in silence.

"She was breathtaking," Garian confessed, placing a hand on hers as he stared into her eyes. "I tried for days to ignore her beauty, but I couldn't stay away from her. I would find every excuse to go to her cell and talk to her. Of course, she didn't trust me at first. Why would she? I was one of the soldiers causing her people's pain."

"But then I took over the role of placing her magic into crystals. I wouldn't take much. Just enough to show she was giving. After that, she trusted I didn't want to harm her. We began stealing kisses every night as they were transferred back to their cells. We talked late into the night in whispers, and I would sneak extra food for her and her family. With each passing day, I grew more and more terrified of her safety rather than my own. I knew then that I had to get her out of there."

Nyel crossed his arms and leaned back in his chair. "How did you do it, though? I've been to the castle and there is no easy way in or out without being detected."

They glanced at each other, and Garian shrugged.

"He can't get in trouble if they're all the way out here," he mumbled.

Evanna nodded, and then said, "Your uncle Sargon helped us escape."

Iris gasped. A grin spread across her face, and her eyes lit up with joy. "Really? I should have known he would be behind this!"

Garian chuckled, surprised by her reaction. "I was a nervous wreck, trying to figure out how to get her out of there. Especially when I told her what I was planning. She insisted that if she went with me, then so must her sister and nephew. I didn't know how to get her out of there, let alone two others. Sargon was ordered to observe the process one day, to make sure everything was going to plan and that the magic crystals were still intact and doing their job. I tried very hard not to even look in her direction, but he knew instantly something was amiss. He cornered me alone in a stairwell and questioned me about my intentions with her. I was so scared that we were all going to be killed on the spot until he grinned at me and reassured me he was on our side."

"I couldn't believe it when I found out," Evanna said with a smile. "The very next night, he arranged for my sister, nephew, and I to be moved to work on a project for him with the king's permission. He told the king he needed more magic than he could produce alone. We were covered in those crystals with our hands and legs bound in chains. They loaded us up into an iron-caged wagon to be taken to another fortress..." Evanna's smile faded from her lips.

Garian gripped her hand in his and finished the story for her. "It was a good plan. However, we were discovered. Sargon's wagon was spotted going in the wrong direction when he thought he wasn't being watched. We were surrounded. By then, we had removed the crystals from everyone along with their bounds. We fought them off as best as we could, but an arrow struck Evanna's sister Shara in the chest."

"The wound was too great. My magic couldn't do anything to save her. She died in my arms…" Evanna whispered, tears rolling down her cheeks. Garian wrapped an arm around her small shoulders and held her close. The room was silent for a moment, except for the wind whistling through the large crack in the ceiling. Even after all that time had passed, there were certain pains that would never go away.

"Sargon distracted them long enough for us to escape," Garian continued. "He instructed that he had a boat arranged for us in a remote area to ferry us across the lake into dragon country. We had no other choice but to keep moving with the soldiers on our trail."

Iris cocked her head. "Did he ever say why he sent you here, of all places?"

Garian shook his head. "All he said was that they would never follow us across the lake and left to fight the soldiers off before we could even thank him."

"How did you get this far out without any dragons attacking you?" Nyel asked.

Garian and Evanna hesitated and looked at each other for a moment. Finally, Evanna spoke up, "The journey was rough. We had many close calls. The dragons began picking up our scent the further we traveled into the mountains, so we would do everything we could to avoid heavily populated areas of them."

She stopped and gave them a sudden questioning glare. "Which reminds me, how and why are you out here?"

Garian narrowed his eyes and looked from Iris to Nyel and back again, his hand tightening on the hilt of his sword.

Nyel stiffened in his chair, his eyes fixated on Garian as his skin began to itch from the approaching scales. A gentle hand on his wrist brought him back to reality. He blinked and turned to Iris, who gave his wrist a squeeze. She then folded her hands in front of her on the table and held her head high as she said, "We are here to make peace with the dragons."

Evanna and Garian stared at her in disbelief.

"Is this some sort of joke?" Garian blurted, scratching his beard as he tried to make sense of what Iris had just confessed.

"No," Iris said firmly. "As I said, you do not have to fear us...I am not my father."

"I don't know that I could trust anyone from the royal family," Evanna stated, crossing her arms.

A deep growl erupted from Nyel's throat that startled the couple. Garian jumped from his seat and raised his sword. "What was that?"

Nyel rose to his feet too, with clenched fists, staring daggers into Garian. Garian's sword was inches away from his throat, but he didn't care. "How can you say you can't trust any royals? It was Iris's uncle that granted you your freedom! You don't know what Iris has gone through to get here. She trained with Sargon when the king wouldn't teach her himself. She studied every book in her library, searching for an answer to help save the kingdom her father has ruined. Not to mention her own father tried to kill her when he found out about her quest! I don't want to hear that she can't be trusted because she represents the best chance for Hailwic and its sorcerers to have a better life."

Stunned, Evanna glanced from Nyel to Iris with wide eyes. "Your father tried to kill you?"

Iris nodded with a sad smile. "I've always known he was an evil man, but I wasn't sure if I ever really expected him to try. Nyel and our friends saved me from that fate."

"You should know, princess. The dragons shouldn't be trifled with. They're a stubborn breed and would sooner turn you into a snack than a friend," Garian mumbled as he lowered his sword to his side.

"How do you know that? Have you interacted with them?" Iris asked, intrigued. She and Nyel both knew firsthand how stubborn and prideful they truly were.

Garian nodded. "If what you say is true, then you shouldn't be bothered to know that we befriended a couple of dragons around these parts. Or at least, they tolerate us and protect us from the others."

"That's amazing! How have you been able to communicate with them?" Iris asked, her fascination growing.

Garian scratched the back of his head. "Well, they understand what we are saying…"

"We'll tell you our secret if you show them yours," Shara spoke up, jumping from her bed and gliding towards them. Nyel had forgotten she was there until she spoke up.

Evanna tried to pull her back, but Shara sidestepped her mother's grasp with ease to stand directly in front of Nyel. She looked up at him with cunning, expectant eyes.

"Well? It's the whole reason I brought you down here, after all!" she inquired. Nyel arched an eyebrow at her in amusement. Her father scolded her and dragged her away from him as quickly as possible.

Nyel glanced at Iris, unsure of what to do. All she did was give him a small shrug. What would they lose if the couple knew his secret?

Nyel sighed and stepped around the table to have more room. Garian pushed Shara back and raised his sword yet again. Nyel raised his hands in the air, trying to remain peaceful with him. "I'm going to show you my power, and I want your word that you won't attack Iris or myself. I promise I won't hurt you."

"I don't like the sound of this," Garian growled, but Evanna placed a hand on his shoulder.

"They've been truthful with us thus far, Garian. Let's see what the boy can do," she reasoned, obviously curious. Nyel took a deep breath and glanced at Shara, who gave him a big smile and nodded her head excitedly.

Nyel closed his eyes, and his body shifted. He could hear their gasps as his skin erupted in green scales and his body grew larger and taller. When his wings sprouted from his back, he opened them to their full extent and flicked his tail as it sprouted from his lower back. Pain pulsated through his body throughout the transformation, but he tried to ignore it. He didn't want to show them any weakness. When he finally opened his eyes, he had to look down at them to see their reaction.

"What magic is this?" Garian asked in awe. His eyes wandered over Nyel's entire body in disbelief.

Evanna surprised him when she walked right up to him and placed her hand on his chest. "This is amazing! I've never seen anything like it in my life!"

"They are definitely not on the king's side if he's part dragon," Garian chuckled, placing his sword on the table as he joined Evanna's side. He ran his hand over Nyel's scaly shoulder with wide eyes. "It's not an illusion. He's real. Outstanding!"

"You all act as if this isn't your first time interacting with a dragon," Iris laughed. Her once rigid shoulders relaxed as the tension in the room seemed to evaporate in an instant. Garian scratched his bearded chin as he continued to study Nyel up and down.

"It's not, actually," he admitted. "Seeing a man turn into a dragon, now that's a first!"

"Does the king know of him?" Evanna asked Iris.

Iris nodded. "He almost killed me for helping a dragon escape with Nyel's help."

A look of pity crossed Evanna's face. "I'm sorry princess, I didn't know."

Iris gave her a sad smile. "How could you? My relationship with my father has never been a good one. It was only a matter of time before our differences became too great."

"A sorry excuse of a human being," Garian spat. He placed his large hand on Iris's shoulder. "Are you two hungry?"

As Nyel shifted back into his human form through gritted teeth, Iris said, "We need to find our friends. We got separated from them after shadow creatures chased us."

Evanna and Garian shared another look. Shara sat in one of the chairs and asked, "You've seen those scary creatures, too?"

Iris nodded. "They've killed and stolen a large clan of dragons and were chasing us along with their shadow counterparts. Ivory must be worried about us."

"I'll go look for Lorna and the others. If it's alright with them, of course, you stay here," Nyel added as he looked at Garian and Evanna for support. "Iris is badly injured and could use some rest in a safe place."

"Who are your friends?" Shara asked with excitement.

"We were traveling with a small group of dragons," Nyel explained. The three of them looked surprised.

"You were?" Evanna asked in amazement. Nyel nodded.

"It's a lot to explain, but Nyel, you shouldn't go by yourself," Iris said in a stern voice. He gestured to her tattered bloody shirt, revealing the fresh scars that could still be seen.

"As I said, you need to rest. Besides, it will go much faster if I search on my own," he admitted.

Iris sighed and looked at the others. "Is that alright with you all?"

"You may stay here," Evanna said. Then added, "Just don't lead any dragons or creatures back here. This is our home, our sanctuary."

Nyel nodded. The last thing he wanted to do was put their family in danger. Garian raised his arm and offered Nyel back his sword. Nyel graciously tied the sword back onto his belt.

He then turned to Iris and said in a low voice, "I won't be long. I promise."

"Just be careful," Iris said, her eyes softening. "And don't take too long."

Nyel reached out to her and gave her a tight hug. She had been through enough already. Knowing she would be safe in this cave put his mind at ease. When they pulled away, he smiled down at her and said, "I'll be back before you know it."

"I'll show you the way out!" Shara shouted and leapt to her feet, but her father stopped her.

"No, you won't, girl," he growled in a stern voice. "Don't think you're not in trouble already for wandering off on your own."

Shara plopped back down into her chair and sulked as Nyel followed Garian in a different direction from where they had come in. They moved in silence for a long while, before Garian said, "Those demons have been thick, as of late."

Nyel grunted. "You're telling me. I'd say I'm surprised you've been seeing them out this far, but I saw the havoc they caused in that clan. Who knows how many more are out there?"

"As you said earlier, they are body snatchers," Garian said in a hushed tone. The tunnel began to lead them upward through the cave. "There's a couple of dragons that help hide us away here. There have been more and more sightings of the shadow creatures, drawing closer to a massive dragon clan not too far from here."

"I'm curious to know how you got dragons to help you. My ability to shift into a dragon helped me get this far. I can't imagine how you accomplished so much without being hunted," Nyel replied, matching his quiet tone.

Garian paused for a moment and opened his mouth to reply when a sudden loud shriek tore at their eardrums. The distance further up the tunnel carried the sound of the startling shriek.

"Hurry, someone is in trouble," Nyel urged.

Garian nodded and together they ran as fast as the narrow tunnel would allow. Garian ushered Nyel around one turn and up another passage. Without his guidance, it would have been easy to get lost in the twisting tunnels.

Finally, a small entrance just big enough for them to squeeze through appeared ahead of them. Nyel could hear the sounds of wings beating against the air as they neared the caves opening. They peeked around the edges of the opening to see a lone dragon shooting fire at five other dragons to fend them off. The glow of her fiery breath revealed the brilliant purple of her scales.

"Lorna!" Nyel gasped in horror as he recognized his exhausted friend overhead.

"You can't give away our position!" Garian hissed as he tried to grab Nyel's arm.

But Nyel was already squeezing out of the cave's entrance. Sharp rocks scraped against his chest as he forced his way through. "I won't shift here, but I can't leave her. She's our friend!"

Garian tried to stop him, but Nyel ignored him. He sprinted up a steep rocky hill towards the battling dragons. His lungs burned as he plowed through the rocky terrain, his feet threatening to slip out from under him all the while. Nyel wanted to distance himself from the cave before he shifted into his dragon form and draw attention to himself. A terrible cry of pain escaped from Lorna's mouth as an enemy dragon slashed its claws through the edge of her wing.

Nyel couldn't stand it anymore.

His body exploded with rage. It transformed with sickening pops as he leapt into the air and drove his newly formed wings down to lift him high into the sky. The others weren't paying attention to him as they were toying with Lorna. He realized they were trying to exhaust her so they could steal her body. Nyel took advantage of the opportunity and rammed the first dragon in the stomach with his sharp horns. Fresh, hot blood streamed down his face and into his eyes as the possessed dragon roared in pain.

As Nyel shook him off, the other four dragons began to charge at him. With her remaining strength, Lorna lunged at one of them and grabbed his long neck with her strong jaws. She began to shake him violently until there was a loud snap that echoed throughout the valley. The dragon went limp and crashed to the ground.

Nyel sucked in a deep breath and unleashed a ball of flames into the face of the first dragon to charge him. He dodged the last two as they tried to bite at his neck and wings. He flew around towards Lorna and shouted, "Are you alright?"

"Where the hell have you been?!" she growled in a murderous rage. Nyel winced. He hadn't seen her mad before, and he didn't like that she was directing it at him. But he could also understand her fury.

"It's a long story," Nyel growled in a hurry.

"And Iris?" Lorna questioned as they watched the three circle back together towards them.

"She's safe," Nyel assured her. "Can you fight?"

"We'll see," Lorna hissed.

Nyel charged towards the lead dragon. As the lead dragon opened his mouth to shoot fire at him, Nyel sucked in a deep breath, shifted into his scaled human form, and grabbed his sword in one fluid motion. The possessed dragon's mouth unleashed a stream of fire at him. Nyel ducked past the fire as he fell towards the enemy dragon and grabbed onto his neck with one arm. The dragon roared with displeasure. Nyel quickly brought up his other hand and plunged his sword deep into the dragon's soft throat.

The roar turned into a yelp as the sword met its target. Before the dragon could fall from the sky, a second one grabbed Nyel with his claws and ripped him from the other dragon's neck, along with his sword, as the body fell to the ground. Nyel struggled against the creature's grip, but every time he squirmed, the dragon's sharp claws sank deeper into his scales, threatening to pierce through them. The dragon fled from the battle scene with the last one of his comrades in tow, roaring in triumph over his captive.

Lorna followed them with a vengeance.

With an extra bout of strength, she caught up to the second possessed dragon, grabbed onto his wing with his sharp teeth and snapped it with her powerful jaws. The dragon shrieked in pain as he tumbled towards the ground far below.

Nyel's captor realized he was the last one with a low groan. He pushed forward, faster than before.

Due to her injury and weakness, Lorna was losing momentum fast. Nyel knew it was up to him to escape the possessed dragon's clutches. He took a deep breath and braced himself. His body shifted into his dragon form once again. Every nerve in his body screamed in pain, causing Nyel to let out an angry roar. The dragon's claws pierced through his scales as he grew until he was too big for the dragon to hold on to anymore. He had no choice but to let him go.

Instead of fighting, the dragon turned and fled when he realized he was outmatched. With a snarl, Nyel flew after him and tackled him from above.

The dragon spun around and kicked at Nyel's underbelly with his hind legs. Nyel held on, ignoring the pain. He drove the creature down towards the earth and smashed him into the ground. The dragon's breath was knocked from him and he looked dazed as Nyel stood over top of him. With one swift movement, Nyel dug his teeth into the dragon's throat and ripped through it, ending his reign of terror.

Nyel panted as he stared down at the dragon beneath him. Then he saw it. The shadow creature ripped itself away from the body, trying to flee once again. Only this time it wouldn't get far as Nyel doused it with fire. The shadow creature vanished as its shriek filled the night air.

Nyel cursed under his breath. It wasn't until then that he thought about the shadow creatures. He didn't have enough time to check if they were still lingering around their used bodies. He doubted they had stuck around.

He returned to the sky and searched for Lorna, but she was nowhere to be seen. Fearful for her life, Nyel scanned the ground below until he spotted her lying on the ground not far from where he had killed the last dragon. Nyel hurried to her side, landing in a spray of dirt and pebbles. He nuzzled her side with his bloody muzzle, trying to wake her.

"Lorna are you alright?" he asked, worried she might have succumbed to her injuries. Or worse, a shadow creature had reached her before he could.

Lorna cracked her eyes open a fraction and glared up at him.

"Do I look alright to you, Shifter?" she asked in an annoyed tone.

Nyel sighed in relief and then chuckled. "No, you look like crap, actually."

"Watch your tongue, youngling, or you'll be next," she growled. He continued to chuckle and laid by her side.

"We need to get you some help," Nyel said as he examined her wounds. She had large gashes in her sides and one of her wings was bloodied and torn. "Do you know where Ivory and the others are?"

She shook her head. "We were separated quite a ways already before I lost you."

Nyel stood once more and said, "Let's get you out of sight at least so you can rest in peace."

"You're not going to bury me like the old one, are you? I still have life left in me," she growled.

Nyel laughed again. "No, I won't bury you. I wouldn't want to dig that big of a hole. Now come on, I'll help you on your feet."

Lorna carefully stood to all fours with Nyel's assistance. Her legs shook with exhaustion. He allowed her to lean against him for support. Once they were steady, Nyel led her slowly back towards the cave entrance. He could only hope that Garian wouldn't be angry at him for bringing a dragon to them.

Chapter 12
The Voice of Emerald

Nyel, over here!" called a voice ahead of them. Nyel looked up in time to see Shara wave at him from the top of a large pile of rocks. He helped Lorna limp over to her and she collapsed on the ground beside him, too weak to carry on.

"Is she alright?" Shara gasped. She jumped down from one rock to the next until she could run the rest of the way to them.

Nyel shook his head. "She needs help. I need to bring Iris to her. I think she could heal her," he said nervously after he shifted back into his human form. Shara eyed his bloodied ribs and put her hands on her hips.

"You look like you need healing too," she said, as her brow arched with skepticism.

"Lorna needs it more than I," Nyel argued, ignoring the sting of his own wounds. He gently lifted her wing to examine the damage to her membrane. Her side and wing had blood stains, along with her neck and chest. She yelped as Nyel tried to place her wing back down carefully.

"I'll be fine. I just need to rest a moment," Lorna grunted. She winced as she tried to make herself more comfortable. Nyel opened his mouth to translate when Shara interjected.

"No, you need magic more than you need rest," Shara disagreed. "My mother and I can help you!"

Nyel froze and whipped around to stare at Shara in disbelief. "Hang on...did you just understand what she said?"

Again, Shara arched her eyebrow. "Um, yeah. Didn't we tell you not moments ago that we talk to dragons all the time?"

"How did you understand what she said?" Nyel asked, dumbfounded.

In response, Shara held up her hand, showing off a small silver ring that held an even smaller green crystal in its band. Similar to the one they found in her bag earlier.

"We like to call it the Connection Crystal," Shara said with a smile. "My father found it long ago while digging in the caves of the mountain behind us. He made it into a necklace to give to my mother as a gift and when they had their first encounter with a dragon, the crystal allowed her to understand what they were saying. We never leave the caves without one on."

"That's amazing," Nyel said in awe as he examined the green crystal before she pulled her hand away from his. It didn't escape him that the resemblance in the color of the crystal compared to his dragon scales were nearly identical. Perhaps that was just a coincidence.

"Come on, we have a dragon to save!" Shara grinned, interrupting his thoughts. She started to hurry down the rocky cliffside where he had left Garian. Nyel quickly turned back to Lorna.

"I'll return with help soon, I promise," he said, placing a hand on the smooth scales atop of her head.

She growled at him softly, saying, "You better be back. Who knows when more will show up?"

Nyel nodded and hurried after Shara. They reached the narrow entrance of the cave and Nyel squeezed his body inside. Shara had no problem given her short and slight frame. As they hurried into the tunnel, Garian emerged, looking furious.

"Shara, I told you never to leave the cave without your mother or I!" he shouted. Nyel paused, unsure of what to do, but Shara didn't even flinch.

"Father, there's a dragon out there that needs our help," Shara pleaded. "We need mother and the princess right away!"

Nyel nodded in response to his annoyed gaze, confirming, "It's true, my friend is badly injured."

Garian then spotted the blood oozing down Nyel's abdomen and said, "It seems that you need healing too." Nyel waved his hand, disregarding his statement and the fact that his daughter had said the same thing moments before. As much as his sides stung and ached, he knew Lorna needed more attention than he did.

"I know I'm asking a lot of you and your family. But please, she needs our help as soon as possible," Nyel urged, staring the burly man in the eye. He had to be a foot taller than Nyel.

Garian sighed and without another word, turned and led the way back to the main cave where they had left the others. Shara grinned at Nyel, obviously proud that they got her father to listen to them. Nyel only hoped that he wasn't getting her into trouble with her father later.

They could hear the faint echoes of Iris and Evanna talking before they could see them. When they finally reached the room, Iris took one look at Nyel and gasped, "You're hurt!"

She rushed over to him with her hands already glowing. Before she could touch him, Nyel reached out and grabbed her wrists. "Save your energy, Lorna needs your help. I'm alright."

"Where is she?" Iris asked as her hands faded back to normal.

"I had to leave her above," he replied, glancing at Shara, who was hopping from one foot to the other in anticipation. "She's badly injured."

"Take me to her," Iris ordered without hesitation.

Nyel examined her and asked, "Have you had enough rest since you were injured? I'm worried you won't have enough strength."

"I'll be fine," she said with a wave of her hand, much like he had with Garian

Garian strode over to grab a small wooden box and pulled out some old cloth. He tossed it over to Nyel and said, "Here, at least wrap yourself with this to stop the bleeding."

Iris grabbed the cloth from Nyel's hands and got to work wrapping it around his shoulder and ribs.

"Mother, she needs our help too," Shara urged as she grabbed her forearm. Evanna looked from Shara to Garian, uncertain of the situation at hand.

"I don't know, we shouldn't…" she started, but Shara cut her off.

"Mother, she's fine! She didn't even care that we were standing right in front of her!" Shara exclaimed.

Evanna glared at her daughter and then her husband. "You were up there alone with dragons and demons flying around? Have we taught you nothing? And you let her?!"

Garian raised his hands in defense. "Don't look at me. I didn't allow her to go up there! You know how she is. She's your daughter, after all!" Evanna rolled her eyes.

"I hate to interrupt, but we need to go help Lorna," Nyel said, losing his patience. Iris had finished her work and had already secured her bag with the dragon egg to her back. She was just as eager to leave. All he could think of was one of the shadow creatures or possessed dragons finding Lorna alone and helpless. He wouldn't let her be alone again. He wouldn't forgive himself if something happened to her.

"Very well," Evanna said, grabbing a worn black cloak, and a palm sized crystal. She put the crystal in her pocket and together, the four of them hurried back out of the cave. Once they made it through the narrow entrance, Garian and Evanna studied their surroundings, including the sky. Nyel and Shara were already halfway up the rocky hill before they started after them. Nyel made it to the large pile of rocks and, as he circled around it, he found Lorna lying in the same place he left her. Her eyes were closed.

"Lorna, we're back," Nyel said, placing his hands on her large cheek. When she didn't respond, his heart raced. He pressed his ear to her massive chest and listened. There was a faint heartbeat, but it wasn't nearly as strong as it should be.

"She's lost a lot of blood. We need to hurry," Nyel pleaded as the others joined him. Garian and Evanna stared at them for a moment before sprinting into action.

Garian pulled out his own crystals and threw one to Nyel. "Know how to use them?"

Nyel nodded and hurried to one side. Iris, Evanna, and Shara were already hovering over her worst injuries. Each of them held their glowing hands above her with eyes closed in concentration. Nyel and Garian got to work with their crystals, tracing them along the gash on her chest and side.

After a few moments, beads of sweat formed on Shara's forehead. Her father took one look at her and grabbed her shoulder to pull her out of her trance.

"Stop," he said in a stern, but kind, voice. "You've done enough. Save your energy. Remember to use control."

"I can keep going! I want to help," Shara protested. She got to her feet and nearly stumbled backwards. Nyel caught her before she fell.

"You'll be more helpful by not passing out from exhaustion," he replied. "Trust me. You've done a great job!"

Garian glared at her until she finally groaned, "Fine, I'll rest."

She sat cross-legged on the ground in a pout. Her fingers dug into the dirt as she scowled at her father when he wasn't looking. Nyel returned to his healing crystal and continued to use it until the energy within it depleted and dulled in his hand. After a while, Garian's crystal dulled too, and they had no choice but to step back and wait for Iris and Evanna to complete their work.

"Uncle, what's going on?" called an unfamiliar voice.

Nyel and Garian turned to see a young man with dark skin, curly black hair, and a strong build approaching them from the west. He had a bow slung over his shoulder and some rabbits tied to his belt.

His eyes scanned the scene, first staring at Nyel and then gaped at the women in shock as they continued healing the injured Lorna.

"Where did they come from?" he asked in bewilderment.

"There's much to explain," Garian chuckled as he ran his hand through his beard. He then cleared his throat and said, "Nyel, this is my nephew, Barrett."

Nyel offered him his hand in greeting. Barrett hesitated before reaching out and giving it a firm shake. His honey-brown eyes then went back to the scene behind them. Just then, Evanna and Iris released their magic. Evanna got to her feet as carefully as possible. Iris crawled over to where Lorna's head lay and stroked her large cheek with a gentle hand. Nyel rushed to join her and they watched as Lorna's large eye fluttered open. It took her a moment to fix her gaze on them.

"Easy, Lorna," Nyel said as she raised her head off of the ground. He caught her chin in his arms and supported her head. "They just healed your wounds, but you still need to regain your strength."

Her eyes softened as she realized what they had done for her.

"Thank you for coming back for me," Lorna said in a quiet, tired voice. Iris gasped and she jumped back in surprise. Her eyes grew wide as she tried to comprehend what just happened.

"I heard you! I understood what you said!" Iris shouted in amazement.

Lorna chuckled as her eyes rested on Iris. "Is that so? If that's true, then I don't have to worry about Nyel relaying my messages to you clearly."

Nyel rolled his eyes. "I've told her everything you've said so far."

"Everything?" Lorna teased. Nyel's face flushed. He averted his eyes away from them, still holding her chin in his arms.

"How is this possible?" Iris asked in bewilderment. She crouched beside Lorna once again, astounded that she could talk to her one on one. Shara joined them and pointed to the crystal ring on Iris's finger.

Iris looked down at the ring in amazement and studied it. "I never knew there was such a crystal," she whispered.

"Crystals are a wonderful thing, aren't they?" Barrett said as he strolled up to them. Iris stood to greet him and offered him her hand.

"Hello, I'm Iris and this is Nyel," she offered.

"Barrett," he beamed as he took her hand in one smooth motion. "You're an incredibly beautiful woman, if you don't mind my saying so."

Nyel resisted the urge to growl at the boy when he bent and placed a kiss on her hand. Although he couldn't really consider him a boy. He seemed to be close to their age. Iris returned his grin with one of her own, unfazed by his pleasantries.

"You look familiar to me…but I can't explain the reason. That can't be possible, though," he said with a furrowed brow as he studied her face.

Evanna joined him and said, "It is possible, nephew. This is the princess of Hailwic."

Barrett's eyes grew wide, and he smacked his forehead with the palm of his hand. "You're the princess? Amazing! Why are you all the way out here? You're not here to drag us all back into imprisonment, are you?"

Iris giggled at his easy-going attitude. "No, we're on an entirely different mission."

Barrett sighed in relief. "Good. I'd hate to kill such a pretty face, but I would if it meant my life."

A fraction of Iris's smile faded at his matter-of-fact tone of voice. Nyel's back stiffened. He released Lorna's head and stepped towards the young man with a hand on the hilt of his sword. He was unable to trust him as he did the others. Something about his demeanor unsettled Nyel.

"I dare you to try it," Nyel growled. His skin prickled with the eagerness to attack. It wouldn't take much to take him down, he thought. The dragon blood pulsed through his veins, ready to protect Iris.

Barrett raised his hands in the air in surrender. "Truce, soldier! I wouldn't hurt anyone unless I had to. It seems my aunt and uncle trust you; and I trust their judgment, so we are good, my friend," he explained. His eyes then drifted down to the blood-soaked bandages wrapped around Nyel's ribs and commented, "Where's your shirt? How did you get those wounds? They look nasty."

"Again, we have much to talk about," Garian offered, placing a hand on his nephew's shoulder to pull him away from the fuming Nyel. Nyel was more interested in giving him a few nasty cuts of his own, but he thought better of it. "How about we all return to the cave and out of sight before those shadows come looking for us?"

"Funny you should mention them," Barrett said, turning to face him again. He pointed towards the north and continued. "I saw a pack of dragons I haven't seen before headed towards the dragon's clan on my way back. They were being chased by a bunch of those parasitic creatures. I had to hide in a hole for what felt like ages before I thought it was safe to come out."

"Did you see a dragon with white scales among them?" Nyel questioned, crossing his arms to better contain himself.

Barrett nodded. "Yeah, there was a white dragon leading the way. How'd you know, did you see them too?"

"We traveled here with them," Nyel grunted.

He then turned his attention back to Lorna. She had already begun to struggle to her feet as they spoke. Nyel placed himself against her shoulder with ease to help her regain her balance. Her weight would have crushed him without his Ascendant power.

Barrett's eyes widened as he watched Nyel walk in step with the big, wounded dragon, who leaned against him.

"My, my, I miss out on everything," Barrett mumbled as the group headed back down the rocky hill towards the cave once again.

"Is there somewhere Lorna can rest for the day to regain her strength? Somewhere hidden?" Nyel asked Garian as they moved.

Garian sighed and said, "Sure, there's a bigger entrance we keep hidden not too far from here that will fit her. It used to be the main entrance of the cave, but it was too large to leave open. We didn't want any wandering dragons to make it a home."

He led the way further past the narrow cave entrance until they reached a large boulder resting against the mountainside. Garian stopped and looked at Barrett expectantly. Barrett stared at him for a moment, sharing a look. Finally, he shrugged and raised his hands. His palms glowed an orange hue.

Suddenly, the boulder trembled in its place. Slow and steady, the rock rolled to the right with the sound of smaller rocks crunching beneath its mass. When it settled to a stop, it revealed an opening in the rocky wall big enough for Lorna to squeeze into. Together, Lorna and Nyel led the way into the new entrance.

Nyel was relieved to find that beyond the opening was a cavern tall enough for Lorna to stand and roam around in comfortably. However, she wouldn't be able to go all the way into the tunnels beyond. The further back the cavern went, the smaller the tunnel shrunk until it was only passable for humans.

Barrett was the last to enter the cavern. He backed into the cave as he rolled the huge boulder back into place with his magic. When the boulder returned to its resting place, the cave fell into total darkness. All the magic users' hands lit up in response to illuminate the surrounding darkness. Satisfied, Barrett wiped his hands on his tunic and said, "If you'll excuse me, I have some rabbits to skin."

They watched as he left the room without another word until all they could see was the faint glow of his hand disappear into the darkness of the cave.

"If it's alright with you guys, Nyel and I will remain here with Lorna," Iris said, turning her attention to Garian and Evanna.

"Are you sure? We have a few hammocks we could set up for you back at home," Evanna offered. Her demeanor towards them had relaxed slightly. It was a relief to Nyel.

Iris shook her head. "We need to talk about our next move, and Lorna should be part of that discussion. Plus, I want to make sure she's fully healed before we leave."

"Alright. If you need us, just follow the tunnel. It will bring you into the main passage that leads back to the main cave," Garian said.

They said their goodbyes and the family of three followed Barrett until their lights dimmed and disappeared as well. Only Iris's hand lit the silent cavern they found themselves in. It was comforting and eerie at the same time.

"Place the egg beside me, Iris," Lorna yawned. "It would do it well to have a dragon's warmth beside it."

Iris did as she was told. When Lorna curled up on the cave floor, Iris pulled the dragon egg out of her bag and placed it at Lorna's side. The purple dragon carefully wrapped her tail protectively around it and drew it closer to her side.

"Do you think the others made it to the clan Barrett mentioned?" Iris asked while Nyel sat across from Lorna.

Lorna puffed, sending a small cloud of dust to float from the cave floor into the air. "I can only hope so. There were so many of those creatures. I hope the shadows haven't got to the clan already."

Nyel clenched his fists. "Maybe I should go on ahead and look for them. They could be in trouble, too."

"You're not going alone," Iris protested.

Nyel sighed. "I can't just sit here and do nothing! What if someone else is currently separated and outnumbered right now, like Lorna was?"

In two steps, Iris planted her feet in front of him and leaned down to meet his gaze. Nyel's breath caught as her long, raven hair brushed his shoulders. Her cool hands reached for the bandages around his ribs and unraveled them to examine his wounds. Nyel winced as she poked and prodded at them for a moment.

Before he could protest, Iris's hands glowed. The sudden warmth of her healing magic seeped from her palms into his skin as she traced them along his wounds. The cuts itched as her magic repaired the torn muscle and flesh. After finishing, Iris removed her hands, leaving pink scars in their place. Satisfied with her work, Iris rummaged through her bag and tore an old piece of cloth into a sliver. She poured a small amount of water onto it from her leather canteen and began to wipe the blood from his sides and face.

"You're getting a collection of these scars. We should stick together. Always," she said quietly, once she had finished cleaning the blood from his sides.

"You're starting a collection too," Nyel mumbled as he stretched his arm to trace his fingertips along the fresh scar on her collarbone. Iris's face flushed when their eyes met.

An earth rumbling snore erupted from the ground beside them. Nyel and Iris turned towards the noise and were amazed to find Lorna had fallen fast asleep. Her tail still carefully guarded the small egg at her side.

Iris chuckled as she took a step back. "She's got the right idea. Let's rest and talk about our plan afterwards. We will have to be careful from here on out. I don't want to cause any more trouble for that nice family."

Nyel sighed. "Fine, but after we rest, I'm leaving with or without you guys. I have to know what's going on with the others. They might be searching for us at this very moment."

Iris joined Nyel on the hard floor, sitting close beside him. She reached for the chain around her neck and pulled out the empty crystal from under her shirt. Iris held the crystal in her hand for a long moment, focusing on it. She then took the crystal off her neck and placed it on the ground between them.

The crystal emanated a warm glow around them, just enough to ward off the darkness. It reminded Nyel of the glow stone he bought for Bem's last birthday. He felt a twinge of pain in his gut at the sudden reminder of home; of his father and Mari. Were they safe from Brock and the other angry villagers? Were they thinking about him too at that very moment? Was Bem safe? Were they able to find Sargon's journal? Nyel tried to push the thoughts away. They would only drive him mad with worry.

"You need to rest, princess," Nyel whispered over the snoring dragon. "Your injuries were far worse than mine. And then to top that, you healed a couple of dragons! You must be exhausted. I'll keep watch."

"Iris," she reminded him in a stern voice, glaring at him.

Nyel grinned mischievously. "Do as I say."

A look of disbelief swept across her face before she returned his grin. "Someone is getting bold!"

"Don't anger the dragon, you might get burned," he growled playfully. To exaggerate his point, Nyel let out a puff of smoke from his nostrils that rolled up to the ceiling.

Iris stifled a laugh with her hand. She rolled her eyes at him and turned herself around to lie down, resting her head in his lap. She peeked up at him and said, "I can handle it. You don't scare me, Shifter."

"I was talking about you," he teased. She gasped and slapped his chest with her knuckles as he laughed.

"Heed your own warning, Nyel, and never forget it," she said in a harsh whisper, and then stuck her tongue out at him for good measure.

Although they were teasing each other, the smile on Nyel's face grew wider at her words. In Folke, his neighbors and even the person who he thought was the love of his life feared him and chased him from his own home. But here was this woman he barely knew, who was at peace with his monstrous form the moment she laid eyes on him. It made him feel exhilarated and nervous all at once. And happy to have her by his side.

They laughed at each other, feeling the stress of their day lift off their shoulders. If only for the moment, it was a welcome relief. Finally, Nyel sighed and said, "Seriously, though. Get some sleep, Iris. You're safe with me."

"I know," she grinned. She then turned onto her side and closed her eyes. Nyel hesitated and then placed his hand on her shoulder. He couldn't help to watch her face as she slept and how peaceful she looked. He was glad she couldn't hear his heart hammering in his chest at the sight of her.

Nyel leaned his head back against the cave wall and stared up at the ceiling as Iris's breath grew longer and deeper until she fell asleep. He felt guilty for sitting there and not searching for the others, but Iris was right. They needed to rest before charging into whatever awaited them outside. He just hoped that the rest of the Guardians had escaped with their lives.

He sat there for a long while, worrying about the others until his eyelids grew heavy. Nyel closed his eyes and hoped he could get a little rest.

Return to me...it is time to mend what has long since broken...return to me...

Nyel's eyes snapped open, and he looked around the dimly lit cave in confusion. It was that voice again! He had heard her voice before, but it was just a dream. Wasn't it? Nyel could have sworn she was in the cave with them, but no one else was there.

Unnerved, Nyel settled back down and waited for the voice to speak again. But it never did.

Chapter 13
Sable and The Seer

I still can't believe I can understand you when you speak," Iris exclaimed with joy. She stared up at Lorna and smiled with excitement.

Nyel didn't have any idea what time it was in the day. He had drifted off to sleep shortly after his experience with the mysterious voice. He wasn't sure who she was or why he was hearing her, but he didn't feel confident about telling the others about it. After all, it was probably just a dream. At least, that's what he decided he was telling himself for the time being.

The three of them sat in the dim glow of light the crystal provided. Iris took the dragon egg from Lorna's side and held it close to her chest. After some rest, the three companions seemed to have recovered from their injuries, at least enough for travel. Most of all Lorna, who held her head high with a twinkle in her eye.

"I hope you're not disappointed, princess. In my experience, dragons can be rather dull," Lorna chuckled softly.

Nyel snorted as he replied, "I've yet to encounter a dull dragon. In my opinion, you're all crazy!"

Lorna growled at him, but he knew she wasn't being serious. Iris shook her head.

"I'm thrilled to talk to you one on one! Now, what is our plan?" Iris stated, looking at both of them. "Lorna, do you think the other dragons went to the nearby clan, as Barrett said?"

Lorna flicked a rock across the cave floor with her talon and remained silent for a moment. Finally, she looked back at Iris and said, "Yes, I think if they were being severely outnumbered, as I'm sure they were, they may have flown into the clan for help."

"Then we should go there too," Nyel suggested.

Something shuffled from the tunnel beyond them. Iris held up the lit crystal to examine the tunnel to find Shara approaching them. She took one look at Iris and gasped, "Is that a dragon egg?!"

"Shara, what are you doing here?" Iris asked in concern, tucking the egg into her bag protectively. "Would your parents approve of this?"

Shara waved a dismissive hand. "Hang on, don't change the subject. Did you steal a dragon egg? I thought you were supposed to be one of the good guys!"

Iris frowned at her accusation, but kept a calm demeanor. "No. We found this unfortunate egg all alone. The mother was killed."

"Oh no!" Shara gasped, crouching down beside Iris to get a closer look. "Then we must protect the poor thing at all costs!"

Nyel stepped in and said, "Shara, Iris asked you a question before. Do your parents know you're here with us?"

Shara's nose scrunched up at the mention of them. "My parents always try to keep me out of everything important. I've made friends with dragons a lot better than they ever have or could. I want to help you guys!"

Iris frowned, obviously unhappy with going behind Garian's and Evanna's backs. However, something she had said intrigued Nyel. "You've made friends with dragons?"

Shara smiled and nodded in excitement. "Yeah! They're old and slow, so they keep to themselves. They live not too far from here. I don't think they'd be able to catch me if they wanted to. So over time, we've become good friends."

"And they are accepting of you?" Iris wavered.

Shara nodded once more. "They are. My parents were the first to make contact with them when they first got here. They're the ones who hid them from the other dragons and kept them safe. They only meet with them occasionally now, but I like to visit them every week, if I can."

"Why did they accept you?" Nyel asked.

Shara cocked her head for a moment, as if she hadn't considered it. "I don't know, really. They always said it was their duty to keep us safe. They're really nice, but they won't ever give me a ride in the sky."

"I'd like to meet these dragons," Iris said at once, finally closing her bag around the egg. Shara's face fell, but she didn't say anything more about the egg.

"Shouldn't we be more concerned with finding the others?" Nyel hesitated. The thought of not finding them made him grow more anxious.

"Maybe they can help us find the clan," Iris offered.

"I already know where to find the clan," Lorna yawned as she rested her head back onto the rocky floor.

"They could help convince the others of our presence," Iris continued, not giving up on her vision. Nyel sighed. The quicker they met with the old dragons, the quicker they would be able to get to the clan.

"Fine. Shara, can you tell us where to find them?" Nyel asked her.

Shara shook her head, leaving Nyel and Iris stunned.

"Why not?" Iris asked, a hint of annoyance and confusion in her tone.

"I won't tell you," Shara replied. Then a big, toothy smile formed on her face with a wicked gleam in her eyes. One that was cunning, yet mischievous. "But I can show you!"

Nyel growled and jumped to his feet. "Shara, your parents will kill me if we take off with you."

"Keep your shirt on, they won't kill you," Shara said with a roll of her eyes. She sat beside Iris, untroubled by his response. She then looked him up and down. "Do you even own a shirt? I could steal one of my dad's for you?"

Nyel bit his tongue and leaned against the cave wall. He crossed his arms against his chest, feeling somewhat self-conscious suddenly.

"Just tell us where to find them and we'll be on our way," he sighed in frustration, rubbing his right temple with his fingertips. He hated to start the day with a headache.

Shara shook her head more firmly this time. "No! I'm tired of everybody treating me like a child. I'm a skilled sorceress. I've befriended dragons and I've explored these mountains on my own. I'm old enough and brave enough. I can help!"

Iris placed a kind hand on her shoulder. "I understand and appreciate your enthusiasm. But you *are* still young and might not fully understand the dangers that lurk out there. Especially with the shadow creatures. We just don't want you to get hurt."

"Do you want to meet the old dragons or not?" Shara answered, also crossing her arms as she stared Nyel down. Her answer was final.

"I could just ask your parents where they are," Nyel countered.

Shara's face scrunched in disgust. "You could, but they won't tell you. They don't want to bring any unwanted attention to our hiding place. To them, the less the dragons see of us, the better."

As frustrating as she was, Nyel realized he had a soft spot for Shara. There was no mistake. Shara was a fighter, and she would not take no for an answer. He held back a smile as he said, "Ok, you win. But if there is any sign of danger, we are bringing you straight back here. Got it? I don't need your death in my conscience."

Shara grinned as she leapt to her feet and bounced with joy. "We should go now while my parents are asleep!"

Iris moved the large boulder that blocked the entrance with her magic as quietly as she could and waited while the others exited the cave. She then carefully rolled the boulder back. They watched as Shara forged up the hill beside Lorna, still bouncing with excitement. Iris and Nyel stayed behind, watching the pair for a moment. She seemed so tiny next to the towering dragon beside her.

"I don't feel good about bringing her out here," Iris whispered. Her voice echoed the same concern Nyel felt in his gut.

"We don't have much of a choice," Nyel replied, trying to reassure her. He then allowed himself to shift into his dragon form and waited for Iris to climb onto his back. The pain he once felt when he shifted had dulled, but was still there. He wondered if it would ever go away.

As he caught up with Lorna and Shara, Iris reached down and said, "You're riding with me."

Shara's eyes lit up, and she jumped to grab her hand. With Iris's help, she climbed onto Nyel's back and settled in front of Iris.

"I can't believe I'm about to fly!" she exclaimed with excitement as she wriggled in place. "It won't take long at all to get there like this!"

"Which way do we go?" Nyel asked, glancing over his shoulder at her. Shara pointed up the very mountain they had been hiding under.

"Seriously? We were underneath them this whole time?" he asked in annoyance.

Shara nodded with a sly smile. He had half a mind to take her back to the cave, but he knew it would be a waste of time and energy arguing with the young girl. Nyel rolled his eyes and crouched low to the ground. Lorna took off first into the sky and Nyel followed her, straight up into the air. Shara squealed in delight, throwing her hands up in the air as they climbed higher into the sky.

Nervous, Nyel looked back at her in time to see Iris wrap her arms around Shara and grasp onto one of his spikes to keep her from slipping. The girl was brave. There was no doubt in his mind. But also reckless. He knew they'd have to keep a close eye on her.

They flew halfway up the mountain before Shara shouted, "Go that way, to the left there!"

As they circled around the mountain, Nyel could hear the waterfall they had fallen down in the distance. Lorna called, "I see them now."

Nyel followed close behind her as they flew towards the ledge of a hollowed-out part of the mountain where he saw two dragons relaxing in the morning sun. As they landed on the edge, the old dragons raised their heads, startled by the newcomers. They were male and female dragons. The male, who was much larger, got to his feet and cautiously approached them. His dull black scales struggled to shine in the sun. His dull black scales struggled to shine in the sun, while a vicious scar had sealed one of his eyes shut and his other eye, a brilliant yellow, caught attention.

"We weren't expecting company. I've never seen your faces before," he said in a scruffy voice. "Who are you, and why have you come here?"

Before Iris could stop her, Shara slid off of Nyel's back and said, "They're with me Sable."

The old dragon's eye widened in surprise as she ran up to him and gave his leg a hug.

"Shara, how did you…" Sable began, but she stopped him and backed up to get a better look at him.

"There's more to it than what you see," Shara grinned. She glanced back at Nyel and Iris expectantly. Iris hesitated for a moment, then jumped down and stood by Nyel's side. Sable stared at her in confusion.

"I've not seen that one before," Sable pondered.

The female dragon stirred and joined her partner's side. Her scales were brighter, casting little specks of orange around them. She studied the newcomers closely.

Her eyes fell on Nyel and she said, "You are a halfling, aren't you?"

Nyel gaped at her in silence. Even Shara's mouth dropped open in surprise.

"How did you…? Have you spoken to Ivory?" Nyel asked.

"I've had a vision of you long ago," said the dragon as she approached Nyel. Nyel took an uncomfortable step back while she studied his face up close. As he studied her face up close, he realized that her scales and skin were wrinkled around her eyes, showing signs of her old age. "Would you do this old dragon a favor and show me what the Ascendant's Gift has provided you?"

Nyel hesitated, glancing at Sable, and asked, "You will not harm us? Shara has put a lot of faith in your protection over her and her family."

"I swear we will not harm you," the old dragon promised in a warm voice.

Nyel took a deep breath and allowed himself to shrink back into his human size. Sable's mouth dropped open slightly as the female's eyes sparkled with a knowing look. She glanced back at her partner and said gleefully, "Did I not foresee this happening?"

Sable chuckled through his amazement. "Yes, my prophet, I've never doubted you. Though I must admit, I never thought I'd see the day."

"What exactly have you foreseen?" Iris asked, but a gasp interrupted her.

Lorna took a step forward and said, "You're Aydamaris, the Ascendant who sees visions!"

The elder dragon laughed. "I guess you have heard of me?"

"Of course, I've heard of you," Lorna said in amazement. "You've predicted many disasters the clans could prepare for or avoid. I've heard of many who make it their goal to seek you out specifically to look into their future."

"And you wonder why I've lived the rest of my life in seclusion," Aydamaris teased. Lorna dropped her eyes at that, not knowing what to say.

"I don't understand. Do you have visions? Of what?" Iris asked.

Sable interrupted just then. "I would first like to know what your intentions are here?"

After being taken aback, Iris quickly regained her composure. "I am Iris, princess of Hailwic. These are my friends Lorna of the Ryngar clan, and Nyel, the Shifter of Folke. We are here in search of peace between the dragons and humans."

"Shifter? Do you not call yourself an Ascendant?" Sable turned to ask Nyel with a look of disapproval.

Before Nyel could answer, Aydamaris said, "Though it's true he carries the Ascendant's Gift, he is an entirely different force, aren't you, Shifter?"

Nyel averted his gaze and said, "I don't know. It just didn't feel right to call myself an Ascendant."

"No, you are much more than that. Don't ever forget it," Aydamaris affirmed. Her words confused Nyel, as well as made him feel uncomfortable. He wasn't anything special, it was just a coincidence he got his power, wasn't it?

"Is peace all you seek, young princess?" Sable asked.

"We seek the camaraderie of the dragons to work together to be rid of the shadow creatures that infect our lands," Iris continued confidently.

"The Shadow Man has escaped his tomb," Aydamaris said gravely. Iris paused in confusion. The Ascendant continued, "We've seen the shadows and the possessed. The clan is quick to eradicate any that get too close, but their numbers grow with every passing day."

Nyel took a step closer towards Aydamaris, and Sable growled in warning. Aydamaris, however, was unfazed and even motioned to her partner to stand down. "How did you know I possessed the Ascendent power?"

Aydamaris brought her head down low to his level and stared at him with intense, dark eyes. The darkest he had ever seen on a dragon. "I received a vision of a man who prioritized a dragon's life over his own, and as a result, was granted the ability to become one of us."

"There's no question that was Nyel," Iris said, joining his side once again.

Nyel remained quiet for a moment, pondering over her words. Then a wave of sudden realization hit him and he quickly asked, "Do you know Ivory?"

Aydamaris stared at him with a wicked gleam in her eye. "You're cunning. That's good. We will need your wits to unite us."

"What do you mean?" Iris asked in confusion.

Nyel shook his head in amazement once again. "Ivory met with her. She must have looked into his future and knew he was the one to pass on the Ascendant power."

"I just gave him a nudge in the right direction," Aydamaris chuckled.

"Well, if you can do that, surely you can tell us how to defeat Kollano," Iris exclaimed.

Aydamaris sighed. "I'm uncertain that I can. My power is touchy. Our magic only works on our kind and my visions appear only for those who need them."

"But you predicted what would happen to Nyel, and he was just a human then," Lorna pointed out, just as confused as they were.

"Yes, but our gift is complicated," Aydamaris replied, emphasizing the complexities of the gift. "As I'm sure young Nyel has learned. I believe it followed the path of Ivory's gift to find its next receiver."

Aydamaris looked down at him and said, "You were destined to become a dragon."

Nyel didn't know if he felt honored or uncomfortable by that statement.

"Can you see if he will be the one to kill Kollano?" Iris asked with hope in her eyes. Nyel stared at her in shock. He hadn't considered that possibility, but he would if he had to.

"I haven't felt a vision for him, but I will try to see," Aydamaris said thoughtfully.

Aydamaris lowered her head once more at eye level with Nyel. He watched in wonder as her dark eyes turned pitch black. His eyes locked onto hers and could not look away. Nyel felt mesmerized as he saw speckles of white light dancing in her eyes while she concentrated on him. Like multiple falling stars zigzagging in every direction. He didn't feel any different except for his body being frozen in place, unable to move as she stared into his soul.

Finally, she blinked her eyes a few times until they turned back to normal. Nyel's body relaxed and he could move again. He sighed in relief and backed away a couple of steps. The orange dragon shook her head. "It is quite hard to see…I think that dark magic could make it difficult to see. Or perhaps the fact that you are still human. Whatever the case, I believe you will be there for the end. The outcome of your meeting, however, I can't say for sure."

She then returned to where she had previously rested. Her legs shook the entire way until she laid down once more. Shara rushed up to her and placed gentle hands on her snout.

"Are you ok, Ayda?" she asked in concern.

Aydamaris let out a tired chuckle. "Yes, I'm alright, little one. I'm not as young as I once was. Visions take much of my strength to accomplish these days, especially if I try to seek them out on my own. I don't use my gift anymore unless absolutely necessary."

"I'm so sorry! I wouldn't have asked if I had known," Iris apologized with shame. Aydamaris shook her head as Shara sat beside her.

"It's quite alright. I would have done it anyway," she replied in a tired voice. "I was curious about that as soon as I laid eyes on him."

"Thank you for checking," Nyel said with a slight bow of respect. "I have to ask, though, why have you been helping Shara and her family stay hidden for so long?"

Sable was the first to speak up, perhaps to allow Aydamaris to rest. "We've encountered many humans in our time, both good and bad. We're not so different. When we first met Garian, Evanna, and Barrett, they were exhausted, frightened, and had little protection from the dangers that surrounded them. We pitied them, so we offered to help them after much convincing on our part. It was hard to tell them we would not eat them without them being able to understand us. I was so glad when they found those crystals. It's so much easier now."

"The crystals are amazing!" Iris smiled in agreement, looking down at the ring on her finger.

"How have they remained hidden from the others for so long?" Nyel asked. "Shara was born and raised here. How have they gone undetected?"

"Not completely undetected," Aydamaris said. "Our son, Ragnar, is the Ascendant and leader of the nearby Maeve clan. He spotted them from a distance one day. He was furious when he discovered them, but we were quick to make a deal with him. Every full moon, I return to the clan to provide my magic wherever it needs to be given. As part of the deal, he insists on leaving us in peace out here on our own. And essentially, it keeps others from discovering our little friends."

Sable added, "When Aydamaris was the clan Ascendant, many dragons near and far constantly pursued her power."

"As I said, my age has caught up with me, so I'm unable to use it as much as I had long ago," Aydamaris sighed. "I fear the power will leave me soon enough. I can sense it."

"How awful," Iris said sympathetically.

Aydamaris winked and said, "It is the nature of the gift. As Nyel knows well."

"Not well enough," Nyel mumbled, kicking the ground with his boot.

He then looked up and said, "Your son is the Ascendant of the Maeve clan. Can you convince him to hear us out?"

Aydamaris hesitated. She and Sable glanced at each other with forlorn expressions. Sable turned back to Nyel slowly and said, "Ragnar will be hard to convince, even with our help. You see, wretched dragonslayers killed his mate long ago…when he discovered them with her body, he went mad and went on a murderous rampage until they all met the same fate. He has never been the same since."

Nyel's stomach sank as he looked helplessly at Iris. Even she was at a loss for words. She quickly regained her composure and said, "I'm sorry to hear that. That's exactly what we want to put a stop to on both sides."

"Will you help us?" Nyel asked, more determined. "We've come all this way; I can't give up now."

The old dragons talked amongst themselves. Nyel gave them the space to do so. He looked back to Lorna and whispered, "Do you think Ivory has mentioned us to the clan?"

Lorna shook her head. "I'm not sure, but I doubt it. I think he'd rather have you by his side when he speaks with them."

Finally, Aydamaris rose to her feet and Nyel rejoined them with growing anticipation. She studied him for a moment. He couldn't read her expression. "We will take you to the clan, but I advise only Nyel goes in his dragon form. I don't think we will make it very far with the other humans. Ragnar won't listen to reason if he sees them."

Iris's face fell, obviously disappointed. "I should be there to speak with him as well."

"First, we would like to make sure Ragnar will not have you killed on the spot," Sable replied. "He is very hardheaded, like his mother."

Aydamaris snorted at him, and Sable chuckled.

"We should leave straight away before it gets too late in the day," Aydamaris said as she glanced at the sky.

"Are you well enough, my love?" Sable asked in concern.

Aydamaris nodded. "Yes, I can manage. The journey isn't too far."

Sable stretched his wings in preparation as Nyel turned to Iris.

"I know you don't like this, but I think they're right. I have to do this alone," Nyel said to her softly.

Iris sighed and nodded. "I know. Just be careful, please. Lorna. I know it's a lot to ask, but will you stay with me so we can get to the clan quickly if there's any trouble?"

"Of course," Lorna replied without hesitation.

Nyel patted Lorna's shoulder and smiled. "Thank you."

He turned to speak to Iris, but was met by the princess, wrapping her arms tightly around him in a hug. His face reddened. When she let go she said, "Please be careful, ok? I'll prepare the crystals I have while I wait."

"Don't wear yourself out. You still need rest," Nyel scolded. Then, with a small smile, he added, "I'll be careful."

"I'll take them back down the mountain," Lorna replied, crouching low to the ground to allow Iris and Shara to climb onto her back. Iris adjusted her bag to keep the dragon egg within it safe from harm.

Nyel raised his eyebrows in surprise. "You're letting them fly with you?"

As she stood up, she said, "We are friends by blood and sisters of war. We look after our own, yes?"

Iris grinned from ear to ear. She patted Lorna's neck, unable to shake her grin. "Of course!"

With that, Lorna dove off the cliff and floated down around the mountain until they were out of sight. Nyel looked back and realized only he and the elder dragons remained. He shifted into his dragon form and waited for them near the edge of the cliff.

"Do you think I stand a chance?" Nyel asked, looking back at Aydamaris.

She stared in the direction of the Maeve clan, as if searching for the answer to his question. Finally, she looked back at him and said, "I really hope you do. The future of our kind is about to change. For better or for worse."

Sable leapt from the cliff, followed by Aydamaris. Nyel watched them for a moment. His heart rate quickened in his massive, scaly chest. His claws gripped the stone beneath them, threatening to carve into the rock from the tension. There was no going back now. Nyel took a deep, steady breath, opened his wings, jumped into the sky and raced into the unknown.

Chapter 14
The Forgotten Prince

Bem

C arver!" Bem cried. His desperate plea filled the small, pitch-black room as it bounced off the walls around them.

Bem summoned his magic, prepared to shoot at the cluster of rocks that separated them. But nothing happened.

He shook his hands and tried again, reaching deep within himself to find his magic. Yet still nothing happened. It was then he noticed a tingling sensation throughout his body, as if his whole body fell asleep at once. It was the same feeling he had when he touched the crystals on the wall.

Bem stumbled around in the dark of the small room, clinging to the crystal walls as he searched for another way out. His breaths turned shallow as he clawed at the walls. This couldn't be happening. In his panic, Bem stumbled into Falcon and nearly fell flat on his face.

"Bem, you need to calm down," Falcon growled from somewhere in the darkness.

He felt disoriented. Whether it was from the darkness or the crystals, he wasn't sure. Falcon grabbed hold of Bem's shoulders to keep him steady. "We can't help Carver if we let fear take control. Allow yourself a few moments to breathe. Ok? Breathe with me."

"But Carver-" Bem started, but Falcon placed his hands on either side of Bem's head and shushed him.

"I said breathe," Falcon commanded.

Bem followed Falcon's lead and took in a deep, shaky breath before slowly letting it out.

"Why isn't my magic working?" Bem asked after a moment, unable to contain the fear in his voice. Time felt as if it were slipping away from them. The longer they were trapped in there, Kollano was getting further away with Carver's body. And he had no idea where to look for him. He had to stop Kollano. He had to save Carver!

Falcon moved his hands back to Bem's shoulders and shook him in an attempt to grab his full attention. "Didn't you see the crystals embedded in these walls? Those are the very crystals that the king's men use to stop a sorcerer from using their magic. We can't rely on our magic to get us out of this. Now please, calm down. We're limited on air as it is."

Bem took another deep, shaky breath and slowly let it out. In a quiet voice, he said, "What do we do? How do we get out of here?"

"Let's begin by trying to move the rock ourselves," Falcon suggested. He released his hold on Bem and shuffled towards the entrance of their prison.

Bem felt his way along the crystal embedded walls until he found the pile of rock. He dug his numb fingers into the rubble, hoping that they could somehow claw their way out. Bem grabbed handfuls of loose stones and dug them out, but most of it was too great and heavy for them to budge. After several painstaking minutes of clawing at the rock, Bem gave up with an exasperated sigh and instead felt his way around the room again for something else, anything else.

"I'm so stupid!" Bem groaned. He pounded his fists against the crystal covered wall, cutting his hands against their sharp edges. But he didn't care. "I should have known something was wrong. You even tried to warn me. I should have known Kollano was inside him this whole time!"

Falcon's hand grabbed his arm from the darkness and forced him away from the wall. "You couldn't have known, Bem. Not for sure. None of us did. All we saw were the side effects of him being with the shadows. How were we to know that Kollano could lie in wait like a disease, waiting for a moment to strike? Have you ever seen any other shadow creature behave that way?"

Bem shook his head and then realized Falcon couldn't see him, so he answered, "No, but it doesn't matter. I should have seen it!"

"Kollano is different. Ancient, evil, cunning," Falcon said in a low tone. "Whatever he is, he's more powerful than the others by far. Why else would someone have him locked away in here without any sign or mention of his name? We must be smart about this."

"What if it's too late to save him?" Bem whispered, tears forming in his eyes once more. All he could imagine was the agonized and frightened look on Carver's face when Kollano appeared.

Falcon's grip tightened on his arm. "We'll find a way, Bem. Don't lose hope just yet."

Bem leaned against the wall and slumped to the floor. They had to figure a way out of there. But how?

"I don't understand how these crystals work," Bem said, motioning to the wall in vain. "How do they withhold our magic like this?"

He felt Falcon's leg brush against him as he joined him on the floor. "They're enchanted to repel magic without prompting. But they're different from a normal crystal. They can't store the magic, only contain it to its original source."

"That seems incredibly pointless," Bem growled, placing his chin on his knee.

"For us, yes. However, it's useful for the king's men who want to detain a person they suspect to be a sorcerer," Falcon mumbled. "Keeps them safe in that way. Though I've never seen a set up quite like this."

"What do you mean?" Bem asked.

"Well, one might have a few large crystals nearby; a pendant around the neck or placed within shackles, for example," Falcon explained. "But never an entire room of them. He must have been powerful."

Bem looked around the small room at the crystals. "How long ago do you think Kollano was placed here?"

Falcon shrugged. "I'm uncertain, but it was probably decades ago. If not for centuries. Long before our time."

"Then how is he alive?" Bem whispered, a chill running down his spine at the thought of being trapped in the little room for years at a time.

"I don't know. It's a form of magic that I've never experienced until now," Falcon replied. "I don't know who he was or where he came from. I wonder if there are books or scrolls in the royal library on it?"

They sat in silence, contemplating what they should do next. Then Bem remembered the crystals he brought in his bag. He felt around for it and his stomach sank when he remembered he left the bag outside. How were they going to get out of there?

To help stifle the growing fear within him, Bem tried to think of something else to occupy his mind. "Why are you called Falcon?"

Falcon chuckled slightly and said, "You're thinking about that now?"

"It's better than the alternative," Bem grunted.

"Yes, I suppose you're right," Falcon sighed, leaning his head back against the wall. "It's nothing of great importance. When Sargon took me in, I didn't speak to him for a long time. No matter what he tried. However, I was a quick study of whatever he tried to teach me. When we started hunting together, I would get my kill faster than him. Since I wouldn't tell him my name, he started calling me Falcon. Because in his words, I was cunning, stealthy, and as silent as the hunter bird. It's kind of a ridiculous name, but I've kept it ever since."

Bem grinned. "I don't know. I find it interesting. I'm glad you kept it."

Falcon sighed and stood. "I just wish I was cunning enough to find our way out of this mess."

A sudden muffled boom resounded overhead, that made them freeze in place. Bem jumped to his feet and whispered, "What was that?"

They strained to hear more, but all they heard was the sound of silence. Then, the walls and ground of their tiny room shook. Loud thumps on the other side of the rock vibrated the small room.

"What if Kollano is trying to cause a collapse?" Bem wondered, suddenly filled with dread.

Falcon frantically felt around the room once more while saying, "Then we need to find a way out of this fast!"

Bem put his ear against the rubble and listened. Just at that moment, a boisterous roar echoed from the other side. A spark of excitement and relief ignited in Bem's chest as he realized what he heard.

"Theo!" Bem shouted at the rock. "Theo, is that you? We're trapped in here!"

They heard a deep growl from the other side, getting closer. The sound of rock and claws scraping together filled the silence. Bem backed away from the entrance and dragged Falcon with him just as the rock crumbled away. Then, with a hefty shove, large rock gave way to a red-scaled head bursting into the small room. Falcon and Bem jumped out of the way, pressing their backs against the furthest wall as rocks flew around them.

The faint glow of daylight poured into the room from high above. Theo lifted his head and examined each of them, one at a time. He then let out a hefty sigh of relief. Bem ran to him and threw his arms around Theo's neck, just behind his jaw.

"Thank you, Theo! We owe you our lives! But right now, we need to find Carver. He's in trouble," Bem said as he released the dragon.

Theo growled angrily as he backed out of the cave. He could barely fit inside. His scales scraped against the walls of the passageway. The sound of it made Bem's ears want to bleed.

"Did you see him?" Bem asked, hopeful to search in the right direction.

Theo nodded his head once with a snort as Falcon and Bem followed him out of the cave. As they exited the tunnel, Theo shook his body from head to tail. His frame was just slight enough to squeeze into the mine, but it couldn't have been very comfortable. Bem was relieved to be out of their stony prison. As his eyes adjusted to the light, he realized Theo was bleeding from several small cuts on his cheek, neck, and chest.

"Are you alright? Where are the others? What happened?" Bem questioned him as he examined the closest wound to him.

He growled once again and huffed, rustling Bem's hair with his hot breath. Seeing that they were minor cuts, Bem sighed in frustration and backed away from the dragon. It would be so much easier if they could just talk to one another.

Theo turned and began trotting through the trees, glancing back to see if they were following. Falcon and Bem had no choice but to follow the red dragon out of the area. Bem grabbed his discarded bag on the way up the ravine.

They had to jog to keep up with Theo's long stride. As large as Theo was, it was quite impressive to see him maneuver between the trees. Although, maybe he was just used to seeing Nyel move around as a clumsy dragon? The thought would have made Bem laugh usually, but now all he could think of was Carver. Still, there were places Theo had to force himself through, scraping bark off the trees in the process with his hard scales.

Bem studied their surroundings for any signs of Carver along the way, but he didn't see anything unusual. They followed Theo all the way past the Telling Tree and back to the lone cabin. Falcon looked towards the open field and asked, "Where are the others? Are they still hunting?"

Theo turned his head towards the west and stared that way for a moment. "Are they looking for Carver?" Bem asked.

Theo looked back at him and nodded.

"You need to know that Carver isn't himself anymore," Falcon explained to Theo. "Kollano was hiding within him. I don't know how or why. He's the one who trapped us in that cave."

Theo's eyes widened. He returned his gaze towards the west and growled. It sounded more like a nervous hum than aggressive. Bem didn't like the sound of it. Like he had given up hope for Carver. Bem sprinted to the cabin and burst through the door. He packed his and Carver's bags with the remaining items they had. He grabbed anything extra from the cabin that may be useful; food, crystals.

A moment later, Falcon joined him in the doorway. "What are you planning?"

Bem didn't stop to look at him. "I'm going after Carver."

Falcon hesitated for a moment and then entered the cabin to stand beside Bem. "Be careful with your emotions, Bem. It's not—"

"Don't tell me it's not Carver!" Bem shouted in anger. He whipped around and took a step forward until he was face to face with Falcon. "Kollano may be controlling him, but Carver is still in there. We have to save him before Kollano sacrifices him too!"

Falcon glared at him. "You expect us to go after Kollano like this? Who knows what army he has waiting for him? Have you ever considered that? His shadow creatures have been stealing bodies in the kingdom and the dragon's territory for weeks, if not longer. There's more at stake here than Carver's life."

"I don't expect you to do anything!" Bem shouted as he shoved Falcon aside to dig through the trunk for jars of preserved food. "I'll go after him on my own."

"I can't let you do that, Bem. Don't be foolish," Falcon said, folding his arms across his chest. His voice was stern, but there was a hint of sadness in the harsh tone. He felt sorry for Bem.

"I'm not being foolish," Bem hissed, turning to face him again. "Yes, I want to save Carver. But think about it. If we can stop him before he gets to the shadows, then it's a win-win situation."

Falcon fell silent for a moment as Bem finished gathering their things. When Bem turned to walk out the door, Falcon grabbed his elbow and said, "Fine. We will go after him. Together. But if there is any sign of trouble, any at all, you must promise me to let Carver go. Walk away and live to fight another day. Don't forget how powerful Kollano is."

He shrugged out of Falcon's grasp. Falcon's response wasn't necessarily what Bem wanted to hear, but he nodded in solemn agreement. Bem left the cabin and set his things beside Theo, waiting for Falcon to pack his own bag.

Bem rested his forehead on the dragon's shoulder. A wave of sudden exhaustion washed over him. He squeezed his eyes shut tight and tried to force the growing fear in his heart to go away. He had seen enough of the possessed to know that Carver was in trouble, he just didn't want to accept that he was lost.

Theo nudged his shoulder with his snout. He looked up in surprise and was met by one large, yellow eye staring down at him with concern. Bem could almost feel the sympathy radiating from the dragon. His throat swelled as he forced tears away. Now was not the time to wallow in grief. He had to do something now to save Carver.

"I'll be fine," Bem whispered to Theo. Absent-mindedly, he grabbed his father's crystal that hung from his neck. He couldn't lose anyone else.

Theo puffed another gust of hot air from his nostrils into Bem's face and tilted his head slightly. Bem patted Theo's shoulder and said, "I'm okay. Let's just find Carver and the others."

Falcon emerged from the cabin with his own bag and a healing crystal in hand. He showed Theo the crystal, and the dragon simply nodded his permission. Falcon used the crystal to heal Theo's wounds as best as he could while Theo waited patiently. After finishing, Falcon placed the crystal in his bag and strapped it around his back.

"Let's get on with it," Bem grunted, not so patiently as he hoisted his and Carver's bags over his shoulder. He then climbed up Theo's front leg and onto his back. Bem reached out his hand to Falcon and helped him up.

Once they were settled, Theo extended his wings and propelled himself into the sky with a leap. The weight of the air pushed them down into his back. Bem squeezed his legs tight around Theo's ribcage as best as he could as Theo's wings pushed them forward through the sky. The sun rested high above them in the morning sky, which Bem was incredibly thankful for. It would give him time to look for Carver. They soared low over the treetops, trying their best to search between them, but Bem could already tell it was going to be difficult to spot him through the dense leaves.

Theo let out a small roar, startling Bem from his search. He looked up just in time to see Steno and Syth circling an area of the woods with their eyes locked on something down below. Theo was quick to join them before Bem could say anything. Bem watched the area below, eager for any sign of what they had found.

Below them, standing on a fallen tree trunk, was Carver. But it wasn't really Carver. The blackened veins and twisted smile contorted his otherwise handsome face as he watched the dragons circle high above him.

"Hello, my love, what took you so long?" Kollano cooed at Bem as Theo hung in place above the trees.

"Release him, Kollano," Bem shouted down at him. He grabbed his bow and readied it in one swift motion with an arrow in place. "Carver is of no use to you. Just let him go!"

Kollano laughed. He placed his hands behind his back, totally at ease. "You won't shoot me, Bem. You'd only kill your lover, not me. It would only inconvenience me at the least. And my answer is no. The prince will prove quite useful to me indeed. Listen, can you hear that?" He placed two fingers to his temple and closed his eyes for a moment in concentration.

"My, my, the young prince does care for his sweet Bem, doesn't he?" Kollano chuckled as his black eyes flickered open and fixated on Bem with sick delight. "It would be a shame for us to part. Why don't you come down here and join me? You have a chance to learn from the most powerful sorcerer this land will ever see. I suggest you take my offer. We could do marvelous things together."

Bem's grip tightened on his bow, but he didn't use it. He couldn't. Did Kollano really hear Carver's voice in his head? As much as he hated to admit it, Kollano was right about one thing. Carver was in there somewhere, and he knew Bem wouldn't try to kill him.

When Bem didn't answer him, Kollano's eyes wandered back to the two circling dragons above them. He smiled again. "It amazes me you got the dragons to obey you. It's been a long time since that has happened. After all, it was my royal blood who branded them as the monsters that they are."

"What do you mean by your royal blood?" Falcon questioned, raising a glowing hand. He wasn't afraid to hit the prince with magic if he had to. Bem's heart skipped a beat at the thought.

Kollano paused for a moment and stared off into space. He then smiled once again as he looked up at Falcon. "The prince puts up a good fight, but I can see through all his walls. He is weak-minded. Your king holds his own secrets. Pitiful excuse of a king at that, just like the rest of them. Many, many years ago, I was in line to be king as well. I would have been a glorious king; powerful, wise, respected. All would have marveled at my power and cowered at my feet. We took great pride in our magic, as they do now.

However, I was more interested in refining my magic into greater things; to become more powerful and indestructible. And I was on the path of enlightenment, but my foolish family feared me. Somehow, they locked me away in that godforsaken tomb, alone…forgotten. Hoping I'd die with my secrets. But they didn't know the powers I held."

"What do you want? How are you here now?" Falcon asked.

"I want revenge, power…I want to be feared. I want what is rightfully mine! Most of all, I want the life that was taken from me. I've spent many excruciating long and painful years as a silent shadow. A whisper of what I used to be. Now that I'm free and whole once more, I won't let anyone stop me," Kollano said in an icy tone.

A shiver ran down Bem's spine. The more Kollano spoke, the more Carver's voice changed into something else that wasn't his anymore.

"Let's make some sort of deal," Bem called frantically, afraid that time was short for Carver. Falcon smacked him in the back to silence him, but Bem ignored him. "Release Carver and we will let you go."

"We can't just let him go!" Falcon hissed. Bem elbowed him in the stomach, causing Falcon to grunt in pain.

"*You'll* let *me* go?" Kollano laughed. He raised his hand in the sky and pointed his palm towards them. "What a childish offer. Here's my deal, *love*. It's quite simple and requires little thought, so it should be easy for you to understand. You won't have to live in fear and secrecy under my reign. You only have to serve me, help me on my quest. Or die."

Before Bem could answer, a roar erupted from Theo's jaws. A jet of fiery flames shot towards Kollano as Theo flew higher into the sky. A split second later, a stream of black magic pierced through the flames that resembled a bolt of lightning and shot through the space they had just been. As the flames and smoke cleared, Kollano disappeared.

"Where did he go?" Bem yelled. His eyes frantically scanned the wooded area below them. Theo searched as well. An angry growl rumbled from his throat.

"Bem, we need to regroup and talk about this," Falcon snarled in his ear. There was no mistaking the fury in his voice, but again, Bem ignored him. All he could think about was Carver. And the thought of Falcon not caring about him made his anger boil over.

Bem's head pounded and he couldn't contain himself anymore. "What is there to discuss? Kollano has Carver and we have to save him. That's it! Theo, fly that way!" He called, pointing to the right.

Theo listened without protest. The other two dragons hesitated and then followed close behind them. They flew just over the trees as they searched for the imposter prince.

"There," Falcon growled, pointing to the left.

Kollano darted through the undergrowth and trees. His pace was much faster than any human should be able to go. Bem locked eyes on him, wondering how it was possible for him to move so fast. Kollano dashed through the trees, keeping enough distance between him and the dragons. The trees thinned out as they approached the edge of the Troden Forest. Bem readied himself. They had a chance that was quickly approaching. If they could swoop in on him, Bem and Falcon could use their magic to contain him and-

Suddenly Syth and Steno roared in unison.

Startled, Bem whipped his head around at their warning to find they were no longer following them. Instead, they were climbing higher into the sky, into the clouds. In the same moment, Kollano called out in Carver's voice, "Dragons in the kingdom! Help your prince, shoot them down!"

Bem turned back in surprise. Theo halted mid-flight. He pulled back so quickly that Bem and Falcon slid into his long neck. One

of the spikes on the back of Theo's neck poked into his belly, but only enough to bruise him. Below them, forming two lines in preparation for fighting, was a small group of soldiers. The soldiers dressed in their finest dragon scale armor and armed themselves with bows, spears, and swords, each weapon adorned with glistening magic crystals.

"The king's army! What are they doing out here?" Bem groaned.

"Theo, get out of here now! And close your eyes, both of you!" Falcon yelled as he summoned his magic.

The soldiers aimed their weapons, but Falcon wasn't going to give them the chance to use them. The sorcerer released a flash of blinding white light as Theo spun around, dazing the soldiers long enough to make them temporarily lose their sight. Bem knew this because he had ignored Falcon's instruction while he watched Kollano run into the safety of the army before the light flashed in his eyes.

They could hear their angry shouts of disbelief as they flew away, of the dragon with men on its back. Bem tried to look back to search for Carver, but all he could see were white stars in his eyes. His heart grew heavy as the realization hit him. He had lost Carver.

"We need to go back. They need to know that's not Carver and-"

"NO!" Falcon interrupted in a stern, angry voice. "We've tried it your way, and we failed. There are more lives at risk than your precious prince. Do you think they'll take kindly to a group of dragons? You saw what they were wearing! You are putting all our lives at risk, Bem. If we go back now, we are as good as dead. We need a new plan and we need one fast!"

"I can't see," Bem mumbled in defeat, tears welling in his eyes. Though it wasn't because of his eyesight.

"Once again, you ignored me," Falcon growled. He let out an exasperated sigh and when he spoke next, his voice softened. "It will return in a few minutes. Theo, we'll be safer if we fly back over to dragon territory. The cabin will be the first place they'll search for us…we need to plan our next steps carefully. Most importantly, Iris and Nyel need to know what happened."

Theo huffed in understanding and silently led the others back north. Bem squeezed his eyes shut and focused on the wind against his face and the expansion of Theo's rib cage with every breath beneath him. The thought of seeing his brother again comforted him slightly, but more than anything, he wanted to go back. He tried to focus on anything else, but his mind wouldn't relinquish the image of Carver's frightened face when he realized what was happening to him. Bem's heart sank once more and the warm tears slid off his cheek and pummeled to the ground below. Only one thought replayed itself repeatedly in his mind. How was he going to save Carver before it was too late? Or the thought he didn't want to acknowledge. Was it already too late to save him?

Chapter 15
Point of No Return

They landed in the dragon's territory just on the shore of Lake Peril. Bem slid off Theo's back and went to the water's edge without acknowledging any of their presence. He watched the ripples of the water as the wind blew over it. There was a storm coming, in more ways than one. Bem sighed and squeezed his eyes shut, trying to force the pain to go away.

He failed Carver. All along, he failed to keep him safe from the evil and darkness that was Kollano. He should have known that Kollano had never disappeared. He used Carver as a vessel to build his strength until the moment was right. And Bem fell for his tricks! He couldn't fight the feeling that it should have been him and not Carver who he had possessed.

"Bem," Falcon called. The pebbles along the lake's shore crunched beneath Falcon's feet as he approached him. A hand fell onto Bem's shoulder and waited until Bem turned to look at him before he spoke again.

"Don't blame yourself," Falcon said, sensing his inner turmoil. "It's ok to feel sad, angry, afraid; any of it. Just don't put those feelings against yourself. Kollano is the one at fault, not you."

Bem nodded his understanding and looked away, back towards the kingdom that felt further away than ever before. Falcon was right. He had to pull himself together if they were going to figure out a way to save Carver. But he didn't know what to do. His mind was numb with hopelessness.

He turned back to Falcon and asked, "Why did Kollano run towards the army? Doesn't he realize that Carver is considered a traitor to the king?"

"Unless he saw reason in Carver's mind that told him otherwise," Falcon offered with a troubled look.

Bem crossed his arms across his chest. "Carver wouldn't betray us, least of all Iris. What would make Kollano think he was safe?"

"I don't know for certain, Bem," Falcon sighed. "Remember, I've known the prince much longer than you have. Carver is…complicated. He always has been. Yes, he left to protect his sister. But it has always been engrained to him that one day the kingdom would be his to control. His to protect and command. And from where I could tell, he had always held his father in the highest regard. I'm just saying he may still feel that he would be welcomed back."

Bem gritted his teeth and looked away from him for a moment. He didn't want to think about that. Instead, he asked the other thing that troubled him, "Kollano went there for a reason. He could have hid from us easily in the forest. But he went to the king's soldiers instead. What does Kollano want from the king? Surely, he can't think he can hide his possession of Carver from his own father? Even those soldiers should be able to see the markings on his skin, or the color of his eyes."

Falcon looked just as troubled. "He hid it well enough from us. I think we need to find Iris and Nyel. They need to know what's happened."

"We won't be any safer from the dragons," Bem replied. "Would it be wise to fly into their territory without warning?"

"I don't see any other choice at the moment," Falcon sighed again. They stared at each other in silence, trying to think of the best course of action.

"Do you still have Sargon's journal?" Bem asked.

"A few of them," Falcon said, motioning to his discarded bag on the ground beside Theo.

"What if we search through them again? Maybe there's something in them that could help us stop Kollano," Bem suggested.

Falcon pinched the bridge of his nose and sighed. "We can, but we can't stick around here twiddling our thumbs! The others need to know that Kollano survived."

"I agree! And you should go tell them," Bem grunted, rummaging through Falcon's bag until he found the journal with the ripped pages.

Falcon stared at Bem like he had gone mad. "And just what are you going to do, pray tell?"

"I'm going to save Carver," Bem answered, returning his gaze with a look of defiance. Falcon shook his head.

"Don't be foolish Bem," he warned.

Bem crossed his arms. "It might be foolish, but I can't leave. Not yet. There has to be something else in Sargon's notes, or in the tomb itself. We didn't get a good look at it."

Falcon cursed under his breath and spun on his heel, sending a spray of pebbles flying behind him.

"What do you expect to find? A list of instructions on how to take Kollano down?" Falcon shouted. His patience had worn thin. "I think if Sargon would have known what to do, he would have done it to save his own life!"

"It doesn't mean there isn't something there that might give us a clue!" Bem retorted. "I will not argue with you. Theo and I can do just fine on our own. You report back to Iris and Nyel. I can't waste anymore time."

Falcon sighed once more and stalked away along the edge of the lake. He was done with their conversation just as much as Bem was. Bem turned away from him and opened the journal to the first page.

A loud huff resounded behind him, rustling the hair on the back of his head. Bem closed the book and glanced over his shoulder to find Theo had joined him.

The crimson dragon tilted his head at him. Whether it was out of confusion or concern, Bem didn't know.

"Will you help me?" Bem pleaded in a near whisper.

Theo's eyes darted to his companion Guardians as a nervous hum reverberated in his chest. Then his eyes settled back on Bem. His hesitation only confirmed to Bem that he didn't seem confident with his plan either.

Falcon returned a moment later, his face stoic. However, instead of addressing Bem, he faced Theo and asked, "Can one of you send word back to Nyel about what's happened with Kollano and the prince?"

Theo's eyes widened in surprise. After a moment of thought, he turned to the other Guardians, and they whispered amongst themselves. When Theo turned back to Falcon, he nodded once.

"Who will you send?" Falcon asked.

Theo grunted at the others. Syth immediately stepped forward and rumbled in response. Theo then returned his gaze to Falcon and waited.

"Falcon, what are you doing?" Bem asked. But Falcon ignored him.

Falcon's eyes flickered to Syth with uncertainty. "Will you swear to get our message to Nyel? This is of the utmost importance to dragons and men alike. Can I trust you?"

Syth lowered his head to eye level and growled his answer. Falcon stared into his unwavering eyes for a moment longer and then nodded his approval. "Very well."

Falcon finally turned to face Bem and said, "The rest of us are coming with you."

"But I thought—"

"Yes, you thought right. I still think we should return to the others. But I know I can't force you to," Falcon replied. "And I can't leave you here in good conscience, either. You're not even well trained in your magic to go off on your own in battle. But you must promise that if things go awry, we leave for the Dragon Mountains at once. I'm not going to allow you to put the rest of us in danger. Do we have a deal?"

Bem considered Falcon's words carefully. He was hesitant to agree to those terms. The thought of leaving Carver behind scared him. He was determined to go, even if he had to go alone. But he knew Falcon was right. It would be foolish of him to go on his own to face a powerful sorcerer and a seemingly unlimited amount of shadow creatures at his disposal. "Yes. We have a deal."

Falcon nodded in approval. He then dug out two crystal necklaces he took from Sargon's cabin. Each crystal necklace, resembling the one Bem wore around his neck, had a dark color with a swirl of amber running through its core. He held one in each palm and closed his eyes. The crystals glowed in his hands. He touched the crystals together, and they shined brighter.

Finally, he opened his eyes, and the light faded from his palms. Falcon placed one of the necklaces around his neck, and then walked over to Syth and said, "I need you to give this to the princess. May I tie it to your horn?"

Syth growled, perturbed. Theo growled back at him and without further protest, Syth bowed his head and allowed Falcon to tie the crystal around his horn. As he did, Falcon offered an explanation. "Sargon was a master at enchantment. Iris and I learned much from him. He enchanted each of these crystals to locate the other. I've just activated them to use a small amount of our energy to work. Whoever wears one necklace can find the other. Be careful with it."

This time, Syth rolled his eyes and grunted, although Theo and Falcon both seemed satisfied. Falcon stepped back and said, "Well, then…that settles the matter. No sense in waiting around here any longer than necessary."

Theo nodded, and a series of deep sounds rumbled in his throat as he spoke to Syth. Syth snorted and shook his head in response. Their conversation was short. As soon as Theo had finished, Syth let out a grunt and opened his wings. Before either Bem or Falcon could thank him, the eager Syth soared into the air and turned northbound towards the Dragon Mountains.

Bem watched him leave, still amazed at how amazing and frightening it was to see a dragon fly high above him. A twinge of sadness burned in his heart. He would have loved to return to Nyel and Iris, making their group whole again. But it wouldn't be whole. Not without Carver. His focus snapped back at once to the journal in his hand. He opened the book and studied the first few pages carefully.

Sargon's writing was more frantic in this journal than the others he had skimmed through. Like he rushed to get his thoughts down on paper. Bem read the scribbles carefully as Sargon described the description of the mine itself. Something about it grabbed Bem's curiosity.

"I think we need to go back to the mine," Bem said.

Falcon looked over his shoulder at the journal and nodded.

"We would have found something at the cabin if anything was there," Falcon agreed. "Then to the mine, it is."

Bem wrapped the leather cord carefully around the book and returned it to Falcon's bag. He then approached Theo. "Ready?"

Theo grunted and crouched low to the ground to allow him on his back. They returned to the sky and turned south once more. Falcon rode with Steno this time, allowing the dragons to fly faster than when they crossed with two on Theo's back. They remained silent throughout the flight. Bem glanced at the sun's position; he couldn't believe it was nearly nightfall. The day had taken a turn he never would have expected when he woke that morning.

Returning to the area at night would be risky. More so with Kollano nearby. But he couldn't wait for daybreak. The thought of waiting made his skin crawl. It gave Kollano more time to get further away with Carver. That thought made Bem wonder if Kollano got away or if the soldiers took him captive. Even though Carver was the prince, he had betrayed the king by helping save Theo's life and accompanying Iris and Nyel into dragon territory. One thing he was certain of, Kollano wouldn't allow them to kill him. He didn't take over Carver's body only to be killed by the king's men.

The dragons made quick work crossing the lake. Perhaps eager to be over solid ground once more. By the time they made it back to Troden Forest, the sun had set. Bem kept his eyes glued to the surroundings below, clutching his father's crystal against his chest. All he could see were trees, but still he kept a wary eye on them. He wasn't about to lose anyone else to the shadows or the king's army. He had to stay calm and watch for any signs of danger. As they drew closer to Sargon's cabin, Steno drifted closer to Theo's side.

From Steno's back, Falcon shouted, "There could be soldiers in Sargon's cabin. We should have the dragons take us to the Telling Tree. They can't land there, nor should they. But we should be able to jump to the tree."

"Alright," Bem replied, his eyes still fixated on the land below. He had hoped there would be a sign of a campfire or torch in the wooded area. It had to be dark within the canopy of the trees. But he saw nothing.

Theo led the way to the small open field where the old Telling Tree stood tall. He flew in close above the tree, avoiding the branches as best as he could. Bem looked for a good-sized tree branch until he spotted one thick enough to support their weight. He adjusted his bag on his back and muttered, "Here goes nothing."

Bem pulled himself up and placed his feet on Theo's back. He steadied himself and locked eyes on the branch below him. It was high in the tree, but still seemed like a far drop from the dragon's back.

Bem took a deep, shaky breath and jumped. He was met with a moment of weightlessness before he crashed down onto the branch. His feet scuffed the bark and his torso fell forward. Branches and twigs scratched at his forehead and cheeks as he plummeted to the ground below. As the ground raced towards him, Bem brought his arms out to catch himself.

A yelp of surprise escaped his mouth as something shot up from the ground at him and caught his wrists and ankles.

Bem blinked once. Twice. Stunned. He looked down at his wrist in confusion. The tree's roots had exploded out of the ground to catch him mid-fall. Bem looked over his shoulder sheepishly at Falcon, who stood on the branch far above him with ease. His hand glowed purple as he lowered Bem to the ground with the tree roots.

Once Bem was placed stomach-first onto the ground, the tree roots returned whence they came. Bem sat up and brushed himself off as Falcon carefully climbed down the tree the rest of the way. When Falcon joined him on the ground, he whispered, "You're not very sure-footed, are you?"

"It's not often that I've jumped off a dragon several feet in the air," Bem mumbled. His cheeks grew hot with embarrassment. "Thank you for catching me."

"Anytime, but let's not make it a habit," Falcon chuckled softly. He patted Bem's back and then waved at the dragons. Theo and Steno, who waited above them for Falcon's signal, flew away and out of sight.

"Where are they going?" Bem asked in a hushed voice. They had to be quiet now. Who knew what men, or creatures, were out in the quiet dark of the woods?

Falcon started heading in the direction the Telling Trees light had taken them earlier that day. "I instructed them to keep closer to the area of the mine, but high enough to avoid detection. If they can help it."

Bem followed close behind him. He hoped Falcon remembered the way to the mine. Bem would have needed the trail light, like before. But he knew if Falcon used the light now, it would draw unwanted attention to them.

They wove through the trees with quick, determined steps. Occasionally, Bem checked over his shoulder to ensure they weren't being followed. The area became more familiar to him once they started down the steep hill towards the old mine's entrance.

Halfway down, Falcon paused for a moment and studied the entrance from a distance. He crept closer, focused on the surrounding area for any sign of intruders. The wooded area remained eerily quiet. Not even a gust of wind blew through the trees.

Satisfied they were alone, Falcon motioned for Bem to follow him the rest of the way to the mine's entrance.

"What should we be looking for, exactly?" Bem asked, dropping his bag to the ground.

Falcon ran his hands along the entrance. "Anything really. Signs, crystals, any kind of marking that would tell us who made this prison."

Bem joined him, looking close at the cool stone wall. He ran his fingers along the side until he felt something beneath the moss. Bem pulled the moss away to reveal an old carving of a triangle and sword. "Falcon, look at this!"

Falcon hurried over to him and studied the carving closely. "I've seen that before. In the castle library. I think it is an old insignia the royal family used to use!"

"Used to use? Why did they change it?" Bem wondered aloud.

"I don't know. Or at least, I don't remember," Falcon confessed. "Iris might know. She knows her family history better than I do."

"So, the royal family did trap Kollano here, just like he said." Bem said. "And if the insignia is as old as you say it is, then that means…"

"Kollano spent over a century imprisoned here," Falcon finished.

Falcon left the mine entrance and gathered a long, sturdy stick, an old rag from his bag, and some twine. He bound the cloth to the end of the stick and, with a glowing hand, lit the rag on fire.

"What are you doing?" Bem asked.

Falcon made his way back to the entrance and answered, "It's the only way we will be able to examine the crystals. Come on, we don't have much time before our light goes out."

With that, Falcon disappeared into the mine. Bem hurried after him. A shiver ran down Bem's spine as they crept down the tunnel towards the makeshift prison. He had to stop himself from looking over his shoulder, almost expecting to see the possessed Carver standing there once more. As they entered the prison, a familiar sensation swept over Bem. A tingle shot from his belly to the end of his limbs. He realized then as he examined the walls, that it was the crystals trapping the magic within his body.

Falcon held his torch to the wall and closely examined each crystal. Many of them were huge, some even taller than Bem. Bem placed his hand on the crystal wall and felt along their smooth edges. The crystals were a mixture of clear and smoky-gray in color. His hand vibrated as he touched each one. "I've never seen crystals like these before."

"Be grateful you haven't," Falcon said in a troubled voice. "I was first introduced to them as a boy. When the king's men took my mother from me."

Another shiver ran down Bem's spine at the thought. "I'm sorry."

"It's in the past," Falcon said with a wave of his hand. "Let's focus on the present for a moment."

Bem nodded and continued to search the area. He moved to the center of the room and stopped when something on the ground caught his eye. He crouched to the ground and rubbed his fingertips on the rocky floor. His hand flew back instinctively when a piercing cold zapped his fingers. The ground was pitch black and ice cold. Bem looked up at the ceiling above the spot and saw webs of black there as well.

"Falcon, what do you make of this?" Bem asked in awe.

Falcon joined him and examined the area. "Interesting. I can't be certain, but I think Kollano was still using some form of dark magic in here. Even with all these crystals in place. I don't understand how he could have done such a thing!"

"Or be alive for so long," Bem added. "Is he even human?"

Falcon paused in deep thought. He then pointed to the crystal walls and said, "The only certainty I have is that a royal had these crystals placed to trap him in here. They use similar crystals in The Keep."

"What's The Keep?" Bem asked, though the name sounded familiar.

"It's one of the king's most guarded prisons for his captured sorcerers," Falcon explained. A look of disgust etched itself across his face. "Most civilians are told it's a high security prison for murderers, traitors, thieves, and the like. In reality, it's a horrific place used to farm magic into small crystals that are sold in markets throughout the kingdom. It's a way to keep gold in the pockets of retches like the king and a death sentence for enslaved sorcerers. And a slow one at that."

"How awful," Bem shuddered. He couldn't imagine being locked away for having a power he was born with. It was barbaric.

A sudden noise echoed down the tunnel from outside that stopped them in their tracks. Bem hurried to the tunnel and strained his ears, unsure of what he had just heard. Moments later, he got his answer. Voices. He could hear voices getting louder as they approached the area. Bem locked eyes with Falcon, his face going pale. Falcon understood immediately.

Falcon smothered the light of his torch and returned them back to darkness. They quickly made their way towards the entrance of the tunnel. The sun had nearly set, making it even more difficult to see their surroundings. But they could hear a group of men stomping down the hill. Bem glanced around the boulder and could make out around a dozen or so headed towards them. He cursed under his breath. How did they know to come all the way out to this part of the forest?

"Do we really have to do this now?" one man grunted in annoyance. His voice was gruff, as if he had smoked a bunch of tobacco before taking the long hike through the Troden Forest.

"You heard the commander," a deeper voice answered. "We have to search the area for some sort of tomb, or whatever."

Another younger man sighed heavily. "Let's just get this over with. My feet are killin' me."

Bem's mouth dropped in disbelief. Some of those voices sounded familiar to him, but he couldn't place where he had heard them before. Who would he know that lived this far away from his home, where he had resided most of his life? Falcon grabbed his arm and dragged him away from the mine.

"What was that? Did you see that?" someone gasped from further up the hillside.

"Hang on," the first man said. The man pulled out a crystal from his robe pocket and held it above him. A sudden bright blue orb shot out of the crystal and zoomed straight for Bem's chest. He yelped and fell backwards in surprise, but the orb only hovered in place. It was a tracking orb that lit up their entire surroundings.

"It's them, the dragon riders!" The familiar deep voice shouted. "Get them!"

Falcon snarled, "Go!"

His hand glowed purple and Bem took off running. A flash of brilliant white light lit up the forest behind him, but Bem learned from experience not to look back. Footsteps followed close behind him and Falcon appeared by his side.

"We need to find the dragons," he huffed.

Before Bem could reply, an arrow shot past him and sank into a tree trunk mere inches from his head.

Bem yelped and dove for Falcon as another arrow flew towards them. They tumbled to the ground behind a large tree, trying to take cover. Bem reached for his own bow and arrows while Falcon grabbed his sword. They exchanged another glance and nodded in silent agreement. There was no running from this fight.

Bem grabbed an arrow and set it in place. He peeked around his tree, only to pull back as another arrow soared towards him. He noted the direction. Bem held his breath, stepped out, and shot an arrow in that direction. A cry of pain echoed in the air as his arrow found its target.

Falcon's hand glowed as he summoned the roots from the trees. They shot up and wrapped around three men at once. They screamed in surprise and hacked at the bark with their swords.

The first man, who was the oldest of the group, held a large crystal in his hand the size of an apple. With a growl, he summoned the magic from within it and shot a ball of fire at Falcon. Falcon rolled sideways across the ground to avoid the fireball. But the cloaked man was relentless. He shot another ball of fire, then another at him. The distraction was enough for the twisting roots to cease. The men cut the roots away and charged towards them once more.

With a shaking, uncertain hand, Bem called upon his own magic. Once it was in his grasp, he reached out his hand and grabbed at a large boulder that rested behind him. The rock began to glow a mixture of blue and white. Bem lifted his hand and it slowly rose and hovered in the air for a moment. With a war cry, he swung his arm at the men and the boulder raced towards them.

They cried out in alarm and leapt backwards to avoid being hit. Bem followed the boulder with another round of arrows hurling towards them, one after another. He aimed and shot three at the cloaked figure with the crystal. One arrow plunged into the man's outstretched arm.

The cloaked man screamed in pain, and with a thud, his crystal dropped to the ground. Falcon seized the opportunity to take control of the tree roots once more and wound them tightly around the Caster before he could grab for another crystal.

Bem reached for another arrow, only to find that his quiver was empty. He swung his bow onto his back and pulled out his dagger from his boot. Bem hurried to Falcon's side.

"I'm out of arrows," Bem gasped. Three men charged towards them with their swords drawn.

"Use your magic," Falcon replied. "I know you can do it."

With that, Falcon grabbed a tree branch with his magic and lunged it at them, pinning them to the trees behind them.

A crack ripped through the air. From the corner of his eye opposite to Falcon, a bolt of lightning flew towards them, aimed at Falcon's back. Without a second thought, Bem grabbed Falcon to pull him out of the way, but it was too late.

An explosion of heat and pain hit Bem in his left shoulder. The air escaped from his lungs in a rush as a current of electricity rippled through them at once and sent them sprawling to the ground. Bem's muscles seized throughout his entire body, sending him into an uncontrollable panic. He writhed on the ground in pain, unable to regain control of his limbs or get a breath. As stars of bright white flashed in his eyes, he prayed this wasn't the end for them.

Falcon's body spasmed violently beside him until he went eerily still.

After what felt like an eternity, Bem's tremors subsided. It left him gasping for breath as sweat drenched his face. Bem wanted to lie there, to succumb to the waves of pain that washed over his body, but he knew they were in trouble. And Falcon was too quiet. His limbs trembled as Bem tried to bring himself to his hands and knees.

"Falcon," he croaked. When there was no reply, Bem grit his teeth and tried to crawl towards him. Footsteps approached him and a boot stomped down onto his back, shoving him back against the ground.

"That'll teach you, serpent-loving freak!" the soldier growled.

The soldier grabbed a fistful of Bem's hair and yanked his head up to expose his throat. The man sneered as he put the edge of his sword to Bem's throat. Bem squeezed his eyes shut, unable to find the strength to escape his demise. The cold, sharp blade began to draw blood as it pressed against his throat.

"Stop! I want him alive," a calm, icy voice commanded.

Bem's blood ran cold. That voice was one he could never forget.

The soldier growled in frustration, but did as he was told. Instead, he grabbed Bem's wrists and tied them behind his back. When the soldier was finished, he shoved Bem's face into the dirt for good measure.

A pair of black leather boots entered his view, then a knee. A hand grabbed his hair and pulled his head up. Bem yelped as the roots of his hair was yanked for a second time and met the eyes of Carver. But they weren't Carver's eyes anymore. It was Kollano's eyes. Cold, black, and calculated.

"My, my, what have we here?" Kollano smirked.

Bem felt as if his heart could burst through his chest. A flurry of emotions swept over him. He was relieved to see Carver, but also terrified that it wasn't him. Why wasn't he tied up? Didn't the soldiers know Carver left with him and his friends willingly to the dragon's land? Then he realized the black veins that had appeared across his skin had vanished. He almost looked normal except for the darkness of his eyes.

"I can see the gears in your head turning, my young friend," Kollano grinned, leaning close to his face. Bem flinched, unable to find his voice.

In a low whisper, Kollano said, "Don't worry, love, I won't let them harm you."

Bem's gut twisted at those words. Kollano used Carver's voice almost perfectly. Almost. He struggled against Kollano's grasp and his head fell to the ground at his feet.

Kollano stood. "We only need one traitor. Kill the other."

"With pleasure, my prince," said the soldier with glee. Bem pulled against his restraints. When that failed, he squirmed on the ground, trying to find his dagger, but his hands only found grass and twigs.

The soldier moved to hover over Falcon and twirled his sword in a circle at his side. He seemed to enjoy his duty as the assigned executioner. Bem called on his magic, but he couldn't reach it. He didn't have enough strength after that lightning strike he endured. All Bem could do was shout, "Leave him alone! Falcon, get up! Please get up!"

In a display of inhuman strength, Kollano grabbed the back of his collar and dragged Bem to his feet with one arm.

"Hush, now," Kollano hissed into his ear. "Let's watch the first of your friends perish, shall we?"

Bem tried to pull away from his grasp, but Kollano's grip only tightened. The soldier plunged his sword downward.

"Falcon!"

A burst of fire suddenly shot into the air from Falcon's hands. A wall of flames that shot up at least eight feet in the air entirely engulfed the soldier. The man screamed in agony as he disappeared from sight. Falcon kicked him out of the way and leapt to his feet, sword in hand. In his other hand was a crystal he brought from Sargon's cabin.

Bem grinned from ear to ear, relieved to see that his friend was alive. But on closer inspection, Bem's stomach sank. Falcon's body shook, weak from the hit he also took. It suddenly clicked in Bem's head why he had a crystal in hand. Falcon didn't have the strength to use his own magic, either. Which also meant he didn't have much strength to fight.

Their eyes met and Bem knew what had to be done. Without uttering a sound, Bem mouthed one simple word to him, "Run!"

An inhuman growl rumbled in Kollano's chest and he spat, "Kill him!"

The rest of his soldiers raced towards Falcon at once. Falcon's face twisted in an unusual show of emotion. His eyes locked on Bem, helpless. Bem gave him a small smile and nodded.

"I will find you," Falcon muttered.

Falcon raised the crystal high into the air. Bem had only a fraction of a second to squeeze his eyes shut before a flash of blinding light filled the area, followed by a pulse of air that pushed towards them. The soldiers shouted in alarm and fell backwards.

Bem opened his eyes and gasped. Falcon had surrounded them in a ring of light that circled the ground and went high above the trees in a wall of light. The sorcerer was nowhere in sight.

Kollano dragged Bem to the nearest soldier and shoved him into the man's chest. "Deal with him. I'll rid us of this sorcerer."

With that, Kollano leapt through the ring of light and out of sight. Bem struggled against his bindings, but it was no use. The soldier shoved Bem backwards onto the ground and he landed hard on his rump.

"Well, well, well…if it isn't my old pal Bem," said the familiar voice.

Bem glared up at the man who had shoved him and froze in disbelief. "Brock?"

Brock grinned down at him. "This day just keeps getting more interesting."

Before Bem could say anything else, Brock brought down the hilt of his sword on the back of his head and everything went black.

Chapter 16
Dark Shadows and Familiar Faces

Every nerve in Bem's body ached as he came to. His stomach lurched as he swayed back and forth on his belly. He slowly opened his eyes in confusion, only to be met with a blinding headache. Bem squeezed them shut again and instead tried to focus on his surroundings. His muscles were stiff from being in the same position for an extended period of time. His hands had gone numb from being tied behind his back.

He opened his eyes once more and realized he was high above the ground. Periodically, a hoof entered his vision. While he was unconscious, the soldiers had thrown him, belly first, onto the back of a horse. And by the feel of it, they had taken away his bow, quiver, and his bag as well. He had nothing to use to defend himself.

Bem's stomach churned with the sway of the horse's movements, threatening to spill its contents onto the dark dirt road below. He stifled a groan, not wanting to bring attention to himself. He knew he was in trouble and needed to escape the situation fast. Bem tested the ropes that bound his wrists together, but was surprised to discover they had replaced them with shackles. It was of no use to break them; he was still too weak from the fight.

"Looks like someone finally woke up," said a snide voice from behind.

Bem turned his head to find Brock riding a few paces behind him. His yellow-toothed smile widened with glee when Bem met his russet eyes. "You were out for quite a while, kid. How's the noggin? I must admit, I don't know my strength sometimes."

Bem's eyes narrowed at him in disgust. Brock's face was one he wished he would never see again. He had slicked back his usual shaggy brown hair and trimmed his curly beard to be more presentable. "What are you doing in the king's army?"

"You haven't heard?" Brock boasted, puffing out his chest with pride. "The king has offered big rewards for dragon slayers to join his ranks. After one kidnapped the prince and princess alongside your traitorous serpent-brother, the king is hell-bent to slaughter them all. And I'm happy to provide my service for such a noble cause. How is Nyel by the way? Did he finally get gobbled up by those monsters?"

Bem ignored his last statement. On closer inspection, he noticed Brock was dressed in crimson red dragon-scale armor. And embedded in the chest plate were three palm-sized amethyst crystals.

"I thought you hated magic and anyone who had anything to do with it," Bem growled in disgust. He tried to ignore the fact that the scales he wore resembled Theo's.

Brock shrugged. "Those are the rules. It's a small price to pay to rid ourselves of these creatures. Plus, I suppose it helps protect me in battle...like I'd need it."

"Will you shut your yaps," commanded the rider sitting in the saddle in front of Bem. "Or I'll knock you both out."

Again, Bem was surprised to recognize another voice. "Thane?"

Thane grunted an affirmative. Brock was the one to ultimately stab his brother when he defended the dragons, but Thane was no better in Bem's eyes. He had stuck close to Brock's side and even stole Nyel's love, Carina, away from him. Seeing both of them again left a sour taste in Bem's mouth.

Bem tried to look around for the other soldiers, but couldn't see anyone else from his position. "Who else followed you into this mess?"

Brock opened his mouth to respond, but from somewhere up ahead, someone shouted, "Halt!"

They came to an abrupt stop. Then the leader called, "Set up camp. We will rest here for the night."

"About time for a rest," Thane grumbled as he dismounted. Thane wore similar dragon-scaled armor as Brock, but his was more of a golden-brown color. With rough hands, he grabbed hold of Bem and said, "Come on!"

Bem barely had time to react as the ground raced towards him. His legs crumpled to the ground, but Thane held up his torso by his collar. "On your feet!"

"Quite the gentleman," Bem grunted. He struggled to regain his balance as Thane dragged him away from the others.

In response, Thane pulled him to a halt, dug into a leather pouch around his waist, and stuffed an old dirty rag into his mouth. With a smirk he said, "There, that'll shut you up."

As Bem's captors dragged him off the path and towards a rocky landscape, he clenched his teeth on the rag to contain his anger. Ahead of them, Brock held an iron pin with a loop and hammer in his hands. He inspected the rocky terrain until he found what he was looking for. Brock placed the pin against the rock and hammered it.

Thane held Bem by the neck with a powerful grip as they watched Brock hammer the pin into place. After finishing, Brock grabbed the loop and gave it a tug. The pin wouldn't budge.

Satisfied, he straightened up and grinned at his work. "That should do it!"

Bem stared at the loop of metal sticking out of the ground as the realization of the situation sunk in. They were going to leave him here on his own, at night, with no protection from the shadow creatures.

Panic grabbed hold of Bem. He tried to pull away from Thane, but the soldier's grip only tightened on Bem's neck. With a grunt, Thane forced Bem to his knees while Brock strung a chain through the loop and hooked it to the shackles on Bem's wrists.

"Wait," Bem said, "Can I at least have my arms in front of me? I can barely feel them."

Brock laughed. "How's that my problem?"

Thane rolled his eyes. He reached down to his boot and produced a hunting knife. He then straightened up and pressed the knife to Bem's throat.

Bem gulped as he felt the cold of the blade against his skin and fell silent. Thane studied him for a moment. His blue eyes seemed void of emotion. Then he said, "Move his arms forward, Brock."

"Why should we cater to him?" Brock sneered. "He's just a prisoner!"

"Just do it! The prince instructed us to take care of him as well," Thane growled. His icy glare turned to Brock. Bem stared at him in shock. He had never heard Thane address him that way before.

Brock mumbled something unkind under his breath as he gave in to Thane's demands. Bem didn't dare move, as Thane's blade remained pressed against his throat. When Brock finished and had him secured to the chain, he straightened up and spat on the ground at his feet.

"There, try to get out of that," Brock boasted with a loud laugh. He shoved past Bem and as he walked away, he shouted, "It'll be impossible without your filthy magic. Nighty night!"

Thane backed away from him and sheathed his dagger. As he turned to leave, Bem quickly asked, "Why is the prince not a prisoner? I thought the king wanted him captured too?"

He stopped and looked over his shoulder at Bem. "The prince had every intention of turning you and your friends over to the king. Didn't you know that?"

Bem stared at him in shock. Thane shook his head with a smirk. "It seems you don't really know your friend as much as you thought, huh?"

With that, Thane turned and strode away. It felt like someone knocked the wind out of him. There was no way that Carver was going to turn them into the king. Thane didn't know Carver like he did. He tried to push that thought from his mind.

Bem watched him stalk back towards the other soldiers, who were setting up small tents and starting campfires yards away. He was all alone. Bem grabbed the chain with both hands and pulled with all his might, trying to get the pin to move. He dug his boots into the ground and pulled again, but it was no use.

He took a deep breath to calm himself and called upon his magic. A sudden sensation tingled from his wrists, down his arms, and into his gut. Yet his magic remained dormant.

Confused, Bem studied his wrists closely. His heart sank with dread. The same magic repelling crystals they had found in the mine were embedded in his shackles. He was completely helpless if any shadow creatures showed up. After a few more attempts at straining against the chain that held him, he gave up in defeat.

How could he have let this happen? Falcon tried to warn him, but he wouldn't listen. Bem's eyes grew wide. He frantically scanned the campsite. There were two people missing. Where was Falcon? Did he escape? Bem tried to stifle the fear that was building inside him with little luck. What if Falcon didn't escape?

Bem shook his head. No, he couldn't think that way. Even though they were both injured, Falcon was stronger than him. Falcon should be with the dragons by now and soon, they would be in the air looking for him.

With a sigh, Bem found a spot where the chain would reach and sat awkwardly against a large boulder in the hillside. It allowed him to at least observe the soldier's campsite. Bem grabbed the blue crystal around his neck and held onto it tight, drawing little comfort from it. He leaned his head against the cold stone and closed his eyes. The sun had already set. It was going to be a long night.

Footsteps startled Bem from his sleep. He cursed himself for dozing off, though it couldn't have been long. He could see his every breath rise in the chilly night air. The stars twinkled overhead. But when he searched for the moon, it was nowhere in sight. All he could see was the glow of distant campfires and the silhouette of a figure walking towards him.

Bem scrambled to his feet, ignoring the pain in his legs from sitting on the rocky ground. Defenseless, the only thing he could think to do was fold the chain on itself and hold it at the ready. As the stranger approached him, he brought back his arms, ready to swing the chain at them.

"Easy Bem, I'm just here to bring you some food," said another familiar voice. Bem gasped and lowered the chain.

"Taiden?" Bem whispered in bewilderment.

Taiden stopped a few feet away from him and placed a small bowl of stew and a chunk of bread on the ground. He then backed away from Bem as if he were a wild animal. Bem stared at the food for a moment, but didn't move from his spot.

He and Taiden had grown up together as good friends. Until that is, Bem realized he had feelings for him that Taiden didn't share. After Bem confessed his feelings to him, Taiden had kept his distance ever since. It tore his heart to shreds knowing he had lost a friend. It was both painful and comforting to see his former best friend standing before him now.

"Why are you here?" he asked, looking back up at Taiden.

"Same reason as Brock," Taiden mumbled. He crossed his arms and averted his gaze.

Bem raised an eyebrow and studied him. "Why are you still following orders from that lunatic?"

Taiden's eyes flickered back to his and he frowned. "You, of all people should know. Brock took me in when my grandmother died years ago. He's kept food in my belly and a roof over my head. I owe him my life for all he's done for me."

For the first time in a long time, Bem saw the old Taiden that he once knew. And he looked worried. But what or who he was nervous about? He wasn't sure.

Bem sighed and relaxed a bit more. He took a few steps forward and knelt beside the food on the ground to examine it. It was more broth than anything else. A chunk of meat or potato floated around the surface. But it was enough to make his stomach growl.

"Did you poison it?" Bem hesitated.

Taiden scoffed, "Do you think I'd risk my own neck? No thanks."

Bem picked up the bowl and welcomed the warmth on his hands. He looked up to Taiden and gave him a small smile. "Thank you."

Taiden looked surprised by his appreciation, but hurried to hide it. "It's nothing."

"Will you get in trouble for bringing this to me?" Bem asked after he took a sip from the bowl. The warmth of the broth trickled down his throat, warming him from the inside. It was a relief he didn't know he needed until he had it.

Taiden hesitated, then shook his head. "No. It's better to keep prisoners strong enough for the journey."

Bem lowered his bowl. His stomach twisted at the word prisoner coming out of his mouth. "Journey to where, Taiden? Where are they taking me?"

Again, Taiden hesitated. He nervously looked over at the campsite where the others boomed with laughter. "I really shouldn't be talking to you about this."

"I know you don't consider me as your friend anymore," said Bem after a moment of awkward silence. "But you should know that I still care about you. And I don't want you to get hurt for helping me…but I also hope that there is a small part of you that still cares about me too."

Taiden met his gaze once more. This time Bem could see the inner turmoil in his eyes. Finally, Taiden stepped closer to him and whispered, "The prince wants us to take you to The Keep."

"The Keep?" Bem wondered out loud. The name struck a chord in him, but he couldn't remember where he had heard of it before.

As if reading his mind, Taiden said, "It's a place where they take the most powerful sorcerers and hold them captive until they either find a use for their magic or...they execute them."

The realization hit Bem like a kick to the head. Falcon had just told him about that horrible place. It was where they took sorcerers to farm their magical energy for the small crystals the kingdom sold to their citizens to make them feel like they were sorcerers. A shiver ran down his spine.

Bem gulped, suddenly losing his appetite. He scanned the camp once more. "Where is the prince?"

"He left not long after you were captured. He said he had to check on something before meeting back up with us," Taiden replied.

Bem's heart sank. What business could Kollano have? He obviously had gained the trust of the king's soldiers. Whatever he had in store couldn't be good.

"What about my friend? Did he escape?" Bem asked.

"I don't know. I think the prince might have gone after him," Taiden shrugged. He glanced back at the others and took a step back. "I better go before they see me talking to you."

A twinge of fear went through him. He had so many more questions for him. And most important of all, he needed to warn Taiden about Kollano.

"Wait, about the prince," Bem blurted out. "He's not what you think he is. He was-"

"TAIDEN! Leave the prisoner alone or I'll string you up beside him," Brock shouted from the camp.

Their eyes met and for a split second, Bem hoped his old friend would help free him. But his hope didn't last. Without another word, Taiden turned and hurried back to the others.

Bem watched him leave and ramble something to Brock that he couldn't make out. Brock growled something back at him and smacked him upside the back of his head in frustration. As he watched their interaction, it made Bem wonder that even though the shackles were on him, was Taiden just as much of a prisoner as him?

Bem finished his bread and stew in a few bites. He left the bowl where it sat and returned to his place against the stone. It wasn't much, but at least it warmed his belly. He leaned his head back against the boulder and closed his eyes in contemplation. Should he try to warn the soldiers about the prince being possessed? He doubted they would believe him. Even if they did, what would happen? Would they try to kill Kollano? With a sinking feeling, Bem knew he couldn't tell them. If they tried to kill him, they would kill Carver too.

He wrapped his arms around his knees and watched the remaining handful of soldiers still awake around their fires. They shouted and laughed and drank, seemingly without a care in the world. Bem wished he had a fire to warm himself by. As the night dragged on, they retreated to their tents one by one until a lone soldier remained, keeping watch over their camp. He didn't recognize him, and the man never looked Bem's way. Bem wasn't a concern to him.

Bem sighed and hugged himself tighter to keep warm. It was going to be a long night. He looked up at the sky. Clouds had rolled in, hiding the stars from sight. And without the moon, the night was truly dark. It sent an involuntary shiver down his spine. Instead, he kept his eyes on the soldiers' camp. Taking what little comfort the fire could provide him.

As he watched the flicker of the small, distant campfire, a sudden stillness of the environment interrupted his thoughts. Bem scanned his surroundings, but all he could really make out were the shapes of the hillside.

A whisper in the cool breeze made every hair stand up on the back of his neck. Bem jumped to his feet and grabbed his chain once more as a weapon. He whipped his head back and forth in search of the source of the noise. He wished he had more light.

He could make out a glow on top of the hill behind where he sat. Bem squinted, trying to focus on the faint light. Suddenly, a high-pitched whisper resounded down the hill towards him. Every muscle in Bem's body stiffened. Bem had heard that sound before, he was sure of it. His grip tightened on the chain, but he knew it was a useless weapon.

Soon another faint glow joined the first, and then another. Bem took several steps back. The blood drained from his face as three figures descended towards him in an eerie silence. Shadow creatures. And he had no magic or fire to defend himself from them.

He brought up his chain and swung it at the first creature. It shrieked at him as the loops of the thick chain passed through it, but its body regained its shape a second later.

"Get back! Stay away from me!" Bem shouted. He couldn't hide the fear in his voice as three pairs of eyes that glowed like embers stared at him. They each bore a wide malicious grin as they descended upon their easy target.

One Shadow Creature raised its hand and grabbed Bem by the throat.

Bem froze in place, a sudden cold like ice raced through his body. The loop of chain dropped from his hands. His brain screamed at his legs to run, at his arms to fight. But the creature's grasp paralyzed him. All he could do was watch in terror as the others drew closer to him. The Shadow Creature reached for his chest, hungry to possess him. To use his body as its own.

White light exploded around him, making it almost impossible to see. The shadow creatures shrieked in unison and dissipated into the air in wisps of smoke. Everything went dark and eerily quiet once more.

Bem collapsed to the ground, shivering uncontrollably as if he had leapt into freezing water. Tears streamed down his cheeks before he could even realize they had formed. He gasped for breath as the panic of what almost happened enveloped him.

A pair of powerful hands grabbed him by the shoulders and lifted him into a seated position. Bem raised his gaze and nearly froze once more. Carver's face glared down at him with an expression that wasn't his own. Of course, it was Kollano. But why did he save him?

"You really are useless, aren't you?" Kollano growled, still holding Bem by the shoulders.

Bem could only gasp for breath and avert his gaze. He couldn't look at Carver's face at that moment, knowing he almost shared the same fate. It also made him feel ashamed that he couldn't protect Carver from his own possession.

"When I address you, I expect you to comply," Kollano hissed. He grabbed Bem's jaw and yanked his head back to look at him. "Otherwise, I WILL leave you for my creatures to consume. Understood?"

Bem nodded. He wished his body would stop trembling.

"Speak," Kollano ordered in an icy tone.

"I understand," Bem spat.

Kollano smirked. "You should be grateful, my dear. I just saved your life. So I'd suggest you work on your attitude as well."

Bem hesitated, and then asked, "Why did you?"

Kollano stared at him, almost surprised by his question. "Because I have other uses for you than allowing one of those pathetic beings to use up your potential."

He released his hold on Bem and stood. Bem caught himself with his hands before his face could hit the ground. Then a sudden realization sparked a flutter of hope in his heart. Bem raised his head and looked Kollano in the eyes. "Or maybe it wasn't you who saved me. Carver did."

Kollano's eyes narrowed on him, his face turning from calm to murderous in an instant. Just before he could answer, multiple footsteps ran towards them.

"My prince, what happened?" Brock shouted as he barreled towards them with his sword drawn.

Kollano raised his hands and in a blink, his face shifted expression once more. When he spoke, it was in a casual tone that was closer to Carver's. "Shadow creatures tried to possess our prisoner. Don't worry, I disposed of them."

Thane and another man with dark skin and jet-black braids stopped behind Brock. They scanned the area for any potential threats. If only they were that concerned before, Bem thought with bitter resentment as he forced himself to his feet. But his legs were still numb and shook uncontrollably. Instead, he fell forward.

In one swoop, Kollano shot forward and grabbed Bem by the back of the neck and steadied him.

"I want a fire built here for our young friend," Kollano commanded, pointing to a spot on the ground close to the chain.

Brock's eyes drifted to Bem. He frowned. "But he's a prisoner. Who cares…"

"Are you ignoring my orders?" Kollano suggested. His tone was calm, but there was a cold threat beneath his words that even Brock couldn't ignore.

"It will be done," Brock said with a short bow and hurried to fetch some wood.

In minutes, the three soldiers utilized the magic of a crystal to build a small fire and then returned to the campsite one by one once they had finished. Kollano shoved Bem to the ground beside the fire and stalked away to sit on the other side of it. Bem peered over the fire trying to understand Kollano's actions. It made him uneasy.

"Carver is no longer here, Bem," Kollano sneered. His pale face and dark eyes haunted him from across the fire.

Bem clenched his fists to steady his nerves. He wouldn't let Kollano intimidate him. "I don't believe that. Carver saved me from those shadow creatures just now, not you."

Kollano chuckled. "You're so naive. Do you really think he has any control here? What remains of him now is nothing more than a ghost of a scared little boy hiding in the recesses of his mind. I pull the strings. I make the rules. You're in my game now, my young friend."

"You're cruel! What makes you think you have the right to take away someone's life for your own gain?" Bem exclaimed.

"You accuse me, yet you're so quick to destroy any other possessed creature you come across. And why is that, do you think?" Kollano asked, tilting his head.

Bem hesitated, unsure how to answer his question.

Kollano smirked and said, "We're not so different when you think about it."

Bem swallowed past the lump in his throat. Then he whispered, "What do you want with me? Why not let one of your creatures take over my body?"

The fire danced in Kollano's cold, black eyes. The possessed prince grinned at him as he leaned forward with a watchful gaze. Like a wolf watching an unsuspecting rabbit. "Why spoil the fun?"

Bem shivered in spite of the fire. He never felt so helpless in his life. The look on the prince's face was wild and inhuman, more than he could have ever thought possible. All he could do was try to get answers. And figure out a way to escape.

They stared at each other from across the fire, studying each other. Kollano tilted his head once more and finally broke the silence. "What are you thinking now?"

The question caught Bem off guard. He released a breath he hadn't realized he was holding and answered, "Why did you stop the shadows from taking me?"

"I've ordered them to follow close behind us. However, I didn't give those imbeciles permission to possess anyone. Simple as that," Kollano replied in an instant.

"I don't believe you," Bem argued. His heart began to race when Kollano's smirk disappeared from his face. But he didn't let that stop him. "No matter what you say, I believe Carver wouldn't allow you to let me get possessed."

Kollano leaned back and put a hand to his chin. The flames flickered in his lifeless pupils as he glared at Bem. "Ah...I see. You're still hoping to save the love of your life. You can give up on that dream, my young friend. He's mine now."

Anger surged through Bem at his words. "I won't let you have him."

Kollano grinned. "You already have."

Bem's face burned red, and he balled his hands into fists once more. He wouldn't allow that thought to overtake his mind. It was true Kollano possessed Carver, but he wouldn't give up hope that he could save him. Somehow.

"You're so certain that your prince will keep you safe, but he certainly didn't keep your silver-haired friend from an untimely end," Kollano continued with a gleeful smile. "What was his name, Sparrow? Hawk?"

Bem felt as if a hammer slammed into his gut. "Where's Falcon?"

"Ah yes, Falcon!" Kollano chuckled, shaking his head. "That Sargon held his orphan in high regard. I didn't see what the fuss was about, his magic was mediocre. He never stood a chance against me."

"You're lying!" Bem shouted as the beat of his heart boomed in his ears.

Kollano smiled, though it did not reach his eyes. "Call me a liar all you'd like, love. He's never coming to save you from your fate."

Bem stared at him, feeling his world crumbling away from him once more. No, Falcon couldn't be dead. Kollano was messing with him. He must have gotten away. But the fear wouldn't leave his heart. This was all his fault.

"You might as well get some rest," Kollano said as he stood, nonchalant. "There's a big, exciting day planned tomorrow. You don't want to miss out on the fun!"

Bile rose in his throat. Bem tried to stay strong as he rose to his feet as well, finally able to steady himself. "What do you mean?"

Kollano grinned once more and turned his back on him. "Never mind that, young Bem. Good night, sweet dreams. Oh, and don't worry. The fire should keep those pesky shadows at bay. Hopefully."

With that, Kollano stalked away towards his tent the soldiers set up for him. Bem watched him until he disappeared inside. Bem spun on his heel and vomited into some brush not far from his reach. As he wiped his mouth on his sleeve, he reluctantly sat back down beside the fire. Was he telling the truth? Did Kollano really kill Falcon? No, he couldn't have. Falcon was smart enough to get away from him, at the very least. But Kollano was gone a long while; he had plenty of time to find him. And Falcon was in a weakened state...

A whisper echoed behind him.

Bem whipped around to find multiple pairs of eyes watching him from a distance, away from the light of the flames. Eyes that glowed like embers.

Chapter 17
The Keep

Morning was brutal. Bem didn't sleep much, knowing that a group of shadow creatures watched over him. Their whispers echoed towards him most of the night, forcing him to sit between the small fire and the distant soldier campsite. His fire didn't last very long, either. He only fell asleep for a brief hour when the sun rose and the shadows disappeared. Until Brock woke him with a kick to the ribs.

Now the soldiers were on the move once more. This time Brock unhooked his chain and secured it to his saddle, forcing Bem to follow behind his horse on foot. Bem stared daggers into the back of Brock's head while he bragged loudly about his past dragon kills. Bem could only assume to impress the pseudo-prince.

He experienced body aches and hunger pangs since he had eaten no breakfast. But he pressed on. There were times he caught a glimpse of Kollano leading the group on horseback. Carver.

He had to stay strong for Carver. Whatever Bem had to endure, Carver had it much worse. He was a prisoner in his own mind. That thought alone gave Bem the strength to march behind them without protest. There had to be a way to save him. He just had to figure out how.

What was Kollano up to? Why did he want to take him to the Keep? Was Bem just an excuse to get into the prison? But for what reason? Why else would he want to keep him alive for so long? So many questions swarmed around Bem's head it made him dizzy.

He wished he had something to eat before the forced march. Taiden didn't dare approach him as he did the night before. He tried not to feel disappointed, but he couldn't help it.

Bem sighed. The terrain beneath him went from a smooth walk to climbing up and down waves of hills, grass, and the occasional boulders as far as the eye could see. It made keeping up with the horses difficult at times. Bem gritted his teeth and forged ahead in silence. He had to stay focused. He wouldn't let Brock or Kollano have the satisfaction of seeing him struggle.

He spent much of his time the night before studying his shackles. They were far too tight to squeeze his wrists out of them. The tingle of the crystals embedded in them never seemed to go away. Bem had never experienced a crystal like them. How were they able to stop him from using magic for such a long time? It was infuriating.

Bem glanced over his shoulder to find Taiden watching him from a distance. As soon as they locked eyes, Taiden turned away from him and urged his horse ahead. But there was no mistaking what Bem saw in his eyes, and he didn't know if he should feel worried or hopeful. Taiden was concerned.

The sun was at its highest point when they finally reached the fortress that Bem could only guess was the Keep. Bem studied it thoroughly as they approached it. It was a large castle, though not as big as the king's own castle. The fortress was built with blocks of gray, weathered stone that towered high over the walls that surrounded it. He could only make out a few windows on the top of its highest tower. A massive iron gate was the only way in and out that Bem could see. Several guards circled the perimeter at the top of the walls and the grounds below, while at least four remained outside the gate.

Bem's heart sank. How could he get out of a place like this without a weapon or magic? He reminded himself he was capable of living without the magic. Bem pushed that thought away from his head. He lived most of his life without it.

As they drew near, the four guards outside the gate brandished long spears and angled them towards the group. Amber colored gems were embedded in each spear.

"Halt!" commanded the lead guard. The group of soldiers did as they were told while Kollano dismounted his horse.

The four guards stared at him in surprise. They glanced at each other with stern expressions written all over their faces. Then the leader said, "Prince Carver. I have strict orders to bring you into custody of the king himself."

"I'm sure you do," Kollano replied in a polite voice. "That is why I have brought you an offering, along with my deepest apologies to the king."

The lead guard hesitated and then lifted his spear. "What is your business here, sir?"

"I've brought with me a prisoner," Kollano motioned to Bem as he spoke. "He is the brother of the dragon shapeshifter that turned my sister against her kingdom. He would make excellent bait for the king."

Bem clenched his hands into fists with anger. He could hear his heartbeat in his ears. So, this was his goal. To capture Nyel. Or perhaps it was to get into the king's good graces. But why? What did he need the king for?

The guard's eyes slid over to Bem. "Bring him forward."

Brock leapt off his horse and undid the chain from the saddle. He then yanked Bem forward until they were side by side with Kollano. Bem could feel Kollano's eyes on him, but he didn't give him the satisfaction of acknowledging him.

Instead, he stared ahead at the heavy iron gate that loomed over him with his head held high. He wouldn't give any of them the satisfaction of witnessing the fear that he tried to bottle inside him.

The guard stepped forward and studied his face closely. He was older. There were age lines around his honey-brown eyes and graying hair in his russet mustache. "You're sure this is one of them?"

"Of course," Kollano replied without hesitation. "I'm sorry to say I traveled with him all the way to the Dragon Mountains."

The muscles of Bem's jaws tightened. *No, you didn't. Carver did. Carver wouldn't subject me to this.*

"Very well," the guard said, taking a step back. "We'll take him from here. But you do understand that you must present him to the king for further judgment on your part. I still have my orders, you understand?"

"Of course," Kollano said again with a polite smile. "In fact, I'd like to be the one to bring him in myself."

The lead guard narrowed his eyes in consideration for a moment. Then, he shrugged and said, "If you must."

Kollano extended his hand palm up and Brock placed the chain in it. The guard stepped aside and waved to someone overhead along the wall. After a moment's pause, the iron gate creaked as it was lifted up halfway. Enough to allow them to enter. The guard then said, "This way."

Kollano stepped forward with a display of authority as he dragged Bem behind him. The first guard led the way while the other three fell in behind them. Kollano's soldiers followed silently behind them and the iron gate closed once more.

As the gate landed with a hard thud against the ground, Bem felt a tingle run down his spine. How was he going to get himself out of this? The others wouldn't even know where he was or if he was alive. He cursed under his breath at his foolishness for getting himself into this mess.

The lead soldier of Kollano's group ordered the rest of his men to follow him around the fortress. They spoke amongst themselves, completely at ease. Except for Taiden, who never took his eyes off of Bem until he vanished from view with the rest of his companions.

They entered the dark castle into a strange, empty, circular room. There was a spiral, stone staircase that went up towards the ceiling, wound down to the floor and out of sight. A large, double doorway opposite of the entrance sat silently with its doors firmly shut. Torches surround the room, mounted to the round walls, providing the only source of light in the cool room.

The lead guard grabbed the closest torch off the wall and said, "Follow me."

He then ventured down the stairs. Kollano turned to Bem and in one swift movement, he undid the chain from his shackles and tossed the chain off to the side. Startled by his sudden closeness, Bem stumbled backwards a few steps. The prince's skin was cold as ice. It made Bem that much more afraid for Carver.

Kollano noticed his unease and smirked. His eyes shone bright in chaotic delight. Bem grit his teeth, suddenly feeling sick to his stomach.

"Follow the guard. Unless you want me to shove you down the staircase myself," Kollano suggested in a low voice.

Bem grit his teeth and did as he was told. What else could he do?

Kollano fell in step just behind Bem and the rest of the guards followed with another torch. The flames of the torches licked the cool stone walls as they moved further down into the earth. Bem expected to come across multiple floors, but the surprise awaited him as they kept descending further and further down into the earth.

The air grew cool and damp as they neared the bottom of the winding staircase. Soon, Bem could hear noises when he couldn't before. Although they were muffled, Bem's breath caught in his throat at the realization of what those noises were. The sounds of moans of suffering and pleas for help from prisoners.

The leader stopped at another iron gate and held the torch closer to his face. Someone from the other side leaned into the barred door and nodded. Without a word, the mute guard pulled out a ring of keys from within their black cloak and unlocked the door.

As they went through the doorway, Bem noticed that the iron of the door had the same smoky crystals embedded in it, just like his shackles. His body vibrated when he passed through the door. The sensation made his brain foggy and his head spun. There was no chance of using his magic around it.

They entered a long corridor, where the ceiling arched way overhead. As they ventured forward, they passed cell doors, each embedded with a large smoky crystal. Each door had a small rectangle on the top with iron bars, and a small door on the bottom sealed shut. There was a torch lit every few yards, but there still wasn't much light to see very far ahead of them.

At the end of the corridor, it split in two opposite directions. To the right, Bem could make out more cells running the length of another long corridor. To the left, he could hear more sounds. Shouts and clanging. He tried to strain his ears to hear more, but Kollano shoved him towards the right. They moved down the second corridor for what felt like forever. How could they have so many tunnels built underground? Bem wondered. Until finally, the lead guard stopped.

He turned to face them and motioned to the door on his right. "We'll leave him here."

One guard followed behind them and hurried forward, already holding the correct key from his own ring. The lock clicked, and the door swung open. Another guard grabbed Bem by his biceps and thrust him inside.

Bem stumbled and caught himself against the back wall. He spun around and his eyes locked onto Kollano's. If Bem would have blinked, he would have missed the flash of horror on his face. On Carver's face.

In an instant, the coldness returned in his eyes, and Kollano said, "Welcome home, young Bem."

And the door slammed shut, leaving him in darkness.

Hours had passed since they brought Bem into The Keep. He kicked at the door, shoved his weight against it with his shoulder, anything he could to open it. But the metal door wouldn't budge. The only accomplishment he gained out of it was a bruised shoulder.

Only the dim glow of a torch across the hall gave him a small amount of light through the small, barred window of his cell door. There was no window to the outside. He was far beneath the earth, away from the daylight. And far away from his friends.

His cell was small, maybe eight feet by eight feet if he had to guess. There was a wooden slab mounted to the wall held up by thick chains that was meant to be his bed. Someone had thrown a dirty blanket onto the bed and placed an even filthier bucket in the corner that gave off a foul odor.

The guards didn't bother to undo the shackles on his wrists. The skin underneath them had long since chaffed from the metal rubbing against them on his journey. Bem clutched his head as his heart raced. How did he allow himself to get here? And how could he possibly escape? They had been holding sorcerers captive in The Keep for years. He banged his fists on the door and let out a cry of anger and frustration.

"Hey new guy! Save your strength. You're going to need it," called a soft muffled voice.

Bem froze against the door. He hadn't seen a single captive on the journey down to his cell. He strained his eyes to look across the hall into the cell across from him, but couldn't see anyone there. Bem couldn't tell if the barred window was occupied because it was too small and too dark.

"Hello?" Bem called, peering out his barred window. "Who's there?"

"Shut your yap, kid," the voice warned. It was a woman's voice. She sounded older, closer to his mother's age; if not older. "Do you want the guards to punish you?"

Bewildered, Bem stood in silence for a moment. He realized the voice was coming from the cell next door to the left of him. He wished he could see who she was, but it was impossible. "How long have you been here?"

Silence greeted him. After a few moments, Bem was about to give up when finally, the woman replied, "I'm not certain. It's been a couple of years."

Bem gasped. Years? How was he going to find a way out of there if people had been held captive for years without escaping? He had to keep calm.

"Are you a sorceress?" Bem asked in a quieter voice.

She scoffed. "Well, what do *you* think?"

Bem rested his forehead against the cool metal of the door and absorbed what she said. "So all the prisoners are sorcerers, then?"

"Aren't you?"

Bem sighed. He wasn't getting anywhere. Perhaps if he familiarized himself with her. "My name is Bem of Folke. What's your name?"

Another moment of silence. Bem squeezed his eyes shut as a dull ache pounded in his head. "If we are doomed to be trapped in this prison for the rest of our lives, can you at least tell me who I'm speaking to?" Bem said, breaking the silence.

"Eryi," she replied in a near whisper. Bem opened his eyes and stared down at the stone floor. She was nervous, almost scared to even say her name.

"It's nice to meet you Eryi…even under the circumstances," he said.

Heavy footsteps echoed down the hallway. Eryi shushed him as he heard her clamper away from her own door. Bem stepped back just as the jingle of keys resounded on the other side.

The door swung open and in strode a tall, armor-clad man with a hood over his head. Before Bem could react, the man pulled his arm back and swung the back of his hand against Bem's cheek.

Bem fell backwards against his bed. He brought his hands up just before another blow landed on him. Bem lifted his leg and kicked as hard as he could into the man's stomach. The man grunted and stumbled back a few steps towards the door.

He scowled, clenched his fists, and charged at Bem once more. Bem hurried to his feet and swung his shackled hands at the man's face. The cloaked figure easily grabbed his wrists with one hand and sent a punch to his face with the other.

Before Bem could react, the man landed another punch and then another until he fell to the dirty floor. All he could do was shield his face with his arms as the man throttled him into a corner of the small cell.

"Enough, Deodar," commanded a voice from the corridor.

Bem's attacker, Deodar, stopped at once and stepped aside to allow the second man to enter. Bem's face and chest pounded. He spat blood from his mouth and glared up at the men, angry and ashamed he couldn't defend himself.

Deodar towered over both Bem and the second man and was built like an ox; his thick arms and legs sprouted from his body like tree trunks. The older, second man was scrawny compared to him. He slicked back his long, greasy gray hair on his head. He dressed in brown cloaks as well, but his hands were adorned with silver rings embedded with crystals of different colors on each finger.

His face was rather handsome for his age, but his pale blue eyes were cold and uncaring. The man took one look at Bem lying on the floor and smiled.

Kendra Slone

"Where are my manners? I am Thesnic, and I'm one of the keepers of the Keep." He chuckled at his own words.

Bem resisted the urge to roll his eyes, but remained silent.

"I apologize for my friend here," Thesnic continued. "He did not realize you were a new contributor to our cause. While you are here, you must follow certain rules. The first rule of course, is to not speak to the other contributors. Under any circumstances."

Bem dragged himself up onto his bed and wiped away the blood from his nose. "Contributors?"

Deodar took a step towards him, but Thesnic swatted him away like a fly. Thesnic turned back to Bem and glared at him, his smile gone. "The second rule: do not speak unless you are told to do so. Understood?"

Bem glared back at him. His eyes flickered to the huge guard behind him, and he nodded in response.

Thesnic grinned in delight. "Wonderful! Now let's get you settled in. I'm sure you'd like to get your hands out of those cuffs."

Bem looked down at his shackles and then up again at Thesnic. He would remove them? Just like that?

Out of his robes, Thesnic revealed a large metal ring with a lock on it. On the opposite side of the lock, Thesnic embedded the same smoky quartz crystal into the ring. He handed the ring to Deodar, who, in turn, strode up to Bem with determination.

Bem instinctively tensed and pulled away from him as he approached. Deodar grunted and slapped Bem upside the head. His head spun as Deodar wrapped the ring around his neck and locked it firmly into place with a small key. He then grabbed another key from the same ring of keys and unlocked the shackles on Bem's wrists.

When the shackles fell from his wrists, Bem rubbed the inflamed skin in relief. It wasn't much, but it was at least more comfortable. The metal ring around his neck was a different matter.

He felt like it was close to choking him and instead of the tingling sensation around his wrists, it now moved up to his neck.

"There! Much better, yes?" Thesnic applauded. Bem gritted his teeth and nodded.

The sound of more footsteps resounded down the corridor, followed by cell doors swinging open one by one. Thesnic spun on his heel and as he exited Bem's cell, he said, "Now then, let's get you to your post. It's time for you to contribute to your king!"

With a forceful yank, Deodar pulled Bem off the bed and propelled him out the door, nearly causing him to lose his balance. As he straightened up, he noticed a thin older woman exit the cell beside him. Their eyes met for a moment, before she turned her gaze down to the floor and joined the line of other prisoners moving down the corridor.

"Off you go," Thesnic said in a cheery voice.

Deodar gave Bem another shove towards the line, causing Bem to curse under his breath. He quickly fell in line behind the woman before Deodar could get another swing at him.

Bem glanced over his shoulder and noticed Thesnic and Deodar fall behind as they moved down the dark corridor. The other guards were at the front and back of the line. Seizing the opportunity, Bem leaned forward and whispered, "Eryi?"

With a swift kick back to his shins, the woman hushed him. Bem cursed under his breath again and stumbled as his leg throbbed in pain.

"Have you not learned your lesson yet, boy?" the woman hissed at him. "I warned you to shut your yap!"

"You spoke to me first!" Bem hissed back at her.

Eryi glared at him over her shoulder. "A mistake I shant make again. You're nothing but trouble."

"Where are they taking us?" he whispered, checking to make sure the guards hadn't heard them.

"As they said, to contribute. Now hush!" Eryi sighed.

Bem did as he was told and followed her down the corridor he had come from hours before. Only this time they didn't turn down the corridor towards the staircase, but went straight into the unknown. At least, it was unknown to him.

This corridor was even longer than the last. He noted there were doors down the path that weren't cell doors. Bem wondered what could be behind them? He shuddered at the thought. Maybe he didn't want to know. At the end of the hall was a stone staircase as wide as the corridor itself. They descended the stairs into the darkness below. Bem could barely see where he was going. He focused his attention on each footstep, hoping he wouldn't trip and fall into the people in front of him.

Finally, they reached the end, and the line of prisoners separated in two directions. Two hallways going different directions. A guard at the end pushed them towards one path or the other. When Eryi approached, the guard shoved her to the right. She tripped over his boot and fell to the floor.

"On your feet, witch!" the man growled and sent a kick to her ribcage.

Eryi whimpered in pain and tried to crawl up the wall to get away from him. Enraged, Bem knew he couldn't stand watching the poor woman being tortured. He lunged forward and pinned the guard against the wall with both arms. "Leave her alone!"

The guard sneered and raised his left hand to Bem's eye level. On his hand, he wore a gauntlet with crystals embedded on the knuckles. They glowed and a sudden flash of power sent Bem crumpling to the floor. His body writhed in pain as the burst of magical energy surged through him.

It felt like he was on the ground for eternity in pain until a small pair of hands grabbed his arms and tried to pull him to his feet.

"Get up!" Eryi urged, yanking on his arm.

"Listen to the witch," the guard laughed. "If you know what's good for you. Or do you want another?"

Bem forced himself up on his feet, even though his body felt suddenly weak. Eryi placed his arm over her thin shoulders and carried some of his weight as they stumbled down the hall. "Hurry up, move your feet."

When they were well enough away from the guard, moving down the torch-lit hallway, she scolded, "That was foolish of you."

"You don't deserve to be treated that way," Bem winced through his pain.

Eryi snorted. "Yes, well...that's how life is down here. You better get used to it."

Bem shook his head. "I won't. It's not right. We're just as human as they are. Maybe even more so."

"Yes," she replied in a sad tone. "But they fear our power."

His body tingled all over. The metal collar around his neck tightened. Or perhaps it was the way Bem wanted to use his magic that made the presence of it more noticeable. He realized Eryi wore the same collar with the embedded crystal.

"Where do they even find crystals like these?" Bem asked, motioning to his throat.

Eryi shook her head, although her eyes flashed with anger. "Something else they stole."

The hall they stumbled down ended and they entered a spacious room with tall ceilings. Bem gazed up in wonder at the bluish glow that ran along the ceiling. More crystals, he realized, to light up the room without the use of torches or fire of any kind. If he didn't see what else the room held, he would be impressed.

On either side of the large room, there were cages with a single chair in each one. In the center of the room were tons of crystals of various shapes, sizes, and types sitting on tables and piled in large carts. More than he had ever laid eyes on.

Bem watched in horror as the prisoners in front of him were blindfolded, one by one. As one guard did this, the others would grab the blindfolded and lead them away to a cage. His heart raced as they slowly approached him.

When they finally got to him, one man pushed the black cloth over his eyes and tied it tightly at the back of his head. Someone then grabbed him by the shoulders and led him out of the line. Bem tried his best to stay calm and focus on his feet, hoping he wouldn't trip. They stopped and the guard carefully turned him around and said, "Sit."

Bem reached back and felt the armrests of a wooden chair. He sat down and waited as the guard shackled each wrist and ankle to the chair. The metal was cold against his wrists. The man checked each one twice over before finally saying, "Good. Wait here."

Where else could he go? But he didn't dare utter a word as he felt the presence of the guard disappear. Within a few moments, he returned and grabbed at the collar around Bem's neck.

"I'm going to replace your collar with the one on the chair and we can begin," the guard said as he fumbled with the lock on Bem's neck.

"Begin what?" Bem asked before he could stop himself. He waited for a blow to the head, but none came. This prison guard was at least nicer than the others he had encountered so far.

"You'll know all too soon. Now listen," the man said as he removed the metal collar and replaced it with another one. "Never try to attack me or my colleagues. You won't be able to use your magic and you certainly won't have the numbers to back you up. We will kill you if it comes down to it."

Despite the circumstances, Bem realized the man was trying to warn him. Maybe he was even trying to be kind to him. Bem nodded in response.

"Alright, let's begin," the man said. He left the caged area and Bem could hear a click as the door locked behind him. "I'm going to place the crystals we need into the device, and it will force the magic from your body into the crystal."

Bem's mouth dropped in surprise. "What?"

"Relax, it will be fine," the man responded.

Without another word, Bem heard a *clunk* of something behind him and his body tingled once more. But this time it was different. The tingle vibrated as his magical energy surged through his body and gathered at his wrists and neck. Suddenly, the energy exploded into the shackled areas.

He gasped as pain swelled inside his chest. The metal ring around his neck turned icy hot until his skin went numb around it. Bem attempted to draw a shaky breath, but it felt like someone had knocked all the wind out of him. Finally, he heard another *clunk* and all at once, the pain and vibration of the magic draining from his body stopped. Bem gasped for breath as the guard moved around him. He wished he could see what the man was doing.

The guard returned to his place behind him and this time he didn't speak as the *clunk* resounded once more. Bem sucked in a deep breath to brace himself and held it as the pain, tingle, and numbness returned throughout his body. The process dragged on for what felt like ages, but it couldn't have been more than a few minutes before the guard switched it off once more.

Bem released the breath he was holding and gasped once more. His head was dizzy and disoriented. A sudden realization occurred to him as the guard prepared once more with new crystals. Bem was growing weaker with each round of his 'contribution to the king'. This is how sorcerers died in The Keep. The guard drained their energy until their bodies wasted away.

Another *clunk* and the pain in Bem's chest expanded slowly throughout his body, even more painful than the last. His head ached and his muscles cramped. He groaned and clenched his fists in agony. "Stop!" he whispered.

Through the whirring in his ears, Bem could have sworn he heard the guard whisper back in a sorrowful tone, "I'm sorry, I can't."

But it didn't matter. Bem bit his tongue until it bled as they started the process once more.

Chapter 18
The Ascendent of Maeve

Nyel

The Maeve clan was only a few miles away from the small family's hideout. This surprised Nyel that other dragons hadn't discovered them. Perhaps their respect for Aydamaris and Ragnar was very high. It made him grateful to have met Aydamaris when he did.

It wasn't long before the Guardian dragons spotted the three of them approaching and announced their arrival to the entire clan with low, steady roars. Nyel scanned the area where the Guardians resided in confusion. Ivory's clan never announced anyone that approached in that manner. Then he realized as one of the Guardians joined their flight and flanked Aydamaris that they weren't interested in him. They were announcing her arrival. She was special to their clan. Nyel was glad to have her on his side. He just hoped it would help.

At first glance, Nyel didn't see the Maeve clan any differently than the last. Just like Ivory's clan, Ragnar's home was on the tallest mountain for miles around. Far below them in a small ravine was the river that flowed from the far off waterfall where they had met Shara. The current had slowed to a more peaceful flow, allowing a grand river to fish. Lush grassy fields rested atop of the ravine on either side, where he spotted a few dragons resting.

Nyel followed close behind Sable as they climbed higher and higher into the sky. Nyel looked below them to see many dragons stop what they were doing and stare at the newcomers. Some even decided to join them; they followed them or raced ahead to

Ragnar's home. Nyel cursed under his breath as his heart hammered in his chest. He had hoped there wouldn't be a big audience for their first encounter. He took a few deep breaths to steady himself, not wanting his nerves to get the better of him.

When they finally reached the top of the mountain, Nyel noticed once again that it looked almost identical to Ivory's lookout. A large open area big enough for multiple dragons to gather. Further back was a large cave where the clan Ascendant lived. Dragons were simple in that respect, Nyel realized. As long as they had a dry place to lay and eyes on the skies, they seemed content.

As the three of them landed, a voice erupted from the cave.

"Why are you here? The moon is not yet full," called a rugged, deep voice from the darkness of the cave.

Sable growled a warning, while Aydamaris held her head high.

"Is that anyway to greet your mother?" she called in a stern voice.

A large, silver dragon emerged from the cave. It was obvious by his stance that this dragon was proud in nature, with a fierce aura about him. He walked steadily towards them with sharp, yellow eyes and a scowl on his face. His silver scales gleamed in the light like metal armor.

Nyel's tail twitched as his anxiety grew. This was not the welcoming he had hoped for, and judging by Sable and Aydamaris's reactions, they were of the same mindset.

"For one who can see into the future, I would think you would know why I am unhappy right now," Ragnar growled as he glared down at her. Sable, who was around the same size as his son, was quick to get in his face and bare his teeth.

"I will not tolerate your disrespect!" Sable snarled. Ragnar growled in return, exposing his sharp fangs.

"Enough, both of you," Aydamaris ordered. She nudged Sable back with her head and faced her son once more. "What troubles you, my son?"

He glared at his father for a silent moment, before turning on his mother and saying, "Ivory and his followers charged into my territory not long ago with those soulless dragons on their tails. We had to help fend them off, and they injured some of MY Guardians in the process! You've caught me at a bad time, mother. I am furious that he arrived unannounced, endangered my clan, and after all of that, refuses to give me an answer why he's here in the first place! Ascendant or not, I'm ready to rip his throat open with my teeth!"

Ragnar's cold eyes then flickered to Nyel and studied him. He sniffed the air and let out a sudden snort. "And now I see you are somehow a part of it...as usual. What is the meaning of this? Why is Ivory here and who is this youngling cowering behind you?"

Nyel huffed and took a step forward. "I'm not cowering. I am here to speak with you, Ascendant. I'm the reason Ivory and our clan arrived unannounced."

Ragnar's eyes narrowed. He sniffed the air once more. "You reek of many scents," he rumbled. "It gives me a headache. You say you are of his clan, but are you truly? I've never seen you before."

"Yes, I am here with Ivory. Amidst the chaos, shadow creatures attacked us and we got separated. I was lost until I met Aydamaris and Sable," Nyel replied, motioning to his parents.

"Then perhaps *you* can tell me why Ivory is here," Ragnar said. He circled around Nyel as he spoke. Nyel stood motionless as Ragnar studied him. He had to be careful with his next choice of words.

"Where is Ivory? I'd prefer for him to be present," Nyel hesitated. He kept his gaze fixed on Ragnar's face, searching for any sign of danger.

Ragnar growled at his words. His foul, hot breath hit Nyel's face as he drew closer to him. "You are in my territory now, youngling. I am your Ascendant. Speak or I will rip *your* throat out instead."

Nyel gulped without meaning to, but he didn't back down from Ragnar's intense glare. He did, however, look at Aydamaris, who quickly joined his side. Ragnar glanced at his mother and, with a sigh, took a step back and said, "What now?"

"Ragnar, this is Nyel," she began. "I have seen him in one of my visions long ago. A very significant vision at that. He has received a great power that will help us unite with the humans to defeat the shadows that are wreaking havoc in Hailwic."

Ragnar's booming laughter echoed all around them. Nyel was only thankful that his throat wasn't being ripped out.

"This puny dragon received the gift? He's an Ascendant? Even so, I'm now expected to believe that his power should bring us and the humans together? Mother, I've let your curiosity get the better of you," Ragnar roared with laughter once more. His surrounding clan members joined him, leaving Nyel feeling smaller than before.

"What she says is true," Nyel growled. Ragnar's laughter died in an instant. The angry Ascendant got in Nyel's face once more.

"I'd choose your next words carefully," Ragnar hissed.

Nyel took a deep breath. "I am here seeking peace between humans and dragons. And to destroy the one called Kollano."

Whispers echoed amongst the dragons who had joined them. Many were angry, as Nyel had expected. Although his main concern was staring at him mere inches from his face.

"Why would you want to unite with those abominable creatures?" Ragnar asked, his voice layered with hatred and disgust.

Another deep breath. "Because I am human."

This time, there were gasps and roars of outrage amongst the spectators around them. Ragnar lifted his head and let out a loud, monstrous roar that silenced their audience at once. He then turned back his fuming gaze on Nyel and growled, "You lie. That's impossible!"

"I'd show you, but I'm afraid you'll eat me," Nyel half-joked.

Aydamaris said, "Ragnar, if you would just listen—" but another angry roar interrupted her.

"Bring me Ivory!" Ragnar roared furiously at his Guardians.

They quickly bowed their heads and dove off the cliffside in search of Ivory. Ragnar glared unblinking at Nyel. His fury filled eyes stared into Nyel's soul. This was a dragon who undoubtedly loathed humans. Anger seeped from every inch of his body at the very mention of them. Nyel knew he wouldn't have stood a chance with him if he had shown up in his human form. He shuddered, thinking about shifting in front of him even now.

Doubt crept into Nyel's mind. Did he really think he could convince every dragon he encountered? His mind raced as he tried to think of how to get out of this situation if needed. And he suspected that he needed to come up with a plan fast. Another short roar from below sounded. Ragnar's Guardians returned, with Ivory and the rest of the clan following close behind him.

Relief washed over him as he scanned his clan and found everyone accounted for, besides Lorna. Her sisters looked at Nyel with worry. He nodded his head quickly at them with reassurance, but didn't dare speak about where she was. Now was not the time for questions.

Ivory joined Nyel's side as soon as he landed. Nyel took that opportunity to check him over for injuries. Ivory had some scuffs from fighting off the possessed, but otherwise, he seemed in good health.

"We were making plans to search for you," Ivory said in a low, irritated voice. "Where's-"

"This…*Ascendant*…claims to be human! Explain this to me. Or are your younglings so incompetent, they seek death to ease them from their suffering?" Ragnar spat at Ivory.

Ivory's eyes flickered from Nyel to Ragnar, obviously surprised Nyel had already told him.

"It's true. Nyel is now part man and part dragon," Ivory replied in an even tone. An angry uproar resounded from the observing dragons. Ivory's Guardians drew in closer to their Ascendant, ready to defend him. As Nyel watched Ragnar's face change from anger to hatred, he wondered if they were going to have to fight their way out of the hostile clan.

"That's impossible! I've never heard of an Ascendant's power granting the ability to shapeshift," Ragnar continued to argue. "Besides, the Ascendant's Gift would have never chosen a human over a dragon!"

"He defended a dragon's life over his own. It was my power that chose him, and rightfully so," Ivory announced with pride.

Ragnar's angry roar thundered around them, causing members of his own clan to flinch. "Then your gift was a weak link in our line! It's a curse to our kind! If what you're saying is true, we need to destroy it and the human, before it spreads its tainted human essence any further among us!"

His clan roared in agreement and closed in on the small group. A nervous growl erupted from Nyel's throat before he could stop it. As the small group slowly surrounded him, he darted his eyes in all directions. This had gone horribly wrong.

Aydamaris let out a roar that silenced the entire group in an instant. All eyes fell on her as she held her head high and announced, "Whether or not you like it, I have foreseen man and dragon working together."

Ragnar's clan hissed and grumbled to themselves, apprehensive of their all-seeing Ascendant. She continued, "You are all aware by now the devastation the creatures of the night have wreaked amongst our kind, and continue to do so. They are attacking the humans as well. Imagine the numbers these creatures have over us? We can't face this darkness on our own. However, it is possible. There is hope. We can work together to defeat the darkness; we can be allies with the humans once more."

"Humans only seek us out to use us for their armor and glory," Ragnar growled. "Your visions only show possibilities, nothing more."

"My visions provide us a great opportunity to aid ourselves in choosing the right path," she replied gently. Ragnar snorted and averted his gaze.

"Your vision is worthless. It did not help my family escape the wrath of your precious humans," he growled, fixing his gaze back on her with anguish and anger in his eyes.

The group went still. The silence was deafening as all eyes were fixated on the mother and son. Aydamaris's eyes brimmed with tears and she looked down at the ground in shame.

"As I said, my visions are true. We all must choose our actions carefully if we want to meet that conclusion in the end or change it," she replied with sorrow.

Ragnar roared in fury. "Are you saying their deaths were my fault?!"

Sable pushed Aydamaris to the side as Ragnar's claws came down in a flash. Blood spattered on the ground as his claws ripped through Sable's shoulder. He roared in fury and rammed his horned head into Ragnar, sending him backwards a few feet. Pandemonium quickly ensued as the observing dragons bellowed and shoved each other as they watched Ragnar and Sable circle each other with teeth bared.

Ragnar charged at Sable and rammed him in the shoulder, sending the old dragon onto his side. As Ragnar opened his jaw wide to go in for the kill, Nyel shouted, "Stop!"

Ragnar hissed as he turned his attention to Nyel. His eyes gleamed with a wild, murderous rage. "You dare speak to me, creature?"

"Yes, I dare," Nyel growled before Ivory could stop him. He stepped out into the open away from the others as Ragnar stalked towards him. "How can you treat them this way? These are your parents."

"They are fools, just like you," Ragnar growled. "You think you know more than I do? I have tolerated their way of life. I have hidden their secrets and respected their boundaries, but no longer! I will never join forces with any human, no matter the cost. And anyone who gets in my way will meet their untimely end."

"Ragnar, enough! Hear him out," Aydamaris pleaded as Sable struggled to his feet.

Ragnar roared again. "I will not, mother! I will destroy him and all your precious pets you have been hiding under your mountain! I will drain their blood on the border of our worlds as a warning to them all. No human shall ever be allowed into our lands ever again!"

Nyel snapped the air with his sharp teeth and hissed. Ascendant or not, he was done with Ragnar. He wouldn't let him harm Shara and her family. As Ragnar rushed towards him in a blind rage, Ivory jumped forward to Nyel's defense and snarled.

Ragnar stopped in his tracks as Ivory said, "If you threaten Nyel, then you also threaten his clan and his Ascendant."

The rest of Ivory's Guardians gathered around Ivory and Nyel in a show of loyalty. Even the Guardians who didn't want anything to do with Nyel were by his side. He was thankful he didn't come here on his own, or with Iris.

"Don't risk war between our clans over this pathetic creature," Ragnar growled at Ivory.

"I don't want that any more than you do, Ragnar," Ivory spat. "But I also won't have you threatening my kin."

Ragnar laughed. "You claim this *thing* as your own? He's a hairless rat disguised in stolen scales. He's not a member of your clan Ivory, you're just amusing yourself for the sake of the Ascendant's Gift that was taken from you. Be rid of both before he destroys us all. How can we be sure he's not bringing in armies of his filthy parasites right now to round us up while we're not looking?"

"I trust Nyel with my life," Ivory answered with confidence. "Give him a chance to prove himself to you and you'll see for yourself."

"He has no chances here. He has one option, and that is to die by my teeth and my claws," Ragnar bellowed, staring daggers into Nyel. An uncontrollable shudder ran through Nyel's body at the thought.

Ragnar turned his attention back to Ivory and said, "If you continue to defend him or any human, I will declare war on your clan, here and now!"

Nyel's stomach twisted into knots as he looked around them. Ragnar's clan was vast compared to Ivory's clan, with many more full-grown, furious dragons behind it. Nyel couldn't put the entire clan in danger for his sake. Nyel opened his mouth to speak his concerns when suddenly a loud, long roar echoed in the distance.

Both of the clans froze and looked towards the sound in unison. Even Ragnar halted and turned his head towards the call. One of the Guardian dragons from earlier was closest to the sound and stared for a moment in that direction.

Suddenly, he bellowed, "Dragons approaching from the east!"

Ragnar hurried to his side and squinted to get a better look. The Guardians in the distance then bellowed a more urgent cry and Ragnar growled. "The possessed are returning. And there are more of them!"

There was a nervous tension amongst the group as everyone looked towards the east. Ragnar huffed as he jumped up to a higher point on his mountain. "What are we waiting for? We must defend ourselves and our home from these intrusive parasites! Hurry after them, don't let them into our borders!"

His dragons let out a battle cry and many took flight. As they and many others from other places in the clan flew in their direction, Nyel watched the approaching threat. He could tell that there were many more possessed dragons hurtling towards them. More than he had ever seen before. This must be the missing dragons from the destroyed Malachite clan, he realized with dread.

Ragnar turned his gaze on Ivory and his clan and growled, "I spare your lives this day. Leave now and I will forget this. Stay and I will kill you after I've killed the rest."

"We can help!" Nyel urged. "You need the numbers."

Ragnar roared in his face, "I don't need anything from you, filth!"

With that, he joined the rest of his clan in the sky as they flew towards the oncoming danger. Ivory sighed in relief and turned towards the others. "I don't think we will get through to him. Perhaps it's best we leave while we have the chance."

"You'll never get through to him if you leave now," Aydamaris said in a hushed voice. She watched the clan rush to defend their home with a deep sadness in her eyes. It was then Nyel remembered she used to be their leader before her son took charge.

"Do you think it wise that we stick around only for him to declare war on our clan when he returns?" Ivory argued as he paced the ground.

Aydamaris turned her head towards the Ascendant dragon and said, "My visions from long ago hold a possibility."

"IF we choose the right path," Ivory growled in frustration.

Sable limped over to his mate, who quickly nuzzled her head into his neck. Nyel looked towards the distant hoard of enemy dragons once more. "I will stay and fight. Ivory, go back to the clan. Leave them out of this. I'll try to convince him…somehow."

Ivory sighed. "We're not leaving you here on your own. We are with you, Shifter."

A few of his Guardians grumbled with distaste, but didn't argue with their leader.

"Aydamaris," Sable mused, turning his attention to his mate. She looked up at him expectantly. "You saw for yourself once long ago a vision that we thought had long since passed. But now I see we were wrong. This is your moment to decide."

"What do you mean?" she asked, cocking her head in confusion.

"You are the rightful Ascendant and leader of this clan," Sable said, his gaze fixed intently on her. "I think it's time that Ragnar stepped down from his role as clan leader."

Everyone went quiet as Aydamaris stared at Sable. Her gaze was distant and sad, torn between two choices and unsure of which choice to make.

"Ragnar has done a splendid job as leader," she protested.

"He's a true defender of his clan. But he is also arrogant and reckless. Ragnar leads with brute force and fear. He can just as easily be their downfall. It may be the only way to keep our clan safe and join forces with Nyel," Sable replied in a gentle tone.

Nyel stepped up. "I will follow you, Aydamaris. I will fight for you."

"That's very kind, but…" she began, but Nyel cut her off.

"I'm going to go help the others. I'll try to persuade him to understand," Nyel explained. "I will do everything in my power."

Aydamaris nodded without another word and Nyel took off into the air before anyone could stop him. It didn't take long before the other dragons of Ivory's clan followed him one by one. Nyel looked to his right and found Ivory hurrying to catch up with him.

When Nyel gave him a questioning look, Ivory simply stated, "We have to try."

Nine dragons flew towards the battle that raged in the eastern sky. Nyel could hear the dragons even from a distance, roaring, clawing, and smashing into each other midair. Nyel cursed under his breath when he noted what little daylight remained.

That's why the possessed dragons had waited until then to arrive. They wanted to capture even more dragons as hosts for the next round of shadow creatures. How could there be so many of those diabolical creatures? Nyel couldn't leave, not when he knew the dangers the clan was about to face. He only wished his friends could be there by his side. But they would be in more danger than anyone else, especially with Ragnar's hatred.

"We need to conserve our fire," Nyel yelled to Ivory over a gust of wind that rushed towards them. Ivory glanced back at the setting sun and nodded without question.

Soon they were amongst the battling dragons. Ivory commanded his Guardians to stick together to protect each other. Nyel nodded as he studied the sky. He had to be certain that the first dragon he attacked wasn't one of the two clans.

Everything moved so fast in every direction; it was hard to focus on just one fight. It made his head spin. He fixed his search on the familiar glow of possessed eyes, hoping it would help his search. A flash of blue caught his eye as it raced towards him. Nyel was ready. He dodged the dragon's open maw lined with sharp teeth by mere inches. With adrenaline coursing through his veins, Nyel whipped around and grabbed the creature by the tail.

The dragon wailed in anger. Nyel confirmed it was possessed by the orange glow of its eyes as it glared back at him. Nyel kicked his hind legs into the blue dragon and sent it tumbling downwards. The possessed dragon was quick to regain its balance. Nyel dove towards it, ready to deliver the final blow.

Before Nyel could finish his attack, another possessed dragon with scales of mossy-green snuck up from behind and bit him in his thigh.

Nyel yelped as pain shot through his leg. Blood rolled down his leg as the green dragon's teeth sank further into the muscle, holding him in place. He attempted to wriggle out of the dragon's grip, but he was compelled to redirect his focus to the blue dragon as it targeted a lethal bite at his throat. His throat stung as he summoned his fire breath in an instant. Nyel roared as a stream of fire blew from his mouth and into the creature's exposed face.

In the same moment, Ivory appeared out of nowhere behind the green dragon and grabbed it by its neck. He yanked the dragon off of Nyel and shook furiously until a sickening snap filled the air around them. Nyel panted and nodded in thanks as Ivory let the dragon drop. They watched for a moment as a shadow creature emerged from the dragon's body and then disintegrated in the remaining sunlight with a hiss.

"They've not learned to protect their necks," Nyel gasped.

Ivory snorted. "No, they have not."

They were separated as more of the possessed dragons came after them. Nyel continued to fight against several shadow dragons. He was able to injure them, but every time he got the upper hand, another one was there to add to the fight.

As he clawed his way out of the grasp of one shadow dragon, his eyes locked with someone familiar a few yards away. Ragnar. His sides heaved with each heavy breath he took while he glared at Nyel with unmistakable hatred. Blood spilled from his open mouth, dripping through his sharp teeth and down his chin. Nyel was certain it wasn't his own blood, and it sent a chill down his spine.

Ragnar's eyes gleamed with rage. He snarled and rushed towards Nyel, forgetting the possessed dragons that circled his Guardians. His jaw opened wide and a ball of fire flew towards him. Nyel leaned to the right and spun away from the flames and out of Ragnar's reach before the furious Ascendant could sink his teeth into him.

"I'm not your enemy!" Nyel roared in anger at the stubborn dragon. "We need to protect the clan first!"

Ragnar whipped around to confront him once more. Nyel tried his best to watch his surroundings for any other dragons. The shadow creatures, the possessed, and even Ragnar's clan could catch him off guard at any moment; and from any direction.

Ragnar, however, had other plans.

"How dare you speak to me, as if you were a real dragon? You're a disgrace to our ancient magic! A leech! You're nothing!" Ragnar seethed.

A deep, instinctual growl rumbled in Nyel's chest. "We don't have time for this! We can settle this later, after we protect the clan from the shadow creatures!"

"I *am* protecting my clan," Ragnar roared and dove at Nyel in a blind rage.

The two collided with each other, locking talons as they kicked at each other's stomach with their hind legs. Ragnar tried again and again to sink his teeth into Nyel's neck and failed each time. Nyel had to use all of his strength and skill to keep Ragnar at bay while also trying to stay in the air as long as possible. Ragnar, being the stronger, bigger, and more experienced of the two at fighting, angled Nyel downwards, and they began plummeting towards the ground.

A slow realization brought Nyel into a panic. Ragnar was going to crush him.

Desperate to free himself, Nyel rammed his head into Ragnar's as hard as he could. At the same time, he kicked Ragnar with both of his hind legs. It was just enough force to drive Ragnar off of him and give Nyel a chance to escape. Nyel spun a few times to the left, and the world spun with him. He closed his eyes and pulled to the right with his wings was all he could to steady himself.

His vision became blurry and his head fuzzy. He blinked once or twice, trying to get the world back into focus. Suddenly, there were two of Ragnar floating around instead of one. Nyel tried to ignore the spinning of his head. Instead, he hurried to create some distance between the two of them.

Ragnar kept up with him with ease. The Ascendant breathed a blast of fire in his direction. The flames licked the scales on his back and he dove out of the way before they could burn him. His breathing grew labored as he looked around for something to use against Ragnar, but he found nothing. Nyel looked back up and his heart sank. Ragnar was above him once more, with a glare of sick satisfaction on his scaly face. The Ascendant dove at him, baring his teeth, reveling with the fact that he had injured Nyel.

A sudden flash of white light followed by a loud crack filled the air. The light blinded them for only a second until a bolt of lightning found its way to Ragnar. He roared in pain as he spiraled towards the ground, stunned by the powerful bolt that coursed through his body. Nyel looked around in confusion until his eyes landed on the most welcoming sight he had ever seen.

Iris and Lorna zipped past him, already on the hunt for the next threat. Iris locked eyes with Nyel for a second, only long enough to smirk at Nyel as they went. As grateful as he was for her help, Nyel feared Iris was now in the reach of the human loathing clan.

He sucked in a huge breath of air and braced himself. He circled back as he caught sight of Iris and Lorna fighting a shadow dragon. Balls of fire and lightning rushed out of her palms, keeping the possessed at bay. Darkness began to creep across them and Nyel could see shadow creatures stirring beneath them in the crevices of the mountains. He took another deep breath and dove towards them. Once he was within range, Nyel released a torrent of fire on them. As if his boiling hatred for them was released within the fire. They vanished instantly with a screech wherever the fire hit.

When his breath ran out, Nyel flew back up into the sky and joined Lorna in a battle against three possessed dragons. They made quick work of them, either knocking them out of the sky or scaring them off. Nyel took that opportunity to look around and, to his relief, he soon realized that most of the possessed dragons retreated. Ragnar's clan chased them as far as they could without completely leaving their territory. Nyel sensed if they were not defending their home, every one of them would have hunted down the possessed and exterminated them.

Nyel returned to Lorna and Iris once more, finally getting a chance to breathe. "Why didn't you wait for us to return?" he panted.

"We flew straight here after we realized we couldn't let you go alone. And I'm glad we did," Iris answered as she watched the rest of the possessed dragons retreating in the direction they had come from.

"Thank you for coming to my aid," Nyel said. "Ragnar is strong and filled with hate."

He studied the dragons flying around them, still fighting off the remaining possessed. Ragnar was nowhere in sight. This worried Nyel on many levels. Was he planning to ambush them? Or worse, if Iris injured him, would the clan turn on her next?

"Come on, follow me before Ragnar comes to his senses," Nyel growled. He turned back towards Ragnar's mountain, where he had left Aydamaris. Without another word, Lorna and Iris followed Nyel. There they found Aydamaris and Sable watching the battle intently from where they stood.

"Thank the stars you're alright," Aydamaris exclaimed as Nyel landed. The weight of his body intensified the aches where he had been hit, bitten, and bloodied, causing him to wince. Nyel tried to ignore the pain as he eased himself onto the ground for a quick rest.

Iris slid off of Lorna before she could completely land and ran over to Nyel. She raised her hands and healed the worse, more bloody wounds as best as she could.

"Save your strength," Nyel said as Iris worked on his neck.

Iris shook her head. "I'm fine, Nyel. Let me help you for a change."

Nyel grinned. "For a change?"

Iris rolled her eyes. "You saved me from being crushed and drowned by a waterfall. The least I can do is heal your wounds from battle."

He nuzzled the top of her head in response with his snout. Then, remembering the reason for some of his wounds, Nyel turned to Aydamaris.

"Ragnar is reckless," Nyel growled. "He is unfit to lead the clan. He was more concerned with trying to kill me than protecting his people."

"Nyel, enough," Ivory said as he glided to land beside them. He folded his wings and continued, "As much as I agree with you, we are not of this clan. To challenge him would mean a fight to the death."

"He already tried to kill me!" Nyel shouted, startling Iris, who had moved onto his thigh to heal the puncture wounds. "I don't care if he likes what I have to say or not. I think Aydamaris should take her rightful place as Ascendant of the Maeve clan."

The others stared at him in surprise. Sable was the first to speak up. "True, it is her rightful place. If she wants it. However, she chose our son to lead long ago. She can't just take it back; it would mean a fight to death for her too. Ragnar is too strong and, in our age, we have grown too weak to challenge him."

Nyel got to his feet, already thinking ahead. "That's true, but it would be different for her. She is special to the clan, yes?"

Sable nodded slowly, narrowing his eyes at Nyel as he spoke.

"They wouldn't want to see her fight against him then," Nyel declared.

Ivory sighed and said, "Nyel, that's not how it works for us. If we are challenged, we will fight whoever it may be."

Nyel locked eyes with Aydamaris and said, "I will help you become Ascendant of this clan and I will gain their trust. Look into my future and see what you find to be true."

"A possible truth," she corrected. Nyel only stared at her expectantly.

Without another word, Aydamaris stepped forward and stared into Nyel's eyes as she had before. Nyel felt the same sensation of being unable to look away from her or move. However, after a moment, Aydamaris gasped and stumbled sideways. Sable hurried to steady her and growled.

"She's too weak to use her power so close together! This is why we left the clan in the first place," he scolded Nyel.

Nyel lowered his head in shame and said, "Forgive me. I wasn't thinking."

She panted for a moment, trying to catch her breath. Finally, she looked up at him and replied, "Don't apologize, you were only trying to help."

"Let me spare you the shame of your weary age then," growled a voice from behind them. Nyel whipped his head around and a growl rumbled in his chest. Ragnar landed heavily next to Lorna and glared down at Iris, who had returned to Lorna's back. A long, red burn ran down his neck from where her lightning had struck him.

Without averting his gaze from her, Ragnar declared, "I, as the Ascendant of the Maeve clan, command that all humans be killed on sight."

Chapter 19
The Call

Lorna and Nyel sprung into action. As Lorna leapt back away from Ragnar, Nyel rushed forward to put himself between them and bared his sharp teeth at the clan leader. Ragnar's Guardians arrived after driving off the possessed dragons. They landed on either side of their Ascendant and crept towards Nyel with murderous glares locked onto him. They hissed and snapped their teeth at the air to intimidate him.

"You can't attack Nyel unless you want the fury of our clan against yours," Ivory warned once more, hurrying to Nyel's aid.

"Do you really think I care about your clan?" Ragnar laughed. "I don't fear you. You're outnumbered. And your weakness as a leader has infected everyone within your clan. It would do more good than harm to be rid of you!"

A low hum stirred around them. Confused, Nyel looked around for the source, but couldn't find anything. To his surprise, the only others following his lead were Aydamaris and Ragnar.

The hum grew in volume and intensity. Nyel winced as the sound grew. He closed his eyes and shook his head, trying to rid himself of the noise. It hurt his head to listen to it.

"Ascendant, are you alright?" a blue and black speckled dragon asked in concern.

"Does that sound not hurt your head?" Ragnar spat, also shaking his head.

The blue dragon cocked her head in confusion. "What sound?"

"Aydamaris?" Sable asked, still supporting her weight.

She met Nyel's gaze, and he knew she could hear it too.

"*Do not fear, be still my Ascendants,*" called a voice from the hum.

Nyel gasped. He realized the voice that reverberated in his head was the same one that had called to him in his dreams. Even Ragnar stared at him in shock for a moment, realizing they were experiencing the same phenomenon.

"*Return to me,*" said the voice. A female voice that was as strange to him as it was familiar. "*The time has come for you to return to me.*"

"Who are you?" Nyel asked aloud. The spectators around him stared at him like he was crazy, but he ignored them. Only looking at the sky as if she was there.

"*Return to me,*" she repeated. "*Your true duty has yet to be fulfilled.*"

Nyel's body tingled all over. His anger and hatred towards Ragnar only moments ago dimmed, and something else took their place. A need to obey this strange voice.

"Where are you?" Aydamaris asked. Members of both clans started mumbling to each other in confusion.

The humming faded just as quickly as it had started. "*Return to me where it all began…*"

And then all went silent in his head. Nyel let out a shaky breath and looked at the others, trying to understand what had occurred. He was thankful he wasn't the only one, as Ragnar turned away from the group, mumbling to himself. Aydamaris leaned in close to her mate and spoke to him in a hushed tone. The strange feeling continued to flow through Nyel's entire body. It was something he had never experienced before. Like the warm glow of sunshine seeping from his snout, down his neck, and all the way to the tip of his tail. And with that unfamiliar sensation was accompanied by an overwhelming urge to fly home. But Folke wasn't the destination.

Something bumped against his chest. In a daze, Nyel looked down to find Iris standing in front of him with a look of concern.

"What happened? What did you hear?" she asked.

Nyel blinked, still unsure. "So…you really didn't hear it?"

"None of us did," Ivory answered, motioning to their own clan.

"It was a voice," Nyel explained. "I've heard it before. She said-"

Ivory cut him off. "Wait, you've heard a voice before and you didn't tell me?"

"This is the first I'm hearing of this too," Iris stated, crossing her arms against her chest.

Nyel shook his head. "I didn't think much of it at the time. She's spoken in my dreams, but always the same thing. She said to return to her. But I don't know who or where she is; or why I even heard it. Only this time, I was able to speak to her in return."

Aydamaris stared at him in surprise. "Strange, this is my first time hearing the voice."

Aydamaris continued, "The ones that heard the voice cannot ignore the connection." All eyes turned to her. Even Ragnar remained silent, just as confused as the others. "Only the Ascendants heard the call."

"Ivory didn't seem to hear it," Casca rebutted. She stood close to Lorna, protective of her sister.

Aydamaris nodded. "Yes. Which means that only the Ascendants that still hold the Gift were the only ones to hear it."

Ragnar snorted and pointed a claw at Nyel. "That creature is not an Ascendant."

Nyel growled, but it was Ivory who spoke first. "Nyel may not use that title, but he has the Ascendant's Gift coursing through his veins. Which means you are one and the same."

An earth rattling roar erupted from Ragnar's mouth. "Do not ever compare me to him. He is lower than the dirt beneath my claws!"

"Enough, all of you!" Aydamaris shouted angrily. "I need a council with the Ascendants at once. Guardians, return to your posts and make sure there are no shadows or possessed creeping about. Now is not the time to be distracted."

Ragnar's Guardians hesitated and instead turned to him. He growled, furious that his mother was commanding his clan. But he must have wanted the same thing, because all he could say was, "Go!"

One by one, Ragnar's Guardians and the rest of his clan flew in different directions to protect their home. Eventually, Ivory ordered most of his Guardians to do the same, only requesting a few to remain close by. Aydamaris led the way to the entrance of Ragnar's cave and sat in front of it, waiting with Sable by her side.

Nyel crouched low to the ground and said, "Iris, climb onto my back."

"I can stand," she said. She walked towards the others, but Nyel put a paw in front of her to stop her.

"Please. I don't mean any disrespect, I just don't trust Ragnar. I'd feel better if you were already on my back in case I need to get you to safety," Nyel explained.

Iris scowled, but said, "Very well."

Without another word, Iris climbed onto Nyel's back and together they joined the others at the cave entrance. Ivory waited for them there. He stood between Nyel and Ragnar in their circle. Even though he had not heard the voice, Nyel was grateful Ivory joined them. Perhaps he could provide some insight on the matter.

"What do you think this council will solve?" Ragnar grumbled, fidgeting his feet. "None of us know what happened."

"But don't you feel it too?" Aydamaris questioned, staring them each in the eye.

"Feel what?" Ragnar spat. But there was a hint of disturbance in his tone of voice, like he wasn't speaking the whole truth.

"I feel it," Nyel offered in a quiet voice. "I suddenly felt almost homesick. The desire to return home is intense. It's twisting my guts into knots just thinking about it. But what bothers me is that when I think of my home, of Folke, of my parents…I know that it's not the destination I suddenly yearn for."

Ragnar stared at him in silence. Aydamaris nodded with enthusiasm. "Precisely."

"So this voice is calling you home?" Iris asked. "But you don't know where this home is?"

Nyel nodded. He shuffled on his feet uncomfortably. "It's strange. The longer I concentrate on that feeling, the more it grows. I want to follow it."

"You'd be even more of a fool than you already are to listen to voices in your head," Ragnar grunted. Nyel growled, but Ivory stopped him with a look. Now wasn't the time to get into another fight.

"Have we not considered the legends that have coincided with the Gift throughout time?" Ivory offered, turning to Aydamaris.

Her eyes widened in shock. "I had not thought of that."

"What are the legends?" Iris asked.

Ragnar glared at her and hissed, "The human should not be meddling in our affairs. Neither of them!"

Aydamaris growled and stepped forward to get in Ragnar's face. "Your anger and hatred are blinding you, my son! There are more important things to worry about than these two. You must push your feelings aside and help us figure this out. The voice called to you as well."

"It didn't call to the human," his deep voice rumbled.

"We all want the same resolution, Ragnar. Don't make things harder than they already are," Aydamaris scolded. Ragnar growled once more, but this time, he said nothing. Nyel hoped Aydamaris was getting through to him, even just a little.

"Please, what is the legend?" Nyel insisted after a moment of silence.

Ivory cleared his throat. "It's a story that generations have passed down since the formation of the Ascendant's Gift, one that I failed to pass on to you. Horrible, ruthless creatures roamed the land high and low in search of power. Hailwic used to be a land that thrived with magic. It flowed freely and naturally. But these beings originated from the dark magic, and their hunger for power grew until they could no longer control it. They craved more than what they already possessed and couldn't bear to let any other creature outmatch them.

"Their greed nearly wiped out the magic they so eagerly tried to consume. Eventually, they turned on us after growing stronger. For our Queen guarded a sacred magic crystal that connected every dragon to each other in mind and spirit. For this reason, they named it the Draconian Crystal. Soon, our enemies surrounded the dragons, and a long and devastating battle ensued. Many lives were lost in the bloody battle. The dark creatures proved to be stronger than the Queen could have ever imagined. In a desperate attempt to defeat the evil forces, the Queen of the Dragons absorbed the crystal's power and used its magic to destroy their leader and the creatures that followed it. The Queen of the Dragons restored peace to the land, and the dragons rejoiced at her saving them. Soon after, the Queen laid a clutch of six eggs. In doing so, the power of the Draconian Crystal flowed out of her body and separated into her six children. And thus, the Ascendant's Gift was born."

"And the Ascendant's powers have passed on from those six children?" Nyel asked in awe.

Ivory nodded. "Yes. There are always six true Ascendants at any given time. Despite having received and lost the power, some of us, including myself, are still referred to as Ascendant out of respect for being worthy of its power. But there are always only six who hold the power."

"Where are the other Ascendants?" Nyel asked.

"I've not seen them in a long while now," Ivory turned curiously to Aydamaris and Sable, but they shook their heads. After a moment's thought, he said, "In fact, I can't recall who the sixth is."

"Other than Ragnar and Nyel, we haven't seen anyone lately," Sable replied. Then his eyes widened. "Oh, I saw Blagun last season when I was out hunting. We spoke for a little while, but he had something urgent to attend to. You've not seen him Ivory? His clan is much closer to your territory."

The mention of Blagun's name made Nyel's stomach twist. He knew what had happened to Blagun and his clan. His bright gold scales and haunting orange eyes were hard to erase from his memory.

"The shadows possessed Blagun. He was with Kollano the first time we met," Nyel said bitterly. "They slaughtered anyone from his clan who wasn't possessed."

Aydamaris gasped, and Sable growled in anger. "These creatures have to be stopped!"

"So the shadows have captured an Ascendant's power?" Iris asked in dismay.

"It would seem so," Nyel growled. "The last time I saw him was when they captured Azar, one of Ivory's Guardians. There was so much happening, I have no idea where he disappeared to. I haven't seen him since."

They all sat in silence, thinking about everything they had discussed. It was Iris who broke the silence. "Do you think the other Ascendants heard the call, too?"

"They must have," Ivory said. "We need to think of a plan of action. We can't ignore this."

Ragnar snorted. "Plan what you will. Let it include the removal of your group from my territory!'

Aydamaris sighed. "Ragnar, be reasonable."

"I am being reasonable!" Ragnar growled. "Ivory and his pathetic followers think they can come in here and take charge of MY clan and MY guidance, all because some parasites have joined his rank and whisper ideas into his thick skull. My plan is to give you all one last chance to leave this place and never return."

"If you would just listen-" Ivory started, but Ragnar cut him off.

"I'm through with listening! Begone, or I will kill all of you!" he shouted.

Nyel held his head high and said, "Don't tell me you don't feel it, too."

Ragnar growled at him, insulted that he would speak to him again. But his curiosity got the better of him. "Feel what?"

Nyel met his glare. "I can't get rid of the buzzing in my head. It's like an annoying horsefly. Ever since we heard that voice. Something is pulling me to follow this...instinct. To search for the mysterious voice. To answer her call."

Nyel knew he was right. Ragnar glared at him in annoyance, but couldn't deny his words.

Aydamaris nodded in agreement and said, "I feel it too. It's been hard to ignore. Even now, I feel the urge to fly into the unknown."

"You've both lost your sanity if you're willing to listen to voices in your head," Ragnar growled once more.

Nyel shook his head. "Try to ignore it then. See how that plays out for you."

Ragnar roared, seething. "Your arrogance will get you killed, arrogant leech! Do you know where it leads? Or if it's even genuine? For all we know, those shadow creatures could be behind it. Or you, for that matter! You filthy human who stole our magic! It didn't happen until you arrived."

Nyel growled in return. "Of course I'm not behind this! Do what you want. I refuse to join forces with you any longer."

With that, Nyel spun around and flew into the air, leaving the circle behind. Iris gasped and wrapped her arms around his neck. "Nyel, what are you doing?"

"He can't be reasoned with, Iris," Nyel growled angrily as he flew out of Ragnar's territory.

"We can't just give up. We need all the strength we can get," Iris replied.

Nyel snorted. "He tried to kill me, Iris. And if we didn't protect you, he'd have tried to kill you as well. We can't trust him to join forces with us."

"So you're going to leave just like that? What about Ivory and the Guardians? What about Aydamaris?" Iris shouted over the wind as Nyel picked up speed.

"I'm not leaving, I just need to be alone," Nyel shouted back.

Iris fell silent and Nyel felt a twinge of guilt for yelling at her. The stress and anxiety of constantly dealing with the dragons and fighting off shadow creatures had left him on edge. More than anything, Nyel wanted his life to go back to normal. Away from everyone and everything else. But he knew that couldn't happen. Not until all the evil went away. He slowed to a glide and said, "Iris, I'm sorry for-"

"We're being followed," Iris interrupted, looking over her shoulder.

Nyel followed her gaze and spotted a lone dragon approaching them from the south. He studied it carefully, readying himself for another fight.

"Is it one of Ragnar's?" Iris asked as Nyel turned to face it.

A slight breeze blew in his face and he sniffed the air. Nyel's eyes narrowed and he sniffed again. The scent smelled familiar, but he couldn't quite place it.

"No, I don't think so," he finally answered.

Iris's hand began to glow as she readied herself for a fight. Nyel flew towards the dragon. Why wait to be attacked when they could have the upper hand? His anger was enough to fuel him for battle. Iris raised her hand, ready to send out a blast of magic.

A strong gust of wind blew towards them again and Nyel gasped. "Wait!"

She froze and stared ahead. "Do you recognize him? Who is it?"

Nyel's eyes widened and his heart began to race. "It's Syth!"

Chapter 20
An Unexpected Visitor

W hat?" Iris exclaimed in surprise. She lowered her hand and squinted. "Where are the others?"

"I intend to find out," Nyel mumbled, picking up speed. Something was wrong. Why would only one dragon come back? Were they attacked? Captured? A million possibilities rushed through his head as he raced through the sky.

Ragnar's Guardians alerted their clan of the strangers' approach, which only made Nyel fly even faster. Two Guardians perched closer to Syth descended from their places on the mountain range and approached Syth. Nyel cursed under his breath. The Guardians reached Syth first and after a moment's confrontation; they made him change his path towards Ragnar's cave.

Nyel growled in frustration and spun in a half circle to return to where he had left the others. He landed with a thud, spraying dirt and rock around him, and waited. The Ascendants hurried towards him and scanned the sky.

"What is the meaning of this?" Ragnar roared angrily. "Is this another one of yours, Ivory?"

Ivory nodded. "Yes, but we weren't expecting him. Please allow him passage. I believe he is here with a message."

Before Ragnar could object, Syth and the two Guardian dragons landed in front of them. Nyel was the first to hurry to his side. His heart sank as soon as he saw there was no rider on his back.

"Where are the others?" Nyel asked, searching Syth's face for any sign of bad news. "What happened?"

Syth gasped for breath and met Nyel's eyes with a tired gaze. From what Nyel could tell, he must have flown non-stop to find them. He folded up his wings and opened his mouth to speak, but Ragnar interrupted him.

"You do not have the right to speak here, filth!" Ragnar growled. He was so close to his face that Nyel could smell the stench of his breath. Nyel stood his ground, too angry and desperate for answers to be fazed by Ragnar's brute force.

He then turned to the newest addition and growled, "Who are you? What is your business here?"

"I am Syth. I'm a Guardian of the Ryngar clan," Syth grumbled, obviously annoyed to have to speak to the new Ascendant. "I must speak with Ivory and Nyel at once."

Ragnar growled. "You're in my territory, runt. You do as I say if you know what's good for you."

"And what is your command?" Syth challenged, a spark of hatred flashed in his eyes for a brief moment. He was more prepared for a confrontation with Ragnar than Nyel could have guessed.

Ragnar roared, "Don't talk back to me! You're here in my clan, so deliver your message to me. I'm waiting."

Syth glanced at Ivory out of the corner of his eye, and Ivory shrugged. It would take forever to hear the message with Ragnar calling the shots otherwise. Syth turned back to Ragnar and said, "Theo sent me back to deliver a message. Kollano took the prince. We tried to return as a group, but the youngling wouldn't abandon him. So the others stayed behind with him to chase after the prince."

Iris let out a horrified gasp.

Bile rose in Nyel's throat. "Bem, you idiot…"

"What is that around your horn?" Ragnar huffed after a moment of silence.

Syth hesitated, and then said, "Something I must deliver to the princess."

Nyel's eyes shot up to Syth's horn. He hadn't realized it before. Tied tightly around the base of his horn was a crystal necklace. In the same moment, Iris slid from Nyel's back before he could stop her. "Wait!"

Ragnar growled at her approach. "How dare you interfere in our business!"

"With all due respect, Ascendant, this is my business," Iris announced, with her head held high.

He roared and swung his paw at her. Nyel shot forward to defend her, but stopped in his tracks. Syth had beaten him to it, ramming his head into Ragnar's throat just enough to knock him backwards. Ragnar's Guardians hissed and charged towards Syth. Nyel changed direction and rammed into the nearest guardian he could reach. Syth swung his tail at the other and together they held their pursuit off.

Ivory leapt between the furious Ragnar and Iris. "That's enough, Ragnar! I will tolerate your arrogance no longer!"

"You are in my clan, Ivory!" Ragnar roared. "I will have you slaughtered!"

"We are leaving," Ivory announced. He turned to stare at Nyel and Syth. "Now!"

Syth snarled with a murderous glare. With one last look at Ragnar, he leapt into the air and let out a short roar, calling the rest of Ivory's Guardians to follow him. Nyel hurried to Iris and crouched to allow her to climb onto his back once more.

"You're a fool if you think I'm going to allow you to live," Ragnar warned with a menacing glare.

Ivory growled. "Don't threaten what you cannot back up. Those shadow creatures will be back with more numbers. What's more important, your clan or your pride? You'd be a fool to not join forces to fight them off. At least think about it before you send your Guardians after us."

With that, Ivory and Nyel flew into the air and followed their clan back towards the south. Nyel kept an eye on Ragnar's Guardians, who flew close behind them. However, it only seemed they were escorting them out of Ragnar's territory. He sighed in relief, somewhat thankful that perhaps the fight with the possessed dragons had exhausted them. Or if nothing else had made them consider saving their strength.

After a few miles of flying south, Ragnar's Guardians fell back and watched them to make sure they left their territory. Aydamaris and Sabel crossed his mind as they neared their mountain, but he couldn't worry about them now. The news Syth had brought them enveloped Nyel's mind. Nothing else mattered to him but the thought of Bem in trouble.

Once they seemed to be safe from Ragnar's wrath, Nyel sped up and joined Syth's side. Before he could even open his mouth, Iris blurted out, "What happened to my brother?"

Syth acknowledged her with just a flicker of his eyes. "As I said. He was possessed by Kollano."

"How is that possible? I thought Carver killed him," Nyel joined in. "Were you attacked?"

Syth shook his head with a worried look in his eyes. "He just…turned. Like he was there the entire time. I didn't even sense the danger that was so close to me."

"Knowing my brother, I know why he wanted to stay behind and help Carver. Didn't Falcon or Theo try to talk any sense into him? Or force him to regroup with us?" Nyel asked. His head was spinning with unanswered questions as his anxiety grew. Where could they be? Were they safe? What was Kollano up to now?

Syth growled in annoyance. "Falcon tried. And Theo would have too if he could communicate with him. In the end, they agreed to go after the prince. Falcon tied this silly crystal onto my horn and sent me back to find you. Last I heard, they returned to the cabin in the forest. That's all I know."

From the front of the group, Lorna let out a quick call to follow her lead, and together they landed in the clearing where Nyel and Lorna had fought for their lives. As Nyel folded his wings, he glanced over at the base of the mountain and spotted the hidden entrance that led to the small family. Garian would not be pleased to find a small group of dragons so close to his home.

"Why are we landing?" growled Orden. "We haven't put enough distance between us and Ragnar's clan."

Lorna moved towards Nyel and Ivory while saying, "There are things that need to be addressed."

She then looked at Nyel and asked, "Where do you go from here?"

Nyel stared at her in shock, then glanced at the others. Most of the Guardians seemed annoyed that she addressed him with the question. As if in response, he felt a strong need to fly west. At the same time, all he wanted to do was find his brother.

"We must answer the call that Nyel and Aydamaris heard," Ivory answered after a moment's silence. "Nothing like this has ever happened in our history. The Ascendants are to gather as one and find the whereabouts of the origin. It would be unwise to ignore it."

At the mention of this, his instinctual urge grew even stronger to agree with Ivory and to leave at that very moment in search of answers. But he still couldn't ignore his heart.

"I'm sorry, Ivory, but my brother must come first," Nyel answered, trying to bury the rest to ignore the call to action.

Ivory turned to him with a look of anger he rarely wore, but this time it was directed at Nyel. "I have stood by your side in all of this Shifter. So far, we have made little progress in your hopes of uniting our people as one. And now you want to just up and leave, when we don't even know if he's in danger?"

"Not just Bem," Nyel countered, standing his ground. "But Falcon, Steno, and Theo, your own blood! Not to mention Kollano is on the loose once more. Who knows what he has in store for the people of Hailwic?"

Ivory snorted. "I understand your bond with your family, but need I remind you that your blood bond with us is just as real? Let me reiterate the importance of the circumstances we now find ourselves in. What you heard back there is something that hasn't happened in the history of the Ascendants. You cannot desert us now."

Nyel swallowed past the lump in his throat. He felt torn between what his instincts told him and what his heart begged him to do. He shook his head, dropped his gaze, and took a deep breath.

"I'm sorry Ivory. I know I have promised my allegiance to you and your clan. But I know my brother. I fear he is in great danger," Nyel answered as he slowly met his eyes.

An uproar erupted from the Guardians surrounding them.

"I knew he didn't care about us!" Lunar shouted.

"He only used us to learn how to mimic us!" Niko yelled.

"How dare you betray your gift!"

Nyel's eyes darted to each of them, but he didn't know what to say. He knew he was right for wanting to protect his brother. But it didn't make him feel any less guilty.

Suddenly, Iris leapt off his back and went to stand in the center of the ring of angry dragons. The ones that hated her hissed at her approach, but they didn't dare attack her with Ivory watching. Nyel kept a close eye on her, but didn't move to hold her back. He knew better than to get in the princess's way.

Iris stood in front of Syth and motioned to the necklace tied around his horn. "May I?"

Syth lowered his head and allowed her to untie the leather cord from his horn. She held the crystal between her hands for a moment and closed her eyes. When she opened them, she looked around at Nyel with hope in her eyes. "Falcon sent me this to find him."

"How does it work?" Nyel asked, ignoring the others for a moment.

"This crystal has been enchanted to connect with another crystal," Iris explained, holding it up by the cord for all to see. "It's made for finding the other when separated. When used properly, the crystal will use the magical energy from both of the wearers to provide enough power to find the other. And the person who wears the second crystal will know you're looking for them as well. It's tricky to use. If worn too long, it could exhaust you of all your energy."

Nyel sighed in relief. "So there's hope of finding them quickly?"

Iris nodded. "As long as Falcon is wearing his, the odds sound good. And Falcon would never take his off, I'm sure of it."

"Great! We should leave right away," Nyel urged, stepping towards her to allow her to climb up onto his back once more.

Iris held up a hand to stop him. "I'm going to them. You're going to stay here."

Nyel froze in surprise. "What?"

The group went silent, all eyes on them. "Ivory's right. You need to follow the call and find out more about your own power. I can handle finding the others."

"But what if you run into Kollano? If he truly has your brother, it seems he has an obsession with the royal bloodline. He could be after you, too," Nyel argued. "I can't let you go alone. How do you even plan on getting there?"

"I will take her," Lorna declared. Iris smiled and nodded her thanks.

Nyel stared at them in silence, trying to think of a better way to make it all work. "What about my brother?"

"I will do everything I can to make sure he is safe," Iris vowed. "The best thing you can do, the right thing, is to find out if there's something within your shared power that can help defeat this evil."

Nyel hesitated. "You know Bem will want to save your brother."

Iris nodded sadly. "As do I. But I will do what I must to protect the people of Hailwic. It's time for me to stop chasing these big ideas and dreams I've planned over the years. My true purpose is to be the princess I'm meant to be, and protect my people."

Syth stepped forward. "I will join you."

Nyel and Iris stared at him in total shock.

"You will?" she asked.

Syth nodded. "We didn't start off on the right foot. As annoying as you humans are, I have formed an attachment with the ones I left behind. I wouldn't be doing my duty as a Guardian to leave my brethren behind. Even the human ones."

Iris smiled. "Thank you!"

"Nyel, will you agree to these terms?" Ivory asked, his unwavering gaze fixated on him.

Nyel stared at Iris, feeling torn. But the feeling inside of him burned at the thought of joining her to find their friends. Even though that was more important in his heart. It unnerved him that the sudden hold the dragon magic had on him was too great to ignore.

"I'll be fine," Iris whispered so only he could hear.

With a sigh, Nyel tore his eyes away from her and nodded once to Ivory.

"Then it's settled. We should make haste," Ivory announced. His tone softened slightly.

Nyel closed his eyes and reached within for his power. Within seconds, he shrank back down into his human form. When he looked up again at Ivory, he cocked his head in confusion. "What are you doing, Shifter?"

"There's one thing I need to take care of before we go," Nyel announced. He grabbed Iris's hand and pulled her towards the mountain where the hidden entrance was.

"And you expect us to wait here for you?" Ivory called in annoyance.

"It won't take long," Nyel shouted. He felt bad for not explaining his motives, but he didn't feel like wasting anymore time arguing with Ivory. They sprinted down the rocky hill towards the boulder before Ivory could stop them.

They stopped when they reached the boulder that blocked the tunnel entrance and gasped for breath. Iris glanced over at him and between breaths asked, "What are we doing here?"

"I didn't want to leave without saying goodbye," Nyel explained. "And to warn them about Ragnar."

Iris frowned at the mention of the Ascendant and nodded in understanding. Without a word, she moved the boulder with her magic just enough so they could squeeze inside. She did not replace it, perhaps to make it easier to leave. With a lit palm to guide her, Iris led the way into the tunnel system, back to the small family.

As they traveled further into the cave, they could hear voices in the distance grow louder and louder. They slowed their pace, not wanting to alarm anyone. Nyel took the lead and was about to call out in greeting when a figure jumped out in front of him and shot a ball of fire at his head.

Nyel's scales instinctively formed across his face, arms and chest as he crossed his arms in an X to shield his face. Iris gasped and her glowing hand changed color, preparing to use her magic on his attacker.

Nyel yelled, "Stop, it's me!"

As he lowered his arms, he saw Barrett staring at him in surprise. Finally, he lowered his glowing hand and said, "Sorry, I wasn't expecting it to be you."

"Who did you think it would be?" Nyel growled angrily as his scales faded back into his body.

"There have been a lot of shadow creatures nearby," Barrett offered. "I'm not taking any chances. I suspect they are here because of you."

Barrett's eyes shifted from him to Iris. His brow furrowed in suspicion. He studied both of them and he asked, "Where have you been? You both look so serious."

"It's a lot to explain. But trust me when I say the shadow creatures aren't just passing through. They're looking for anyone, and I mean anyone, to possess," Nyel replied, his voice gruff with annoyance. He tried to look around Barrett to see if the others had noticed their arrival.

"I'm not sure that I trust *you* yet," Barrett growled. "You think you can just come and go as you please? Be more considerate than that. This is our home!"

"I know, I'm sorry. But there are more dangers that they need to know about. Where are your aunt and uncle?" Nyel asked.

Barrett motioned with his head over his shoulder and reluctantly stepped out of the way. Nyel stalked past him, finally making his way down the last tunnel to the main room.

"Nyel, you're back!" Shara shouted with glee. In her arms, she held Iris's bag. And within it, the dragon egg. "How's Aydamaris?"

In all the chaos of the past day, Nyel had forgotten about the egg. He wondered if Iris had asked her to watch over it when she left?

Garian and Evanna looked up from their seats at the table and immediately got to their feet. On the table were a dozen crystals arranged by size.

"How did it go?" Garian asked, crossing his arms in anticipation.

"I think you may need to consider leaving the mountain," Nyel spoke up, cutting to the chase. All eyes turned to him.

"What? What about the dragons? I thought you were working something out with them?" Garian asked, perplexed.

Nyel nodded. "I was…I am. They are going to take some convincing. In the meantime, I believe it would be wise to move somewhere safer. The leader of the Maeve clan already knew of your existence and our being in his territory has angered him. I just don't want anything bad to happen to you."

"Why would we have to leave?" Barrett asked as he came in. "We have the protection of Aydamaris."

Nyel hesitated because Ragnar did not approve of his proposition. "He tried to kill me when I was helping fight off the possessed dragons. Iris saved me and knocked him out of the sky. Aydamaris and Sable are kind and care about you, but now that I've met Ragnar and his followers, they are no match for him if he attacks. They also may leave their mountain for the time being. I'm sorry, but I don't think it's safe to leave your family here."

"That's just great," Barrett grumbled. "We were doing just fine on our own until you came along! Where are we supposed to go? Returning to the kingdom means they will kill or imprison us once more. I will not allow myself to be captured after my mother sacrificed her life to free me from that place!"

"We will leave," Evanna stated calmly, stopping Barrett in his tracks. He glared at her, furious.

"How could you say that? This is our home. It has been for years; we should fight for it!" Barrett shouted.

Evanna shook her head. "No, this isn't our home. The princess and I spoke for a long time before she left to find Nyel. She has made me realize that there is hope for Hailwic yet. You're right, there is a home we must fight for. But it isn't here. We've been hiding for far too long. Our place is in Hailwic. We deserve to live without fear. We must fight for the rights of the imprisoned sorcerers and sorceresses. They deserve their freedom too."

Iris smiled at her and nodded enthusiastically. "And we will help you do it. We will need the numbers."

"You expect the king will let you walk right into his prisons and let them go?" Barrett accused. "Have you forgotten how locked down they keep their prisons? Besides, even if you make it in, the prisoners wouldn't trust you. Especially with a royal at your side."

Evanna went to him and placed a gentle hand on his stubbled cheek. "My nephew, have you forgotten? It was a royal who helped us escape that fate. We have to try, Barrett. For us, for them, and for your mother. She wouldn't want you to live out your life hiding in a cave. You deserve a better life than this."

Barrett angrily pulled away from his aunt's touch and stalked back down the tunnel without another word. She watched him go with sadness in her eyes. Iris placed a caring hand on her shoulder and said, "We can do this. I know we can. But I must tell you my first duty is to find our friends who are in trouble. We just found out that the leader of those shadow creatures, Kollano, may still be alive and has captured my brother."

Evanna gasped. "I'm sorry to hear that! I understand. We will follow your orders, princess."

"Please, just call me Iris," she reminded her with a smile.

Nyel's eyes roamed around the cave, taking in the family's home. It would be hard for them to leave the safety and comfort of their cave. But he also knew it would only be a matter of time before Ragnar's Guardians arrived to wipe them out. He tried his best to push aside the guilt he held for the part he played. If he hadn't been trying to reach out to all the clan leaders, they would have never had to leave. But he couldn't change it now. It was too late for that.

"I think we should all prepare to leave," Nyel announced, turning to Garian. "No use waiting around any longer than we have to. I'll talk to Ivory about allowing more Guardians to accompany you. It will be quicker and safer that way."

"Are you sure that's wise? Aydamaris and Sable are the only dragons who I can trust," Garian asked.

Nyel nodded. "I know of a few Guardians that may help that I know for certain they will not harm you. Don't worry, I wouldn't send anyone I wouldn't trust to assist you."

Garian nodded in return. His face turned noticeably paler than before. He clearly showed his fear, but he didn't want his family to notice. He turned on the spot and began gathering some leather bags. With Evanna's help, he gathered food, clothing, and other materials and carefully packed them away into their bags. Shara emerged from wherever she had been hiding with two leather corded necklaces in hand. They each held the same green crystals that Iris wore on her ring.

She handed them to Iris and said, "Here, for your friends! I made them after you left. I was hoping you'd come back to us."

Iris smiled with gratitude and gave Shara a big hug. "Thank you! This will make it so much easier for them. Are you sure you have enough crystals, though? I wouldn't want to take something you might need."

"We have a few more," Evanna answered. "But I'll hold on to those for now. I told her to make those for you to use however you'd like."

Iris tucked the necklaces safely away in her pocket and said, "I appreciate the thought. Thank you!"

Nyel watched as Iris helped Evanna gather up her most important crystals. Garian helped Shara pack her own bag and gather up their weapons. He then locked eyes with Iris and sighed. Nyel reached out to her as she walked past, his fingers tracing against her arm. She stopped and turned to him with a questioning look.

"I better go to Ivory before he sends someone in after me. I'll talk to him about the Guardians."

Iris nodded. Her smile disappeared into a frown, her eyes sad as he turned to leave.

Nyel hesitated. "What's wrong?"

"I'm sorry. I failed my quest and brought more trouble for you in the process," she said, lowering her voice so that only he could hear.

Surprised, Nyel stared at her. "What? Why would you say that? You haven't failed. Nor have you brought any trouble to me I wasn't already in."

Iris shook her head. "I suppose. But I didn't accomplish what I set out to do. You're stronger than I am; and braver. I had a dream, my uncle's dream, to unite with the dragons. I realize now that my dream needs a revision. It was never me who would accomplish this, but you. You're the one who will unite our races once more."

He chuckled. "You're putting a lot of faith and expectations on me, princess."

Her cheeks flushed and in a scolding tone, she said, "Iris!"

Nyel stopped laughing and placed his hands on her shoulders, staring into her eyes. "No! Princess. Princess Iris of Hailwic. If you're going to hold me to my destiny, then I will hold you to yours. It's time to stop running from it. You are the true heir to the kingdom. Your father failed your people long ago. But not only them; he failed Sargon, your mother, your brother, and most importantly, he failed you! It's time to fight for what's rightfully yours. Find our brothers, save the imprisoned sorcerers. Don't hold back! Give it your all! And I promise, when the time is right, I will find you. And I'll bring all the fire and the rage of the dragons with me."

Tears formed in her eyes. Iris wiped them away with a quick motion of her hand and pulled Nyel into a tight hug. Nyel closed his eyes and held her close, not wanting her to see the pain he fought so hard to hide from her. He wanted so badly to follow her and find their friends together. He felt it in his heart. Bem was in danger. It killed him that he wasn't flying back to find him at that very moment. But he had to stay and find an answer to who the voice was inside his head and what it could mean.

They let go of each other, only this time Iris looked fierce, confident, and determined. She grinned at him and said, "Well then, Shifter, prepare for your new quest. The quest you were born to follow. And may good fortune shine on us both."

"You too, my princess," Nyel grinned back, placing a fist to his chest in a salute. With that, he turned and made his way out of the tunnels to find Ivory.

Chapter 21
The Duty of The Shifter

Nyel stood in the field at the bottom of the mountain that hid the small family's home. It felt strange to be standing on two legs again with the warmth of the sun on his bare skin. The knee-high grass swayed around him in a gentle breeze as he watched Garian and Barrett secure their bags to their respective Guardian companions that elected to accompany them.

It was no surprise to Nyel that, upon the request of additional dragons, Lorna's sisters volunteered immediately. It made him feel better they could stay together and help Iris keep the others safe. He studied the Guardians as they interacted with the others. Lorna was the most receptive to conversation with the humans. She, Iris, and Garian discussed a plan of action as they prepared for their departure. Casca and Aura seemed nervous, but would help when needed. Syth seemed annoyed as usual, although there was something about him that was different from the last time they spoke. He seemed eager to leave. Concerned, even.

Nyel made his way over to Syth and stopped beside him, following his gaze southward. "What's on your mind?"

Syth turned his gaze onto Nyel, startled by his approach. Then he snorted and said, "I have a bad feeling about how I left the others. I truly hope they would have found their senses and followed me back by now."

Nyel nodded and crossed his arms. He felt it too. Something wasn't right. "Thank you for playing the role of messenger. I'm sure it wasn't your first choice."

Syth huffed. "Of course it wasn't! But on my way here, the further I got on my journey, the more I felt like I abandoned them.

They should have sent Steno instead. He wasn't the one that carried the prince."

Nyel's eyes widened as he stared up at Syth. "You're worried for Carver?"

Syth growled and shook his head. "Of course not! It's only…he was my responsibility to keep an eye on and I never suspected that Kollano was inside of him. I never caught a scent of anything different."

He sounded embarrassed by Nyel's question. But most of all, he sounded ashamed. Nyel placed his hand on the dragon's scaly leg and said, "It's not your fault. He fooled us all."

He then lowered his voice to a whisper, "And it's ok to care about Carver."

Syth snorted and pulled away from Nyel's touch. "Are we ready to leave yet?"

Nyel smirked and shook his head. Whether or not Syth wanted to admit it to himself, Nyel suspected he had cared for the humans he traveled with. A massive improvement from when he started. It gave Nyel a small amount of hope that perhaps he could convince more dragons to change their minds with time.

"I think so," Garian answered Syth. He tightened the last rope around Aura's chest.

Iris gathered them around and clasped her hands together. "Alright. I'll be flying with Lorna. Garian, I think you'd be best with Syth. Evanna will go with Casca and Barrett with Aura. Questions?"

"Yeah, who am I riding with?" Shara asked, bouncing up and down with excitement. "Shouldn't I have my own dragon to ride to?"

Iris shook her head. "I think it's safer if you ride with someone else."

"Can I ride with you?" she asked, her eyes lighting up.

Iris hesitated and looked at her mom for answers. Evanna shrugged.

"As long as it's alright with Iris," she looked over to the princess, who nodded. "Then yes. But you must behave yourself and listen to what she tells you! If I hear one complaint from her about you misbehaving, I'll tie you to the tail of one of these dragons myself!"

"Yes!" Shara shouted in excitement.

She raced over to Lorna. Amused, Lorna lowered her head and allowed Shara to wrap her arms around her snout as she laughed.

Aydamaris and Sable joined them and bowed their heads to them.

"Safe travels, my young friends," Aydamaris said.

"May the wind be in your favor," Sable agreed, bowing his head.

Garian and Evanna bowed to them in return. "My family would like to thank you humbly for your protection over these long years," Garian said as he rose once more. "We will never forget your hospitality and your sacrifice."

Aydamaris chuckled. "It was a privilege, dear ones. I hope we can meet again one day."

Garian smiled. "I hope so too."

With that, Aydamaris and Sable turned and leapt into the air. Nyel watched them fly back north. Earlier, Aydamaris had told him and the others that they planned to talk to Ragnar once more. She thought it important that he should not ignore the voice that called to them. Nyel hoped Ragnar wouldn't listen. It would be easier to travel without having to look over his shoulder the entire way. Anymore than he had to, anyway.

"Well, let's mount up!" Garian boasted, giving Barrett a slap on the back. The brooding Barrett sulked over to Aura without a word. Nyel watched him carefully. He was the only one he was concerned about, as he didn't know much about him. The young sorcerer was still against leaving their home, but he wasn't going to stay behind.

Nyel and Iris remained as the others climbed onto their dragons and got settled. Garian grabbed Shara and hoisted her into the air, both of them laughing as he did. Nyel watched them, suddenly feeling homesick for his own family.

Behind him, Ivory bellowed out a long farewell. It was also the final call for him to leave. He turned and watched as the remaining Guardians followed Ivory into the air back towards the north. Towards Ragnar's clan. He was glad they had each other. He slowly turned to Iris and found she was already watching him with sad eyes.

"I guess this is it," she whispered.

Nyel nodded, a lump formed in his throat. In one swift motion, he pulled Iris into a hug and held her tight. He squeezed his eyes shut and breathed in the scent of her hair. How long would it be before he saw her again? He whispered, "Please be safe."

"You too," she sighed.

An overwhelming sadness washed over him as they parted. This was it. The moment he had been dreading. Iris would leave to find their brothers, and he had to stay behind. The thought of it could drive him mad. But that whisper, the feeling that had haunted his thoughts for days, told him he was doing the right thing. He had to trust it. Iris was capable of helping the others on her own. He knew that to be true.

As she turned to walk away, something inside him snapped. Nyel stepped forward and grabbed Iris's wrist. "Iris."

She turned around in surprise. His breath caught in his throat as their eyes met once more. Before he could back down out of fear, Nyel placed his other hand on her cheek and leaned in. Their lips brushed in a delicate kiss. His stomach filled with butterflies when Iris lifted her hand and gently placed it on his cheek.

Nyel's eyes opened wide, and he pulled away in embarrassment. "I'm...I'm sorry. I should have asked. Please forgive me."

Her cheeks flushed, and she said, "It's ok."

He looked up at her in amazement as she leaned in and rested her forehead against his. "I only wish you hadn't waited until this moment to let me know how you feel about me."

Nyel lowered his gaze. "I'm sorry."

Iris held his face in her hands and said, "We will revisit this later. Just promise me you'll be safe. Do you swear it?"

Nyel stared at her intently, his heart racing in his chest. "I swear. I'll find you soon."

She leaned in once more and their lips met. Only this time, neither one of them wanted to pull away from the other. Finally, Nyel pulled away from her, grabbed her hand, and looked into her eyes once more. They held each other's gaze, silently praying for the other's safety.

Then, with a last squeeze of her hand, Nyel turned and ran. He couldn't face her any longer, or else he wouldn't be able to let her go. As he ran, he transformed into his dragon form and threw himself into the air. Only then could he allow himself to turn and watch as Iris climbed onto Lorna. One by one, the dragons and their riders flew into the sky with their backs to him, going the opposite direction. Leaving him behind.

He let out a long roar filled with a mixture of hope, despair, and anger. For Iris. For Bem. For himself. And then he turned his back on Iris and hurried to join his clan on their next endeavor.

Nyel sat silently by himself and watched the remaining Guardians interact with each other. The friends he had made within the group had all left with Iris. Despite easing his worries about her, the thought also left him feeling alone. The rest of the Guardians of the Ryngar clan didn't like him. Or at the very least, they weren't ready to accept him as one of their own. And he couldn't blame them for that.

Even Ivory was angry with him for wanting to leave. But Nyel couldn't bring himself to apologize for wanting to help his brother.

So he offered to take first watch over the group, along with the Guardian called Trunic.

Trunic was older and didn't take part in the younger dragons' talks about their glory days of hunting and battling other clans for territory or finding their mates. In fact, the only time Nyel had ever heard him speak was when they wanted to play a game of wit and recite old riddles to each other. Trunic was the sharpest and quickest to answer the others' riddles. In turn, his proved to be the most difficult to solve.

Nyel stared past the group of Guardians and found Trunic perched high above them, atop a rocky cliff. He kept his unwavering gaze towards the east, where Ivory and Lunar had left for Ragnar's territory to find Aydamaris and Sable. They had not returned to their home by nightfall, so Ivory was determined to recruit them into their group.

As much as Nyel respected Ivory, he didn't appreciate how the Ascendant had treated him since he discovered the mysterious voice had called to him. Nyel couldn't help but wonder if the old dragon was jealous that he had received the call instead of him. But he would never accuse Ivory of such things. The thought made Nyel feel guilty. Even if that were true, Ivory was right about one thing. It would be wrong to ignore something as important as the Ascendant's Gift.

Ivory was his only true ally out there now. Nyel had to seek his forgiveness, even though he didn't feel like he was entirely wrong for wanting to find his brother. Without Ivory, he didn't have many others to talk to. Most of the Guardians that remained ignored him or were hateful towards him behind Ivory's back. It was going to make for a long trip.

The world spun around him. Nyel had to close his eyes and take a deep breath. When he opened them once more, his eyes wandered around until the dizziness wore off. This had happened more than once throughout the day. And every time it subsided, he kept his gaze fixated towards the west.

He thought back to the voice that echoed in his head. How it called him to search for it. Nyel's heart raced as he realized the connection. The dizziness stopped once he faced towards the west. Was that the direction the voice echoed from? Was he meant to travel that way? He couldn't be certain of anything.

Trunic grunted and met Nyel's gaze from above. "Ivory approaches."

Nyel turned his head and spotted Ivory floating towards them with Lunar close behind him. Behind them, to Nyel's relief, were Aydamaris and Sable. The others stirred from their rest and waited for the four of them to land. Nyel and Trunic remained at their posts, but eagerly listened.

"Welcome back," Orden said, assuming charge. As Ivory folded his wings against his sides, he continued, "Did Ragnar give you any trouble?"

Ivory shook his head. "No trouble. We met Aydamaris and Sable outside of his territory."

"Ragnar refused to listen to the call," Aydamaris said. She then met Nyel's gaze. "What are you going to do, young Shifter?"

All eyes fell on him. It made his scales itch. Nyel answered, "I will follow the call, if you will go with me."

Aydamaris's eyes beamed with delight. "Of course I shall."

Nyel let out a sigh of relief. At least he wouldn't be the only one who heard the voice. Ivory let out a puff of smoke and said, "We should get moving. We've wasted enough time as it is."

"Very well," Aydamaris replied. She then turned to Nyel and asked, "Tell me, what do you feel? Where do your instincts guide you?"

Nyel jumped from his perch where he had kept watch and moved away from them, pointing towards the west with his claw. "I can't explain it, but I feel like I'm being pulled in that direction."

Aydamaris nodded, intrigued, as she followed his gaze. "As do I."

"Then it's settled. We travel west," Ivory announced. "To the skies!"

Without another word, Ivory and the Guardians leapt into the air. Nyel watched them for a moment from the ground. His nerves twisted his stomach into knots. He hated how anxious he felt about the whole thing. Sable and Aydamaris joined him on either side of him.

"What troubles you, Shifter?" Sable asked in a kind voice.

Nyel turned to him and sighed. "I've created tension with my clan when there didn't need to be any. Even Ivory is angry with me. I hate feeling blind to where we're supposed to go. Now I feel like I'm just their broken compass."

"Things will get better, young one," Aydamaris encouraged. "We are with you. I believe whatever calls to us will reveal itself. Have faith. And don't forget, whether they like it or not, you are their Ascendant and you do have a voice. Even Ivory will look to you when the time is right."

Nyel smiled at her, comforted by her words. Sable opened his dark wings. "I suppose we should join them before they come back for us and pluck us off the ground."

Aydamaris chuckled and said, "Right, as always, my love."

Together, the three dragons soared into the air to follow their companions into the unknown. Nyel stayed close to them as they rejoined the rest of the clan. All seemed well. The weather was perfect for flying and nothing seemed amiss on the ground below them. The gentle cool breeze of spring was welcoming against Nyel's face.

"Do you have an idea of where we may be heading?" Nyel asked Aydamaris.

She shook her head. "It's been a while since I've traveled anywhere further than my home. There is another clan farther west of here, but we've lost contact with them long ago."

"Why's that?" he wondered aloud.

When Aydamaris didn't answer, Sable replied, "Ragnar became an Ascendant and the new leader of our clan. And as you have come to learn, he's not very eager to welcome newcomers into his territory."

Nyel chuckled under his breath. He certainly was not.

"Why do you think Ivory is upset with you?" Sable asked after a moment.

Nyel sighed. His heart felt heavy once more. "Something urgent came up back home. Carver, the prince, my brother Bem, and our friends are in danger. Syth said the leader of the shadows may have possessed the prince's body and my brother went after him. I wanted to go back and find them. Ivory became upset when I wanted to leave."

"Why did they not wait for more help?" Aydamaris asked. The concern in her voice reminded him of Mari, Bem's mother and his stepmother. Which made him feel all the more worse.

"I think my brother loves the prince," Nyel replied. "It's as simple and as complicated as that. Who wouldn't do whatever they could for the people they loved?"

"And you love your brother. Why not go to him?" Sable asked.

Before Nyel could answer, Aydamaris said, "Whatever Nyel and I heard is not just a voice. I think I can speak for both of us that this presence is something that has always been a part of the Gift. It's not just a duty to find this presence, but a privilege."

"That reminds me, what happened with Ragnar?" Nyel asked, trying to change the subject. "He heard it too. Do you think he can really ignore the call?"

Aydamaris sighed. "Knowing my son, he will try. But I'm not so sure that he can."

They fell silent. Nyel pushed the thought of Bem, Carver, and Iris from his mind. He had to focus on his own mission now. The faster he figured out the meaning of the call, the quicker he could return to his friends and help them. He had to remind himself that they were more than capable of handling themselves.

"So, what can we expect in the west?" Nyel asked.

"More mountains," Sable shrugged.

Nyel sighed. As beautiful as they were, they were exhausting to fly around. Not to mention all the crevices and ravines the shadow creatures could hide in.

Sable chuckled. "What did you expect of us? The mountains are dangerous, exhausting, and some have proved impossible for humans to climb. The further in we go, the less likely we'd run into a dragonslayer."

"I understand the logic behind it, but it doesn't mean I'm excited about it," Nyel grumbled.

Aydamaris laughed. Nyel took one look at her and couldn't resist the dragon-like smile that formed in his face. He was glad to have them on this journey.

"Nyel, Aydamaris…join me," Ivory called from up ahead.

They fell silent and did as they were told. Aydamaris joined him on the left while Nyel at his right. Nyel could feel some of the Guardians' eyes on him, but he tried his best to ignore them. "Yes, Ivory?"

"Do you have a sense of where the voice wants you to go?" Ivory asked, turning his head to each of them in search of an answer.

Aydamaris shook her head. "Not precisely, but I sense we are moving in the right direction."

Ivory nodded. He then turned to Nyel. "And you?"

Nyel sucked in a deep breath. "I have the same feeling as Aydamaris."

"Hmm," Ivory pondered, deep in thought as he stared ahead of them at the land ahead. "For now, we will continue to fly until perhaps you receive another sign. We will just have to be cautious."

"How so?" Nyel asked.

Ivory turned his gaze on him and huffed. "We will have to watch out for the possessed and shadows, of course. We also have to be mindful of the last clan. Who knows what their condition is."

"I forgot there was another clan until Aydamaris reminded me. Are they as big as Ragnar's clan?" Nyel asked.

Ivory shook his head. "The Asya Clan. It's about the same as ours, I would say. And they are more willing to talk to other clans if the situation is peaceful. I worry about them."

"Why not go to them first?" Aydamaris suggested. "We have a responsibility to warn them of the dangers that are running rampant through our land. If they haven't faced the shadows yet, we need to inform them and help them prepare."

Ivory paused in consideration. "Perhaps that is the best course of action. We'd then have the chance to ask Mairwen if she also heard the voice."

"Mairwen is the clan's Ascendant, I assume?" Nyel asked.

Ivory nodded. "The youngest Ascendant that I know of currently. Besides yourself, I suppose."

With a warm glow in her eyes, Aydamaris added, "Her father granted her the Ascendant power. He is still the leader of the Asya clan until she's ready to take over."

Nyel thought it over, a bit confused. "But it seems that if a dragon is an Ascendant, they're usually the clan's leader as well. Is that not the case?"

"Most Ascendants step up and become the leader of their clan," Ivory explained. "The ancient power that flows through an Ascendant's blood also compels us to protect our own, even more fiercely than we already do. But her father decided she was not ready to take his place. And he is also an Ascendant, even without his power. The drive is still there to protect our own."

Nyel studied Ivory, and the realization hit him. He finally understood why he was so determined to figure out why the voice had spoken to them and called them into action. He respected him more for it.

"Ivory, can I ask you something?" Nyel hesitated.

Ivory looked at him and nodded. "Yes, of course."

Nyel gulped. "I don't mean this out of disrespect. But who will take your place as the clan leader when the time comes?"

It was now Ivory's turn to study him with intense eyes. Nyel winced, wondering if he was out of line for asking the question. He was glad none of the other Guardians heard him.

Finally, Ivory said, "That's a decision I've not yet made."

"Is your decision final?"

"Not exactly," Ivory replied, turning his attention forward once more. "It can be the final decision, but the clan has a right to determine who they want to lead them as well. Someone could fight me for it too. But I don't fear that from any of them. Choosing the wrong leader could be what destroys a clan's structure. Whatever I decide, it must be the right choice."

Nyel nodded. Ivory carried more on his shoulders than he let on.

"So, what is the name of this clan's leader?" Nyel asked him.

"Talon."

"How does he feel about humans?" Nyel laughed half-heartedly. He held little hope after the last encounter.

Ivory was silent for a moment. "I'm actually not sure. We've spoken on many occasions, but never about that. We're not close. I'm not even sure if any humans have ever made it that far. I would think the trek would be treacherous. It makes me thankful to have wings, come to think of it."

"I suppose we will find out how he feels when we get there," Nyel sighed.

Ivory huffed. "You still plan to expose who you are?"

"I must. For Iris and for the Ascendant power," Nyel said simply.

Ivory chuckled. "Very well. I had hoped you would agree to it. I was concerned your encounter with Ragnar had put you off of that quest."

Nyel snorted at the thought. "Ragnar is a hateful and maddening creature, but he won't scare me from doing the right thing. At the very least, the other Ascendants deserve to know who I am. We share the same line, after all."

Ivory studied him for a moment. His eyes grew soft, and he said, "I'm sorry for getting cross with you before."

Nyel fell silent, so Ivory continued. "I'm fully aware of how important family is. But you must understand, the power you hold is important to us. All of us. And with this mysterious voice appearing to you, I couldn't bear the thought of you ignoring it."

"I know," Nyel answered. "I will do everything I can for our clan. But please understand that I will be rejoining my friends when this is over, even if it's just for a moment. I have to know they're alright."

Ivory nodded. "Agreed."

Nyel grinned, relieved that they could put the awkward tension to rest. They continued to fly in silence, but now Nyel felt more at ease. The mountains seemed never ending. However, they began to change from rocky terrain to lush forests near the base. A mist floated up from the tall trees and created a dense fog that made their line of sight harder to see through. The group started to slow down without prompting. More cautious than they were before.

It made Nyel nervous. What if the fog was enough to hide the shadow creatures from the sun? And from sight? They'd have to be on constant guard day in and day out if it kept up. He sighed in frustration. They already were on guard from any possessed dragons that might be looking for more bodies. So he kept his eyes moving to watch for any potential threats that might come their way.

The clan journeyed in complete silence, too focused on their senses to create idle conversation. By the end of the day, they traveled miles towards the west. Ivory finally made the call to find a place to rest as the sun set. They found a quiet plateau where they could rest and keep watch from high off the ground.

"Orden and Lunar will take the first watch," Ivory ordered. The group nodded or grunted in agreement.

The two Guardians found a place on either side of their group while the rest of them began to curl up to sleep. Nyel avoided Orden's glare as he passed by. He was still not happy to include Nyel in their clan. Nyel wasn't ready to talk to him, either. He still hadn't recovered from the icy rage that Ragnar presented. He was afraid that if he pushed Orden too much, he might end up in the same predicament as he had with Ragnar. As long as he had Ivory on his side, Orden would behave himself out of respect for his Ascendant.

Lunar was a different matter. They spoke briefly once when they had stopped for a drink of water from a cool stream. Her scales were a light gray that reminded him of the moon, especially in its glow. Her name suited her well. However, her beautiful scales bore the marks of old scars and scorch marks. She had seen battle and from the looks of it; she wasn't one to mess with.

When they spoke, she was very quiet and didn't want to talk much. With her, he didn't sense hatred towards him. Only sadness. Her brilliant blue eyes flickered over at him and then scanned the rest of the group as she looked for a good place to keep watch over them.

"When will we next hunt?" asked Orden from the other side.

Ivory glanced at the setting sun and shook his head. "I don't want anyone hunting at night. We will decide who will go out in the morning." Nyel sensed an opportunity.

"I will," Nyel offered. Perhaps if he helped contribute to the clan, they would warm up to him more. So far, all he had provided them was to escort him around the country. If he wanted to get to know them and, in turn, for them to know him, he needed to make more of an effort.

The others snickered at his comment. Confused, Nyel turned to them and said, "What? You don't think I can hunt?"

"As one of us? Doubtful," snickered Glyder, one of the younger Guardians. "Don't you need a stick or a rock or something?"

Nyel rolled his eyes. "Sure, if you want to put it that way. I grew up using a bow to hunt for food. But I can just as easily hunt as a dragon, too."

"I'd like to see that!" Glyder laughed. "Hey Ivory, if Nyel goes hunting, I'm going too!"

Orden growled from where he sat. "We'll leave here with empty stomachs if he sends you morons to hunt for our food."

"Ah come on, Orden! You can trust me. I'm a skilled hunter!" Glyder smirked. "I want to see this man-dragon in action! Besides, I can easily catch enough meat for everyone all by myself."

"He's not one of us, Glyder. Don't let him fool you," Orden growled in a menacing tone.

Glyder rolled his eyes, unfazed. "Take a breath, Orden, I know. Everything will be fine."

"Very well," Ivory said, stepping in before things got too heated. "Nyel and Glyder will hunt first thing in the morning. Now let's get some rest."

"Yes!" Glyder whooped in excitement. He nudged Nyel's shoulder with his head as he walked by him. "We'll see how great of a hunter you are in the morning then, man-dragon!"

"My name is Nyel, you know," Nyel said with a roll of his eyes. But their encounter left him hopeful again. Maybe he would make more friends amongst the Guardians after all.

As he found a place to lie for the night, he looked up and found Orden glaring at him. Even though the old dragon's intense glare made him uncomfortable, Nyel locked eyes with him. He wouldn't give Orden the satisfaction of scaring him off.

A low growl rumbled under Orden's breath before he finally turned away and studied the surrounding area. Nyel let out the breath he was holding. One thing was certain. No matter what, he couldn't let his guard down. There were too many dragons who'd rather see him as the prey instead of the hunter.

Chapter 22
Imprisonment

Bem

Bem stared at the ground as the stone floor passed beneath him. It had only been a couple of hours in the chair, but it felt so much longer to him. When they finished, the guard placed the magic-repelling collar back on his neck and removed his blindfold. But he didn't budge, too weak to move. His body was exhausted, like he had run miles through a treacherous landscape. Two guards dragged him out of the cage when he couldn't find the strength to stand on his own feet. What did they do to him?

As they approached the stairs, someone burst out in laughter. He recognized the man's voice as the one who had kicked Eryi earlier. "Couldn't handle the work, eh? I guess you're not as tough as you thought you were."

"How about next time, don't weaken him before a contribution? You're wasting your crystals for nothing," growled the guard on his left. It was the one who locked him in the chair. He sounded younger than the others.

"Remember your place, boy, or I'll use it on you next time! That's what he's here for, to recharge our crystals for the good of the kingdom," the man sneered. "Now move along. You received your orders. You know where to take him!"

"Yes sir," the guard grumbled and fell silent as they dragged Bem up the stairs.

They reached the corridor and approached one of the middle wooden doors that Bem had spotted before. The door swung open, and they shoved Bem into another armchair and left him there. He didn't bother to raise his head as they left the room without a word.

The room glowed a soft blue, just like the last one he was in. Maybe they were preparing to take more magic from him already. Bem sat there for a moment in complete silence, trying to regain his composure. *Come on Bem*, he thought. *They left you alone. Get up, now's your chance!*

Slowly, he placed his arms on the armrests and hoisted himself upright. He had to get a hold of himself. Maybe he could find something to help him escape or at least defend himself with. He took a deep breath and lifted his head to look around.

"Hello, love," said an all too familiar voice from across the room.

Bem's blood ran cold. He focused his eyes on a figure that sat behind a large wooden table. There, behind stacks of parchment and books, sat Kollano.

"What are you still doing here?" Bem uttered. He tried to force himself onto his feet, but he wasn't strong enough yet.

Kollano flicked his wrist as if batting away a fly. "Don't feel obliged to stand on my account. I'm sure you've had a rough day."

His smirk made Bem's face flush with anger. He swallowed past the lump in his throat and growled, "What do you want?"

"Are we past the pleasantries already?" Kollano said, resting the scroll he had been reading on the table. "Where have your manners gone, young Bem?"

Bem only glared at him in response. Of course, he wanted to save Carver. He felt it with every fiber of his being. But he wouldn't allow Kollano to toy with him any further. Kollano's smirk vanished as he took in Bem's appearance.

Kollano stood and moved around the table to stand in front of Bem. He bent over to inspect him. His cold, dark eyes burned into Bem like hot daggers as he studied him. After a moment, Kollano let out a sigh of relief and straightened. "Good, they haven't taken your spirit. You're stronger than you appear."

"What do you care what they've taken from me?" Bem countered, balling his hands into fists.

Kollano chuckled. "It infuriates you to not understand me, doesn't it? Don't worry. If you prove yourself to me, I'll let you in on every little secret I have."

Bem stared at him in shock. Did Kollano think he wanted to join him? Help him and his shadow creatures take over everything? He had to know all Bem wanted was Carver. And that certainly would thwart any plans he had. Kollano took one look at Bem's dumbfounded expression and grinned once more.

"Let's just say I'm waiting for someone," Kollano finally offered.

This caught Bem's curiosity. He had to keep him talking. "Who would you be waiting for in a prison?"

"You're smart. I'm sure you can figure it out."

Bem let his head rest against the back of the chair, too exhausted to keep the charade going. He wasn't getting anywhere trying to question him. He needed time to rest and think.

Kollano raised an eyebrow at him. "Do I bore you?"

Bem let out an exasperated laugh. "Trust me, you have my complete attention."

He winced as a pain shot through his body. "What are they doing to the prisoners here? I feel drained."

"Exactly that," Kollano shrugged, sitting against the table. "They drain you of your energy and magic to use for themselves. Haven't you ever wondered how they sell so many crystals throughout the kingdom? They don't grow magic in a field. No, they enjoy harvesting their magic from people like you and I."

Bem's stomach churned at the thought. "They could kill us."

"And they have," Kollano said, his voice suddenly icy cold. "The men and women who were born weak have kept our magic at bay. They've killed countless sorcerers for their own gain. But I'll make them pay for their greed. They don't even know what true power is."

Bem realized he had touched a nerve. Thinking fast, Bem said, "You care about the wellbeing of sorcerers?"

"Most of them are weak too," Kollano answered. "They'd rather hide or serve their pathetic king to save their own skins. Their lack of strength prevents them from reaching the real potential of what a true sorcerer can do. They even lack the strength to protect themselves."

The room seemed to spin around him, but Bem tried to ignore it.

"So it's power you want," Bem said, trying to ignore the dizziness in his head.

Kollano smirked. "You're on the right track. I told you that you were smart."

He approached Bem once more and knelt in front of him. Bem tensed, and he turned away from his deathly gaze.

"One day, you'll see the world the same way I do," Kollano whispered. He grabbed Bem's chin and turned his face back towards his. His skin was as cold as the gleam in his eyes. "And you'll be begging to learn all that I know of our world. To serve me."

Bem's eyes narrowed. "You're wrong. One day, I'll bring Carver back into his own body. And you'll be dead."

Kollano patted Bem's cheek a little too aggressively. "Promises, promises. Keep that spirit, young Bem. You'll need it to survive what I have in store for you."

With that, Kollano stood and placed a glowing palm on Bem's forehead. And everything went black.

Bem woke to a throbbing headache. He groaned and rolled over, only to tumble onto the floor below. He opened his eyes and realized he was back in his small cell. It was quiet. He had no way of knowing what time of the day it was or how long he had been out.

He slowly sat up and noticed a small wooden bowl and a mug that rested inside the door. Bem crawled over to it and examined their contents. The mug held murky water within it and the bowl contained something that resembled porridge. Or so he thought. The smell alone was revolting.

Bem rested his back against the wall and held the bowl in his hands. With a deep breath, he grabbed the spoon and forced the bland, cold food down.

It was terrible, but as Bem washed it down with his mug of water, he knew he had to keep up his strength. He had to find a way out and figure out what he needed to do about Kollano. For whatever reason, Kollano had something in mind for Bem. But what, he didn't know. It was possible he was using him to get to Nyel or Iris. Or maybe his history with Carver was amusing to him. Although the possibilities made his stomach sick, he knew it would at least keep him alive. For the time being.

"You alright kid?" whispered a voice from the cell beside him. It was Eryi.

"I thought you weren't going to talk to me anymore?" Bem whispered back, setting his empty dishes next to the door.

There was a pause. Then she replied, "You're trouble, there's no doubt about it. That's why I must talk to you. There's something else going on with you. So out with it, what's your story?"

"What makes you say that?"

"Where did the guards carry you off to? The only time anyone disappears around here like that is if they're dead or dying," Eryi scoffed.

Bem thought about it for a moment. Would it hurt to tell her the truth? Finally, he settled on, "It's a long story."

Eryi chuckled. "Well, I suppose I can cancel my trip to the market…Do you really think I have anything else to do?"

Bem grinned and shook his head. "You've been here awhile. Do you even know what's been going on out there recently?"

"I've heard rumors of a sickness, yes," she answered.

"It's worse than that," Bem said, staring into the darkness of his cell. "People are being possessed by shadow creatures. And their leader has possessed my friend."

A long moment of silence followed. Bem wondered if she'd believe him. It sounded insane, even to him.

"Why didn't I recognize the signs before? It's Kollano, isn't it?" she asked suddenly.

Bem's jaw dropped, and he turned to face her, even though he couldn't see her. "How did you know? Did you hear his name from the guard or something?"

"No," she said, her voice grave. "No, he's quite the legend where I'm from."

Bem stared at the wall, dumbfounded. How could she know anything about him? He and Falcon had determined that he existed over a century ago. "Where are you from? What legend do you speak of?"

"My people need to know what's going on!" she said, her voice growing louder. "Bem, we need to get out of here."

"Your people? You've been here for years, and now suddenly you're ready to escape? Tell me what you know!" Bem said. He stood and grabbed the bars of his small window. "Eryi, talk to me!"

"Not now," she suddenly whispered. "I have to think. The guards will be making their rounds soon. Don't get into any trouble in the meantime, alright?"

With that, Bem could hear a scuffle as she moved away from him and silence met him once more. Eryi was a puzzle to him. What did she know about Kollano that even the princess and prince didn't know? The mine they had found was ancient. How could anyone know anything about his imprisonment there?

Footsteps echoed down the long hallway outside, so Bem hurried away from the door and laid down on his cot. He stared up at the dark ceiling as guards passed by with torches. He watched the light of their flames flicker across the walls of his cell as they went.

He wasn't going to get anything out of Eryi now; he knew that. All he could do was close his eyes and hope his mind would stop racing so he could get a proper rest.

Bem opened his eyes for what felt like seconds after he fell asleep. At first, he wasn't sure why he woke until he heard whispers in the hallway outside his door. He grit his teeth as he sat up. His body ached in protest at the torture of his magical energy being taken from him. Carefully, he rose out of bed and tiptoed over to the cell door.

He strained his ears to listen, but he heard nothing. Bem wondered if he had dreamt it when a familiar voice spoke.

"Haven't you been here long enough to figure a way out? Don't you use your brain at all?" Eryi hissed in annoyance.

"Of course I have! I've thought about it every godforsaken day since I've been here," said another familiar voice. Bem gasped. It was the man who had hooked him up to the chair to take his magic away from him. Why was Eryi talking to him?

Eryi scoffed. "Hawthorne, I may be old, but I'm not senile! It seems to me you've been enjoying your job entirely too much. Have you forgotten why you're here?"

Hawthorne slammed his fist against her door and growled, "Don't patronize me, Eryi! I hate myself for what I must do to these people. To watch them cave in on themselves with every passing day in that dungeon. It's barbaric! I'll never forgive myself for what I've done to them, even under the circumstances."

A moment of silence allowed Hawthorne's words to sink in. When Eryi spoke again, her tone was softer and more warm. "I apologize, Hawthorne. I know you are here on my granddaughter's request. Your loyalty to her is truly remarkable, and I'll be forever grateful to you for all you've done. But now we must put those long-awaited plans to action. I've learned of a terrible discovery that we must tell the Shielder. We can't wait any longer."

"But I'm supposed to gather more sorcerers before we escape," Hawthorne said, uncertain.

Eryi sighed, her voice sad. "I know, dear boy. And you've done tremendously. But this is of the utmost importance. The fate of all lives, magic and non-magic, are in jeopardy."

Hawthorne sighed in return. "Very well. I'll make the arrangements."

"The boy in the next cell must come with us," Eryi ordered.

"The newcomer? He's only been here a couple of days. Why is he so important? We haven't even looked into him yet," Hawthorne asked in surprise.

"He knows more than you realize. Haven't you wondered why you carted him away after the contribution?," she answered.

"That was him? Do you realize we were ordered to present him to the prince?" Hawthorne gasped.

"The prince?" Eryi asked in astonishment. "Even more reason to bring him along."

Hawthorne moved away from her door enough that Bem could see him. He was young, close to his age. And he looked troubled. Their eyes suddenly met. They were dark brown and his skin was pale. Three jagged scars ran down his left cheek. Bem said nothing, only stared at him. He wasn't sure what was going on, but he realized he might have a way out of The Keep if this guard truly was friends with Eryi. And of course, if Eryi was an ally to him. After all, he didn't really know her either.

Finally, Hawthorne turned his gaze back to Eryi and said, "Very well."

Chapter 23
A Matter of Life or Death

Bem followed close behind Eryi as they trudged down the long corridors. He wanted to talk to her about Hawthorne and their 'plan'. What were they planning? Who were they and how did they know so much about Kollano? A few days had passed since Eryi and Hawthorne's conversation. But he couldn't get a word in before the guards would appear down the corridor or march them along to contribute their magic to the king. The thought of it made Bem sick.

They strode down the corridor in silence towards the dungeon, where they stole their magic once more.

His chest tightened as they passed the door where Kollano had been when Bem was brought to him. Bem wondered where he was now? He shook the thought from his head as they descended the staircase. They followed the same path as before, and Bem waited in line as the guards blindfolded the prisoners one by one.

Bem's eyes flickered up and landed on the face of the guard who would take him to the chair. It didn't surprise him to find that Hawthorne was once again the guard who would take him to the chair. They stared daggers at each other, sizing each other up, wondering if the other could be trusted. Hawthorne scowled and roughly tied the blindfold over Bem's eyes.

Hawthorne grabbed Bem by the shoulder, led him to the chair, and firmly strapped him in place. With the collar in place around his neck, he could hear Hawthorne fumbling with something behind him. A click resounded and the same tingle happened as before. Bem held his breath as his magic trickled out of his body and into the empty crystal.

Another click and the machine stopped, allowing Bem to release his breath. Some more fumbling behind him and another click.

Bem braced himself, but this time, the tingling sensation never came. He sat in confusion as the seconds passed by. Finally, he heard the click again and Hawthorne casually moved crystals around once more, as if nothing had been disturbed. When he started the process again, Bem's curiosity grew. Was he doing this on purpose?

As if in answer to his thoughts, Hawthorne leaned so close to Bem's head that his breath tickled his ear when he hissed, "Would it kill you to act like you're in pain or something?"

Surprised, Bem gave a slight nod and held his breath. He clenched his hands into fists and waited for the sound of the next click. They did this repeatedly. The farther along the process went, the more Bem acted exhausted.

Finally, Hawthorne ripped the blindfold from his face and studied him closely. Bem hung his head, trying to feign sickness from the contribution. He then went to the next chair and studied another man. Bem peeked through his eyelashes and examined the dungeon. It looked like each guard was in charge of three chairs at once. He looked to the right and saw Eryi sitting beside him with her head hung low as well. Her long, white hair covered her face.

"Leif! I've used up all of mine for the day," Hawthorne called. "Take them to their cells."

Bem tucked his chin to his chest. He peeked out of the corner of his eye as a man, maybe in his forties, moved towards them. Hawthorne helped the man, Leif, replace the metal rings with the crystal collars and un-shackle them from their chairs. Leif grabbed Bem's shoulder and pushed him towards the exit, followed by Eryi and the third man, who remained silent.

"Move," Leif ordered.

Bem did as he was told and led the way back towards the stairs. He was careful to keep from going too fast and appear exhausted as he passed the other guards. They didn't give him a second glance as he made his way up the stairs.

They ascended the staircase and made their way down the hallway. Bem noticed the door to where he met with Kollano was open once more. As they passed, he couldn't stop himself from sneaking a peek into the room.

Kollano stood in front of the table talking to a commander. Bem clenched his jaw to contain his anger. He was using Carver's body to gain authority and power, just as he said. The soldiers had orders to capture the prince, but Kollano had convinced them otherwise. The thought made Bem's stomach twist into knots.

As if sensing his inner turmoil, Kollano's eyes flickered towards the doorway and met Bem's for a fraction of a second. Bem's blood ran cold, while Kollano's eyes burned with delight. And then he turned away and resumed his conversation with the soldier.

A chill ran down Bem's spine. He had to get out of there. He couldn't take that look in Kollano's eye. Something about it made him wish he would rather kill him than toy with him. Bem took a deep breath and stared at the floor until he reached his cell door.

Leif opened the door for him and shoved him inside. Bem went without protest. He turned, expecting to have the door slammed in his face, only to find Leif turning his head from the left to the right, searching for something. Bem's brow furrowed in confusion.

Without warning, Leif charged inside the cell at Bem and grabbed him by the throat.

"Hey, what are you doing?!" Bem exclaimed. He didn't wait for a reply. Bem swung his fist at the man's face, but Leif caught it with no trouble.

"Stop it," Leif said in a calm voice. "I'm here to help. Accept it, or I'll leave you here to rot. It doesn't matter to me."

"What are you talking about?" Bem growled. It didn't seem like he was helping.

Leif raised his right hand and showed Bem a small key. "I don't have time to explain, so do me a favor and stop asking ridiculous questions."

He then grabbed Bem's neck and fit the key into the lock. Bem felt a click as the crystal collar was unlocked. He grabbed it and felt the collar loosen in his hands.

"Leave it around your neck, so it seems like it's still on," Leif instructed. "We're leaving tonight."

With that, Leif left his cell and locked the door behind him.

Bem stared at the door in shock as Leif hurried into Eryi's cell next. A moment later he was gone, leading the third prisoner away, who suddenly didn't appear as exhausted as he seemed before. He moved to the barred window of his door and tried to peer out as far as he could.

The corridor was silent once more.

"I can smell the smoke billowing from your ears from here," Eryi chuckled from her cell. "Just trust the process."

He could feel the tingle of the crystal lift from his body as soon as he put some distance between him and the crystal embedded collar. Bem examined it in his hands with a sense of relief. He finally had a way to defend himself. He just wished he had learned more from his friends about how to use his magic properly. In that regard, he was still vulnerable.

"I don't know any of you. How do I know I can trust you?" Bem replied, still holding the collar in his hands.

She chuckled softly once more. "Well, kid, put it this way. What choice do you really have?"

Bem smirked and shook his head. She was right, after all. He moved away from the door and sat on his cot. This could be his only chance out of there. He doubted even Falcon didn't know where he was, let alone the others. If Falcon was...no. He had to believe that he had gotten away from Kollano. He had to escape if he wanted to help the others and save Carver.

With that thought fueling his courage, Bem carefully placed the crystal collar back onto his neck and waited.

Hours passed while Bem lay on his cot and stared up at the dark ceiling. He still didn't know what time of the day it was or how many days had passed since he was imprisoned. It couldn't be longer than a week, he assumed. In quiet moments like this, he wondered where Falcon and the dragons were. Did he escape Kollano's wrath? Bem hoped so. Though Kollano's words still haunted him. Maybe Falcon didn't escape…Bem shook his head at the idea. He had to believe they were out there looking for him. Or, at the very least, returning to Nyel and Iris.

Guilt had been building inside of him for not thinking of his brother when he recklessly chased after Kollano. He should have known that things wouldn't have ended well. And if he was being honest with himself, he was lucky to be alive. Only Kollano's unusual fascination with him saved him from certain death. He shuddered at the thought.

But what purpose did he have keeping Bem close by? Was it Kollano, or was it Carver's mind and feelings that triggered something within the shadow man to keep him alive? Carver had to be in there somewhere, Bem could feel it. He sensed it the day Kollano brought him to his cell; he saw the concern written all over his face.

Whatever the reason, Bem knew one thing with absolute certainty. He couldn't do anything to help Carver locked away in a deep dark, magic draining prison. He had to escape and get rid of Kollano without also killing Carver. Eryi knew something more than she was letting on. Maybe she could set him on the right path to figure out how to be rid of all the shadow creatures.

Or maybe she just needed some extra manpower to fight their way out of this hell.

Bem let out a sigh. He sat up on his cot and stared at the door. He had to try.

The sound of footsteps echoed down the corridor. His spine stiffened as he listened to their approach. It sounded like there were two people this time. The warm glow of orange light cascaded in the corridor, reflecting small shapes on the walls and ceiling. A key slid into his door and creaked as it opened, revealing the tall silhouette of Hawthorne. On his hand was a black gauntlet with three crystals embedded along the top. One crystal emitted the orange glow Bem had noticed approaching them.

"Ready then?" Hawthorne whispered.

Bem took a deep breath and nodded. He stood and fiddled with his collar, ensuring it fit on his neck just enough so it seemed to be intact. Once he stepped outside his cell, his heart raced from the adrenaline that coursed through his veins. Hawthorne joined the second man unlocking Eryi's cell. Bem followed close behind and wasn't surprised when he saw Leif hurrying with a ring of keys.

When the door finally opened, Eryi emerged with a victorious grin on her face. "Let's get out of here!"

"Hold on, ma'am. We still have two others to release," Leif countered. He gestured with his head further down the corridor. Bem had never been that far down. Going further into the dungeon made him more nervous. And from the annoyed expression on her face, Eryi felt the same way.

"We need to go now, before the next round of guards show up," she hissed.

Hawthorne joined her side and draped an arm around her shoulders. "It will be quick, gran. I promise."

Eryi scowled at him. "I told you not to call me that. I'm not an old lady."

Hawthorne smirked but held his tongue.

"Very well, let's be quick about it then!" she growled, suddenly leading the way down the corridor.

Hawthorne hurried after her and placed a hand on her upper arm. "Don't wander off. You'll get yourself killed that way. Let me take the lead."

Bem silently followed them, matching the pace with Leif. They followed the glow of Hawthorne and Leif's crystals down the corridor until it curved to the left and revealed another long corridor. Bem's heart raced when the distant glow of a torch slowly approached them.

"Now what?" Eryi hissed.

Hawthorne only tightened his grip on her and pushed her forward. Leif latched onto Bem's arm and shoved his head down.

"What are you doing down here with those prisoners?" called the guard as he got closer to them. He seemed to be in his thirties or forties, with a smooth bald head and a short dirty-blond beard on his face.

Hawthorne stopped and carefully put himself between Eryi and the guard. "They're depleted. We are taking them to solitary to allow them to regain some of their strength before they're completely useless."

The man studied Bem and Eryi, unconvinced. "The commander told us we didn't need to store them once they were depleted," said the man, studying Bem and Eryi, unconvinced. It's just a waste of time to replenish them. You'd better dispose of them before someone reports you. He doesn't want any unnecessary numbers."

"Of course, sir. We'll dispose of them at once," Hawthorne said, giving the guard a slight bow.

"Hawthorne, right?" the man said after a moment's thought.

Hawthorne kept a straight face, but Bem could hear the slight catch in his throat. "Yes, sir."

"I know you haven't been here long," the guard said, moving closer until he was arm's length from him. The flames of his torch danced in his pale blue eyes as he studied Hawthorne closely. "You're probably still a bit green with the disposal process. The commander doesn't take well to weakness, Hawthorne. Luckily, you have me to look after you. So I'll tell you what, I'll take over from here and you go get yourself a nice warm ale to calm your nerves?"

Bem's heart thudded against his ribcage. The man grabbed Eryi's other arm and began to pull her away, but Hawthorne kept a firm grip on her.

"No, I can manage," he grunted, pulling her back towards him.

With a quick flick of the wrist, the guard shot a blast of magical energy from his own crystal gauntlet that smacked into Hawthorne's chest. Hawthorne flew backwards against the wall and slumped to the floor.

The guard chuckled at Eryi's shocked expression. "That will teach him to back talk me-"

But he wasn't able to finish the sentence. Eryi threw her crystal collar to the floor and shot a bolt of bright yellow magic from her fingertips. The guard yelped in surprise and flew in the opposite direction. His torch spiraled through the air and clanked to the floor.

"I've heard enough out of that fool's mouth," Eryi scowled, wiping her hands on her torn brown dress. Bem and Leif hurried to Hawthorne's side, who was already pulling himself onto his feet.

"Well, that didn't go well," he grunted, rubbing the back of his head.

Eryi scoffed. She hurried to the unconscious guard and pulled the gauntlet off his hand. She rested her hands over the crystals and absorbed what was left of its magical energy. "He won't be needing this. Now, what do we do with him?"

"I have an idea," Leif answered. He grabbed shackles from his belt and fit them around the man's wrists. He looked at Bem and said, "Grab his feet."

Bem did as he was told and together they hauled the guard down the corridor until they reached an empty cell. They tied his ankles together with old scraps of blanket and stuffed a bit in his mouth. Leif locked the door behind them as they left and joined Eryi and Hawthorne once more.

"We need to get out of here. We're wasting too much time," Eryi urged.

Leif shook his head. "I can't leave her behind."

"Who?" Bem asked. He looked over his shoulder, almost expecting more guards to come charging after them at any moment.

"His girlfriend," Hawthorne frowned.

Leif's face went red as he said, "She's not my girlfriend. But I can't leave her here to waste away."

Hawthorne rolled his eyes and started down the corridor once more. "Now we're wasting time talking. Let's move people!"

They hurried after him, Eryi a little more begrudgingly than the rest of them. At another cross in the path, Hawthorne held up his hand to stop them. He checked down both hallways and nodded, satisfied no one was there.

"Leif, go get your girl," he said. "I'll grab Hyram. You two wait here. It won't take long."

With that, the two men split up and hurried down opposite hallways until the glow of their crystals went faint or disappeared entirely. Bem fiddled with the collar on his neck, keeping an eye on each corridor for any signs of someone approaching. He didn't know how the soldiers kept track of the tunnels. They all looked the same to Bem.

"I swear, they better have a decent plan out of here," Eryi sighed with a shake of her head. "For the time they've had to plan, they didn't do a good job of it."

"Why aren't we trying to set more people free?" Bem asked. The guilt of it had been weighing on him ever since he put the plan in motion.

Eryi's eyes shone with tears, but she forced them back. "I know how you feel. I wish we could, but there's not enough strength to get them out of here alive. Most of them have been here for months or years at a time. They don't have a lot of fight left in them to escape. Hawthorne allowed me to regain my strength the past couple of weeks, but if he did that to multiple people, the others would take notice."

"That doesn't mean we shouldn't try," Bem argued.

Eryi sighed. "Let's worry about us escaping with our lives first. Then we will get more reinforcements to come back for the rest. We'll only get them and us killed in the process if we try now."

Bem laughed to himself. "How do you suppose we'll find the numbers for that? They have a stockpile of crystals filled with stolen magic to use against anyone who dares to try."

"You haven't met my people," Eryi grinned. "You don't know what we are capable of."

Bem couldn't help the smirk that formed on his face at the thought of Theo and the other dragons soaring through the skies towards the Keep. "I suppose I don't. As you don't know what my people are capable of either."

She raised an eyebrow. "What's so amusing?"

Bem shook his head. "Trust me, you wouldn't believe me if I told you."

Footsteps echoed down the corridor once more. Eryi and Bem stiffened and pressed themselves to the wall on either side of the hallway. Eryi looked at Bem and whispered, "Take that ridiculous collar off. If it's a guard, it won't save you from the repercussions of being out of your cell without a guard."

Bem nodded in silence and placed the collar on the floor so it wouldn't make a sound. Eryi's hands glowed faintly, so Bem called upon his own magic.

The combined rush of adrenaline and the flow of his magic energy were enough to make him feel giddy. Without the crystal on him, Bem was amazed by how much it had absorbed of himself for days on end. It coursed through his veins and heightened every nerve throughout his body. It made him feel alive. He would never take his magic for granted again.

They readied themselves, raising their hands to unleash their magic on the sorry individual who would wander up to them. When the footsteps were close enough, Bem and Eryi pounced. They rounded the right corner and pointed their glowing palms at the approaching couple.

"Wait, it's me!" Leif yelped in surprise.

They stopped just before the flow of their magic could leave their palms. Bem let out the breath he held while Eryi scowled at Leif.

"Why the hell didn't you announce yourself, you great oaf?" she scolded. "We almost killed you!"

"I didn't think I'd have to!" Leif growled. In his arm, he held a slender brunette woman close to his side.

Bem studied her with a sinking stomach. Now he understood what Eryi meant by the lack of strength the other prisoners had experienced. The woman was skin and bone, with dark circles under her eyes. They had already removed her collar, revealing a red ring around her neck where the metal had chafed her skin. If Leif wasn't holding her up, Bem wondered if she'd be able to stand on her own. She was near death.

"Where's my brother? Where's Hyram?" she asked in a weak voice.

Leif held her close and answered, "Hawthorne is getting him. Then we're getting out of here. I promise."

"What's your name?" Eryi asked, her usually stern voice softened as she gazed upon the poor girl.

When she didn't respond, Leif replied, "Her name is Rae."

Another pair of footsteps hurried down the opposite hallway towards them. Soon, Hawthorne and the man who was in the chair beside Bem earlier that day joined them in the crossway. Panting, the man took one look at Rae and tears formed in his eyes.

"Hyram!" she smiled, her eyes lighting up as soon as she recognized him.

Hyram took two giant steps and pulled Rae into his arms. He was taller than the rest of them with large muscular arms that threatened to snap Rae like a twig. His thick shoulders and torso engulfed his little sister until Bem couldn't see her anymore. They had the same golden-brown hair and hazel eyes.

"This is a touching reunion, but we need to go before we're discovered!" Hawthorne urged, already heading back down the corridor they had come from before. Eryi was hot on his tail.

Hyram nodded and, without asking, lifted his sister into his arms and followed close behind. Bem couldn't help but notice the look of disdain Leif had watching Hyram walk away with Rae in his arms. But as quickly as it came, the look disappeared. Leif and Bem hurried after the others, watching and listening for any signs of guards.

They hurried past the cell where the guard was tied up. It remained quiet. Bem hoped it would stay that way so the guard wouldn't draw any attention towards them. They hurried down the corridor and passed Eryi's cell and then Bem's. Still no sign of any other guards.

Bem felt a pit in his stomach form. Shouldn't there be more guards? What if they suspected them? Finally, they reached the last hallway leading towards the spiral staircase and their freedom. Hawthorne rounded the corner and froze. Everyone skidded to a halt as the small hallway came into view.

Waiting for them halfway down the hallway were approximately twenty guards, all wearing full armor ordained in crystals.

The commander stood in the front of his small battalion with a sly grin on his face. "Well… well… well…we have a couple of traitors in our hands, don't we?"

Hawthorne drew a dagger from his belt and readied his right hand with his own gauntlet of crystals. Then he grunted, "Commander Norris."

Commander Norris cocked his head to examine the rest of their group. "Hawthorne and Leif, is it? I should have known you wouldn't last long here. Or do you know these people? That would make your capture and punishment all the more fulfilling."

"Let us pass. No one has to die this day," Hawthorne demanded, keeping a strong stance. Bem and the others followed suit, readying themselves for a fight. Hyram held his sister tight to his chest, as if frightened she would vanish from his sight otherwise.

Commander Norris smirked once more. "I'm afraid I can't let you do that. Do you think you're the first to disguise themselves amongst my troops? It has never worked. None of you will leave here alive. You sealed your friends' fate the moment you tried to escape this prison. Now you'll watch them die, one by one, before you will ultimately follow them."

Then his eyes landed on Bem. A frown formed on his face. "What possessed you to steal the Prince's prisoner?"

Bem felt many eyes fall on him from both sides of the hallway, but he tried to ignore them. They had to get out of there before Kollano found out about their attempted escape.

"What does the prince want with him?" Hawthorne pressed.

The commander shrugged his shoulders. "Should have asked the prisoner yourself before you let him out of his cell. Can't trust everyone you meet, can you?"

Hawthorne's fist tightened on his dagger. His eyes flickered over to look at Bem, a hint of uncertainty flashed across his face.

In the same moment, Commander Norris raised his hand and three amber colored crystals glowed. A flash of orange lit up the hallway as a ball of fire launched from his palm and soared towards Hawthorne.

Bem leapt in front of him and caught the fireball with glowing hands. He grit his teeth as the flames licked at his skin. He forced his magic to create a barrier between the fire and his palms. His magic flowed freely throughout his body, becoming one with his mind.

With a war cry, Bem flung the fireball back at the commander, with another of his own soaring behind it.

It all happened so fast that the commander didn't have time to react. The fireball crashed into his upper chest and engulfed his face. He screamed in pain as he clawed at his face, falling back onto the floor.

A split second later, both their group and the guards shot magic at each other. Bem and Hawthorne crouched low to the side of the hallway to avoid the first few blasts of fire, gusts of wind, and the stray bolt of lightning that danced through the air.

Eryi leapt back and forth with the energy of a much younger woman, laughing wickedly with joy as she lifted two guards into the air and smashed them against each other. Leif stood guard in front of Hyram and Rae, deflecting any blasts of magic that flew their way.

The guards shot blast after blast of magic at them, some charging forward while others stayed a little behind. Bem realized that even though they had a bountiful storage of sorcerer's magic locked away in their crystals, it didn't mean they knew how to use it or how much of the energy they were wasting.

A few of the guards who fared better with their arsenal of crystals crept closer towards them. Bem knew they couldn't remain sitting there forever. He leapt to his feet and summoned his magic once more. With both his hands, he pushed a ball of energy towards the guards with a powerful gust that sent them hurling back into the others. They fell on top of each other in the chaos.

Hawthorne shot a bolt of lightning at them. They shrieked in pain until their bodies went limp. Leif leapt forward and shot a fire blast at another group of guards. Not knowing how to deflect the magic, the guards tripped over themselves, trying to get away from it.

Eryi stood firmly in the center of the hallway with a wicked gleam in her eyes. "Enough of this. Help me move them!"

Hawthorne and Leif joined her on each side and together they slammed the guards against either side of the hallway. The remaining few still pushing to fight stood on their feet once more, but this didn't deter Eryi. With a deep breath, she pointed her hands at the ground and swung them high into the air in front of her.

Two spouts of fire shot from her hands and created two walls that surrounded the guards, leaving a clear path down the middle towards the exit.

"Let's go!" she shouted.

They followed her path without question. As they dove into the flames, it felt like the heat of the fire would burn every inch of exposed skin. Bem covered his face with his arms as he ran and tried his best to ignore the screams of the guards as they passed.

When they reached the locked door, the crystal embedded door made Bem's limbs tingle once more. Hyram stepped forward and grabbed the handle with the glowing gauntlet. With one swoop, he ripped the crystal embedded door off its hinges and tossed it to the side.

A man in a black cloak stood on the other side, carrying a pile of scrolls. He took one look at the group and screamed in terror. He turned to run up the stairs, but Hawthorne grabbed the back of his cloak and pulled him down. With a quick swipe of his dagger, he silenced the unfortunate man. Once the door was clear, Eryi hurried down the hallway to rejoin them.

Without another word, the group ran up the spiral staircase until they reached the main floor of the tower. Thankfully, no one was there waiting for them.

Bem hurried towards a window and looked outside. It was dark. Heavy rain pelted the glass windows and distant thunder rumbled overhead.

"The storm should help cover us," Hawthorne noted as he joined Bem at the window.

Bem nodded. He turned to address the rest of the group. "We still have to be wary of shadow creatures."

Hyram looked at him in bewilderment. "You mean the stories of the sickness are true?"

"Unfortunately, yes," Bem frowned as he turned to him. "If you come across one, don't let it get too close. Use light or fire to be rid of it. Otherwise, it will take over your body."

"Why do they need to possess someone?" Hyram asked in confusion.

"They're lost souls searching for their body," Eryi intervened.

Bem was the one who was surprised this time. "Lost souls?"

Hawthorne scowled and pointed at a lit lantern approaching the doors outside. "We don't have time to discuss this. We're not out of danger yet!"

"Right, where do we go from here?" Bem asked, focusing on the matter at hand.

"We have enough manpower to blast the gates wide open," Hawthorne said.

Eryi shook her head in disapproval. "That may be true, but will we have the strength to escape afterwards?"

"I know where they keep their horses," Leif cut in. He hurried towards the back of the room and pointed down another hallway. Only this one had windows in it instead of cells. "They made me muck the stalls for weeks when I started. We'll have more of a chance on horseback!"

"Then let's be on our way!" Hawthorne urged. He followed Leif down the hallway with determination. Bem glanced back at the figure with the lantern. To his relief, the man turned and walked another way. Maybe he was doing regular patrols of the grounds? Bem hoped that was the case.

Bem hurried after the others and raced down the hall towards what Bem could only assume were the stables. Leif halted at the end of the hall and held up his hand, stopping the others. Ahead of them to their right was a lit double doorway, where a group of angry voices echoed from within.

They glanced at each other, unsure of what to do. Until Bem heard a voice that was all too familiar. The possessed Carver's voice that he hated was becoming so ingrained into his head.

"Why did the king not come here personally?" Kollano shouted, his usual cool tone abandoned. Bem didn't know which was more frightening.

The first man stammered over his words. "The king is not permitted to travel with his company."

"Does he not have enough soldiers to accompany him?" Kollano growled.

A second man spoke up, his voice more stern and unfeeling. "Sir, with all due respect, he doesn't trust you. You followed the traitorous princess into dragon territory against the king's orders. You abandoned your king and your people! Why would he choose to risk his life to appease your feelings? Why not turn yourself in to him if you want to redeem yourself?"

Something smashed against the wall, causing a few of their group to flinch in surprise. The fire that lit the room burned brighter as Kollano shouted, "It's not my feelings I'm concerned about! He's wasting precious time. I've brought him a gift to prove my loyalty to him and mend that broken trust. I've provided him leverage to bring the princess and her pet dragon straight to his doorstep!"

Bem gasped and immediately covered his mouth. Leif glared at him and mouthed, "Quiet!"

The room was still for a moment. Until finally, Kollano asked angrily, "What does he command then?"

The first man let out a sigh of relief. "He's instructed us to accompany you back to the capital. In chains, of course. Just until you've proved your worthiness for his forgiveness. You can bring your prisoner along as well. Look at the scroll I've brought. I have it all here in writing."

Bem's heart sank. So that's why he kept him alive. But why was Kollano so determined to gain the king's praise? It didn't make sense. The scroll of parchment crinkled as the man unrolled it for Kollano to examine for himself.

Hawthorne held his breath and peeked around the corner. Keeping his eyes fixated on the room, he waved his hand to the others, signaling for them to go. Leif and Hyram hurried past the doorway with Rae pressing her hands to her mouth. Eryi went next, glancing over her shoulder at Hawthorne with worry. They rounded the corner to keep out of sight and, hopefully, out to the stables, gathering some horses.

Bem gathered his courage, bouncing in place. He moved forward, keeping his footsteps light, when suddenly, Hawthorne's arm shot out in front of him. The force of his arm nearly knocked the wind out of his chest. Bem's boot barely hit the light spilling from the doorway before Hawthorne wrapped both arms around him to keep him steady and dragged him backwards towards a pillar in the hallway.

Just as they retreated into the shadows, Kollano stormed out of the room towards them with the two Kingsmen in tow. Each of them wore traveling cloaks with the king's insignia etched in the back. Hawthorne and Bem moved as one around the pillar as they passed, holding their breath.

"Sir, it would be wise to follow the king's order as instructed," the first man protested, hurrying after him.

Kollano turned on his heel and grabbed the man by the throat. "How dare you speak to me like that! Do you really think *you* have authority over *me*?"

"Sir!" the second man gasped. He hurried towards them with an outstretched hand. However, he had second thoughts and kept his distance from the shadow prince.

"My prince…I didn't mean-" the first man struggled, clutching Kollano's wrist with both hands, trying to pry him off.

Kollano only grew angrier. He lifted the man into the air with one arm and said, "Neither him nor you can command me. I came back on my own terms and he will welcome me with open arms. I will not play prisoner to my own blood! I refuse to let them cast me aside and forget about me! I want what is rightfully mine!"

The man clawed at Kollano's hand, unable to speak. But it was no use. Without a second thought, Kollano squeezed the man's throat with a glowing hand until a sickening snap filled the air and the man went still.

Kollano tossed the man's limp body to the floor and glared at the second man. The man trembled with fear as he struggled to find words. Bem watched as black veins crept around his dark eyes, the only real sign he had ever lost his cool demeanor. It lasted only for a second, but the second man didn't seem to notice.

"Do you understand me, filth?" Kollano sneered, his cold eyes alight with rage.

"Ye-ye-yes, sir," the man breathed, shaking violently.

Kollano reached towards him.

"P-p-please, sir. I understand fully. Have mercy on me!" the man squeaked, fumbling backwards.

This time, Kollano only patted the man's cheek rather forcefully with his hand. "Good. Then we shall prepare for departure. Don't disappoint me again…Off you go."

The man didn't need any other coaxing. He scuttled back to the room, nearly tripping over his own feet, and closed the door firmly behind him. As the doors latched into place, it left the hallway dark except for a few lit torches and the occasional flash of lightning in the night sky.

Kollano stood in place for a moment longer, staring at the room where the man had disappeared. And also towards the pillar where Bem and Hawthorne hid.

Bem clamped his mouth shut, just as Rae had moments before. He didn't realize he was shaking until Hawthorne grabbed his shoulders to calm him. They dared not peek around the corner as Kollano seemed to study the area from his spot. Bem squeezed his eyes shut. *Please walk away. Please walk away. Don't find us!*

What felt like an eternity later, quiet footsteps moved down the hallway, back towards the spiral staircase where they had escaped.

Once Kollano descended the stairs and out of view, Hawthorne dragged Bem down the opposite end of the hallway as fast as he could.

"It won't be long before he finds the dead guards," Hawthorne panted as he ran. It was the first time Bem saw true fear in his eyes. At least he wasn't the only one who was frightened of Kollano.

They followed a passage that led to a rather large stable filled with horses. Some with the saddles on them, and some without. Any other time, Bem would have found it disgusting that anyone would leave the gear on their horses. This time, however, he was thankful the soldiers were careless. Leif and Hyram had already pulled the horses with gear on them out into the open. They found three for themselves. Hyram lifted Rae into one and offered the reins to Leif.

"It would be better for me to have my own horse. Guard her with your life," Hyram instructed in a serious tone.

Leif took the reins and nodded. Eryi and Hyram climbed onto their own horses while Hawthorne grabbed another from its stall. Leif looked around and his face fell.

"There are no others with their tack on. Can you put the gear on quickly?" he asked Bem.

Bem spotted a mare that reminded him of Mystic, Fridolf's old war horse. He pet her muzzle and said, "No need. Let's just get out of here. We don't have much time."

With that, he pulled himself onto the mare's back and grabbed tufts of her long mane. Bem grinned to himself as Leif got onto his horse behind Rae. If he could ride a dragon without a saddle, he could ride a horse without one.

"Hyram, if Leif and I use what's left of our crystals, do you think we can blast our way through that gate?" Hawthorne asked.

Hyram nodded.

Hawthorne charged forward with his horse. "Alright then, let's-"

Ding!

The toll of a large bell high above them in the tower struck, sending vibrations through the stone.

Ding!

"They know!" Eryi shouted.

"Hurry!" Hawthorne yelled.

Ding!

They stormed out of the stables into the stormy night. Hawthorne led the way, closely followed by Hyram and Leif. Mud flew into the air as their horses' hooves galloped through the wet grounds. The group circled around the tower towards the lone gate in the stone walls. Above them on the wall's edge, guards ran and readied their bows to attack. Bem wished he had his own bow. Instead, he'd have to rely on his magic, something he wasn't as familiar with as he'd like to be.

Ahead of them, a group of soldiers spilled out of the tower and charged towards them. Bem took a deep breath and called upon his magic. It flowed through his body even more naturally than it ever had before. He wondered if the crystal collar blocking his usage of his magic made the connection stronger. He summoned a ball of fire to his hand and flung it at the closest guard on the wall, catching him by surprise.

Eryi joined him, shooting lightning and fire at the guards one by one. Hyram, Leif, and Hawthorn defended themselves against the footsoldiers, who thankfully didn't have their magic crystals equipped. Their armor was clean and the king's insignia was sharp on their chests. Bem wondered if these soldiers had come from the capitol to escort the prince back to the king?

"Hyram, get the gate!" Hawthorne shouted. He then sent a guard flying backwards against the tower.

Hyram kicked his horse's sides and hurried towards the gate. Bem and Eryi followed him, keeping the guards on top of the walls off of him. When Hyram got close enough to the gate, he threw his hands outwards and sent a blast of magic towards the gate. But nothing happened.

As Bem got closer, he felt a shudder race down his body. He looked up at the gates and gasped. Embedded in every other bar were the same crystals that repelled their magic. Bem brought his horse back around until he felt like he could call upon his magic once more.

"Eryi, stay away from the gate!" he called.

She nodded, her face ashen as she shot down another man from the wall. Behind them, they could hear more soldiers pouring out of the tower. They were going to be outnumbered sooner than later.

Hyram glanced back at the tower and then back to the gate. Bem spotted what he was looking at the same moment. A wheel that would open the gate manually. Hyram leapt off of his horse and ran towards the wheel.

He grabbed hold of the wheel and pulled with all his strength. The gate creaked as it slowly rose off the ground. The remaining guards on the walls rushed towards the gate and aimed their arrows at Hyram. Bem and Eryi kept their distance from the gate and shot balls of fire at them, knocking them down.

A pair of soldiers emerged from an opening near to where the wheel of the gates rested. Without a second thought, Bem urged his horse forward. The familiar tingle crept through his body as he approached the gate once more. The strength of it made his limbs feel numb. He leapt from the horse's back and tackled the first man to the ground, knocking him out cold.

Bem grabbed the man's sword from his hand and spun around just in time to block the second soldier's sword that was aimed at Hyram's neck.

Hyram faltered and looked over his shoulder in shock.

"Keep going! I'll hold them off. Open the gate!" Bem yelled as his adrenaline took over. He shoved the soldier backwards and swung the sword at the man's face.

The soldier clenched his teeth and ducked out of the way. He then turned direction and rammed his head into Bem's stomach. Bem gasped as he toppled over onto the ground with the man on top of him. The soldier raised his sword to deliver it into Bem's chest.

Bem twisted underneath him and brought up his knee into the man's groin. The soldier grunted and rolled off of Bem, giving him the chance to get on his feet. Bem sent a kick into the man's chest and knocked him down onto his back. He swooped down and grabbed the man's sword, and pointed it at his throat.

"Spare me!" the soldier pleaded, lifting his hands to block his face.

Bem hesitated. The soldier wouldn't have spared his life if it was the other way around. His decision didn't take much thought. He growled, "Get out of here, before I change my mind."

The soldier scrambled backwards through the mud to get away from Bem. He then stumbled to his feet and ran back towards the tower. At the same moment, Hawthorne, Eryi, and Leif charged past him on horseback to join Bem and Hyram. They left a bunch of soldiers slumped on the ground behind them.

Bem's heart raced. They were winning. He turned his eyes back towards the man he allowed to flee and froze. Instead of running for safety, the soldier hung suspended in the air with a look of terror in his eyes. His body spasmed and his mouth gaped open as if to scream, but no sound came out. Standing below him with an outstretched arm was Kollano. However, his icy gaze didn't rest on the man he tortured in the air. Instead, he locked his eyes on Bem.

The blood drained from Bem's face. Fear gripped his belly like an iron claw. Bem instinctively took a step back and bumped into his horse.

"The gate won't open any further! You must go now!" Hyram shouted to the group.

Bem looked back and saw the gate was open just enough for them to get through with their horses.

"There should be a lock on that thing," Leif argued.

Hyram shook his head. "It's damaged."

Hawthorne gaped at Hyram. "We can't leave you behind!"

"You must!" Hyram urged. "If I let go, the gate will shut. Then this will all be for nothing."

"There has to be another way," Rae pleaded. Her eyes were wild with fear as she stared at her brother.

Hyram met her desperate gaze with a sad smile.

"There's no time, big sister. Let me save you this time." Then he turned to Leif and his expression changed, more serious. "Protect her with your life."

Leif stared at him and nodded. "I will."

Behind them, they could hear more soldiers racing towards them. Bem looked back and saw the guard drop from the air and lay motionless on the ground. Kollano began to move towards them, his eyes still locked on Bem.

"GO!" Hyram shouted, a mixture of fury and desperation in his voice.

Leif was the first to go. He urged his horse through the gate as Rae screamed, "No! Hyram, please! Don't leave him!"

Eryi hurried after them. Hawthorne gave Hyram one last agonized look and followed with a cry of anger. Bem climbed onto his horse and started towards the gate.

"I'll hold them off as long as I can," Hyram shouted. He released the wheel as soon as Bem cleared the gate. The metal door landed on the ground with a hard thud, separating them forever. His body pulsated by the sheer amount of crystals layering the door, leaving him sick to his stomach.

Bem couldn't bring himself to leave The Keep's entryway. He waited for a moment, looking back at Hyram as he, in turn, looked back at Bem.

"Help our people. This nightmare must end," Hyram said.

Bem didn't fully understand what he meant by that, but he nodded. "I will."

With that, Hyram ran from the gate towards the oncoming soldiers. He ran far enough away from the crystals until his hands glowed. With a battle cry, he called upon his magic. He raised his head towards the heavens as his entire body glowed. The oncoming soldiers faltered and stared at Hyram in disbelief. Bem caught the eyes of Kollano, this time filled with rage.

Bem turned and kicked at his horse's sides and raced after the others. As The Keep fell behind him, a boom filled the air. They halted for a moment and looked back in astonishment and horror. A massive ball of fire and light filled the area where they had just escaped, leaving the soldiers running around in terror as the fire engulfed them.

Bem's heart sank as he realized the sacrifice Hyram had made for them. Rae wept while the others bowed their heads. Now he understood what Falcon had been trying to teach him since day one. Always have control of your magic and know your limits. Now he understood how fatal calling upon one's magic could truly be.

Chapter 24
Something Wicked

Nyel

Nyel woke to a nudge against his shoulder. Startled, he rolled to his feet in a daze, ready for a fight.

"Shh! Don't wake the others," hissed Glyder, who stood behind him. "It's time to go hunting."

Nyel let out a sigh of relief. He stretched his sore muscles. Whether it was the constant flying or from sleeping on the cold hard ground, he wasn't sure. But he wasn't going to complain about it. He needed to get used to the ways of being a dragon.

He studied the surrounding area as he allowed himself to wake up. It didn't seem that he had slept very long. But the sky had already produced a warm glow in anticipation of the rising sun. Nyel looked around at the rest of the sleeping dragons. Orden and Lunar had swapped places with two other Guardians, Meinrad and Niko, who ignored them as they crept through the hoard of slumbering dragons. Meinrad glared at Nyel, just as Orden had. He was the closest companion of the old, bitter dragon. Nyel made a mental note to keep an eye on him as well.

Nyel was extra careful not to step on any stray tails. That would earn him a bite in the leg for sure. Once they carefully made their way past their sleeping companions, Glyder silently leapt from the plateau and glided towards a nearby forest. Once he landed, he trotted to the treeline and stopped to wait for Nyel to catch up.

"If you want me to do the hunting, it may be quicker," Glyder whispered with a mischievous gleam in his eye. "I'll even tell the others you caught a few so you won't look bad."

Nyel rolled his eyes at the young dragon. "You really don't think I can hunt, do you?"

Glyder shrugged. "Maybe you can as a human. But I doubt you're any good as a dragon. It's not natural."

Nyel growled at him softly. "Be ready to be surprised, lizard-brain."

Glyder chuckled. "Is that a threat? You're definitely as hardheaded as a dragon, I'll give you that much. Very well, let's split up. I'll go left and you go right. We'll see who catches the most prey."

Nyel nodded, resisting the urge to roll his eyes again. It was true he would perform better if he had his father's bow and arrow. But he had grown more in tune with his dragon side and he had hunted with tooth and claw before. All he had to do was let go of his human side and trust the animal instincts that the dragon in him provided. It couldn't be that hard. At least, he hoped.

They split ways and flew into the air once more. If the trees had been more spread apart, Nyel would have gone into them immediately. But the forest was dense and his scaly sides would've scraped against the bark of the trees. It wouldn't have done him any good to go that route. The noise would alert the entire forest if he did. His sharp eyes scanned the forest below, looking for a clearing or an easy target.

He glanced up after he circled around the canopy of trees and caught sight of Glyder diving into the wooded area below him. Nyel cursed under his breath. He must have found something already. Nyel doubled his efforts and focused on the forest below in search of anything tasty.

Off to his right he heard the patter of hooves against the ground. Nyel swung his head over to the side and scanned the area. A dash of tan fur whisked through the trees below. Finally!

Adrenaline racing through his veins, Nyel changed his course and followed the animal from high above. He didn't dive in right away. Instead, he remained patient, hoping for the right moment to strike. As he glided over the canopy, an opening in the trees revealed two deer dashing through the woods. He cursed under his breath. They must have heard him, or even caught his scent.

Nyel took a deep breath and allowed his instinct to drive his attack. He dove into the woods and grabbed the first doe's neck with his teeth. It went still in an instant. With a quick swing of his tail, he knocked the other doe down and also finished it with his powerful jaws. He let out a shaky breath when all went silent. Unsettled by the fact that the taste didn't repulse him, he licked the blood from his teeth. He sighed. Hunting with a bow and arrow would be much easier, he thought.

He grabbed his game and flew into the air once more. His body teetered in the air as he struggled to balance the additional weight. He returned to the group to find a few Guardians had awakened and were already waiting for breakfast.

A few of them stared at him in shock as he dropped the two deer on the ground beside them.

Trunic rose to his feet and approached the deer. He sniffed it and looked up at him in amazement. "You got these by yourself?"

"I did," Nyel replied, again resisting the urge to roll his eyes.

Then, to his own surprise, Trunic laughed in amusement. "You returned before Glyder did. And with twice the amount!"

Orden huffed from a distance. "The human probably stole it from him. Wouldn't be the first time."

"What? You're back already?!" came Glyder's voice from above. Nyel hopped to the side as the young dragon dropped a fox beside his deer. Then his eyes grew wide. "How did you manage to get *two* deer?!"

"Glyder, don't be so surprised," Nyel said with a smirk and a shrug. "I told you I could hunt as well as you could, if not better."

Glyder's boisterous laugh echoed around them. "I must admit Nyel, I'm impressed! Come on, the hunt is not over yet. I'll still win this hunting war!"

Nyel chuckled and followed Glyder back to the forest. They spent the next hour hunting for more food for the rest of the group, sometimes grabbing deer, and others grabbing smaller prey such as rabbits, foxes, and a wild pig. Nyel had to admit, hunting with heightened senses of sight, hearing, and smell made stalking his prey a lot easier than if he were tracking them on foot.

As he pounced on his last catch, a young buck with small antlers, a strange scent, caught his nose. Nyel lifted his head and sniffed the area once more. To his right, he spotted a felled tree with four large gashes in it. He crept closer and sniffed the tree, finding it strange the scent came from there. On closer examination, he spotted a strange black goo in the gash marks.

Puzzled, he leaned closer and sniffed it once more. To his astonishment, the goo wiggled in response. Nyel pulled his snout back at once in confusion. Was it alive? What could have caused those gashes? Was the tree down already or did whatever strike it break it? So many questions ran through his head that he didn't realize Glyder had called to him overhead until he repeated himself.

"Come on Nyel, it's time to go back!"

With one last glance at the strange substance, Nyel picked up his meal with his teeth and soared into the air, still uncertain of what he had just witnessed.

Nyel rejoined Glyder, and soon the strange finding left his mind. They landed beside the Guardians once more, laughing and joking about each other's catches of the morning. Nyel offered his deer to the others, settling for a few of the smaller prey.

"Well, who won?" Trunic asked, licking the bones clean of one of the deer Nyel had captured.

Glyder and Nyel glanced at each other. With a sigh of defeat, Glyder said, "I caught more technically, but he grabbed the bigger game. So I think that makes him the winner."

"But you just said it yourself! You caught more than me, so you won!" Nyel argued, giving him a playful shove.

Glyder shook his head, spun around, and locked horns with him in a playful joust. "I said you won, Shifter. Just take the win!"

"Enough! You make me sick watching you associate with the human," Orden growled.

Glyder turned away from Nyel and laughed. "You should give him a chance, Orden. He's not as bad as you think."

Before Orden could speak, Ivory stepped in and said, "You two better eat. We're going to leave soon after. Orden, I need to speak with you."

With that, Ivory walked away with the irritated Orden following close behind him. His share of the food lay untouched, which didn't surprise Nyel. He watched them go and sighed. "I don't think I'll ever be able to have a normal conversation with him."

Glyder shrugged. "To be honest, neither have I. He's always had a bad temper. I just stay away from him when I can. I suggest you do the same."

They ate their meal in silence, a few rabbits to hold them over until they could properly hunt for themselves. Nyel tried not to think about it too much as he ate. It was too disturbing to think about eating raw meat if he dwelled on it too long. But the truth of it was, he was a dragon. And whether his human side liked it or not, the meal didn't bother him at all. He was only glad that Iris wasn't there to see him consume his meal in such a way. Or any of his other friends, for that matter.

After they finished their small meal, they joined the rest of the Guardians who were talking amongst themselves. They went silent when Nyel drew closer. However, to his surprise, Glyder didn't rejoin his own friends, but stayed beside Nyel.

Ivory stood in front of his clan and said, "We should reach the Asya clan before sundown. If we encounter any trouble, we will separate into two groups. The dragons to the right of me will follow Orden, and the rest of you will follow me. Understood?"

Nyel winced. He and three others were in Orden's group. He wondered why Ivory didn't include him in his. But he nodded his understanding instead of bringing attention to himself. He wouldn't get anywhere with the rest of his companions if he didn't work with them. At least Glyder was in his group, too.

"Alright then. To the sky!" Ivory roared.

Nyel roared with his clan and leapt into the sky. The morning wind was cool and refreshing against his scaly face. He closed his eyes and took in a deep breath of the fresh air. It felt oddly peaceful soaring through the air with other dragons. They were the masters of the sky. Everything below them felt small compared to their place amongst the clouds. It made Nyel feel free in some regard.

Throughout his days of living as a dragon, he realized his wings had grown stronger. Nyel was also more confident with his ability to maneuver his muscular body as well. He was pleased to be able to keep up with the rest of the clan with ease. One day, he would have to thank Vail and Scarlett, Theo's young siblings, for their flying lessons.

He glanced out of the corner of his eye to find Glyder watching him curiously. Nyel turned to him and asked, "Something on your mind?"

Glyder blinked, perhaps startled he had been caught staring. But he quickly recovered and said, "I was just wondering what it is you do for fun? As a human, I mean."

"Oh," Nyel chuckled, surprised by the question. "Well, for fun, I liked to explore the woods and mountains near my home. I like to hunt, read, and spend time with my family. My stepmother used to insist that we go out in the meadow on a warm day and have a picnic as a family. I used to find it embarrassing. What I wouldn't give to be together again now."

Glyder pondered over his words. "I don't know what a picnic is, but it sounds like you miss your family terribly."

Nyel nodded. "I do."

"It must be awful not being able to fly," Glyder stated after a moment of silence.

Nyel laughed, glad he could lighten the mood with his random thoughts. "At first, I would have disagreed with you. I was terrified of flying when I first started. But now…I'd miss it if I couldn't."

Glyder was silent for a moment, lost in thought. Then suddenly he burst out, "What is 'read'?"

Nyel gaped at him for a moment until he realized dragons don't typically store books or scrolls in their caves. "Oh. Well, one way we communicate with each other is to write our words on parchment. They can be on anything like a scroll of instructions, a book of stories, or a map of locations. It's a way we store our history and keep a record of legends for the next generation. Does that make sense?"

Glyder's eyes grew large. "Fascinating! We only tell our stories by word of mouth. That must be nice to be able to know the exact thoughts of your ancestors."

"I wish they all kept a history of their lives, but sadly that's not the case," Nyel sighed. "I only really know about my father and his father before him. I don't know much about my mother's family. She died when I was a baby."

"I am sorry for your loss," Glyder said at once.

Nyel met his earnest gaze and knew his words were genuine.

"Thank you, but it was a long time ago. I didn't even know her," Nyel replied.

Glyder shook his head. "A loss you feel every day, nonetheless. Never let go of her memory. Speak of her when you can. Keep her in your mind and in your heart, and she will never be truly lost."

Nyel grinned at the young dragon. He was wise beyond his years. Or perhaps he was older than Nyel realized. It didn't matter, though. Glyder was right. "Thank you, Glyder."

The dragon nodded and gave him a wink with his large eye. They flew in silence for another moment as they soared through the mountains. Then Nyel asked, "What do you do for fun?"

Glyder chuckled. "Explore, hunt, tell stories…"

Nyel laughed.

"I also like to train for battle with my brother," Glyder continued. His face turned more serious and his mood shifted. "In case a clan or rogues ever attack us. Or dragon slayers."

Nyel frowned. "Your brother isn't with us? Wouldn't he be a Guardian of the clan, too?"

Glyder shook his head. "No. Sumner isn't a part of our clan, or any clan. I have to go to him if I want to see him."

"I see," Nyel said. "Why is he not part of a clan?"

Glyder shrugged. "He's not one to put his trust in others. I think he barely even trusts me these days. We used to be close. We looked after one another when we were younglings, but now…"

"I'm sorry," Nyel said in a quiet voice. He didn't know what he'd do without his brother's presence in his life. "Tell you what, while our brothers are away, we will look after each other. How does that sound?"

Glyder's eyes widened, and he turned away in embarrassment. "I'm not looking for your pity!"

Nyel snorted. "I'm not pitying you! I'm being serious."

Glyder's eyes drifted back to him and stared him down. When he searched Nyel's eyes and found he was telling the truth, he smirked. "Very well then, I accept. But that doesn't mean I'll go easy on you next time we hunt together!"

Nyel grinned. "You better not!"

They continued to chat throughout their journey as the landscape passed by below them. The more they talked, the more relaxed Nyel felt around him. They shared funny stories with each other and burst out in laughter. A few of Glyder's friends ahead of them looked back in curiosity, perhaps wondering what their friend found so amusing talking to the Shifter. A few times Ivory shushed them to not draw attention to the group, but Nyel saw the amusement in his eye. He was pleased to see another member of the clan getting to know Nyel.

Their group passed through the Dragon Mountains on a gentle breeze. The weather was warming up, and the skies were clear and blue. Nyel breathed in the crisp, fresh air and sighed. It was something he could get used to if the world wasn't trying to fall apart at the seams.

A sudden shriek from far below yanked him from his thoughts and turned his blood cold. The group of Guardians hissed and growled in alarm. They slowed their pace to search for the cause of the sound.

"What was that?" Glyder gasped.

"It wasn't an animal..." commented one of his friends, a young female with yellow-green scales named Ines.

Orden was already flying into action. "We need to check this out! My group, we fly first. Ivory, bring your group if we need more muscle. Otherwise keep watch."

Without another word, Orden dove towards the sound with his followers. Nyel and Glyder glanced at each other nervously before following them. They dove into a ravine where the forest seemed to dwindle without the light it needed to grow. Nyel's body tensed at the thought of what could be lurking in there. Before he could let out a warning, the dragons ahead of him gasped in horror.

"There's a dragon down there. He's hurt!" called Niko.

Orden growled. "I see him. There's someone with him, too."

Nyel spotted them at last. A dragon with ruby scales laid sprawled on the ground. He was frantically trying to get up, but couldn't find the strength. He fixed his eyes on his companion, who shot blasts of fire further into the ravine.

Their group landed all around the injured dragon and crept towards the other. Nyel hurried to the injured one's side and tried to comfort him. "It's ok, we're here to help."

"Yawna..." he croaked, his eyes still fixed on his friend.

"Nyel, look!" Glyder gasped in horror.

Nyel's eyes moved from the dragon's face down to his left side and gasped. There were bloody gashes all over the dragon's ribs and neck. But what startled him most of all was the thick, black sludge-like substance that oozed and bubbled from his wounds. His eyes went wide when he recognized the substance. It looked eerily similar to the fallen tree with the gashes in it.

Glyder lowered his head to sniff the black substance, but Nyel shoved him away with his head. "Don't touch it! We don't know what it is."

"We have to do something!" Glyder argued, his eyes wild with anger and fear.

Nyel's mind raced, trying to figure out what they could do to help him. "What's your name?"

The dragon's eyes went wide. His slit pupils dilated until they were nearly round. The whites of his eyes seemed to vanish entirely. All he could muster to say was, "Yawna!"

In the same moment, a loud, monstrous roar erupted from the ravine beyond them. A female dragon, who Nyel assumed must be Yawna, hurried backwards as her stream of fire breath dwindled to smoke. Orden and the others hurried to her side at once, ready to face her attacker. And they didn't have to wait long.

From the shadows of the ravine, a huge burly figure barreled towards them. Small trees buckled under the creature's mass, their trunks echoed as they snapped in two. As it grew closer, the group gasped as one.

"It's a bear!" called Meinrad.

Nyel stared at the creature in shock. It was true the creature's body was bear-like in appearance, but it was twice the size of any bear Nyel had seen in his life. The same black sludge-like substance had matted its brown fur. Where its eyes should have been were only two hollow sockets that glared hauntingly at them. Black sludge dripped from its large yellow teeth and sputtered from its mouth when it roared.

"Don't let it escape!" Orden growled at the others. As one, the Guardians rushed forward to strike.

Yawna panted as they galloped past her. Her eyes were wide in terror as she screamed, "Don't get too close! Don't let the slime touch you!"

But the Guardians continued on, ready to meet the monster head on. Nyel snorted in annoyance and leapt into the air. He pushed his wings as hard as he could to catch up with them. Just before the Guardians and the creature could clash, Nyel let loose a stream of fire between them. The bear let out a high-pitched shriek once more and slid to a halt.

"Don't interfere, half-breed!" Orden roared in anger, but Nyel ignored him. He swooped around and let a second stream of fire ignite the land between them and the bear. The bear rose on its hind-legs to its full height and flung a massive paw at Nyel as he passed. Nyel closed his wings and rolled his body to the right to avoid the bear before opening his wings again to catch himself.

He then landed next to the small group of Guardians and watched the bear, who paced back and forth across from the fire. The light of the flames flickered in its hollowed eye sockets as it glared at Nyel.

Orden charged over to Nyel and bared his teeth. "I should kill you for disobeying my orders!"

"If I had let you all attack that thing with brute force, you could have gotten yourselves killed. Or worse…" Nyel growled, thinking of the dragon that lay behind them.

"I'm tired of you meddling into our lives and thinking yourself higher and mightier than all of us," Orden roared, his face just inches from Nyel's. "Perhaps I'll throw you to the bear and find out if your prediction is true?"

Nyel growled. "This isn't the time to argue! That's fine if you don't like me or accept me, but don't endanger the lives of our clan just to prove a point!"

"This isn't your clan!" Orden roared and swung his claws at Nyel's face. His claws connected with Nyel's right cheek and his head swung to the side in a daze. Orden growled and threw his head against Nyel's shoulder.

Nyel's upper body flew backwards into the air and plopped on the ground, knocking the wind out of him. He gasped for breath. He struggled to get back up when he spotted Orden coming after him once more.

A flash of blue scales flew over him and knocked into Orden. Orden stumbled back in surprise, only to growl with fury at his attacker. Glyder stood between Orden and Nyel. He lowered his head and let out a ferocious growl.

"That's enough, Orden!" Glyder growled as the older dragon stared him down. "This isn't the time or place for this."

Breathing heavily, Nyel got to his feet and stared at the two of them. He couldn't let Glyder fight his battle for him. He didn't want to get between them. Orden stepped forward, now ready to fight Glyder.

A shriek broke the trance they were all in. As the group turned their heads to face the noise, the bear launched itself through the fire and landed on top of Orden. The old dragon yelped as he collapsed under the bear's weight. The Guardians shouted in terror, wanting to help, but not wanting to touch the creature.

Nyel cursed under his breath. There was only one thing he could do.

"Ready your fire!" he shouted at the others. He then charged past Glyder, put his head down, and pushed off the ground with his hind legs with all his strength.

His horns connected with the bear's belly as it stood tall above Orden. His head pushed hard against the bear's soft belly and shoved with all his might. The bear roared as it fell over on its side. A split second later, a torrent of fire shot down on the bear from all sides.

Nyel leapt away from the dragon's fire and watched the beast burst into flames. Its maddening shriek echoed around them. He turned and examined the older dragon as he struggled to his feet. "Are you alright?"

"I'm fine!" Orden shouted. He limped away from Nyel and eyed the bear with hatred.

Glyder growled and started towards Orden. "Nyel just saved your life! I think a bit of gratitude wouldn't be too much to ask for!"

Nyel stepped in front of him, but Orden ignored them. Instead, the old stubborn Guardian added his own fire to the bear.

Nyel shook his head in defeat and said, "Just leave it."

"But-" Glyder began, but again Nyel shook his head.

"There are more important things to worry about right now," Nyel answered.

The others yelped as the deranged bear let loose another angry roar and charged after them. His fur was still ablaze, making his hollow eyes seem even more sunken and dark. The bear reared back its arm and swatted at the nearest dragon it could reach.

Ines leapt out of the way just in time, while the others backed away in astonishment and fear. In a shaky voice, she asked, "What can we do to stop it?"

"I'm not sticking around. They're on their own!" Niko growled. Soon, one by one the Guardians flew into the air out of harm's way.

"Cowards!" Orden roared in disgust. He then set his angry eyes on the bear and hissed, "I'll kill it with my teeth and my claws if I must!"

"Wait!" Nyel shouted, but there was no stopping him. Orden charged for the bear as his brethren pleaded for him to fly away. He let out a roar cry as he drew closer to the bear.

A sudden flash of blue whizzed by Nyel and Glyder and soared past Orden. He yelped in surprise as a slender framed dragon flew by him. Nyel didn't know who she was or where she came from, but he knew she was in grave danger. He flew into the air once more and followed after her, ready to come to her defense.

The blue dragon pulled up into the air just above the bear, opened her jaws wide, and let out a fierce breath of what looked like a mixture of blue and white fire. The bear shrieked once more as the embers on his fur fizzled out. In their place, ice crystals formed. Nyel stared in amazement as the bear gradually slowed in his movements until finally, he froze into place on his hind legs.

Once the blue dragon was satisfied with her work, she ceased her icy breath and redirected her gaze towards her wide-eyed audience. Her slate-gray eyes pierced their very souls as she glared at them with displeasure.

"Do you idiots have a death wish, or something?" she asked in a condescending tone.

Orden growled, ready to fight his next opponent. "Idiots? We were trying to protect those dragons over there! Who do you think you are?"

Her eyes flickered to the injured male and Yawna, who sat close beside him in despair. The silver dragon's eyes softened with sadness for just a moment, before she turned back to Orden with a determined icy glare.

"Listen, for you would do well to remember my name with dignity and respect," she said with the authority of a seasoned leader. "I am Mairwen, Ascendant of the Asya Clan. And you will tell me who you are."

Chapter 25
The Ascendant of Asya

Nyel stared at Mairwen in amazement as she strode past them and joined the two strangers. Yawna looked up at her with tears in her eyes. "Mairwen, thank goodness you're here! Can we do anything to save Renvar?"

Mairwen studied the injured dragon, who lay panting on the ground. His eyes were wide and vacant of any recognition of either of them. The Ascendant dragon looked up at the sky and said, "There's one I saw who may be able to help."

Nyel followed her gaze to see Ivory and all his sky-bound Guardians floating down towards them. As they landed, Mairwen approached Ivory with a look of determination. "Ivory, it's good to see you, my brother-in-blood. You have a lot of explaining to do for your sudden arrival, but now isn't the time. I need your help. Can you lend your healing blood to my friend? He may be too far gone, but we must try!"

Ivory turned his gaze to Renvar and let out a sad sigh. "I'm sorry, Mairwen. My Gift has gone to another. I cannot help you with this."

Yawna let out a long, sorrowful cry. As she went to lay her head down on her companion, Mairwen stepped in and gently caught her with her foreleg. "I'm so dreadfully sorry, dear Yawna. I should have gotten here sooner. But I beg you not to touch him. Whatever this sickness is could spread to you."

"I don't care, let it take me! My life is meaningless without Renvar by my side," Yawna wailed. She tried to shove past Mairwen's leg, but she blocked her path once more.

With a nod of his head, Ivory sent Niko and Glyder to help push Yawna back and barricade her from her sick companion. Yawna wailed once more, screaming, "Don't keep me from my mate! Don't let him die alone!"

Renvar gasped a shallow breath, his eyes dilated and vacant. But with his final breath, Renvar whispered, "I'm sorry, Yawna."

And then Renvar was no more.

Yawna collapsed to the ground and sobbed. Mairwen, who flew in with a confident presence, saw it dwindle away and be replaced with something else. It was a mixture of sorrow, fear, and above all else, anger. She shooed the Guardians away from her friend and rested her head against hers.

"I'm sorry I wasn't here in time. What happened?" Mairwen asked with a strangled voice.

But all Yawna could do was weep for Renvar. Nyel hung his head out of respect for the fallen dragon. What could have caused such devastation? It was unlike anything he had seen before.

He wanted a closer look. Nyel lifted his head and examined Renvar's body. The black ooze seemed to stop pulsating along his wounds as soon as his body gave out. He stared in shock as the black sludge seemed to absorb into his body until there was nothing left to be seen.

Ivory and Aydamaris joined him, staring at the fallen dragon.

"Can this have something to do with the shadow creatures?" Aydamaris asked in a low voice.

Ivory shook his head. "I don't know. But anything is possible in these dark times."

"The shadow creatures can only possess a body, not perform whatever type of magic this is. His pupils never changed color, but they were dilated," Nyel pointed out as he moved his eyes across Renvar's body while speaking. "If a shadow creature did this, that would mean…"

"They're getting stronger," Ivory answered what the other two were thinking. He stared at each of them with fear in his eyes. "If they are getting stronger, then we need to be smarter."

"We can't survive being divided much longer. We have to work together to be rid of this evil, all of us," Nyel insisted.

Ivory nodded and turned to find Mairwen. As he did, his eyes widened when he realized she had been standing behind them as they spoke.

"Shadow creatures…so you've seen them too," she stated quietly. Her gaze lingered on Renvar with sadness. "What do you mean by, we can't survive being divided?"

Nyel hesitated, choosing his words carefully for the moment. "The clans need to forget their differences they may have amongst each other. We need to come together and defend ourselves against this dark magic."

"Is that all?" Mairwen asked after a quiet moment.

Her question intrigued Nyel. He was going to wait until they met with her father before revealing his power to them. But there was something about this Ascendant that made him feel…different. Like he could trust her.

"I am the new Ascendant of the Ryngar clan," Nyel said. "My name is Nyel."

Mairwen studied him for a moment, and then said, "Pleasure to meet you Nyel, although the circumstances could have been better. But what does that have to do with our conversation?"

Nyel swallowed past the lump in his throat and finally, he said, "Because I'm not a dragon. Not originally, anyway."

This time, Mairwen stared at him with wide eyes. "You lie!"

Nyel glanced over at Ivory, who gave him a simple nod of approval. They had the numbers if he needed to be protected. With a deep breath, Nyel slowly shifted from his dragon form into his human form. He grit his teeth as every nerve in his body lit up with pain. He tried his best to hide it.

Mairwen gasped as he shrank to a much smaller height and stood on two legs.

"Do you believe me now?" he grinned and held his breath as his pain settled down.

Nyel expected her to cause an uproar and spew hatred at him like Ragnar had done. Instead, Mairwen surprised him when she lowered her head to his and sniffed his hair. His messy brown hair swirled in the breeze of the dragon's breath, tickling his face. She then looked up at Ivory and said, "This power is of our descent? Your Ascendant power has truly passed on to him?"

Ivory nodded. "From my very blood."

"Fascinating!" she exclaimed. Her lips curled back in a dragon-like grin. "Father's going to like you."

Nyel stared at her, dumbfounded. "...That would be a first."

"I can only imagine, young humans. You must all come with me back to the clan," Mairwen announced, turning to the others. "It's not safe to stay out here, especially with night fast approaching."

"That's why we are here, to meet with you and your father," Ivory explained.

Mairwen nodded. "I have an idea why, but we'll discuss that later. Come! I will lead the way."

She then turned to Yawna, who remained on the ground in silence. In a soft tone, she said, "Come Yawna, we must go before anything else comes looking for us. Father will want to speak to you as well."

"We can't just leave him here," Yawna sniffed, her eyes never leaving Renvar.

Mairwen rested her head against hers once more and squeezed her eyes shut, also pained by the loss of their friend. "I will send the others to care for his body in the morning. I promise. But I won't allow you to remain with him. It's not safe. I'm not losing someone else to those things."

Yawna trembled and nodded her head in understanding. Mairwen helped her to her feet and waited for her to gather herself. She then looked back at Ivory and the rest of his Guardians, ready to leave. Without a word, Nyel held his breath and shifted back into his dragon form. He ignored the pain as best as he could, but Ivory eyed him with a look of concern.

Nyel just shook his head and said, "Later."

One by one, they took to the skies. Mairwen waited for Yawna to join the others in the air before she too leapt with opened wings. With a sudden vicious snarl, she flew past the frozen bear and swung her tail at it with a mighty blow.

The bear's body shattered into large pieces like broken glass and crumbled to the ground. Nyel followed her, amazed at her power. How cold would her breath have to be to be able to shatter something with great mass such as the bear? It intrigued, yet terrified, him to think about. All he could do was follow the mysterious young Ascendant and wait for the answers of so many questions that swarmed in his head.

They didn't have to travel much further. Mairwen and Yawna flew side-by-side in the lead, followed closely by Ivory and Nyel. The rest of the Guardians, Aydamaris and Sable, flew behind them in silence. Orden had remained silent ever since their encounter with the bear. He wouldn't even look in Nyel's direction, nor did he take the lead with his group. Nyel didn't mind it. If he could go the rest of their journey with no interaction with the older dragon, he'd be content.

The group ascended to pass over a mountain that quickly approached them. As they did, a strong, cool wind rushed over the mountain top and hit Nyel's face. He sucked in a long, deep breath and let out a gasp. The smell of saltwater hit his nostrils and overwhelmed his senses. He looked over at Ivory in shock.

Ivory chuckled. "I suppose I didn't mention where their clan is located, did I?"

"I think not!" Nyel laughed in response. He flapped his wings harder, driving him forward to match his pace with Mairwen's.

She took one look at him and laughed. "Wanna race, half-blood?"

Nyel snorted. "Just call me Nyel. Or if you're really particular with titles, you can call me Shifter."

Again, Mairwen chuckled. "How about this? I'll give you the title of 'Loser' once I beat you!"

With that flourish of her wings, Mairwen soared higher into the air fast as a bolt of lightning. Nyel growled and flew after her, accepting her challenge. He wasn't about to take such a name, especially from someone he just met. Nyel pumped his wings as fast as he could to catch up to her, but it was no use. Her long, slender frame made her move as if she was as light as a feather. But it didn't stop Nyel from trying his hardest to catch up with her.

They climbed higher and higher until finally they soared over the mountain top. Nyel let out an audible gasp when a large, open ocean welcomed him from afar. The blue water stretched for miles ahead of them. Nyel floated over the last of the mountain range, forgetting their race. He stared in wonder at the ocean beyond.

The soft crash of waves bellowed far below them. Seagulls cawed as they soared over the water, looking for fish. Their white feathers shone brightly in the sunlight. The smell of the saltwater enveloped his senses. Staring at the water gave him a sense of freedom, yet at the same time, made him feel so small. How far could he fly out there until exhaustion overwhelmed him? It was a thought he didn't care to think about.

At the bottom of the mountain below stretched a wide open field that raced towards the water's edge, only being divided by a white, sandy beach. He then noticed something in the distance. A large island filled with tall trees. Something flew over the lonely island that looked bigger than a bird. Nyel squinted and realized that it was a dragon.

"Is that where your clan lives?" he asked, pointing to the island beyond the shore.

Mairwen hesitated. "Not exactly. We stick to higher places. Follow me, this way!"

Before Nyel could ask her what she meant, Mairwen swung to the left and flew parallel to the mountain range they had just crossed. Nyel followed her, confused by her words. Did part of their clan live on the remote island? He was certain it was a dragon he saw over the trees. He wondered why they would separate themselves from each other.

But he had no time to ask her any more questions. There was a bend in the mountain range ahead of them that stretched further north along the coastline. As they approached the bend, he could see specks of light in the setting sun. He squinted, trying to find the cause of the flash, but the sunlight shone right into his eyes. Then he spotted them. Two dragons flew towards them from the bend. Nyel glanced nervously at Mairwen, hoping they were with her.

As if in answer, Mairwen called out to them with a confident roar. In return, they let out another roar and circled back around to fly alongside them. When they got closer to the two dragons, Mairwen called, "Anything to report?"

"No, Mair," said a slight-framed male dragon. He seemed very young, not much older than Theo's siblings, Vail and Scarlett. "All has been well since your departure."

He then looked around at the group she led and whispered, "Where did you find these wanderers?"

"They're not wanderers, Zander," Mairwen chuckled. "They're from the Ryngar clan."

Zander gasped and looked back once more, finally setting his eyes on Ivory. "Oh wow! He's one of the powerful Ascendants, isn't he?"

Mairwen's eyes flickered over to Nyel, before saying, "There's a lot to discuss, little brother. You'll have to forgive me for waiting to answer anymore prying questions."

Zander rolled his eyes. "You're no fun. You know I'll find out, eventually!"

"Then wait for eventually," Mairwen teased.

As Zander grumbled under his breath, Mairwen looked over at the second older dragon and asked, "My brother didn't give you too much trouble while I was gone, did he?"

The second dragon seemed to be closer to her age. His body was lean and fit, his bronze and yellow scales sparkled in the light, and his horns on his head remained sharp and intact. He met Mairwen's gaze with bright yellow eyes that held a touch of slyness in them, but when he spoke he remained proper and calm.

"No more trouble than usual, my lady," said the dragon.

Mairwen rolled her eyes at him.

"Don't call me that. Unless you want me to call you Lord Flint," she growled.

Flint's eyes beamed a sly, cunning gleam. "If you insist, my Lady."

Mairwen growled at him and rolled her eyes once more. "You spend too much time with my brother."

"I vowed to protect him. Which means I am to be with him day in and day out. There's no point in fighting the inevitable," Flint sighed.

He then glanced back at the group behind her. "You've flown a long way. Your Guardians must be tired. We have plenty of room for you all to rest and plenty of terrain to hunt out of. I only encourage you to have a partner with you at all times. We live in unsafe times."

"So you know of the shadow creatures that haunt the land?" Ivory asked.

Flint nodded. "All too well, I'm afraid. We have a constant watch over our clan to help keep us safe."

"First, we must go seek an audience with my father," Mairwen announced. "Then we can all rest. Flint, there was trouble on our own journey."

Flint's eyes widened, and he looked around at the group. "Where's Renvar?"

Mairwen lowered her gaze to the ground and said, "We lost him."

A low growl rumbled in Flint's throat. "Was it those creatures?"

"Worse," Mairwen answered, meeting his gaze again. "It was something else. Some other dark magic that sucked the life out of him. I've never seen anything like it."

"I think it would be wise to find your father," Ivory suggested.

Mairwen nodded and looked to Flint. He met her gaze and, as if knowing what she was going to ask, he said, "Allow me to find him. Wait for us at the Gathering Point."

Mairwen nodded and flew towards the base of the mountains. As they followed her, it surprised Nyel to see Flint and Zander not join them in the same direction. He glanced over his shoulder and saw them hurry towards the island he spotted far from the mainland. Why would they go there?

Curiosity bubbled inside him, but he waited for such questions. Instead, he focused on following Mairwen towards her clan.

It didn't take long for Nyel to spot the clan's Guardians perched along the highest points of the mountain as they soared by. They did not announce their arrival to the others, perhaps because they were with Mairwen. The Guardians nodded at them as they passed, which Nyel returned. A very different welcome than the last clan they had visited.

Mairwen landed in a large clearing of land that was surrounded by a wall of flat-faced cliffs on either side, only allowing one way in and out from the ground entrance. As Nyel landed, he looked out of the narrowed path of the mountain's entrance towards the ocean. And beyond there, he could see the large, lonely island that rested in its waters. Tall grass swayed in a gentle breeze around them. He noticed a trodden path that led from the entrance of the area and moved towards the center of the field where the grass did not grow as tall.

This left Nyel puzzled. Did the dragons walk into this area often? He assumed it would be easier to fly in, just as they had done. He shook his head. There was always something new to learn from every clan. And sometimes, the lesson proved to be dangerous. He needed to keep a sharp mind.

"Here they come," Mairwen announced, watching the entrance.

They turned their attention towards the northern sky to see three dragons flying towards them. It looked like they had left the island. Nyel's curiosity was buzzing, but he held his tongue.

When the dragons drew closer, he realized that Flint and Zander were among them, followed closely by an older, gray-scaled dragon. They passed overhead and landed in the clearing behind them.

As the older dragon folded his torn wings against his body, he turned his cunning blue eyes on them and, in a booming voice, said, "Ivory! It's been far too long, my friend!"

Ivory chuckled and strode towards him. "It has, my dear friend. How are you, Talon?"

The clan leader sighed and said, "Fair, I suppose. Have you come to warn me about those nasty demons roaming our homeland?"

Ivory nodded. "Yes, among other things. Has your defense held firm against them?"

Talon snorted. A puff of dark smoke shot from his nostrils and flew away in the breeze. "We've lost a few brave dragons, I'm afraid. But we've learned the shadows hate our fire. As for the possessed dragons…we've fought them off." His eyes narrowed, and he added, "I don't like to fight our own kind, especially those from our clan. But we do what we have to do in order to survive."

Mairwen stepped forward. "I have more unfortunate news that we need to discuss."

Talon turned his questioning gaze on her and said, "You're back sooner than expected. What's wrong?"

She then explained what had happened on the outskirts of their home. Nyel watched Talon's face as it changed from surprise to sorrow, and then finally morphed into anger. "What does this mean? Are you certain the bear was finished?"

Mairwen nodded. "I smashed it into pieces."

"Very well. I will send a group to take care of Renvar's body," he then turned to the teary-eyed Yawna and said, "I am so sorry for the loss of your mate. We will give him a proper sendoff, I promise."

"Thank you, Talon," Yawna sniffed. Then she bowed her head until the tip of her snout touched the ground.

"Flint, Zander, please gather a group to take care of Renvar for me. I want them to go at first light, not a moment sooner. I must stay here with our guests," Talon instructed.

With his chest puffed out, Zander confidently replied, "Father, I would be honored!"

Before Flint could even speak, Zander leapt into the air and flew towards one of the closest Guardians posted on the mountain high above them. Flint shared an amused look with Mairwen before chasing after the young dragon.

Talon chuckled and turned to Ivory. "It's astounding how fast our hatchlings grow, don't you agree?"

Ivory's eyes lingered on Zander, his mind elsewhere. "Yes, they grow quickly. Keep yours close while you can, my friend. One day, they will fly from your nest and far from your reach."

Talon studied Ivory's forlorn expression. He opened his mouth to say something, but shut it once more. He followed Ivory's gaze, and they watched the distant Zander land next to a Guardian. After a quiet moment, he asked, "What else brings you here, my friend? Surely you didn't leave your clan in these trying times without good reason?"

"Yes, you're right," Ivory said. He turned towards the rest of his clan and continued, "Come join me, Nyel, and Aydamaris."

Nyel took a deep breath and followed Aydamaris to join the lead Ascendants. Sable trailed behind them from a distance, always staying near his beloved mate. Talon's eyes grew wide, and he bowed his head immediately to Aydamaris as she stood beside Ivory.

"My apologies, Aydamaris," Talon fumbled. "I didn't mean to overlook you. It's an honor to have you here in our home!"

Aydamaris laughed. "I took no offense. You did nothing wrong, young Talon. I'm honored to see your spirit shining once more, finally."

Talon let loose a boisterous laugh. "You've not changed a bit! I've missed you dearly. We must catch up sometime."

Aydamaris's eyes twinkled as she said, "I would like that very much."

Talon then turned his attention to Nyel and cocked his head. "I don't believe we've yet. I am Talon, Leader of the Asya clan."

Nyel bowed his head slightly and replied, "It's nice to meet you. My name is Nyel, of Ivory's clan."

Ivory snorted with annoyance and added, "He is my Ascendant."

Talon's eyes grew wide with disbelief as he looked from Ivory to Nyel. "Ivory, I didn't know your power had passed on. And to another youngling, I might add. Just as mine passed to my Mairwen."

"We're not younglings, father," Mairwen commented with a roll of her eyes. Nyel grinned at her.

Talon studied Nyel once more. "May I ask what the Ascendant power bestowed upon you? I'm always fascinated by what it draws out of our souls."

Nyel faltered, caught off guard by his statement. "Our souls?"

Talon nodded. "Yes. I believe that the Ascendant's power brings out our hidden gifts that are buried deep within our souls. Our true selves. What we become in this life and contribute to our kind. With that in mind, would you agree by observing the Ascendant's you already know?"

Nyel studied the small group of Ascendants around him. Ivory was caring, patient, and willing to listen to those in need. A true healer. Aydamaris was thoughtful, wise, and empathetic. A true seer. Ragnar was arrogant, but he was a fierce protector of his clan. His brow furrowed as he realized he didn't know what his gift was. He made a mental note to ask Aydamaris later. With Mairwen. He did not know her well, but he sensed beyond her warmth she had a strong will and iron resolve in her heart. A true leader.

He couldn't turn that same gaze on himself. Whether he wanted to admit it or not, Nyel felt like the Ascendant power was wrong to choose him. He didn't truly belong to their long line of powerful and heroic leaders. He didn't really belong anywhere.

Nyel looked back up at Talon and said, "It makes sense when you put it that way, I suppose."

Talon chuckled. "You don't sound very confident in your answer. Why is that?"

"I've just never really thought about it that way," Nyel said, averting his gaze.

Talon studied him with curiosity. "What is your power, young Ascendant?"

Nyel glanced around and didn't see anymore of Talon's clan other than the Guardian's high above them. He then looked at Ivory, and Ivory nodded to him. Mairwen's eyes gleamed with delight as they fluttered back and forth between him and her father.

With a calming breath, Nyel closed his eyes and shifted once more into his normal self. He could feel himself shrink in size and his scales disappear into his skin. Nyel rose from his crouched position and waited. He expected to hear a gasp of fear or an angry remark from the clan leader. But all was silent.

Nyel slowly opened his eyes and craned his neck back to meet Talon's surprised stare. Talon glanced around at the group behind Nyel and finally his eyes rested on Ivory. He looked impressed by what he had just witnessed.

"The Ascendant's Gift turns him into a human?" Talon asked in a low voice.

Ivory shook his head. "No. It gave a human the ability to turn into a dragon."

This time, Talon's eyes widened, and his jaw dropped slightly in shock. "What? I thought the Ascendant's Gift only went to our own kind! I've never heard of this happening before. I didn't think it was possible! Did you know this would happen?"

Ivory gestured to Nyel, saying, "It is very possible, as you can see with your own eyes. And no, I never dreamed that our power would choose a human. But Nyel was the one our power chose."

Talon returned his gaze to Nyel and asked, "It must have been terrifying when you realized what your gift could do."

Now it was Nyel's turn to stare at him with surprise. Almost every dragon he had ever encountered seemed upset when he revealed who he truly was. They demanded to know how he stole the Ascendant's power. Talon, on the other hand, wanted to know if the experience had scared him. The leader of this clan and his daughter were truly unlike the others.

"And you're all accepting of this man into your own clan?" Talon asked after a moment of silence.

Out of the corner of his eye, Nyel could see many of Ivory's Guardians shift uncomfortably and avert their gazes. A snort resounded in the back of the group as Orden exclaimed, "We are just following the orders of our true Ascendant!"

Talon's eyes narrowed as he stared at Orden. "I assume you are referring to Ivory?"

"Of course I am!" Orden growled in annoyance.

Talon's eyes flickered to glance at Nyel before he said, "I'm thrilled you respect your leader. But Nyel is your true Ascendant now. And I will not have you disrespect him in my presence. If you do so, I will banish you from my territory. Is that understood?"

Nyel gaped at him while Orden growled something under his breath, but said no more to anyone else. Glyder stepped forward and said, "It's true most of us were appalled when we learned Nyel received the Ascendant's Gift. We hated him for it. But speaking for myself, I've gotten to know him better over the past few days and I'm proud to call him a member of our clan. And perhaps one day, I could have the honor of calling him my friend."

Glyder smirked down at Nyel in his human form and Nyel couldn't stop the smile that grew on his face. "I'm honored, Glyder. Thank you."

"So you can understand us even in human form as well?" Talon noted. "This is fascinating indeed!"

Nyel stared at him, unsure of what to say next. He was expecting to have to prove himself to another clan leader, but this time, he was being accepted without hesitation. The change of pace was a relief, yet unnerving all at once.

"Ivory, might I have a word with you in private?" Talon asked.

Ivory nodded and said, "Of course. Lead the way."

Talon and Ivory strode away from their group towards the base of the mountain. Nyel watched them go, wondering what they could possibly be talking about. He never expected Talon to be so inviting. It made his head swirl with a mixture of relief, excitement, and confusion. He wished Iris could be there to revel in this moment with him. She would have loved Talon. And especially

Mairwen. The more he thought about it, the more he realized Mairwen and Iris were kindred spirits.

"That went well," Mairwen grinned, stepping in his line of sight. Nyel nodded. "Who is he?"

When Mairwen cocked her head in confusion, Nyel elaborated, "I just mean…I've never encountered a dragon quite so accepting as he. Does he not fear or hate humans like the others do?"

Mairwen hesitated. "We are cautious of humans. But no, we do not hate or fear them. Not unless they give us a reason to, anyway."

Nyel's eyes flickered over to Ivory and saw a look of astonishment cross his face before quickly extinguishing it. Nyel stepped towards the two clan leaders, but Mairwen moved with him and lowered her head to meet his gaze. "Trust me, just wait."

Her words piqued his curiosity even higher, but Nyel did as he was told and stayed put. It didn't take long before Talon and Ivory returned to them. Ivory seemed troubled. However, Talon's demeanor didn't change.

"It's getting late. I invite you all to join me further into the mountains with the rest of our clan. It will be a safe place to rest from your long journey," Talon offered, his voice warm and unbothered.

Everyone turned to Ivory, who had the final say on the matter. Ivory nodded and said, "That would be wonderful, thank you."

"Let us depart!" Talon grinned. With that, the clan leader flew into the air and soared high over them. One by one, Ivory's clan followed him.

Nyel sighed, realizing how exhausted he felt after the day's events. He grit his teeth through the pain and shifted back into his dragon form to follow the others.

Talon led them all to a valley nestled within the tall mountains. Along the highest points, Nyel noticed their Guardians posted around the perimeter of the valley. It reminded Nyel of Ivory's clan in a way, only with a smaller amount of giant trees that surrounded them. They cleared out the ground to give the dragons more space for a comfortable dwelling. A large freshwater pond sat nestled in the far right of the valley and a small stream ran to it from the south.

Throughout the valley were the rest of Talon's clan. There were dozens of them, clustered into groups of families, friends, and some that kept to themselves. Nyel's heart warmed when he spotted a few younglings playing together near the pond. It was a peaceful and welcome sight to see a happy and healthy clan. It made him want to protect them from the evils that Kollano had unleashed upon the world.

Talon led them towards the pond and landed beside it. Nyel felt the eyes of the dragons below on them as they followed Talon's lead to the pond. Once the group landed, Talon said, "You may rest here for the night. You have nothing to worry about. My Guardians always keep a vigilant watch at all hours. You will be safe here"

"I can keep watch over our own clan," Orden grumbled.

Talon frowned. Before he could speak, Ivory said, "Hold your tongue. He is giving all of us a chance to rest the whole night. And we will happily accept your offer. Thank you, Talon."

"Of course," Talon said with a small bow of his head. "If you need anything else, just let one of my Guardians know. Until tomorrow then."

With that, Talon leapt into the air and flew towards the opposite end of the valley and out of sight. As Nyel watched him leave, Aydamaris joined him by his side. "Nyel, we should speak to Mairwen before she leaves."

"Hmm?" Nyel hummed. His eyelids were heavy at the thought of a full night's rest ahead of him.

"Have you forgotten why we came?" she asked, a serious look on her face.

As if in answer, something within tugged at him. A drive to search for answers. The need to answer the call.

"Hey wait!" Nyel yelled when he spotted Mairwen begin to lift her wings to depart.

With a curious look, she answered, "Yes?"

Nyel and Aydamaris hurried over to her on either side. Nyel glanced around and asked in a hushed voice, "We need to ask you something that might seem strange."

"Did you hear a voice calling to you a few days ago? A voice you couldn't explain the origin of?" Aydamaris asked her straight out.

Mairwen looked startled and folded her wings tightly against her sides. "You heard it too?!"

Nyel let out a sigh of relief.

"Yes, we did. As did my son, Ragnar," Aydamaris replied. "I think something is calling out to all the current Ascendants. For what reason, I do not know."

"How curious!" Mairwen gasped, looking from one to the other. "And now you're on a quest to find the mysterious voice, aren't you?"

"We are," Nyel confirmed. "And also to meet you."

She turned her gaze towards the east with a distant look in her eye. "That's part of the reason we were out there today. I wanted to look further outside of the clan for any signs of something...anything to do with that voice. But I didn't tell anyone about it. I didn't want them to worry about me and think I'd gone mad. It's my fault that Renvar is gone."

"You didn't know what was out there," Nyel offered to comfort her. "None of us knew what that thing was or that it even existed."

Mairwen turned her teary eyes to him and said in a hushed voice, "Yes, but it's still my duty as an Ascendant to protect my clan from danger. I failed Renvar and Yawna in that regard. But thank you for your kindness."

Nyel took a deep breath and let it out slowly. He was at a loss for words. He was beginning to truly understand the emotional and physical toll it took to be an Ascendant. It humbled him yet made him feel guilty for not fully embracing his own power; his own responsibility.

This time, Aydamaris spoke up. "I think it's important that we seek this voice. It's calling out to us for a reason. But for what, I'm not sure."

"While I agree with you, my first duty is to Renvar. Perhaps we can discuss the matter afterwards," Mairwen said. "For now, I suggest you two get some rest. It was an eventful day, after all."

She opened her wings again to leave, but Nyel interrupted her once more. "May I join you in recovering Renvar's body? I promise I won't get in the way. I'd just like to help in this difficult time."

Mairwen was stunned by his offer. "Of course. We are leaving early in the morning."

Nye nodded and said, "I'll see you then."

They wished her a good night before Mairwen lifted her wings and took off into the evening sky.

"I want to get to know her better. I feel like there's something Mairwen and her father aren't telling us," Nyel said quietly as she watched her fly further into the valley.

Aydamaris hesitated. She hesitated and asked, "Do you think they can't be trusted?"

He turned to meet her worried gaze. "I don't know if it's that. I just sense that there's something more to their story. Does your power tell you anything?"

Aydamaris shook her head. "My Gift has weakened over the years. It will only show me visions of something of extreme importance. Like sending Ivory to meet you."

"I see," was all Nyel could say.

After a moment of silence, Nyel and Aydamaris parted ways in search of a comfortable place to sleep. Aydamaris found her place beside Sable in the soft grass beside the pond and settled in for the night. The rest of Ivory's clan had already done the same except for

Orden, who sat furthest away along the pond's edge. He stared into the valley beyond in silence. Nyel realized the older Guardian would never outgrow his stubbornness. He shook his head, curled up into a ball beside the pond, and closed his eyes with the thoughts of the peaceful valley around them easing his troubled mind.

Chapter 26
The Mystery of Renvar

The sweet, cheerful chirps of songbirds woke Nyel from his sleep. He raised his head off of the ground and blinked in confusion. Where was he?

As his vision cleared of sleep, he slowly realized that they were in Talon's territory. He gazed at his surroundings with a sense of wonder. The valley was even more beautiful in the morning sun. Dragons soared in the sky above him. The younglings he spotted the day before splashed around on the opposite side of the pond he rested beside.

One of the younglings' mother walked past him as she yelled, "Get out of that water at once and come eat your breakfast before I roast your hides!"

The younglings giggled and glided over the pond towards her on wobbly wings. She shook her head and turned to lead them away when she spotted Nyel watching her.

"Apologies, I hope I didn't wake you," she said, her voice warm and kind.

Nyel chuckled. "It's alright, I was just getting up."

She nodded to him and followed the younglings, who soared away from them and followed the stream. Nyel rose to his feet and went to the pond for a drink of cool water. A school of small fish swam away from him as soon as his mouth touched the surface. Fish sounded like a fine breakfast, he thought, with a growling stomach. He wondered if there were bigger fish in the pond? Or better yet, what fish could he find in the ocean? He would have to visit the salty waters soon.

A shadow cast over him, interrupting his thoughts. Nyel lifted his head from the water to find Ivory standing behind him.

"Good morning. How did you sleep?" Ivory asked before he dipped his own muzzle into the water below.

"It was the best sleep I've had in ages," Nyel grinned as he stretched his legs. "Did everyone else rest as well?"

Ivory lifted his head and met Nyel's gaze with an irritated sigh. Water dripped from his chin as he said, "Orden stayed up the entire night to watch over our group."

Nyel shook his head and said, "He'll probably be exhausted for the rest of the day, but that doesn't surprise me."

"I'm sending him home, back to the clan," Ivory stated.

Nyel stared at him with wide eyes. "You are? Why?"

"I have my reasons," Ivory said. "But now I must ask you an important question. Who among these Guardians do you trust with your life if I was not around to guide them?"

Dumbfounded by his question, Nyel said, "Well, I suppose a lot of them are coming around to my presence."

"Be more specific," Ivory insisted, studying him intently.

Nyel sighed and observed their group for a moment. Many of them were still sleeping, while the others sat and spoke to each other at ease as they watched over the valley beyond them.

"Aydamaris and Sable, of course. Glyder. Trunic. I think I'd trust Glyder's friends, Niko and Ines. I haven't gotten to know them very well though. Lunar and Meinrad follow Orden's lead in his distaste for my being here," Nyel finally answered.

Ivory nodded. "Very well. Thank you."

"Why do you ask?" Nyel asked again.

Ivory hesitated. Then he replied, "I think it would be best for you to find something to do elsewhere. I have much to discuss with the Guardians, and I think it would be best if you're not here for this."

"Wait, you're sending them all home?" Nyel asked in shock.

Ivory shook his head. "No, just the ones who haven't learned to accept you yet. It's not a punishment. I want more Guardians back at home to protect the rest of our clan. I had hoped to be back sooner, but there are urgent matters we must attend to first."

The mysterious voice echoed in Nyel's mind, always reminding him. Nyel nodded and said, "Alright. I offered to accompany Mairwen to Renvar's body this morning."

"Really? Why, may I ask?" Ivory responded in surprise.

"It felt like the right thing to do," Nyel said. "Plus, I want to get to know her more. She's the only Ascendant I've met that's still new to this Ascendant thing as I am. Close enough to it, anyway."

"Very well, just be careful," Ivory replied, his eyes drifting over to his Guardians. "You best get going, then. Wish me luck."

He then turned and strode towards his group of Guardians. Those who were awake looked up at him with anticipation.

Guilt swelled inside of him for a moment, but Nyel tried to shake the feeling away. It was impossible for him to please everyone. He had to learn that. He was about to leave when he spotted Aydamaris sitting by herself in the shade of a tall tree while Sable slept soundly nearby. Nyel hesitated when he studied her face. She looked troubled.

Nyel walked over to her and asked, "Are you alright?"

Startled, Aydamaris looked up at him and shook her head with a nervous laugh. "I'm not sure. I just had the strangest dream."

"Do you want to talk about it?" Nyel asked.

Aydamaris sighed and looked away. "There's not much to talk about. In my dream, I was lying here just where I slept, and a silent dragon approached me. But she didn't look like us. She was made up of a glowing green aura of light. I stared at her in awe, and she brought her muzzle to mine and examined me. She then shook her head and flew away. I tried to get up to follow her, but she was gone before I could stop her. Then I woke up."

"Wow," Nyel pondered. "That's an unusual dream."

"I wasn't able to go back to sleep," she continued. She then looked at him with tears in her eyes. "I can't explain it, but her departure made me sorrowful. I wanted to go with her, but she didn't want me to."

He stared at her in shock. Her dream really affected her. "Do you think it was something more? One of your visions, perhaps?"

Aydamaris shook her head. "No. I've never had one like that. It was probably just stress after the last few days. I'll be alright."

"Are you sure?" Nyel enforced. He didn't want to leave her in a state of despair.

Aydamaris nodded profusely. "I'm sure. You better hurry and find Mairwen before they leave you."

"You're right," Nyel said quickly, having nearly forgotten his plan. "Just try to get some rest. Please?"

Aydamaris smiled and nodded at him. Nyel lifted his wings and soared into the air without looking back at the group. He found Aydamaris's dream fascinating, especially since it created such a reaction out of her. But now wasn't the time to ponder over it. Instead, he began to scan the valley below, wondering where he could find Mairwen.

He spotted Zander chatting with a group of younglings around his age further down the stream. Nyel glided down towards them and landed a few feet away.

Zander glanced over his shoulder at him and gave him a huge, dragon-like grin. "That's the Ascendant I was telling you about! I told you he was real!"

Nyel raised his brow in confusion as the other younglings turned to look at him in excitement. Then their faces fell as they studied him.

"He looks normal to me," a young girl said as she studied Nyel closely.

Nyel chuckled and turned to Zander. "You don't think I'm normal?"

"My dad told me everything last night," Zander exclaimed, bouncing up and down in his own excitement. "You're a human!"

Nyel froze and stared at him in disbelief. If Talon told his young son about him, would that mean he's told the rest of the clan as well? He looked around nervously, but the only ones around him were the younglings.

When Nyel didn't answer him, Zander continued, "Don't worry. No one will harm you here. You've come to the right clan!"

"I'm not so sure. Can you keep my power to yourself until I talk to your family a little more?" Nyel asked, lowering his voice. "I've come across too many dragons who weren't happy when they learned who I am."

"So you are a human!" exclaimed a red male with small white horns sprouting from his head. He reminded Nyel of a miniature Theo.

Zander rolled his eyes and said, "Like I said, Brolly. You never listen to me."

"You're filled with stories! Who could ever believe a word you say half of the time?" Brolly teased with a roll of his eyes.

Zander growled at him and tackled him to the ground. The others egged it on except for the young female who spoke before. She stared at Nyel with bright yellow eyes and asked, "Can you show us your power?"

The others stopped instantly and turned their attention back on Nyel. "Yeah, show us!"

Nyel let out a nervous laugh and said, "Maybe another time. I'm looking for Mairwen. Do you know where I could find her?"

"I'll take you to her! I think she might be waiting for you with my dad," Zander said as he got to his feet.

Nyel thanked him as they prepared to take to the skies.

"By the way, my name is Wren. It's nice to meet you, Ascendant," said the young girl with a slight bow.

Nyel turned to her and bowed his head in return. "Nice to meet you, Wren. And please, just call me Nyel."

Her eyes twinkled with delight before she turned and started chasing the others towards a wooded area.

Nyel chuckled. To be that young again without a care in the world, he thought.

He flew into the air behind Zander, who guided them back towards the north and flapped his wings harder to gain speed. Nyel realized he may try to match his own flight, so Nyel slowed down to not tire him.

"I thought Flint was your guard. Where is he?" Nyel asked.

"He's meeting with my sister and the others to go take care of Renvar," Zander explained.

Nyel's heart sank. "Did they leave already?"

Zander shrugged. "Maybe. They were waiting for a couple of their friends to join them. Flint doesn't usually go to those kinds of things. His duty is to be with me most of the time. Father thinks I get into trouble too often. But Renvar was a close friend of Flint's and my sister. He wanted to give Renvar the perfect send off."

"I'm sorry for your loss," Nyel offered quietly.

Zander glanced at him. "Did you see what happened to him?"

Nyel explained, "We arrived too late to see exactly how he was injured. But I saw the aftermath."

"Those creatures are getting closer to us," Zander said with a shudder. "There are more and more sightings of shadows and other dark things every day."

Nyel frowned and gazed back in the direction they had met Mairwen for the first time. Zander was right. They were getting closer. The shadow creatures were becoming more abundant and more powerful. He wished he knew a way to get rid of them permanently.

When he saw the frightened look on Zander's face, he said, "You have a powerful clan. And we are here to help protect you, too. Just make sure you go nowhere on your own, especially at night."

Zander nodded. After a moment of silence, he changed the subject, saying, "There they are."

Nyel realized they were back at the horseshoe shaped meeting area from the night before. He spotted Mairwen in the center of the field with Flint and Yawna. There were two others, a male and female, waiting with them.

"What are you doing here? I thought I asked you to stay in the valley with your friends?" Talon scolded Zander as they landed beside them.

Nyel quickly interjected. "That's my fault, sir. I asked him where I could find Mairwen."

"And a simple explanation wouldn't have worked?" Mairwen snorted with a cunning look in her eye. She stared at her younger brother with a stern expression that reminded him of his stepmother, Mari. She gave him and Bem that same look every time they got into trouble.

"You guys get to have all the fun! I was only trying to help," Zander said with an innocent tone as he averted his gaze.

Talon sighed and shook his head. "It's alright Zander, thank you for showing Nyel the way. Now go back to the clan."

"But father, I-" Zander started, but faltered when Talon's gaze turned hard and a low warning growl rumbled in his chest.

Yawna stepped in and said, "Zander, can you accompany me back to the valley? I'd feel better if we could fly together."

With a sigh, the young dragon said, "Fine, I'll go. Only because Yawna needs a guard."

"Thank you for your assistance, Zander," Nyel added, hoping to pep him up.

Zander nodded at him glumly and returned to the air. Yawna bowed to Mairwen and said in a quiet voice, "Please take care of him. I know he would appreciate his friends sending him off into the next world."

With that, Yawna followed Zander into the sky and back over the mountains once more. When they were out of sight, Talon sighed. "He is so eager to grow up and play a bigger role in our clan. He wants to be a Guardian one day, you know. I just want him to live a safe and comfortable life away from all these monsters that have been appearing as of late. Tell me Nyel, have the shadows reached your land as well?"

Nyel nodded. "Yes, they have. And we've met and fought against their leader. He calls himself Kollano. He took over a sorcerer's body, and we thought our friend might have killed him before he could get away. However, we recently learned that he took over our friend's body instead. I fear he is the reason these creatures are getting stronger. I just don't understand how he's doing it."

Talon pondered this for a moment. "If you fought him, do you have an idea how we can get rid of him and his shadows for good?"

Nyel shook his head. "I don't know. They don't like fire and light, but even still they seem to come back in even more numbers. And this new creature…whatever it was, it could withstand our fire and was out in broad daylight."

"We are hoping to discover a way to destroy them all," Talon said, glancing at Mairwen as he spoke. "We've been sending out Guardians to different locations hoping to discover something. But we have had no luck yet."

"My friends went back into the kingdom in search of answers. I'm hoping they found something of use," Nyel said.

"I think we should get going," Mairwen announced after an awkward silence. "I'd like to get to Renvar as quickly as possible."

Flint nodded. "Agreed. Maybe we can search for more clues while we're out there. Find out where these creatures came from."

"Very well," Talon said. "I will return to the clan and watch over things. Please be careful. If anything is amiss, I must demand that you return to the valley at once."

Flint nodded and then bowed to Talon before the clan leader flew away. Mairwen then turned to Nyel and asked, "Are you ready?"

"Yes, I am. Sorry if I kept you waiting," Nyel added, ashamed that he was the last to arrive.

"We weren't waiting long," said the young female. Her scales were the color of coal, yet her eyes were a soft blue. She portrayed an air of kindness. Sensing his eyes on her, she added, "My name is Maghnus. And this is Swithin."

She gestured to the copper scaled male beside her. His yellow eyes studied Nyel closely as he nodded in greeting. He then looked away towards the east in silence. Nyel wondered if he was upset that he had joined their small group. Until Maghnus added, "Swithin doesn't say much. But he's really kind once you get to know him."

"I see. It's nice to meet you both," Nyel smiled.

Swithin turned and met Flint's gaze. Flint nodded and said, "Right. Let's go, everyone."

One by one, they leapt into the air and turned towards the east, back in the direction Nyel and his clan had traveled from. Flint led the way, followed by Maghnus, Nyel, Mairwen, and finally Swithin in the rear. Once they leveled out high in the sky, Nyel turned to Mairwen and asked, "Yawna didn't want to come?"

Mairwen shook her head. "No. I think she saw enough yesterday. She just wanted to ask us to take good care of him and thank us for understanding."

"They were mates?" Nyel asked.

She nodded once more. "They were fond of each other for a long time. I think they even planned on having hatchlings in the future, after Renvar was more settled in his role as a new Guardian. He was going to be in a trial period to guard over the island."

This intrigued Nyel. "The island? Why would the island need to be guarded?"

Mairwen and Maghnus shared a look. Then, Mairwen said, "I've said too much. It's not my place to say. It's just a very special place for us. I ask that you and your clan don't venture over there unless you have my father's permission. Otherwise, we will ban you from our territory forever."

Nyel was taken aback. Without more probing, he responded, "I won't go near the island. I promise."

Regardless of his promise, Nyel stared at the distant island as they flew along the mountain range. Again, he noted two or three dragons circling overhead. Now he realized that they were guards entrusted with the task. His mind went wild with the possibilities that the island must hold. What could be so important to have specialized guards there around the clock? The only thing he could think of was maybe they kept their nests there. But why would that be such a secret?

He didn't get to think much longer about it. Flint led the small group over the mountains and back inland. The ocean and its white sandy beaches disappeared from sight. They headed southeast, this time led by Mairwen. Nyel wanted to ask her more about what she thought of the voice that had called to them, but he remembered she had kept that information to herself. Would she want to talk about it around her friends? He'd have to wait for when they could be alone.

They finally reached the place where Nyel had first spotted Yawna and the bear. As they glided down towards the area, Nyel scanned the ground. Scattered across the scorched earth, he could make out chunks of mush. He realized they were the remains of the shattered bear that Mairwen had destroyed. He shuddered at the memory of those hollow eyes staring at him.

A strange feeling came over him as they quickly approached the ground. He studied the scene carefully. Something wasn't right.

"Nyel!" Mairwen gasped. She halted her descent, causing the others to do the same. She turned to him with a look of terror etched across her face.

His stomach sank as he realized what had caused her reaction.

"Mairwen, what's wrong?" Flint asked urgently.

A growl escaped Nyel's throat as his eyes scanned the ground, the trees, and even the sky. "It's Renvar. He's gone."

Chapter 27
Evolution

W hat?!" Flint gasped. His eyes scanned the area frantically for his friend. "I thought you guys said he was dead."

"He was!" Mairwen insisted in a shrill voice.

They landed on the ground close to where they had last seen Renvar. Nyel searched the ground for any signs of where he went. He didn't see any of the black slime anywhere. On closer inspection, he spotted footprints leading away from the scene. He followed them for several yards until suddenly they vanished.

"The trail ends here," he noted, turning to the others with a look of concern.

"What should we do?" Magnus asked nervously.

Flint studied the path as well. With a shake of his head, he said, "We should return and let Talon know what's happened."

"No," Mairwen growled. She glared in the direction the footprints ended. "We came here for our friend. We can't leave him to that dark magic."

Flint turned to her and snorted. "It's too risky. I'd never forgive myself if we lose someone else to this madness. I must insist that we return home and tell your father at once. We must protect the clan."

"And we shall!" Mairwen growled once more. "I need to know what has become of Renvar. I can't return to Yawna without answers. I just can't."

Flint turned to the others in search of their help with the situation. Maghnus puffed out her chest and stood beside her Ascendant. "I will go wherever Mairwen leads me. She's right, we can't leave him behind like this."

He looked at Swithin, who only shrugged. Even though he hadn't spoken a word, Nyel got the sense that he would follow Maghnus. He wondered if they were mates?

"Nyel, you're my last hope. Please talk some sense into these airheads," Flint begged, at last turning to him.

Nyel let out a sigh as his eyes drifted to the patch of grass flattened by Renvar's body. "I'm sorry Flint. We need to find out where he is. Maybe we can put a stop to whatever magic has taken him before it continues to spread."

Flint let out a defeated sigh. "I was afraid you might say that. Fine, I'm outnumbered. We'll split up into two groups. Report back here if you find something, don't do anything that will get you killed."

"Don't let that slime touch you," Nyel added. "Stay far away from it. We don't know what it can do."

The others nodded in agreement and they took to the skies once more. Maghnus and Swithin veered right towards the west, while Flint, Mairwen, and Nyel ventured eastwards. They spread out wide in the sky, keeping each other in their sights, while also giving themselves more of an advantage to find something.

Nyel scanned the mountains carefully. He glided with the wind, taking his time to search every nook and cranny of the grounds below. He glanced around at the vast mountain range and felt his stomach sink once more. They were way over their heads. The area was too vast, and they didn't have enough eyes to search for Renvar. He could be long gone, having had the entire night to disappear. But they had to try.

Hours passed with no signs of trouble. Nyel ventured further and further away from the others to cover more ground. His wings ached, ready for a break from the constant circling over a radius of land. They were miles away from Talon's clan. He realized they were near the area where his own clan had rested for the night.

He gasped as a realization hit him. When he and Glyder were hunting, he spotted the downed tree with the large marks in them. The marks that held black sludge within their crevices.

Nyel dove towards the forest line and landed in a heap. He winced as a shocking pain ran through his body. What was happening? It felt just like the pain he had been experiencing when he shifted forms. He let out a growl. Now was not the time for his own problems. It would be easier to venture through the woods without his massive body scraping against the trees. However, he wasn't looking forward to it.

He shifted into his human form and let out another yelp of pain. As he shrunk down in size, every nerve in his body screamed in pain. He bit his tongue until it bled as his transformation completed. Beads of sweat formed on his brow and tears stung his eyes. Something wasn't right. He shouldn't have been experiencing this pain for so long. Even though he never wanted to concern Ivory, it was time that he discussed it with him. Nyel made a mental note to do just that when he returned.

Nyel straightened up and spat some blood out of his mouth. His pain slowly subsided into a dull, bearable ache. It was time to focus on the task at hand. Nyel ventured into the woods and headed in the direction where he thought the tree might have been.

The shade of the trees made his walk pleasant. Birds chirped in the canopy of the trees. Small bugs buzzed around him as he stepped carefully through the underbrush. He stepped around a bunch of hanging vines and studied the woods the further he went in. Nothing seemed amiss. He cursed under his breath. Where did he see that tree before?

He pressed onward, picking up the pace. The quicker he found it, the better.

Nyel searched the woods carefully, using his heightened senses for any sign of danger or disturbance nearby. Nearly an hour passed before finally, against all odds, he finally spotted the fallen tree. He jogged over to it and knelt on the ground beside it eagerly.

The scratches were deep. Small remnants of the dark sludge remained, dried into the wood. He didn't dare touch it. The scratches could have been from a bear, or even a smaller dragon. Could it have been from the bear they had encountered? It seemed impossible. The distance between the two locations was huge. Trekking through the dangerous mountains, especially on foot, seemed like an impossible task for a bear. Then again, it wasn't a normal bear either.

Nyel searched the ground around the tree and cursed under his breath. There weren't any footprints large enough to match the scratches on the tree. Just a deer trails a few feet away. He cursed under his breath again and sighed. Back to the sky, he thought with a grimace.

He wasn't quite ready to shift yet, still sore from the last time. Instead, Nyel jogged back towards the tree line and decided to change back once he was in the open again. He jogged for some time, keeping his eye out for any other signs of what had caused those gashes in the wood. But everything else seemed normal.

The edge of the woods drew near. Nyel wondered if he should hunt for a quick meal, since it was nearing the middle of the day when something stopped him in his tracks.

The screech of multiple dragons echoed above him as large, winged shadows darted through the light, shining through the tree branches overhead. Nyel ducked down into a large prickly bush with his eyes aimed towards the sky.

His breath caught in his throat when Nyel realized they weren't ordinary dragons. A group of the unfortunate few, possessed by shadow creatures, soared past his hiding place and landed in the open field past the tree line that was once his exit route.

Nyel's eyes scanned the shaded area around him. He was thankful for the light that spilled through the leaves. He only hoped it would be enough to keep the shadow creatures away from him.

The group of the possessed acted so different than any real dragon he had encountered. They snapped at each other, their limbs trembled and turned in strange directions. He stared at them in confusion as he realized that even for shadow creatures, their actions didn't match the dragons he fought before.

A dragon with cranberry-colored scales let out a painful screech and collapsed to the ground, followed by a sand-colored dragon. Nyel could see their darkened veins had spread from the between their scales and wriggled throughout their body like worms.

The rest of the group laughed maniacally and circled around the two in a frightening, gleeful chant. The scene made Nyel's stomach churn with unease.

Something caught the attention of one sapphire dragon, causing him to pause. The dragon broke away and sniffed the ground leading towards the trees. He stopped and his head darted up so quickly that Nyel had to force himself lower to the ground under the brush. Small thorns scratched against his skin before his scales instinctively grew to protect him.

The possessed dragon's burning orange eyes stared directly at his hiding place. Nyel couldn't breathe. He held completely still, afraid that even one movement would give himself away. The sapphire dragon then turned and joined his group once more. Nyel let out a shaky breath.

The sapphire dragon hissed something to what must have been the leader, and the group froze, except for the two that writhed on the ground in pain. The lead dragon stared into the woods, his lip curling back over his teeth in a menacing, dragon-like grin.

"We know you're there, little dragon," he cooed in a chilling, high voice. "Don't worry, we won't come after you."

Nyel grit his teeth, but didn't budge from his hiding place.

The cranberry-colored dragon began seizing on the ground. His limbs flailed around, and his eyes rolled into the back of his head. Seconds after, the sand-colored dragon did the same thing. Suddenly, their dark, wriggling veins slithered out of their body. Thin black tentacles began to squirm and thrash around, growing longer and grabbing the ground around it. Nyel watched in horror as black slime poured out of the dragons' mouth, nose, eyes, and even through their scales.

The possessed dragons chanted gleefully once more in a language Nyel didn't understand. The leader and the sapphire dragon continued to watch the forest with their menacing grins.

"There's no escape for you now, little dragon," the leader screeched with laughter. "Your life essence will be a delicious host for our brothers!"

Suddenly, two sludge-like creatures yanked themselves out of the possessed dragon's bodies and fell to the ground in a pile of writhing tentacles. The dragon's bodies lie motionless on the ground, no longer a vessel for the shadow creatures. In their wake, something new had emerged. The sludge-like creatures rose, slowly taking the shape of a crude, four-legged creature. Then they would fall, rise once more, only this time taking the disturbing shape of a man.

"Feed, my brothers!" the leader shouted. "Feed! Obtain your true form!"

The new creatures rose once more, both taking on random shapes and forms, and pulled themselves forward with slimy black tentacles. And they came right for Nyel.

Unable to hide any longer, Nyel tore himself from the prickly bush and ran as fast as he could in the opposite direction. The group of dragons shrieked with delight as the sludge of monsters chased after him with their tentacles.

The undergrowth rustled and branches snapped as their slimy tentacles grabbed them to pull themselves forward. Nyel leapt over logs and dodged around trees, hoping that he had enough distance between them to shift into his dragon form. When he looked back over his shoulder, his heart sank when he realized the creatures were very fast. Their bodies rolled as their tentacles grabbed anything in sight.

His heart raced with fear as he urged his legs to move faster. He didn't know what became of the rest of the possessed dragons, only that they didn't chase after him as well. Tall weeds and grass covered the ground, causing his feet to slide along hidden roots and loose sticks that littered the ground.

Nyel dodged between trees and leapt over a large boulder. His body suddenly felt weightless as the ground angled downhill. Surprised by the sudden change, he fell to the ground and yelped when his ankle twisted under him. He toppled to the ground as a sharp pain shot up his leg.

He gasped for breath as he looked back for the creatures. They hadn't caught up to him, but he could hear the snapping of branches as they drew nearer. He grabbed his ankle and grit his teeth. Thankfully it wasn't broken. He only twisted it when he landed awkwardly on the ground.

Nyel frantically looked around and noticed a hollow under the ledge of the rock he had jumped over. Thinking fast, he pulled himself onto his feet and hopped over to it. He crawled under the ledge to hide and curled up into a ball to tuck his legs under the ledge as well.

Moments later, the sludge creatures barreled over him and rolled down the hill. Once they were far enough away, he allowed himself to catch his breath. Nyel's heart hammered in his chest as he waited and watched them disappear. What were those things? What did their leader mean by stealing his life's essence? He shuddered at the thought; he really didn't want to know.

A terrible cry echoed up the hill from far below. Nyel froze. He recognized that sound. It was the cry of a wounded animal, something big. One of the creatures must have captured it. Nyel cursed under his breath. He had to move. They could come back in search of him.

Nyel dragged himself out of his hiding spot, his arms and shoulders covered in scratches and dirt. He winced as he carefully put weight on his left foot. With a frustrated sigh, Nyel started walking back up the hill, in the opposite direction of the creatures. Maybe if he was quiet enough, they wouldn't come back in that direction looking for him. All he knew was he needed to return to the sky.

As Nyel returned to level ground, he heard a grunt from down the hill. He whipped around in search of the noise and froze once more. A large moose stood at the bottom of the wooded hill staring straight at him. Black slime dripped from its nostrils, ears, and mouth. Dark, hollow sockets remained where its eyes should have been, like a skull.

Nyel took a shaky step back and nearly fell over once more. The great moose snorted, then he charged up the hill at an incredible speed.

He bolted in a different direction, forcing his leg to carry on even with the sprain in his ankle. Nyel gasped as beads of sweat rolled down his face and neck. The possessed moose leapt up the remaining hill and barreled towards Nyel. The distance between them dwindled. His fear fueled him as Nyel pushed himself to run faster.

He glanced back and gasped when he realized the moose was only a couple of yards away from him. Black sludge sprayed from his nostrils as its hollowed eyes bore into Nyel. Into his prey.

Nyel sucked in a deep breath, willing himself to change ever so slightly. A burning sensation, much like indigestion, crept up his throat. When he was ready, Nyel whipped around and opened his mouth wide with an angry roar.

Fire spewed from his open mouth and created a wall of fire between them. Startled, the moose skidded to a halt and stared at the flames. Nyel turned his head from side to side to put as much fire between them as he could. Before the possessed moose could recuperate its thoughts, Nyel turned and ran once more.

The ground angled downwards once more. Nyel felt relief for a moment, thinking maybe he could lose the possessed moose. But his victory was short-lived. The sounds of snapping branches alerted him first. Nyel looked over his right shoulder and yelped when he realized the second sludge creature was coming right at him.

Nyel pumped his legs faster, ignoring his ankle as it burned in agony. The hill angled further down, growing steeper and steeper until he was practically sliding down it on his feet, hands, and rump.

A wild bellow resounded behind him. The moose had caught up to him as well.

Nyel ran until he spotted another ledge. He looked back with fear gripping his chest. Both creatures were nearly an arm's length away. The struggled, raspy breath of the moose drew closer. It sent a chill down Nyel's neck. He had nowhere else to go. The trees were too thick to fly out of. And even if he wanted to fly, he didn't have enough time to shift. Nyel took a deep breath, ran with all his strength, and leapt from the ledge.

He was immediately stunned as soon as his feet left the ground. Instead of falling to a lower level of the ground as he had before, the ledge suddenly dropped off of a mountainside hundreds of feet in the air.

The rocky face of the mountain he leapt from whizzed past him as Nyel began to freefall.

A terrible shriek resounded above him. He looked back in horror to find that the moose and sludge creature were directly above him. It seemed he wasn't the only one to not realize the ledge was actually a cliff.

As the moose's legs flailed in the air, the sludge creature splayed out its tentacles and grabbed at the mountainside until it pulled itself to a halt.

Nyel reached within himself to shift, but nothing happened. His body was too tired and hurt. He pleaded with himself, begging it to change to his dragon self. But still nothing happened. Tears stung his eyes as he watched the ground grow closer. This was it. This was how he was going to die. But before he got too far into his dreadful thoughts, a flash of blue scales hurtled towards him from high above.

With one swoop, a pair of clawed paws wrapped around his torso and plucked him out of the air. As he returned to the sky with his savior, Nyel watched in horror as the moose fell the rest of the way to its ultimate demise. Nyel shuddered as it disappeared into the forest below with a loud crash.

"Are you alright?" asked a familiar voice.

Nyel glanced up and was relieved to see Mairwen looking down at him with concern. He gasped in return, "Thank goodness you were here!"

"You didn't answer my question," she scolded.

Nyel nodded immediately. "I'm ok, just a sprained ankle. I have much to tell you!"

"Are you able to change into your other form?" she asked.

Still catching his breath, Nyel replied, "Could I catch a ride with you for a while? I'm exhausted."

"Of course," she said. Though she still looked concerned as she studied him.

With Mairwen's help, Nyel climbed up her leg as she gently floated high in the air. This would have scared Nyel before, but he had flown so much that the height didn't really bother him anymore. After settling Nyel on her back, Mairwen turned towards the north and started flying once more.

Flint met up with them moments later. He stared at Nyel in shock and gasped, "He really is a human!"

Nyel chuckled, just grateful to be alive. "I sure am."

"There are more of those creatures than we realized," Mairwen said. "I think it best that we return home. My father needs to hear about this."

Flint nodded at once. "Let's go find the others."

Mairwen and Flint flew as quickly as they could while Nyel told them everything that had happened to him in the forest. The only thing he left out was the fact that he felt pain when shifting. In the back of his mind, he wondered if it had stopped him from shifting when he fell, but he tried to ignore that thought for now. When he finished, Mairwen and Flint exchanged a look of concern.

"So these new sludge monsters are really just an evolution of the shadow creatures?" Flint asked after some thought.

"That's what I believe," Nyel replied. "The leader commanded them to take my life's essence. I wonder..."

"They need to absorb the lives of others in order to live," Mairwen finished his thought, meeting his eye.

Nyel nodded with a grim expression. "Exactly."

"We must stop these creatures from spreading," Flint growled in anger. "They're going to destroy us all if we stand by and do nothing."

But what were they to do? Mairwen and Flint continued the discussion while Nyel stared ahead as they approached the meeting point. They already knew that their fire didn't affect the sludge creatures. And they chased him through the forest in broad daylight. Something had to be done.

A short roar sounded behind them. They looked back and were relieved to see Swithin and Maghnus had returned from their own search.

"Any sign of Renvar?" Mairwen called.

Swithin shook his head.

"We found nothing. How about you guys?" Maghnus said as they drew closer.

"I'll let Nyel fill you in on the way back," Mairwen said.

Then Maghnus and Swithin froze when they got a look at Nyel on her back.

"I didn't know you allowed the humans on your back," Maghnus said in alarm.

Nyel wasn't expecting that reaction. In fact, he wondered what she could mean by that. Mairwen let out a growl. "You misunderstand, Maghnus. This is Nyel. He has the gift to change into a dragon."

They stared at him in amazement. "Wow! So he's not from the-"

"Stop talking," Flint growled.

Maghnus took one look at him and closed her mouth at once. Nyel stared at all of them in confusion. Finally, he turned to Mairwen and asked, "What's going on?"

Mairwen snorted in frustration. Instead of addressing him, Mairwen said, "We better return to the clan. We have much to discuss."

The others quickly agreed and flew towards their home once more. Their comments confused Nyel, but he didn't have much time to ponder them as Maghnus began asking him about what he found. But as he described everything that had happened to him once more, he couldn't keep his suspicions out of his mind. What were they hiding from him?

Chapter 28
The Island

They returned quickly to the clan in search of Talon. Mairwen led the way to a small overlook in the middle of the valley. It was the perfect vantage point for the clan leader to watch over his clan. There was a hollowed-out nook in the mountain side large enough for him to rest in out of the weather. And from the ledge, the entire valley was in view.

It was there they found him. He sat still as a statue as they approached. The four dragons landed beside him, breaking his trance. Talon looked up at them in surprise and said, "What happened? I was about to send a search party out to find you."

"We ran into trouble," Mairwen replied. "Or at least Nyel did."

Talon's eyes widened when they fell on Nyel. "You're a human again. What happened? Are you injured?"

"A little," Nyel admitted. "But I'll survive. However, you need to know what I saw."

Talon stood as he said, "Let's go retrieve Ivory. He should be a part of this discussion, I'm sure."

"Maghnus, would you mind?" Mairwen spoke up.

Maghnus bowed her head and, without another word, she and Swithin left to find Ivory. After a questioning look from her father, Mairwen said, "Not everyone knows about Nyel's gift yet. I'd rather wait until later to explain it."

"Very well," was all Talon said.

Talon leapt off the ledge, with Mairwen following close behind. They turned towards the horseshoe meeting point once more. Nyel wondered why they liked to meet there so much. Perhaps because it was far enough away from the rest of the clan? He wasn't sure.

They landed in the center of the field and waited for Ivory to arrive. Nyel carefully slid off of Mairwen's back and yelped once his feet hit the ground. He would have fallen to the ground had Mairwen not caught him with her tail.

"Are you alright?" she asked, lowering her head to his level to examine him.

Nyel grit his teeth. "I twisted my ankle running from those things. I probably didn't do it any favors by continuing to run on it."

"Do you not have healing magic?" Mairwen asked, in confusion.

He shook his head. "No. I don't have any crystals either. My friends took care of that sort of thing when we were together."

"I see. So not all humans have magic," Mairwen said thoughtfully. "I didn't know that."

"I don't expect you to know a lot about humans," Nyel said. He carefully took off his boot to get a better look at his ankle. "I knew nothing about dragons until I met Ivory and his family."

Mairwen opened her mouth to say something, but thought better of it. When Nyel looked up at her once more, she averted her gaze. What was she holding back?

The sound of wings beating against the air alerted them to Ivory's approach. With him were Maghnus, Swithin, and Trunic.

He took one look at Nyel and asked, "What happened? Why are you not a dragon?"

"There were some complications," Nyel began.

Mairwen recalled their adventure once they found Renvar had vanished. Then Nyel told them what happened when he was on his own in the forest and how Mairwen had to save him from falling to his demise. After finishing their tale, the group went silent as they absorbed everything.

"I don't know what I expected, but not that," Ivory growled. "Something has to be done about those creatures!"

"Agreed," Talon said. He paced in thought. "If those shadow creatures are evolving, where will it end? How powerful can they become if they possess all the lives they need? What is their end goal in all of this?"

"Father, we need to double our guard duty," Mairwen said. "If one of those creatures appears in our territory, we need to be ready to face it and alert the others to its presence."

Flint stepped forward at once. "I'll assemble more Guardians for tonight. We don't have a moment to lose."

At that, Talon glanced at the placement of the sun. It was entering the early evening hours.

"Very well," he nodded.

"We will lend our assistance on the matter while we are here," Ivory offered. "What's left of my Guardians will help keep watch over night."

Flint bowed to both of them and hurried to find the Guardians.

Nyel turned to Ivory and said, "So, you sent the others home?"

"I did," Ivory replied, turning his gaze to Talon. "Only the Guardians you trusted remain, Nyel."

His face reddened at his words. Did he send them back because of him? If Orden didn't hate him enough already, he will despise him now. Nyel felt the need to apologize to Ivory for causing any trouble, but at the same time, he was relieved that they were gone.

"I want all of you to rest for the evening," Talon ordered to Mairwen and her group. "Tomorrow we will start patrolling the area for any signs of Renvar and those creatures. Understood?"

Mairwen nodded. "Yes father."

"Go on then," he said.

She began to lower herself to the ground to offer Nyel a ride when Talon stopped her. "I want Nyel to accompany me first before he returns for the evening."

Mairwen paused and straightened up. "Does that mean…?"

Talon nodded. "I'm taking him to the island."

Nyel glanced at both of them in confusion. "What? Why? What's out there?"

But they didn't seem to hear him.

"Are you certain you don't want me to accompany you?" Mairwen asked.

Talon shook his head. "There's no need. We won't be there long. You approve of this, yes Ivory?"

Nyel looked to Ivory who nodded his approval. "Now is as good a time as any. I will return to my Guardians and prepare them for their watch."

He then turned to Nyel and said, "Be safe."

"But Ivory, I don't understand what's going on," Nyel protested.

Ivory chuckled. "You'll see soon enough. I'll see you later."

With that, Ivory and Trunic returned to the sky and flew over the mountain towards the valley. Nyel turned to Talon, unsure of what to do. What was so important about that island?

"Father, I must insist that I go," Mairwen argued.

Talon growled at her, losing his patience. "Do as I say Mairwen!"

Maghnus stepped forward and nudged Mairwen. "Come on. Flint will need our help to get the others together for the night watch. And I wouldn't mind a quick hunt for some food. How about you?"

Mairwen growled and said, "Fine."

Without another word to her father, Mairwen left, with Maghnus and Swithin close behind her. When they were gone, only Talon and Nyel remained. Talon let out a sigh and shook his head. "Both of my children are so eager to grow up and take my place. It's not a position they should take lightly."

Nyel winced as he slid his boot back over his swollen ankle. "I can understand Zander. But do you not think that Mairwen is ready to be a leader?"

"She's just so young and inexperienced," Talon said. "I don't want her getting into things she's not ready for."

Nyel chuckled. "I know what you mean. You know what I think? I think our Ascendant's Gifts chose us for a reason. We are both young for such a power, yet it still chose us. That has to mean something, right?"

Talon stared at him thoughtfully. "I suppose you're right. I'm just not prepared for her to leave the nest."

"You'll have to let her go eventually," Nyel replied, hobbling to his feet. "From what I've seen so far, she's an excellent leader."

This time, Talon chuckled. "Alright, enough with this talk. Can you change or will you need a ride on my back?"

Nyel attempted to reach for his power. Every nerve in his body began to ache and he stumbled slightly before giving up. "If you don't mind, I'll take your offer."

"Very well."

Talon lowered himself to the ground, and Nyel carefully climbed his leg and shoulder to his back. Nyel groaned every time his ankle bumped into his scales. Once he was on Talon's back, the leader of the clan stood up and glanced back at him.

"Are you going to be able to hang on?" he asked with uncertainty.

Nyel patted his shoulder. "Don't worry. This isn't my first time flying this way. I'll be careful."

Talon nodded. He leapt into the air and wobbled a bit as he climbed higher into the sky. Nyel wrapped his arms around the dragon's neck as Talon laughed boisterously.

"Now, this is an experience!" he exclaimed with glee.

Nyel shook his head in amusement as Talon continued to laugh. He was glad Talon was enjoying himself. He was probably the first dragon who was excited to have a human on his back. It would most likely be the last dragon to enjoy it as well. Nyel decided to just savor the moment. He threw back his head and arms as the wind whipped through his hair and let out a yell of his own.

They passed over a white sandy beach and soared beyond it over the ocean. Nyel breathed in the salty air once more and listened to the gentle waves that crashed against the shore. The brilliant blue water below sparkled in the evening sunlight. As they ventured further out and the water became deeper, something splashed the surface, catching his eye. As Nyel studied the area, his amazement grew upon spotting a fish bigger than he had ever seen before darting back into the depths. He looked up towards the horizon beyond the island and realized the ocean continued on further than he could make out.

"What do you think is out there?" Nyel asked in amazement as he studied the horizon.

Talon shook his head. "I'm sure there are more islands and more land out there somewhere. I'd never assume that we are the only creatures living in such a vast space as this."

The thought of other worlds and kingdoms intrigued, yet concerned, Nyel. He had never thought about the possibility of anything else existing besides Hailwic. He was so content with his life in Folke growing up that he never even considered the other possibilities out there. How narrow-minded he had been.

It didn't take long to reach the mysterious island that Talon wanted to bring him to. Something sparkled on the similar white, sandy beach as they approached. Nyel squinted and realized two dragons laid in the sun, warming themselves. Beams of sunlight bounced off their bronze and blue scales in brilliant specks of colors. They looked peaceful until one of them noticed them approaching in the sky.

Once they spotted Talon, they quickly got to their feet. Talon landed in a spray of sand and walked the rest of the way to the two dragons. The sound of the waves against the shore were so relaxing and the sun felt comforting against his scales. He admired the life this clan must live in more peaceful times.

"Why are you lounging out here like a couple of sun-lizards?" Talon asked in a stern voice. Nyel realized then that perhaps these dragons were Guardians as well.

"Sorry Talon," said the bronze male. "It was such a beautiful evening. We wanted to enjoy it for a moment after we completed our rounds."

"You were both practically asleep," Talon growled in frustration. "You realize if we were strangers, we could have killed you without you even knowing what hit you!"

"No one comes out here besides you anyway," the blue dragon chuckled, but immediately went silent by the death glare that Talon gave him.

"You're obviously not ready to handle such a responsibility, Dulryg," Talon growled. The disappointment in his voice seemed to cut more than his words.

The blue dragon hung his head in shame. "I apologize Talon. I didn't mean any disrespect. It's just nothing ever happens out here."

"And it's your duty to protect this island when it's assigned to you," Talon sighed. The two Guardians shifted uncomfortably in place when Talon fell silent.

Finally Talon said, "Finish your week here and prove to me you can handle this responsibility. Then I'll decide if you can handle this task in the future. We are doubling our guard inland. There are new dark creatures drawing near our home. We must always be vigilant!"

"Dark creatures?" Dulryg gasped. "If that's so, shouldn't we be home instead of here?"

"I'll make that decision if I need you. Now do as I say."

They nodded in agreement. Then Dulryg said, "I'll go make another round now!"

The bronze dragon followed his lead when Talon said, "Wait, Ash. I need you to find Jaela and have her meet me here, please."

"Yes, Ascendant," Ash said with a slight bow. Then he disappeared down a path that led into the woods. The path was just large enough for his body to fit into, and he soon disappeared from sight.

Nyel watched him leave, even more confused than ever. Why would Talon worry about protecting an island so far out from his clan? He wondered if maybe there were dragons here he wanted to protect that didn't want to be in the clan. Maybe they kept their nests here. But why would he be willing to show Nyel where their nests were?

Nothing made sense to him, but he didn't press Talon for any information. He would learn soon enough. Instead, Nyel carefully slid off his back and landed in the soft sand. He limped around him and turned his gaze back on Hailwic in the distance while they waited. It wasn't too far. If he needed to swim back in either form, he could manage it. At least he thought he could. It would be an exhausting feat either way. The mountains were a breathtaking backdrop behind the ocean. They stretched further to the west for miles.

The island rested near the bottom of what appeared to be a V formation of the land that surrounded it with the ocean. On the eastern side, he could see the mountains they had traveled through. To the northeast, he could make out a large forest that ran far from his sight. To his right, in the northwest, the mountains dwindled and instead turned into a large, vacant plain that stretched on without a tree in sight.

As Nyel studied the landscape around him, he wondered if anyone had been out that far from the Kingdom to make a proper map of the land. The few maps he had studied in his lifetime only reached the bottom portion of the Dragon Mountains just past Lake Peril.

"I've found her, Ascendant," Ash's voice announced, interrupting his thoughts. "She's on her way."

"Thank you Ash, that will be all," Talon nodded.

Ash bowed his head in return, leapt into the air, and flew in the opposite direction of Dulryg. Nyel assumed to guard the island as Talon had instructed before. Then he realized something. Dulryg and Ash never once questioned him about being there. Did they not notice him? Everything about Talon's clan was an enigma to him. Nyel turned his attention to the path, listening for the cracks of tree branches or the shaking of leaves against scales. He heard a small rustle further in heading towards them.

"Ah, here she comes now," Talon said with a pleased expression. "Nyel, I want you to meet a special friend of mine. I'd like to introduce you to Jaela, Chieftain of the Draven Tribe."

At the same moment, a small figure emerged from the island woods. Much shorter and more slender than he would have ever guessed. A figure that only walked on two legs and carried a strong staff by their side. Nyel's eyes widened and his jaw dropped as out from the woodland path emerged a tall, slender blonde-haired woman.

Chapter 29
The Wrath of Darkness

She stopped in front of them, bowed respectfully to Talon, and said, "I see you have brought a straggler to our island. Did we not agree that we would discuss such things before making such a big decision?"

Jaela looked to be in her thirties. Her skin was tan from long days in the sun. She wore thick leather armor over a sleeveless beige shirt and leather-skin pants. Around her neck was a necklace made of small white shells, and in the center was the same green stone that Shara gave to Iris. A mysterious crystal that allowed her to talk to the dragons. In her hand was a strong wooden staff that was slightly taller than her, with something tied around the top of it. It looked to be a bundle of bright, colorful bird feathers.

"This isn't a straggler," Talon said, gesturing to Nyel with a happy gleam in his eye. "This is Nyel, of the Ryngar clan. You haven't met him or its leader yet."

Her face fell slightly, and her grip tightened on her staff. Her left hand drifted down towards her hip, where a long, curved sword rested in a leather sheath. "What is this? You expect me to believe this man has come from another dragon clan? Has your brain turned to mush? He's lying to you!"

Her voice grew angry as she spoke, her hazel eyes burned holes into Nyel. "How could you be so careless, Talon?"

Talon lifted a paw and said, "Wait, Jaela, hear me out! Nyel is unique and I think you could become great friends if you give him a chance. He is an Ascendant with great power, like my daughter. Will you allow him to show you before you make a judgment on either of us?"

Jaela studied Nyel and only gave a stiff nod. She didn't release her grip on her weapons. Talon looked at Nyel and said, "Will you show her?"

Nyel stared at him and then turned his gaze back on her, still dumbfounded that there was another human living amongst dragons.

"Talon, I'm sorry, but I'm having difficulties right now," Nyel apologized. "My body is too weak from the day."

Talon took one look at him and gasped, "Of course! Jaela, I've also come here to ask you to heal him of his injuries. Can you do that for me?"

"Why would I do that?" she seethed, still staring at Nyel like he was the most dangerous creature she had ever laid eyes on. Not minding the massive dragon that towered over both of them.

"Please, Jaela? I promise it will be worthwhile in the end," Talon asked once more. He lowered his head to her eye level.

Jaela stared at him in annoyance. Finally she said, "Fine. But if he attacks me, I'll be serving your hide to the rest of my people!"

"Fair enough," Talon laughed.

Nyel stared at them, dumbfounded as they interacted. It was as if they were old friends, or like they had grown up together as brother and sister. It was so bizarre to him to see a human and a dragon treat each other as equals. It made the corners of his mouth raise into a small smile. This was what he had been looking for.

Jaela approached Nyel with a hard expression and grumbled, "Where are you hurt?"

"My ankle," Nyel answered quickly, pointing down to his foot.

Jaela looked down at his boot and then back up at him. "Well, let me see it!"

"Oh right," Nyel said nervously. He sat in the sand and carefully pried his boot off his swollen ankle once more.

She knelt on the ground and examined his leg. "It's a good thing Talon brought you here. I think you might have broken it."

Nyel stared at her in shock. "Really? Wow, I can't believe I could run on it."

"You broke your ankle and still ran on it? What on earth possessed you to do that?" she scowled as her hands began to glow a faint green.

Nyel held still as she ran her hands over his ankle. "I was being chased by shadow creatures."

Jaela's eyes shot up at him. "Talon has mentioned them before. And you were strong enough to survive?"

"Thankfully," Nyel chuckled.

She took her time to heal his ankle completely. Once Jaela finished, she stood up and moved away from him. Nyel put his foot down and carefully stood up. He was immediately relieved to find that the pain in his ankle was gone. Nyel bounced around on both feet, then one foot, and grinned.

"Thank you so much!"

"It was nothing," she mumbled. Then she looked to Talon and said, "So why did you bring him here if not only for the healing?"

Talon looked at Nyel once more. "Can you try now?"

Nyel nodded, suddenly nervous. He quickly pulled on his boot and took a few steps back.

With a deep breath, Nyel reached within himself for his power. The pain returned, but this time, he was able to fight against it. Jaela yelped and took a few cautious steps backwards as Nyel changed back into his large, green-scaled dragon form. He landed on all fours and flourished his wings while he stared awkwardly at Jaela.

"He can turn into a dragon?" Jaela gasped in shock. "I didn't know we could possess such magic."

"I'm not a dragon," Nyel finally spoke up, causing her to freeze. "Not originally, anyway. It's nice to meet you, Jaela."

"What do you mean, not originally? I don't know any human magic that could turn a man into a dragon," she questioned, keeping her eyes on him.

Nyel stated simply, "I received an Ascendant's power, which allowed me to become a dragon." He didn't dare approach her. She was still on edge by his presence. He couldn't believe he was meeting another human this far out in the dragon's realm. What other secrets did this land hold?

"But you really started out as a human? Truly?" she asked, her expression intrigued yet still guarded.

Nyel nodded.

"Why have you come here?" she asked after a moment of silence.

Nyel hesitated. "To be honest, I didn't know why Talon brought me here to your island until moments ago. As for being here amongst the dragons, I have many reasons that may take a while to explain."

Jaela and Talon exchanged looks. She then studied Nyel a moment longer until finally she straightened up and dropped her left hand from her knife. "Talon is funny in that way—always keeping secrets."

"I have so many questions," Nyel blurted out. His head was racing at this new revelation.

"I can answer some for you," Talon offered, laying on the beach in the warmth of the sun. In the same moment, Dulryg passed by overhead, studied the beach below, and then turned and disappeared over the trees. Jaela didn't even flinch at his presence as she stood pondering over something.

Talon began, "A century or two ago, humans and dragons lived in peace. They worked together to create a better life for all under the rule of their respected leaders. For the humans, it was their king who led them. For us, we had a Queen."

Nyel tilted his head as he said, "I didn't know dragons believed in monarchy."

Talon chuckled. "It wasn't quite the same as your monarchy, I'm sure. The Queen dedicated her life to protecting all of her people for us. She ruled with a powerful magic that kept us connected and unified as one."

"What does this have to do with Jaela's tribe?" Nyel wondered out loud.

"We are the last descendants of the men and women who lived in peace with the dragons," Jaela answered.

"How did you end up here?" Nyel asked in amazement.

Jaela exchanged another look with Talon, before she responded, "The Ascendant of the Maeve clan has always been a friend to our people. Each Ascendant has vowed to keep us safe, and in return we use our magic to help defend them, heal them, and protect something very sacred to us all."

"Sacred?"

Jaela hesitated. "Sacred and secret. I'll leave it at that."

"I see," Nyel said, his mind racing. What would they be protecting that was so important to Talon's clan? No matter what it was, it made Nyel feel more at ease than he had in a while. Their level of trust in each other was a welcome relief.

"I would like to hear your story Nyel," Jaela said suddenly, leaning against a large boulder in the sand. "How did your abilities come to be?"

"I was chosen, much like any other Ascendant," Nyel began.

He then explained his story about how he met Ivory, Seren, and her children. How they saved each other's lives that day. And how Ivory's blood passed on the Ascendant's Gift to him. Talon and Jaela listened intently without interruption. Her eyes went wide as he told his story. After he finished, she asked, "You went against your own people to save those dragons? You lost so much."

Nyel gave her a thoughtful smile. "I lost a lot that day, but I gained more confidence. I'm stronger now in more ways than one and I also made new friends that accept me just the way I am. So, I suppose I no longer regret what I did that day."

"And what brought you here to our tribe?" Jaela asked after a moment of thought.

"It's my goal to meet with all the clans to bring humans and dragons together. We need to be united now more than ever," Nyel stated. Then he added, "I didn't know you were here, but I'm glad we've had the chance to meet."

Jaela smirked. "A heroic journey, indeed. Is that all?"

"What do you mean?" Nyel asked, confused.

"Is that the only reason you came this far in your journey?" she asked again, studying him closely.

He stared at her, unsure what she meant. As Nyel opened his mouth to respond, a sudden distant roar interrupted him.

Talon leapt to his feet and turned towards the mainland. One after another, a resounding call echoed over the blue waters towards them.

"Something's wrong," Talon said with a stone icy glare in the direction of his home.

Ash and Dulryg floated towards them, but Talon shouted, "Stay here and protect the island!"

With that, Talon leapt into the air in a spray of sand and hurried back towards his clan. Nyel turned to follow him when a hand smacked against his right shoulder. He looked down in surprise to find Jaela meeting his gaze with an intense look in her eyes.

"Change is coming, Nyel. You're on the right path. Just follow your instincts," she said.

Nyel opened his mouth to ask what she meant, but Jaela only smirked and said, "Don't worry. We will meet again."

She then released him and, without another word, she ran back into the woods, leaving him alone on the beach.

Her words caught him off guard, but he didn't have time to ponder them. Nyel lifted his wings and soared into the sky, happy to be in his dragon form once more. Talon had already reached the mainland by the time Nyel left the island. He chased after Talon as quickly as he could. When he caught up to him, they flew together the rest of the way back into the valley.

"I'm going to find Mairwen," Talon called. "Return to your clan and make sure they're alright."

Nyel nodded and flew back to the pond at once. Although he knew Ivory sent a few Guardians home, it still surprised him to find that only four of Ivory's Guardians remained, along with Aydamaris and Sable. Nyel landed beside them and asked, "Where's Ivory? What happened?"

Glyder spoke up first. "I don't know what's happening. Ivory went to see Mairwen before they started calling."

Suddenly, a loud commotion echoed from the opposite end of the valley. They fell silent and turned their heads towards the sound. Roars of what sounded like anger and fear built in unison as the clan flew into the air in a flurry of multicolor wings and scales. Nyel leapt into the air without hesitation. The rest of his small group of Guardians followed him at once.

"What's going on?" Glyder shouted from the back of the group.

Nyel searched the sky around the swirl of dragons ahead, but couldn't see what caused them to panic. "I don't know, but it doesn't sound good. Stick together and keep your eye out for any signs of trouble."

Then he spotted it.

Down beside the stream of water was a trembling dragon that stood over the bloodied body of another. The trembling dragon looked crazed. Black sludge dripped from his mouth and oozed through his scales. He stared down at the bloodied dragon, panting as if waiting for something.

Aydamaris gasped as she glimpsed the horrific scene. "Is that…Renvar?"

Nyel looked again, and his stomach twisted in horror. She was right. It was Yawna's mate they encountered from the day before. The one that disappeared before they could return to his body. He was alive. But no, he couldn't be, Nyel thought as he eyed the black slime.

"But I thought he was dead?" Glyder shouted, his voice cracking with fear.

Then the injured dragon shook. Nyel growled, "Something has taken over his body. Look!"

The bloodied dragon rose to his feet, his body convulsing in the process. With three large coughs, the injured dragon hacked up a ball of black sludge and his eyes went wild. In unison, Renvar and the new sludge creature looked up at them and let out a piercing shriek unlike anything he had heard. The only sound that came close was the screech of the shadow creatures when they vanished in the sun. A cold chill ran down Nyel's spine.

He turned to the others and said, "We can't let them make any contact with the others. That's how this sickness spreads!"

"Then let's get rid of it!" Trunic growled, before plunging downwards towards the creatures.

Nyel and the rest of the Guardians flew beside him. They opened their powerful jaws and let out a torrent of flames down upon the two sickly dragons. Their screeches pierced the air with an intensity that threatened to drive Nyel mad.

Then the two dragons started flapping their wings. It made their sludge begin to swirl through the air. Trunic led the Guardians back up into the sky to avoid getting hit with the black slime. As they regrouped higher up in the air, Nyel spotted Talon and his Guardians soaring towards them, along with Ivory and Mairwen.

Mairwen gasped as she caught sight of the first attacker. "Renvar?"

Nyel growled, "Now we know where he disappeared to."

Niko stared at him in shock, obviously not caught up with the news. "But he was dead! We all saw it with our own eyes!"

Nyel shook his head. "This is an evolution of what the shadow creatures are capable of."

"We can't let them roam around here and take anyone else. Let's move," Talon ordered.

Mairwen snarled and dove towards the dragons. As she opened her mouth to let out her frost breath, the second dragon arched his neck and spat a glob of sludge directly at her. In a split second, a flash of bronze-yellow scales whizzed by and pulled her out of the way just in time before the projectile sludge hit her. As she tried to regain her balance, she looked up at her savior and gasped, "Flint!"

Flint stayed close by her side and checked her over. "Are you alright? Did any of it get on you?"

She shook her head. "I don't think so."

He turned his gaze on Renvar and growled, "I can't believe the dark magic got Renvar. And now he's after more of us. This has to end!"

Talon roared, furious that his daughter nearly became the next target. "Destroy them!"

He and his Guardians dove at the sickly dragons and released another round of fire on them. The heat of their combined fire was so intense that Nyel could feel it from his place in the air. The second dragon shrieked as it succumbed to the flames and dropped to the ground. Renvar soared into the air and shot a jet of black sludge at the first Guardian he saw, Swithin. Fortunately, Swithin was faster. He dodged his attack before he, too, became infected.

Renvar arched his neck to spit out another round of sludge, but something stopped him. He froze in place as the dark, hollowed sockets where his eyes should have been searched right and left for something they could neither see nor hear. His head whipped around and stared off into the distance. With another nasty screech, Renvar turned and fled from the scene without looking back.

With an angry roar, Talon exclaimed, "Don't let him get away!"

"Wait! I don't know if that's a good idea," Flint shouted as he rejoined him.

Talon snarled, "We can't let him escape and infect anyone else!"

"I understand," Flint urged. "But he already attacked one of our own, two if you count Renvar himself. Who knows what else is out there? All I'm saying is it could be a trap. I think we should regroup and come up with a plan."

A sudden screech split through the air, and a spew of sludge shot up from the ground behind them. Before anyone else could react, Mairwen spun around and unleashed her icy breath on the second slime creature. Both the creature and the sludge it hurled at their Guardians turned into ice in seconds. The ball of sludge dropped to the ground and shattered around them.

The second creature lay motionless in ice on the ground, its maw still open wide to attack them.

"Flint," Talon ordered in a furious voice. His glare was on the frozen creature.

Flint nodded and swung his tail at the frozen sludge creature. It too, shattered into thousands of tiny pieces and scattered on the ground around them.

Talon turned back towards the direction Renvar had flown, but with the sudden commotion he was no longer in sight. With a frustrated growl, Talon said, "Everyone to the meeting point at once! Round up the rest of the clan. Flint, take a few others and inspect the valley. Make sure there aren't any more of those creatures hiding anywhere."

The Guardians did as they were told and hurried towards the field, once more surrounded by the mountains. There, many members of the clan had already gathered. The younglings cowered under their mother's belly with wide eyes and trembling legs. The clan whispered amongst themselves with urgency in their voices. Once Talon landed, the clan hurried towards their leader and started hurling questions at him all at once.

"What was that?"

"What happened to Renvar?"

"Why did he attack one of our own?"

"Is that what a shadow creature does?"

Their swarm of questions made Nyel's head spin. Talon tried his best to answer each one at a time, but then another voice would drown him out. The closest clan members even started asking him questions about what had happened. He tried to focus on them when suddenly a voice resounded in his head much louder than the rest. *Return to me. Time is running out. Hailwic is in danger. Return to me...*

Nyel's head snapped up, and he looked around for the source of the voice. His eyes met Mairwen's, who looked just as astonished. The others around him didn't seem to notice the voice. With a frustrated growl, Nyel broke away from the crowd and trotted over to a more quiet area.

His heart fluttered as he said aloud, "Where are you? I don't know where to find you."

You know where I am. Return to me...

He knew where she was? How would he know such a thing? Nyel knew nothing different than he did when he first heard the voice

"So you heard it as well?" Aydamaris asked, as she joined him. Mairwen was quick to follow them with a look of astonishment.

"How could we possibly know where she is?" Mairwen sighed in frustration.

Talon began shouting over the uproar of frightened and angry dragons, trying to get their attention. The Guardians of Talon's clan returned in groups with the rest of their family and friends who had strayed from the area.

Mairwen looked back at him and sighed. "I don't have time for mysterious voices. We have too much to worry about as it is."

Nyel's head spun as he tried to think about any clues that might lead them in the direction. Even so, he couldn't think of anything. They sat together in silence as Talon ordered his clan to listen to him.

"Guardians will surround the perimeter tonight. I want everyone else to sleep in packs," Talon commanded. His usual friendly tone had gone hard without a trace of fear. "No one will leave the clan without permission. The surrounding areas are not safe. No one will go anywhere within the clan on their own. In the morning, I will send out groups to patrol the area for any signs of those things. And if we find them, we will destroy them. No matter what. Do you understand me?"

The clan members nodded and stated their understanding, but they were still uneasy. Nyel couldn't blame them, he felt the same way.

"My Guardians and I will also contribute to protecting your clan as long as we stay here," Ivory added.

Flint and his small group of Guardians appeared from over the mountain and landed close to the gathered clan.

"The valley is safe," Flint called to Talon.

Talon nodded. Then he turned his gaze on his clan and said, "You may return to the valley. Heed my warning. We will establish hunting times when we learn more tomorrow."

One by one, the Guardians led the clan back to the valley. Nyel stood, and for a moment, he thought about searching for the voice. But no, that wasn't a good idea, he thought as he studied the setting sun. It was going to be dark soon. It wouldn't be wise to venture outside the clan's territory in the dark without knowing what could be out there waiting for him.

With a sigh, he started towards Ivory instead. "Where do you want me to keep watch?"

Ivory shook his head. "No, Nyel. We have already decided that you need a rest. You went through enough today."

"But my ankle has been healed," Nyel said before he could stop himself. His heart leapt into his throat. Did Ivory know about Jaela and the others on the island? Was he supposed to keep it secret even from him?

In answer to his question, Ivory said, "I know what you encountered on the island. And while I'm grateful that you're better, that doesn't mean you're not still in need of a rest. Don't worry, you'll have plenty to do in the morning."

Nyel sighed. He wasn't going to argue with Ivory. Instead, he gently nudged Ivory's shoulder with his snout and said, "As you wish."

Ivory chuckled. "Get some rest."

Nyel turned to Mairwen, Aydamaris, and Sable, who had joined them when he wasn't looking. "Are you coming?"

Aydamaris shook her head. "I've rested today. I plan to assist with the watch this evening."

"As do I," Sable said.

Mairwen sighed. "I'll rest a little later. I have to make sure Zander isn't getting into trouble and speak to my father. We will find you if we need you."

Nyel nodded, feeling somewhat ashamed that he wasn't helping them. But he knew better than to argue. They outnumbered him.

He wished them a safe night and flew into the air. The events of the day ran through his mind as he flew back into the valley and found his place by the quiet pond. Nyel drank many gulps of the cool water, found a soft patch of grass, and curled up into a ball. He forced himself to close his eyes as the day turned into night. At some point as he ran through the woods from the creatures in his mind for the fifth time, he eventually succumbed to sleep.

The night was still when he woke. To Nyel, it felt like he had just fallen asleep, but hours had passed. Something had unsettled him, but he didn't hear a sound. No birds, no bugs, not even the breath or grunt of a nearby dragon. Nyel opened his eyes and noticed a strange green glow that lit up the blades of grass around him.

He slowly lifted his head and froze. Standing beside the small pond was the slim form of a glowing emerald dragon. He could not see well-defined features, but he could tell it was an adult female. Her entire body glowed like starlight. Wisps of soft green light floated off of her. The gentle glow reflected in the smooth water of the pond. She rustled her wings and lowered her head, as if to study him.

Nyel hurried to his feet and looked around to see if anyone else saw what he did, but no one was around. Was he dreaming?

The emerald hued mirage stepped towards him. Nyel stared at her in wonder until her silent footsteps led her to stand right in front of him. Soft, white orbs floated where her eyes should have been. Nyel knew he should be afraid. He knew he should turn away, to fight her, or to even call for help.

But he wasn't afraid of her. There was something so warm and familiar about her. The emerald dragon leaned towards him and carefully touched her snout to his.

A pulse of light exploded from her body and rushed through the valley, lighting everything up in that magnificent color of emerald. Even so, no one stirred from their sleep. Even the Guardians were not alerted by her presence.

The emerald dragon slowly lifted her head and met his eyes once more with those glowing, white orbs. Then the dragon surprised him as she spoke in a voice that echoed in his head.

At long last, you have returned to me…Nyel.

Chapter 30
The Dragon Queen

Y ou're her!" Nyel exclaimed in surprise. "You're the one who's been calling us! Who are you? Why did we need to find you?"

The glowing dragon didn't respond. Instead, she turned away from him and suddenly sprung into the air without a sound. Nyel blinked for a moment; afraid it had only been a dream. But when he looked up at the sky, he noticed the soft green glow of the dragon waiting for him high above. Nyel took a deep breath, opened his wings, and leapt into the air.

When he had almost reached her level, the glowing dragon turned from him once more and zipped through the air like a shooting star over the northern mountains.

"Hey, wait up!" he called. Nyel pumped his wings and chased after her, afraid that if he lost sight of her, he'd never see her again.

He flew over the mountain tops that bordered the northern valley. As he soared past them, he could hear a voice shouting to him. Nyel looked over his shoulder to see Aydamaris calling to him in concern at her post, but he didn't stop. He was too close to finding out the truth.

Nyel scanned the area, unsure where the emerald dragon had gone. Then he spotted her. A distant glow in the night over the calm, dark ocean. Without a second thought, he hurried after her.

The glowing dragon watched him draw closer to her for a few moments. Then she turned away once more and zipped through the air with a trail of emerald light behind her.

"Wait! I need to talk to you," he yelled. But it was no use.

The emerald dragon shot over the ocean until she dipped downwards and landed on the lonely island. The entire island lit up in a wild display of white and green light and then went dark once more. Why would she lead him there?

Nyel hesitated, wondering if he should go back to find Aydamaris and Mairwen. After all, he wasn't the only one that the voice had called to.

Then he thought of Aydamaris and of her 'dream' the morning before. He remembered she told him that a green dragon had come to her, but had rejected her. Perhaps he was the only one meant to follow the mirage. Either that or it was a trap of some sort.

Nyel snorted as he fought himself over the right choice. He had to find out what she was. He had to try.

With that thought in mind, Nyel flew as fast as he could over the last stretch of ocean to the secretive island. The calm ocean water rushed underneath him as he glided over it. He glanced up at the sky to find it twinkling with thousands of stars. For a split second, he thought of how much Iris would love a night like this. Perhaps one day he could bring her back to see it for herself.

He landed on the white sandy beach and looked around. There was no sign of the emerald dragon anywhere. He cursed under his breath at having lost her when suddenly a growl erupted from the sky.

Nyel leapt backwards as Dulryg landed in a spray of sand and bared his teeth at him.

"What are you doing here?" Dulryg growled.

Before he could answer, he felt a thud behind him. Nyel looked back to find Ash hunched behind him, his sharp teeth gleaming in the moonlight.

"Didn't you see the glowing dragon?" Nyel asked them, looking from one to the other.

"What dragon?" Ash grunted, staring at him like he was crazy.

Nyel was about to respond when he spotted a lone figure with a torch moving in the woods. The figure slowly emerged from the tree line to reveal Jaela. In her right hand she carried her staff and in the other hand, she held a torch in a tight grip.

Dulryg and Ash shared a look of concern before turning to her.

"It's alright, boys," she said to the Guardians. "Let him pass."

The Guardians stared at Nyel skeptically, but did as they were told. However, they didn't return to the sky. They stood by the tree line and watched Nyel intently.

Nyel stared at her in surprise. "Jaela? Why are you out here at this hour? Did you know I was coming?"

"Forgive me for my coldness towards you before. You're more impressive than I had originally thought," Jaela said with a smirk. "Green, I'm sure, but I think she made a wise decision."

"A wise decision? On what? Did you see where the glowing dragon went?" Nyel asked in a rush, more confused than ever.

"Change into your human form and follow me," was all Jaela said as she turned to venture back into the woods.

Nyel shook his head in frustration. "Why won't you answer me? What's going on?"

Jaela stopped and turned to face him. "You'll learn soon enough, young Shifter. You have yet to answer her call."

Nyel's mouth dropped open. How did she know about that? Without another word, Nyel shifted back into his human form. He let out an agonized cry as pain shot through his body. Nyel fell to his knees, gasping for air. The light slowly approached him once more, and a hand entered his view. He slowly looked up to see Jaela looking down at him with a kind smile. "Take my hand."

Surprisingly, he found her hand to be callused as he reached for it. Jaela pulled him to his feet and then released his hand to grab her staff, which she had rested against a tree. "Can you walk?"

"I'll manage," Nyel grunted, his pain subsiding.

"Then let us go," Jaela replied. She then turned to the Guardians and said, "Don't let anyone else pass until I say so. Understood?"

The Guardians grunted and turned away from her.

Together, Nyel and Jaela walked into the dark woods. It was unusually quiet on the island as well. Nyel couldn't hear anything rustling through the leaves or scurrying across the ground. It was as if the entire world had held its breath as he searched for answers.

Jaela led him down a long path towards the center of the woods. The trees closed in on them, narrowing until the path was only wide enough for them to walk single file. Perhaps to keep the dragons away from their home, Nyel thought.

In the distance, he noticed the glow of light. When they got closer, he realized it was a combination of torches and a large campfire. They made it through the last of the trees and entered what appeared to be a small village. Nyel stared in wonder at the small houses that surrounded them. The villagers built small houses with the trees from the forest and many of them were on stilts. He even noticed some houses built in the trees themselves.

It was late, so he didn't see many people out in the village. But he did spot guards, men and women, surrounding the perimeter. They looked at him with curiosity, but didn't leave their positions.

"Come this way," Jaela said in a hushed voice.

They moved through the center of the village down a packed dirt road. When they came to the fireplace in the center of the village, Jaela turned left down another path. This path led to a lone house that was also on stilts and was bigger than the rest of them.

"What is this place?" Nyel whispered.

"This is our village of the Draven Tribe," Jaela said with pride. She then pointed to the large structure. "And this is my home. Every chieftain has lived here, carrying the history of our people for generations within those walls. But it is what lives behind my home that we hold most sacred. Stay close."

They circled around her house down a stone lane path through a large grassy field towards a bluff. At the bottom of the bluff, there was a large opening where guards stood on either side of the entrance with wooden spears at their sides. At the end of their spears were sharp metal tips. When Jaela approached them, they bowed respectfully.

"Who is this?" one man asked, studying Nyel closely. He was tall and muscular, with long brown hair tied back. Around his dark eyes he wore red face paint, along with two stripes that ran down his chin. The other guard, who resembled the first with his dark eyes, short brown hair, and muscular frame, also wore the same face paint.

"This is Nyel. He is here to answer the call," Jaela said with pride. "Nyel, this is my husband, Calix, and our dear friend, Eero."

The two men stared at Nyel in disbelief. "Him?"

"Stand aside, Calix," Jaela said. "You know better than to question her judgment. This is what we've been waiting for."

The first man, Calix, nodded. "Of course, my love. If you are certain."

With that, Calix and Eero returned to either side of the tunnel entrance and waited.

Jaela then turned to Nyel. "From here, you will go alone."

Nyel looked at her nervously. "What's in there?"

"Someone who has been waiting to meet you for a long time," she answered.

He stared into the cave entrance. It wasn't a large tunnel. He wouldn't be able to walk inside in his dragon form. Nyel felt uneasy. What was this all about? What if it was a trap? But it couldn't be, Nyel thought. How would Jaela have known that he had followed a mirage to her island?

Nyel took a deep breath and nodded. "Ok, I'll go."

Jaela grinned, her sun-tanned face glowing with delight. "We'll be here when you return. You can count on us."

He nodded once again, unsure what she meant by that. Jaela handed him her torch and took a step back, eagerly waiting.

Nyel held the torch high in a firm grasp and took a cautious step through the entrance. The rock tunnel was narrow but smooth. He was certain that someone had made it using magic. He took his time to be certain he wasn't walking into something dangerous. Several minutes passed as the tunnel declined further into the earth. The light of his torch danced ahead of him on the walls and the ceiling. He was wondering if the tunnel would go on forever when finally he could make out a faint green glow towards the end of the tunnel.

He took another deep breath and hurried the rest of the way down the tunnel. Once he reached the end, Nyel stopped and stared in amazement.

A huge, cavernous, oval-shaped room greeted him. The warm glow of emerald green, the same color as the dragon who had come to him, filled the room. The space was so enormous that a couple of the homes outside could fit inside it stacked on top of each other. A stream of water trickled far off in the back of the room where he couldn't see. And sitting in the center of the spacious room, on a stone pedestal, sat a large emerald crystal the size of a watermelon.

Nyel rested his torch on the ground, knowing that it wouldn't catch anything on fire, and slowly approached the crystal with a sense of awe.

It wasn't like any crystal or stone he had ever seen before. It appeared shiny and smooth, as though someone had handcrafted it. Nyel stepped closer and noticed there were soft green orbs of light floating around inside it, like gentle fireflies dancing in a jar. The light seemed to pulse in the most comforting way.

"*At last, you have found me,*" said the voice that had haunted his mind for days.

Startled, Nyel jumped backwards and looked around for the source. Until he realized that the voice had come from the crystal itself.

Nyel swallowed past a lump in his throat and said, "Yes, I'm here. Who are you? What is this place?"

"*I was once called Zyere. You may know me as the Queen of the Dragons. This is my final resting place,*" the voice answered in a warm tone. The orbs of light swirled around inside of the emerald crystal as the voice spoke.

"So the legend is true," Nyel said in amazement. "You're the one who created the Ascendants."

"*Yes, there is some truth to that legend Ivory told you,*" she said. "*However, the way the Ascendants were formed differs from what you have heard, I'm sure.*"

"I was told that you absorbed the Draconian crystal and passed the Ascendant's Gift to your six children," Nyel stated.

The crystal light flickered for a moment. Then she said, "*No, not to my children. But to my closest friends and allies in a terrible battle that resulted in my death.*"

"Your death?" Nyel asked, confused. "If you're dead, then how am I talking to you now?"

"*The remains of my spirit are intertwined with the last of the Ascendant's power that lives in this vessel,*" the Dragon Queen said. "*Along with the ties that bind the Ascendants together.*"

"Ivory told me the Draconian Crystal truly connects with all dragons. Is that how you could call out to us?" Nyel asked after a moment's thought.

"*It is,*" she replied. "*However, I can only reach out to the current Ascendants. Our bonds are still strong, although everyone else, I cannot reach any longer.*"

"Why have you waited so long to call out to the Ascendants?" he wondered out loud before he could stop himself. "Every

Ascendant I have encountered has been just as surprised to hear your voice as I was."

"I have laid dormant within this vessel for many, many years," she began. *"Until the dark magic from long ago was awoken once more. It was then that I knew it was time to act. And the time for my era of protector of this power, to finish once and for all."*

This took Nye aback. "What do you mean? How did you know the dark magic returned?"

"Because I can feel it. Long ago, my friends helped defeat the evil that was threatening to destroy us all and stole one of the Ascendant's powers from my reach. You see, I tried to face the Shadow Master on my own. But the Shadow Master fatally wounded me in his attempt to take my power for himself. To preserve our sacred magic, I gave a portion of the power I held to my six trusted allies. In doing so, my soul fused with the Draconian Crystal and our bond was forever sealed."

"I had hoped by splitting up the power, the Shadow Master wouldn't be able to easily obtain it. But one of my friends lost his life to that despicable creature, allowing the Shadow Master to absorb a piece of the Ascendant's Gift. But he was still no match for the remaining power of the Ascendants and their fury. After the darkness was defeated, and the Shadow Master was sealed in his tomb, I thought the sixth piece of the Ascendant's Gift was lost forever. And the Draconian Crystal would never hold the full strength of our magic again. However, recently, I felt the sixth Ascendant once more, just as I had all those years before. But it isn't as whole and pure as before. The gift is now deformed and corrupted into something evil and filled with darkness. And what's worse, a second Ascendant has fallen to the Shadow Master."

Nyel gasped as the realization hit him. "Kollano was the Shadow Master even then, wasn't he? He possesses the sixth Ascendant's Gift! But that also means…the shadow creatures could possess the Malachite Ascendant Blagun as well!"

The Dragon Queen hissed, causing the emerald light to flicker like a wild flame. *"Yes, I heard his name from Blagun's mind right before I* lost connection with him. I don't know how, but I fear Kollano used the Ascendant's Gift to make himself more powerful in more ways than one."

"You don't know how he's been able to use the power?" Nyel said.

"All I know for sure is that he used our power to bring himself back to his full potential," she said. "I knew my Ascendants would need help against this new threat that has corrupted our bloodline. They have no one to guide them to work with your kind as we did so long ago. That is why I chose you, Nyel."

Nyel's eyes widened. "Me? How could you have chosen me? I only got this power by mistake."

"No," she replied gently. "It was no mistake. Throughout the past centuries, my only duty, my only purpose, was to help guide the Ascendant's Gift to those who were worthy enough to wield its power. Once chosen, the power takes on the form of the individual's true soul. And you, my dear boy, have the soul of a dragon and a heart of courage."

"So what you're saying is, you knew Ivory would find me?" Nyel asked in bewilderment.

"I did," she answered. "After Kollano awakened the lost Ascendant power, I ensured Aydamaris would direct Ivory to your kingdom and followed Ivory to you."

"But why?"

"Because I knew my Ascendants would not attempt to contact the humans on this matter. They didn't even know what happened with the Shadow Master. How could they? My story was twisted throughout the years and our bond had been severed when the sixth Ascendant went dormant with Kollano," she explained.

Nyel snorted in annoyance. "But you could have reached out to any of them, just as you have done now. Ivory is more understanding of humans. He could have led your cause!"

"Even though our bonds have strengthened since the awakening, my connection to the Ascendants is weak unless they come together," she said.

Nyel fell silent, his annoyance vanished in an instant. "Most of the Ascendant's live apart from each other in their own clans…"

439

"And who brought most of them together thus far, in only a short amount of time?" she asked.

Nyel's mouth fell open. "You chose me to bring them together, didn't you?"

"I did," she answered with pride.

He shook his head in amazement. "You realize I didn't want to do this. Princess Iris convinced me to talk to the dragons to bring us together. I never intended to bring the Ascendants together when I left Folke. I set out to your homeland intending to find Ivory to rid myself of this power."

"A wise princess, indeed," the Dragon Queen said. *"I know you did. I felt the fear and the loneliness in your heart. And I'm sorry for what you went through. But now you know what your purpose is, through and through. The reason you were the one to be gifted the Ascendant's power. You're the one to bring the Ascendant's together, and with their help, the dragons and humans as well. This darkness will destroy us all if Kollano continues to capture and control our power, not to mention any magic from the human realm he could be after."*

"What will come of bringing all the Ascendants together? Why is that so important?" Nyel wondered.

She fell silent for a moment. Then she said, *"I knew when your blood joined with ours that you were special. I knew you would be the one to find me here. It is my intention to pass on the rest of my power to you. If you're willing to accept it."*

Nyel stared at the crystal in shock once more. "Pass on your power? Haven't you already done that? Isn't that how the Ascendants were created in the first place?"

"I was once the sole wielder of this great power," she explained. *"I used it to protect this land and all that dwelled in it from a darkness similar to the threat Kollano has unleashed. We cannot let him get that far ever again. I could hold him off, but in the end, the power was too much for me and it ripped me into pieces. The crystal before you is all that remains of my consciousness. It also contains the key to uniting the rest of the power back into one being."*

"Wait…I don't understand," he said, thinking over her words carefully. "You want the Ascendant's power to rejoin into one dragon?"

"*I believe it's the only way to stop the madness that is taking over both of our people,*" she replied quietly. "*I was too weak to bear the power and deliver the final blow. But I think the next wielder of this great power will have the strength to do what I couldn't.*"

"The Ascendant's would never allow that," Nyel exclaimed and shook his head. "They are proud of their bloodline. They would never give it up."

"*With my power,*" she said with conviction, "*You would be their new leader. You would be their Dragon King.*"

Nyel's jaw dropped once more as the blood drained from his face. Dragon King?!

"I can't be their leader! It wouldn't be right. They'd never allow that."

"*It is more right than you know,*" she said. "*I chose you from the beginning, Nyel. You are the one to carry on my legacy and do something I could not do. You must take back the two stolen Ascendant powers to rid our land of this darkness once and for all. Don't doubt your capabilities, young Shifter. You know I'm right.*"

He fell silent, allowing her words to sink in. Having that much power didn't seem right to him. How could he be the one to carry such a burden? He was grateful for the acceptance he finally received, but the dragons would never see him as their king. He didn't even want to think of himself on such a high level. The very thought made him sick to his stomach.

"I'm sorry, but I can't accept this task. You'll have to choose someone else," Nyel stammered. His heart raced with panic. "Mairwen isn't far away, perhaps she could-"

"*NO!*" the Dragon Queen roared in a blaze of brilliant green light. Nyel flinched from the harshness of her voice and fell silent. She continued, "*You might not understand it now, but you must be the one to take on this responsibility. The others are too prideful. Even your refusal to take on this great power shows me I am right to have chosen you. You cannot defeat these shadow beasts without it. I sense the worst is yet to come. There is more treacherous darkness that will soon be released upon all of Hailwic. Kollano has a second chance to finish what he started. You must be prepared to face him!"*

Nyel stared at the crystal once more. With a heavy sigh, he said, "Very well. I accept. What must I do?"

The crystal returned to a comforting glow, like a warm fireplace on a cold day. *"You must swallow the crystal. Once you do, it and my power will fuse within your body. And you will learn the true potential of being an Ascendant."*

Swallow it? He thought with dread. But he knew better than to argue with her. With a deep breath, Nyel reached within himself and shifted into his dragon form. He let out a cry as pain surged through his body once more. Once he was in his dragon form, he gasped for breath.

"Kollano tried to use his stolen power against ours," the Dragon Queen growled in anger.

"The pain has been getting worse," Nyel gasped. "I don't know how to fix it, or if I can stand it much longer."

"While he tried to corrupt your gift, I'm afraid that might not be the only reason you are feeling such pain," she said.

Nyel stared at the crystal skeptically. "What do you mean?"

The green orbs floated silently in the crystal, threatening to drive Nyel mad. Then, she finally said, *"The Ascendant Gift has never willingly chosen a human as its host. There is so much we don't know about this marriage between you and our power. I believe that it's possible that the power may try to reject you."*

"What? But it chose me! Why would it choose me only to reject me?" Nyel asked in confusion.

"As I said, there's a lot of unanswered questions," she explained. *"I believe if you absorb my power, it will help the pain go away and make your*

transition easier. But along with this is another consequence you must face. If you accept my power, you must also take back the other Ascendants' powers as well, including the stolen gifts. However, if you wield all the Ascendant's Gifts as I have asked, you may not return to your human form."

Nyel's mouth dropped open, and he stumbled to the floor. How could this be? If he did what the Dragon Queen asked of him, he might bring an end to Kollano once and for all. But to do that, it could mean he may be stuck as a dragon forever?

"I don't know if I can do this," Nyel finally stammered. "What about my friends? My family? I can't just leave them behind and live out my life as a dragon."

"You have the power to bring humans and dragons together, remember?" the Dragon Queen reminded him. *"I know this is a hard decision to make, and I'm sorry I've forced this decision on you. But I've followed the path of many Ascendants over the years, and none of them had the soul that you possess. You are the true Dragon King, Nyel. But only if you accept it for yourself."*

He shook his head as tears formed in his eyes. "Are you sure this is the only way? As I said, Mairwen would be a fine choice as a leader. She comes from a dragon clan that has worked with humans in secret for years!"

"The Ascendant's Gift never chooses wrong, Nyel. I'm certain you are the one," she said firmly.

A single tear rolled down his scaly cheek. "I'm scared."

Waves of emerald green washed over him from the crystal. *"I know, young one. But you will see in time that you were always meant to be standing right where you are."*

Nyel took a shaky breath and slowly approached the crystal once more. He stopped a few feet in front of the crystal and hesitated for a moment. "What will become of you? Will your conscience become a part of me as well?"

"No," she said in a content voice. *"I will be no more. But knowing that you will carry on this role will help bring me peace."*

Nyel nodded and slowly lowered his head until his snout was inches from the stone. With one last look, he whispered, "You've put a lot of trust into a simple trapper's son from a small village. I hope I make you proud of your decision."

"*I know you will do the right thing for our kind,*" she answered warmly.

Before he could talk himself out of it once more, Nyel gently grabbed the crystal with his powerful jaws, threw his head back, and swallowed it whole in one gulp. He winced as the heavy, smooth crystal slid down his throat. It felt heavy at first, and then suddenly vanished, as if fusing deep inside of his chest.

Suddenly, his entire body trembled. Every inch of his body vibrated as the Dragon Queen's power seeped out from the crystal and surged throughout his entire body. A tingly sensation like small needles pricking his skin crept through his limbs and body until they went completely numb. His head spun as whispers filled the cavernous room.

Nyel shook his head as fear filled his heart. The whispers reminded him of the shadow creatures and, for a split second, he wondered if he had fallen into Kollano's trap. But his fear didn't last long. The numbness died down and the feeling returned to his limbs.

Not realizing he had been holding his breath, Nyel gasped for air as he hung his head low to the ground. His legs trembled as he stared down at the stone floor of the cave. And then everything went still.

With a quivery voice, he gasped, "Are you still there?"

But there was no answer from her. The Dragon Queen was no more, just as she said. Her sudden absence made him feel an overwhelming sense of sorrow, which he had not expected. Nyel took a deep, shaky breath to calm himself.

The whispers subsided after some time had passed, except for one. He couldn't make out what it was saying, but he was shocked when he recognized the voice.

"Mairwen?" he squeaked in surprise.

"*Nyel?!*" Mairwen called, her voice distant.

He lifted his head and looked around for her, but no one was there with him.

"Where are you?" he asked.

"*Where are you?!*" she shrieked. She sounded relieved and angry at the same time. "*I can't see you anywhere. Did you go into the woods?*"

"Wait…" Nyel said, lifting his head and searching the cavern. Then he looked back at the tunnel entrance, but still didn't see her. "You're not here?"

"*Where is 'here'? I'm on the beach of the island. How am I hearing you in my head?*" she demanded in a terrified voice. "*Are you dead?!*"

Suddenly, another distant voice called out to him. Nyel hesitated before he cautiously focused on the unfamiliar voice. It didn't take long for him to recognize who it was.

"*What's happened? Why won't you let us through? Nyel!*" Aydamaris shouted in concern. Again, he looked around, but didn't see either of the Ascendants anywhere.

His eyes widened with realization. Their voices echoed in his head, just as the Dragon Queen had when she had called to him. By taking in her power, Nyel was now more connected to Mairwen and Aydamaris than he was before.

Nyel let out a nervous laugh, suddenly feeling exhausted. "Aydamaris, I'm alright! I'm not dead. Far from it. I have so much to tell you both."

"*Where are you? Dulryg and Ash won't let us enter the woods,*" Mairwen growled.

"I'm with Jaela. Wait for me there, I'll come to you," he finally answered.

Mairwen was silent for a moment, then she said, "*Hurry.*"

Nyel let out a sigh and glanced back at the pedestal where the emerald stone had once rested. What had he done? Why did she trust him with such a heavy burden, above all of her Ascendants? It made little sense to him. He had more questions now than he had before. One thought floated through his mind above all others that caused his stomach to twist into knots. Was he going to be trapped as a dragon forever?

He shook his head. No, he couldn't dwell on that now. The Dragon Queen had only said there was a chance that he'd be trapped in his dragon form. Perhaps there was a way that he could help reunite the Ascendant's Gifts without having to bear the full weight of it. He needed to talk to Jaela. And to Ivory and Talon.

Nyel turned back to the entrance and realized he was too big to fit through it. He sucked in his breath to prepare himself and shifted once more. To his amazement, he returned to his human form with ease.

Nyel stared down at his hands and flexed his fingers. He summoned his scales to his arms, and they appeared at once. Then, without a second thought, he focused on just his wings, and they sprouted from his back with a flourish. A grin formed on his face as he balled his hands into fists. His pain was gone. The Dragon Queen's power had strengthened his bond with his Gift so much that even his ability was as natural as breathing. Finally, he could shift with no pain.

The flames of the torch Jaela had given him dimmed, but Nyel didn't need it. Instead, he focused his eyes until they morphed in order to see in the dark on his own. Nyel's wings disappeared into his back and he climbed up the tunnel the way he had come. There was a lot to do if he were to truly fulfill the Dragon Queen's wishes. He had to find the rest of the Ascendants, especially the captured ones. He needed to find his brother and Iris.

The shadow creatures were getting stronger and more abundant. But now he was more determined than ever to destroy every last one of them. Now he was certain what his true purpose was from the start.

His thoughts went to Jaela, and another grin formed on his face. Her tribe could be the key. They could be the first to band with the dragons and change history forever. He needed to learn as much as he could about them as soon as possible.

The glow of the rising sun illuminated the tunnel entrance. How long had he been in there? Nyel stepped out into the calm, early morning air and took a deep breath. He was ready to face whatever the future held for him. As long as he had his friends by his side.

Jaela spotted him and hurried to the cave opening. To his surprise, he saw that a small crowd from Jaela's tribe had gathered behind her house. Word must have gotten around about his arrival on their island. How much did they know about the Dragon Queen and the Ascendants? Perhaps even more than he did.

She stopped a few feet in front of him and studied his face intently. "At long last, the Dragon Queen is at peace."

Then, to his surprise, Jaela knelt to the ground, followed by her people. Then, in a clear, loud voice, she announced, "We have protected her crystal for many generations and now the time has finally come for a new era. Welcome to our home, Nyel. The newborn Dragon King."

Chapter 31
A Fork in the Road

Bem

Hawthorne led the silent group southeast towards the safety of the Troden Forest. They kept a fast pace, hoping to get far ahead of any pursuing soldiers. The storm raged around them as strong as ever. Lightning lit up the surrounding hills for a brief moment. Bem strained his eyes with every flash, watching for any soldiers or shadow creatures that could follow them.

Bem couldn't stop the image of Kollano's murderous glare on Carver's handsome face from invading his mind. It sent chills down his spine. Even though he couldn't see anyone pursuing them now, he knew deep inside of him that Kollano wouldn't let him go. Similar to how Bem knew, he wouldn't let Carver go.

He glanced over at Hawthorne, who rode alongside him. Hawthorne's face was grave, his eyes wide with anticipation and sorrow. As much as they were all exhilarated to be free of such a wretched place, it had cost them dearly. Most of all Rae.

Another flash of lightning revealed the dark tree line of the Troden Forest. They slowed to a trot as Hawthorne led the way into the trees. Bem followed him, though he was hesitant. He was free now. As much as they had helped each other, he had a responsibility to Falcon. Theo. Nyel. Carver...

"Hawthorne, wait," he said, bringing the group to a halt.

Hawthorne looked over his shoulder at him. "We shouldn't stop our progress. What is it?"

"I can't go with you," Bem finally said. "I have my own people that need me."

Hawthorne studied him and then turned his questioning gaze to Eryi.

Eryi moved her horse to stand beside Bem and looked at him with tired eyes. She had used a lot of energy in the fight. She looked sick, like she could pass out at any moment. "I'll cut to the chase. Are you sure Kollano possessed your prince?"

Bem nodded. "Yes. He tricked my friends and I for a long time. We fought with him and his creatures. We thought Carver had killed him, but he finally revealed himself, proving us wrong."

Eryi's brow raised in surprise. "You thought he killed him? You fought him? How?"

Bem scratched the back of his neck, unsure if he should tell them everything. "It's kind of a long story. Kollano possessed Carver's uncle Sargon, the king's brother, first. We fought him and his shadow creatures. And we thought we had won. Until we didn't."

Eryi and Hawthorne shared a look.

"What?" Bem asked.

"You mean to tell me this is his second contact with a royal body?" Eryi asked, her voice becoming more panicked.

Bem stared at her, surprised by her reaction. "Well, yes. Why is that important?"

"Eryi, we need to keep moving. We don't have time to sit here and listen to these stories," Hawthorne urged.

Eryi crossed her arms against her chest. "Don't pretend you're not concerned about this, too. You remember the Shielder's tales of the ancient guard?"

"Yes, but that's all they were. Children's tales. Silly traditions. Don't tell me you believe in them?" Hawthorne argued, tapping his horse's ribs with his heels to continue further into the woods. The rest of the group followed.

"I've learned firsthand not to question such stories," Bem countered. "There's always some truth to them."

Eryi leaned over and smacked him on the back. "You see? The boy gets it!"

"You haven't answered my question," Bem said, bringing the conversation back on track. "Why does it concern you he has possessed more than one person?"

"It's not that it's more than one person. It's that he has possessed more than one member of the royal family," Eryi explained. Our people took on the responsibility of guarding his prison long ago when he was first locked away. The way they sealed him was so intense that even if he got out, he'd be too weak to do anything. But he's discovered a way to possess them, anyway."

"And command an army of shadow creatures," Bem pointed out.

Eryi nodded.

"Is it wise to bring Bem back to our home?" Leif questioned from behind them. He had been quiet until that point, consoling Rae and keeping her safe. "Did you see how the prince was staring at him? It seems where he goes, the shadow man will follow."

Hawthorne halted and turned in his saddle. "Leif has a point. No offense, Bem, but I heard how he spoke of you back in the hallway. Perhaps it is best we go our separate ways. You should go find your friends."

"The Shielder will want to hear from him!" Eryi argued. "He's had firsthand experience with everything that is happening in Hailwic. Maybe he even knows of something that will kill him!"

"We can tell him ourselves," said Leif.

"I agree with Leif and Hawthorne," Bem spoke up, silencing them all. "For now, at least. But I'd like to bring my friends back with me if I can. We need to learn more about Kollano's origin. Even the prince and princess were unaware of his existence."

"The answers you seek about Kollano could be with the Shielder," Eryi protested. "It's possible he may know a way to help your prince!"

Bem hesitated before answering. All he wanted was to get Carver back. And she was right. He was torn, although her people were the only lead he had to find the answer.

"I know. But I've realized that I've been selfish in all of this. I need to find my friends and work together on this. I can't do this alone," Bem finally said.

Eryi glared at him, but said nothing. She faced overwhelming odds.

Bem gave her a small smile and continued. "I appreciate everything you've done for me. But I feel the best I can do right now is to make sure Kollano doesn't follow you back to your family because of me. And I won't let him hurt Carver in the process. This is something I have to do."

"Very well," Eryi grunted. "You can find us south of Troden Lake. In a village called Bao."

Leif glared at her. "You can't just tell him where we live. What if he becomes possessed or Kollano captures him? He could lead them straight to us!"

"Leif, you may not realize it, but we have a duty to take partial responsibility for this sickness that has been unleashed on this unsuspecting land!" Eryi shouted, losing her patience with him. "If something like that happens, then we must be ready for him!"

Hawthorne stopped the group once more and turned to look at them. Leif grit his teeth and averted his gaze to the ground. Bem understood.

"This is where I leave you now," Bem said with a sad smile. "I won't forget what you did for me. Thank you all so much."

"Just promise me you'll find us soon," Eryi insisted.

Bem nodded. "I promise."

"Farewell and safe travels. Be a light amongst the shadows," Hawthorne said.

With that, they turned once more and headed south towards Bao. Bem watched them leave as the rain spilled off of the canopy of the forest around him. He wondered what his next step should be. It was the first time in a long time that he was completely alone. He patted his horse's neck, although he was really comforting himself.

He had to keep moving. The soldiers, or even worse, Kollano, could be after him at that very moment. He turned his horse towards the north and gazed into the trees beyond.

"Let's look for Falcon first," he said out loud to the mare. His stomach sank as he thought of Falcon. He didn't know about Falcon's fate after they captured him. He could only hope that when he found him, he was still alive.

Chapter 32
The Shadow Master

Bem didn't get very far northbound before the woods fell silent all at once. Even the drops of rain seemed to disappear into nothingness. He froze and checked his surroundings. His horse whinnied nervously and let out a snort. Bem's breath caught in his throat. He couldn't see them, but he knew they were there. Shadow creatures.

"Let's go, girl," Bem urged his horse, leading her down a narrow deer trail through the trees.

Part of him hoped that the shadow creatures would follow him instead of the others. He didn't want them to get into any trouble because of him. He was certain Kollano sent the creatures after the group. Although he wasn't sure if Kollano would allow the shadow creatures to possess him, he was certain they would take the others.

Then again, Bem was alone and who knew how many creatures were lurking in the darkness of the woods?

A faint hiss wafted through the trees behind him. Bem's head whipped around and for a split second, he thought he saw the faint glow of ember-eyes staring back at him through the trees. He would not take a chance to allow them to catch up.

"Go!" he shouted, kicking hard at his horse's sides in a panic.

The horse snorted once more and broke into a full gallop through the dense trees. Bem used all his strength to squeeze his legs against the horse's ribs to keep from falling off. The combination of rain and the lack of a saddle made it almost impossible to hold on, but somehow, he did it.

A shriek erupted behind him in response. This time, when he looked back, he could clearly see the shadowy figures racing behind him, trying to catch up. Their haunting eyes and wicked grins sent a chill down his spine. Bem sucked in a breath and grabbed hold of his magic within.

With a thrust of his hand, he sent back a ball of fire towards them. They hissed with displeasure, but dodged his attack with ease. Bem cursed under his breath. Everything was against him. Days of little food and lack of sleep, along with his magic draining and the fight to escape, had left him without enough energy to defend himself. He didn't even have a crystal of magic to use against them.

Instead, Bem faced forward once more and hunched low on his horse's neck. He prayed she was fast and nimble enough to get them to safety. As they raced through the woods, the trees and the brush grew more and more dense. Bem faced a quick decision, either turning back into open land or taking their chances pushing through the woods. So he redirected his horse back to the edge of the woods.

As soon as they broke free from the trees, his horse doubled in speed and raced along the edge of the tree line. Bem let out a sigh of relief as the sound of the shadow creatures faded away. He didn't dare let his guard down yet. Bem urged his horse to go as fast as possible, hoping to put some distance between them.

However, his relief was short-lived. Once he was out of the cover of the woods, a new sound took the shadow creature's place. The faint sound of multiple hooves pounded the muddy ground in the distance. Soldiers from The Keep were searching for him too.

A flash of lightning illuminated the area around him. In the distance, he could hear a man shout, "Over there!"

Bem cursed and ducked down once more. But it was too late. The soldiers had spotted him. Thunder rumbled overhead, followed by a clear hiss.

His head whipped to the right just in time to see a shadow creature peel away from the dark woods and slam into him. The sudden force knocked him from his horse and sent him hurling into the mud. His horse let out a panicked squeal. Her eyes were white with terror as she stumbled, then bolted out of Bem's reach.

Bem gasped for breath as stars danced in his eyes. His face landed on the muddy ground. Hot blood pooled into his mouth from his split lip. He spit it out and coughed as he tried to catch his breath.

A sudden icy chill overcame him and his body went stiff. A dark, shadowy hand entered his field of vision as it rested on the ground beside him. Bem's heart hammered against his chest as the shadow creature slowly knelt until it stared him in the eye. Its menacing grin widened victoriously as the shadow grabbed his throat to keep him still.

"I've got youuu," it gloated in a drawn-out whisper.

Bem's vision blurred as the creature crept closer to his face. It was going to possess him. He was going to lose his body before completely losing his mind. He wanted to scream, but nothing came out. Paralysis rendered his entire body helpless, leaving him unable to move. He couldn't even close his eyes and hide from the horror in front of him. The sound of the soldiers grew louder as they drew nearer, and for a moment, Bem hoped they would get there in time to save him from this terrible fate.

"Back off, or I'll end you," someone growled.

The shadow creature immediately vanished from Bem's vision. He blinked in confusion as the paralyzation slowly disappeared. A rough hand grabbed the hair on the back of his head and yanked him out of the mud.

Bem winced from the pain, but he still couldn't move enough to defend himself. Replacing the Shadow Creature was the cloaked figure that was Kollano, his face twisted with rage.

"Where do you think you're going?" he spat.

Bem could only groan in response. His body ached from pain and exhaustion.

"I had a plan for you, dear Bem. But you've ruined those plans. Worry not. Someone has brought something to my attention. Something that has made me realize that you and I could work wonders as a team. I can't just let you go now," Kollano grinned, but his wicked eyes did not match his smile. It made Bem shudder.

"You're insane. I'd never work with you!" Bem said through gritted teeth.

"I know you wouldn't, not willingly..." Kollano chuckled.

Kollano knelt in front of him and grabbed Bem around his head. His thumbs rested on Bem's temples, and he glared into his eyes.

Bem screamed as his head suddenly exploded with pain. He tried to pull from Kollano's grasp, but to no avail. All he could do was watch Kollano's pleased face as a loud ringing pierced his ears. Bem couldn't look away from Kollano's face. He could see his lips moving as he spoke to him, but the only thing he could hear was the ringing in his ears.

And then his mind went blank. The ringing in his ears increased as he floated in the darkness. He wondered when he fell asleep...did he fall asleep? Was he having a bad dream? Wasn't he just with someone?

Cold rain pelted his face and body. Something didn't feel right. He couldn't move.

Slowly, Bem forced his eyes open and nearly gasped. A shadow creature floated over him, staring down in his face. It was keeping him frozen on the muddy ground. Bem's heart raced as he realized the creature reached towards him, eager to take over his body as his own. Didn't this happen before?

Then he remembered. Where was Kollano? Had he imagined him being there? Perhaps the impact of being tackled off his horse had caused him to hit his head too hard.

Then he heard screams of terror as a loud, booming wave of thunder rolled over them. Bem's heart skipped a beat. That wasn't thunder, he realized. It was a sound he had heard many times before. Another roar erupted over him just as a blinding flash of white light lit up the area around him. The Shadow Creature shrieked as it faded away, cursing the light as it did.

Bem's body trembled as he finally regained control over his limbs. He forced himself to rise to his hands and knees as the ground thudded beneath him. He couldn't look up, instead he let out a series of violent coughs as blood spewed from his mouth.

"Bem!" shouted a voice just inches away from him.

He raised his head, expecting to find Kollano or one of his soldiers racing towards him. Instead, his exhausted gaze met the worried amethyst eyes of Falcon. The sorcerer knelt beside him and lifted Bem's arm over his head.

"Falcon?" he wheezed, unable to take his eyes off his face. "You're alive!"

"Yes, let's continue to keep it that way, shall we?" Falcon smirked as relief washed over his face. He heaved Bem out of the mud and onto his feet.

Bem finally looked up and found Theo hurrying to his side. The dragon pressed his snout against Bem's chest, happy to see his friend once more.

"The soldiers, they're after me," Bem croaked as Theo pulled his head away. The crimson dragon crouched low to the ground, eager to get Bem out of there at once.

"I know. Steno is distracting them, but we don't have much time," Falcon explained in a hurried voice. He helped lift Bem onto Theo's back. Bem looked back towards the soldiers and to his amazement, saw Steno circling over them and letting out stream after stream of fire at them.

They tried shooting arrows at him when they weren't shielding themselves with magic from the torrent of fire. Kollano must not be with them, Bem realized in surprise. He would have fought the dragon in an instant. But if he wasn't there, where was he?

His head spun suddenly as he thought of Kollano. Why wasn't he with the soldiers chasing him? When was the last time he saw him? He thought about it. The Keep. He saw him last when he escaped The Keep.

When Falcon sat behind Bem on Theo's back and shouted, "Let's go!", it interrupted his thoughts.

A low rumble reverberated in Theo's chest before he leapt into the air and climbed high above the ground. Rain pummeled against Bem's face as distant lightning lit up the night sky. He welcomed the cool water and the crisp winds that whipped around his shaggy hair. It made him feel happy to be alive. But he knew they weren't out of harm's way yet.

Theo let out a roar, calling to Steno.

Steno sent another blast of fire at the soldiers before turning around and joining Theo. With a few grunts to each other, the dragons quickly redirected and started flying towards the northern Troden Woods. The soldiers regrouped and let out ball after ball of magic at the retreating dragons. But they were too late. The soldiers quickly disappeared behind them, allowing Bem to let out a sigh of relief. Until he heard Steno let out a vicious snarl from his left.

Bem and Falcon looked back and, to their dismay, they spotted a hoard of shadow creatures flying after them.

"Will they never quit?" Bem sighed in frustration, beginning to call upon his magic.

Falcon took one look at Bem's glowing hand and grabbed his shoulder to stop him. "Save your strength, Bem, you're injured. Here."

From his pocket, Falcon pulled out a small yellow crystal and handed it over to Bem. "It's not much, so use it to heal yourself."

Bem nodded and got to work right away. He drew the power out of his newly gained crystal and held it against his chest. The gentle warmth of the healing magic seeped into his skin and flowed throughout his body. All of his aches and pains slowly disappeared as he absorbed the entire crystal's magical energy. However, his head remained foggy from exhaustion.

As he did this, Falcon and the dragons prepared to fight off the shadow creatures. Steno spun around and soared towards the creatures, letting out another blast of fire from his powerful jaws. Their shrieks filled the night air as the fire connected with some of them. Theo growled and Steno returned to him, letting out a puff of smoke.

From the darkness of the woods below, they heard another screech as more shadow creatures rose from the treetops directly underneath them. Theo and Steno breathed a wall of fire at them before quickly flying away from the area.

Falcon twisted around completely until he sat back-to-back against Bem. From his palms, he unleashed fire and beams of light at any creature that got too close to either dragon.

"There are too many of them," Falcon gasped after a moment of repeated bouts of magic in multiple directions. "I can't keep track of them. Theo, can you go any faster?"

Bem could see the panic in Theo's eyes when he looked back at them.

"Where are they all coming from? I've never seen so many at once!" Falcon shouted as he tried his best to fight them off.

"They follow their master everywhere," Bem said through gritted teeth. "I think Kollano's close."

Falcon looked back at him for a second and said, "Can you see him?"

Bem shook his head. "No, but he was too angry to just let me escape without a fight."

Suddenly, a massive roar resounded from the sky ahead of them. Like the clouds themselves might crash down on them. Bem's stomach dropped as he thought this could be Kollano. Somehow, he had a dragon hidden nearby and was flying after them.

Until Theo and Steno let out a victorious roar in response. Falcon glanced over his shoulder with wide eyes. Bem squinted through the rain and to his amazement he spotted four dragons flying straight at them. And on each of their backs sat a rider.

Bem grinned and shouted, "It's Nyel!"

Then he spotted Iris sitting upon Syth, her raven hair swirled in the rain filled winds. Her hands glowed with magic, with a look of determination on her face. Before Bem could say anything more, Falcon roared, "Iris!"

"Come on! Let's show these Shadows who they're messing with!" the princess shouted as Syth whizzed past them.

Without hesitation, Theo and Steno circled back around and let out war cries of their own. Behind them were unfamiliar dragons and riders, but they had no time for introductions. Who had they found that would ride a dragon? But he didn't have time to think about that. Bem could only be grateful that they had reunited with their friends.

Two of the riders behind him started using magic on the creatures while their dragons let out fire blasts. The shadow creatures shrieked as, one by one, they disappeared in a blaze of light. The group of six dragons and their riders fought against the shadow creatures until eventually those that remained turned and soared away to save themselves

"Shall we give chase?" Iris cheered, reveling in their victory.

"No, there are soldiers back there after us," Falcon replied. His eyes lit up by her presence and his shoulders seemed to relax. "And Bem thinks Kollano is nearby as well. We should regroup elsewhere."

"Sargon's cabin?" she suggested hopefully.

Falcon shook his head. "It's too dangerous. Maybe we should return to the dragon lands?"

"No," Bem said. "I might have a lead to help us defeat Kollano once and for all. But it means traveling further south into the Troden Forest."

"Let's go to the cabin just until we have a plan. They won't be able to get that far before we leave. Plus, if we lead them north, they may not expect us to change direction later," Iris insisted.

"Very well. But only for one day," Falcon sighed.

"We can show her the mine we found too," Bem offered.

Falcon nodded, and Iris looked at him expectantly. But Bem couldn't ignore the absence he felt any longer. "Where's my brother?"

"He had to stay behind to fulfill a promise he made. He's chasing a lead with Ivory," she answered. There was a sudden sadness in her voice as her eyes cast downward.

A frown emerged on Falcon's face. He noticed it, too.

Bem let out a sigh of relief. At least Nyel was alright. Then an overwhelming feeling of shame washed over him for asking about his own brother. "I'm sorry I didn't protect Carver. I failed you both."

"No, you didn't," she scolded. "Kollano is admittedly clever. But so are we. We'll stop him and save my brother. You mustn't lose faith!"

Bem forced a smile. He wished he could share in her confidence at that moment. Suddenly, his head spun and a feeling of nausea threatened to empty his stomach. Bem swayed and nearly fell off Theo's side. Falcon had to grab him and hold him in place.

"You need rest," Falcon said, his voice filled with concern.

"I'll be ok," Bem said, but he knew deep down Falcon was right.

"Try to sleep. I'll watch over you," Falcon offered, keeping a firm grip on his arms.

"But- "Bem started, then Iris cut him off.

"Rest Bem. I have so much to tell you when we get to Sargon's. Including you as well, Theo," she smiled. She motioned to a green crystal on her neck with a proud grin.

Theo looked at her in surprise, but Bem didn't understand the reason. He had already closed his eyes as the dragons and their riders flew to the safety of Sargon's cabin. As the world faded away from him and he succumbed to his sleep, a cool voice whispered to him from his dreams. It was almost too low for him to hear, but there was no mistaking the threat behind its words.

Yes, get your rest, my dear Bem. Soon enough, the real fun will begin.

Acknowledgments

What an experience it has been to have written my second book! Even though the wait was an unfortunately long one, I'm so grateful to my beloved readers for supporting me along the way. Your patience, kind words, and excitement for The Shifter was the drive I needed to bring you an even more adventurous and thrilling story of Nyel and Bem. I hope you enjoyed The Forgotten Prince as much as I did writing it!

Now to start, I'd like to first thank my editor Crystal, for always being available to answer my questions and run ideas by her. And of course, for editing my book! Without her, this book wouldn't sound half as good as it does now! I hope we can continue working together in the future.

To my cover designer, Christian, thank you once again for an amazing book cover! It was so easy and painless to work with you. I gave you just a little description of what I wanted, and you knocked it out of the park on the first try! I am in awe of your work. I can't wait to see what we'll come up with for the next one!

To my beta readers, thank you for your dedication and taking time out of your busy schedules to read over my story and provide honest feedback! A special shout out to Lori and Deedee once again, who have been great sources of this feedback and good friends throughout the years.

To my family, whom there are too many to list without having to create another book: thank you for always supporting me in my dreams. You've always been there to listen to my ideas, my rants, my worries and concerns, and also have been there to promote my book. I'm grateful for you all and love you bunches!

To my husband Pete, thank you for supporting me through everything. From helping me lug all of my equipment to book shows to bragging about my books to friends and family, you always have my back in this, and I couldn't do it without you either! Love you!

And to my young nephews, when you're able to read this. Follow your dreams! It will more than likely take a lot of hard work and determination, but please never give up on yourself! You are stronger than you know and capable of doing wonderful things in life. Know that I will always believe in you and will be rooting for you every step of the way!

That's all for now! I hope you enjoyed reading *The Hailwic Chronicles: The Forgotten Prince*. Now it's time for me to get back to work and finish book 3. Until next time, my lovely readers!

Sincerely,
Kendra

Also by Author:

The Hailwic Chronicles: The Shifter

About the Author

Kendra Slone loves to live in fantasy worlds in her free time. From reading and writing books to playing video games, she is always searching for the next best thing to grab her attention.

She is the author of *The Hailwic Chronicles*, a YA fantasy series that she started writing when she was young. An avid reader in the same genre she writes in, Kendra has always wanted to publish a book of her own. She made that dream possible by self-publishing her first book, *The Hailwic Chronicles: The Shifter*, in October of 2020.

Kendra lives in a quiet, small town in Illinois with her husband, three cats, and two dogs. Want to know about her future projects and life updates? Follow her on social media for more!

Follow Me on Social Media!

Facebook: www.facebook.com/authorkendraslone
Instagram: authorkendraslone
TikTok: authorkendraslone
X: AuthorKendraS

Made in the USA
Columbia, SC
26 June 2024

559fa5d2-8b4d-4a2e-8b54-fd205c0516f8R01